THE SWIMMER'S PROMISE

MARK L. HARDY

The Swimmer's Promise

Mark L. Hardy

ISBN: 978-1-967375-12-7 (Paperback)
ISBN: 978-1-967375-13-4 (E-book)

Library of Congress Control Number: 2025911310

Printed in the United States of America

Published by:

info@thequippyquill.com
(302) 295-2278

CONTENTS

INTRODUCTION

T he Library opened and a sophisticated, beautiful, older, blonde woman with bright green eyes moved to the front desk. She enquired about "home movies". The librarian pulled an older 8mm projector from the closet behind the front desk and directed the pretty woman to a private room in the rear. The room was occupied by family and friends. She directed them to be seated behind her; face forward. The woman sets the projector on a table and pointed it to the opposite wall where she pulled down a white screen from a roll affixed to the ceiling above. She affixed a six-inch reel of fully developed 8mm film onto the empty upper mechanical arm. The lower arm already carried an empty six-inch reel that stood ready to receive the story soon to be told.

The home movie projector – an ancient relic of filmography - fired up. The room darkened and the portable movie screen lit up to cast a white glow across the room. The exposed 8mm film clicked and tickled its' way around and through the well-timed gears as it drops from the upper six-inch reel to the lower. Except for the mechanical clickety-clack of the projector, the room was quiet and would remain quiet except for the giggles, guffaws, and miscellaneous small talk that would continue until the upper reel emptied and the lower reel was full. Abruptly, a large number "3" flashed up on the screen, then a "2", a "1", and a ZERO. The scene opened with these opening lines:

"IVORY"

"The god of the angry deep
Arises too early from the porcelain sea

Mere mortals do disturb his rest
They shall not now withstand his test

To splinters he doth smash their ships
Tis kindling he doth make of boats

But Mom doth throw the Ivory in
And the Ivory floats!"

*****

PREFACE

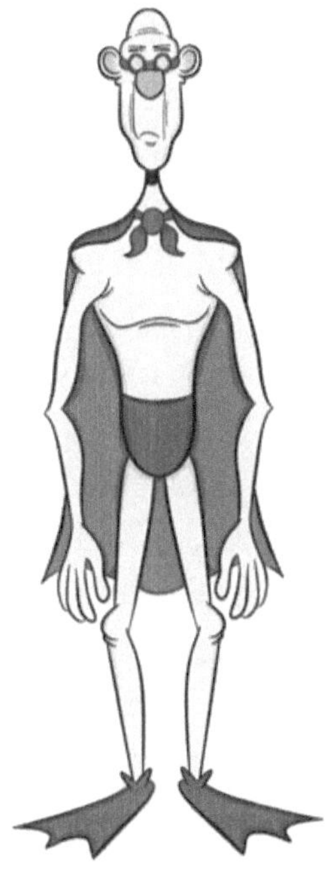

Marty swam, still not sure why he'd left the island. All of a sudden, the bananas were bland. The mangoes had lost their tang, especially since Marty had cut all but the last of the trees for firewood. The fruit from the one remaining tree failed to get his juices flowing. The last of the coconuts came down about the same time he'd cut the last coconut tree. The milk from the green ones was effervescent; the meat was so soft you could scoop it with your thumb. All that was left now were a few brown ones, fallen to the ground long ago and either returned from the ocean on the waves or found partially buried in the recently disturbed sand following the last tropical downpour. The meat was rock hard and the milk, sickeningly sweet; a bit like his former partner – always so damn cheerful in the morning. *Did that guy ever lose his temper?* Marty wondered. *Did anything ever frustrate him?* Somehow, he couldn't trust a guy who wouldn't say crap even with a mouthful.

Maybe that's why he'd come to this island in the first place, to get away. Who knew? He had been here now for ...how long? He couldn't really recall. The food had been good and easily available, at least at first. An accurate lance with a homemade trident into the crashing waves at the deep water side of the atoll, away from the more placid lagoon yielded Mahimahi, soft enough to be eaten raw; a quick reach into a mango or banana tree added a side dish that gave nutrients; and, a slice of papaya with a squirt of lime was a tasty desert. That was all gone now.

On lazier days, scallops taken from the lagoon meant an easy meal. The scallops were collected from just offshore at the protected side of the island and boiled in the sweeter milk taken from the older coconut in the dark brown shell. This brown shelled coconut was harvested with no real effort from the ground. No one could say until opened for just how long it had laid there. The meat was hard and white, and when scraped from the inside, it helped to render an acceptable alternative called Pahua, an island staple. Pahua was like mush to islanders: ubiquitous. A hard-boiled taro root was drab like unbuttered toast but filling. On some days, drab and unbuttered was all that was needed. More recently, life was drab and unbuttered in general. Marty commiserated. What he wouldn't give for a good cup o' Joe: black no sugar. He'd tried espresso: too fancy. He couldn't handle the Yuppie crowd, the Gen X-ers, the Millennials. The Starbucks Society was a bit overwhelming. Laptops, smarter-than-smart, phones with immediate access and instant gratification, but with no real communication, not really. Hell, Marty used to carry every phone number he ever needed in his head. Even some he didn't need. Susan didn't care now if he ever called her again, so why remember?

People say that time heals all wounds; that time erases all; or sometimes they say: "give it time", when the immediate outcome is considered disagreeable or unwanted. "Patience is a virtue", they counsel, as if the mere act of waiting is somehow a positive character trait.

But Marty had come to the island – first and foremost – to erase Time and its consequences. He could do without the lasting regret, the ever pressing guilt, or even the idea that delayed satisfaction over time heightens expectation and enhances the ultimate reward. Absence did nothing to make Marty's heart grow fonder; it just hurt. So, why should he remember? "Well," he concluded, "after all is said and done, Time can be intoxicating."

What Marty wouldn't give now for a good long commercial advertisement during halftime. His wife would DVR every NFL game and even some of the college teams. She preferred to watch the games straight through – skip the commercial interruptions- in a blatant attempt to manipulate time, to erase it. She would simply fast forward through the commercials to get right back to the action. But to Marty, TV commercials were a respite; a time - if you will - to grab a cold one from the fridge; to eat a chunk of bologna; or, maybe grab a slice of cheese. TV was supposed to be the real "timeout", a timeout from....well, thinking of difficult memories. Commercials were a step removed: a timeout from a timeout.

Marty would press this point, but of late his days here on the island were too much drab and too much unbuttered. Of late, the island offered neither peace, nor excitement. Of late, life - at best was lackluster. Of late, Marty felt that his time here had run out and he resented it. He needed to escape. He needed to swim. He donned his flippers, hiked up his Speedo, and adjusted his goggles. The water was calm and placid. The reef was far away. The distance reduced the roar to a slight murmur. The night was moonless. The stars here in the South Pacific were countless and bold. He pushed off silently into the void. He stroked effortlessly and kicked every now and then. His long red swimmer's fins easily propelled him forward. The lapping of the waters against the shoreline grew quiet. The roar of the open seas grew louder. He wasn't sure how long he'd been here, in this place. He had found some advantage here. It seemed such a very long time ago that he'd stopped worrying about...well... about time, itself. The days of the week, the months of the year, the years themselves had been washed away with each succeeding wave. He couldn't remember exactly when or how long ago he had forgotten about time. He couldn't recall exactly when he stopped celebrating holidays, stopped marking his calendar, or stopped checking his wristwatch. His wristwatch...a memory flashed. In high school, he earned the Ivan C. Bills award not a trophy, but a self-winding wrist watch--very nice. One year after graduation, he was set to board a plane. He would be gone for two-years. As a going-away gift, Susan gave him a new battery-operated Timex. The circumstances forced him to replace his favorite watch with the new one. Reluctantly, he unfastened his self-winding treasure. His younger sister kindly offered to take it home for safekeeping. With hesitation, he handed it to her and asked her to keep it safe. He never saw it again.

With some trepidation, he had pulled the new watch onto his wrist and smiled a difficult smile. He set the time and wound it. He wasn't used to winding his prize watch, and this action felt strange. Several hours later, as he boarded the plane, he thanked Susan again and kissed her goodbye. He trusted that she would wait for him. Shortly after take-off, he saw that the hands on his brand new, electronic wrist-watch had not budged. The time still read as he had initially set: 2:32 pm. He reset the watch to correct the time and for the next 15-minutes or so, he bumped and shook, rattled and rolled his new watch- all in an ultimately unsuccessful effort to keep the hands moving. With each bump, the second hand would move forward a few seconds, just enough to get out of the way. He finally managed to keep the hands moving and over the course of a few days or so, sometimes a few weeks, the hands continued almost reluetantly, and the watch kept decent time. But, over the course of 6 months, it never ran consistently, until at the end of 6 months, it stopped for good. In the days following, Marty received a letter.

"Dear Marty", it read. "This wouldn't be so difficult if you both weren't so neat".

Yeah right, Marty had thought. That guy was about 3,000 miles neater than him when she penned those words. He was there and Marty wasn't. End of story. Another dropped pass. Another errant shot at the buzzer. Another missed block that brought the linebacker crashing down onto Marty's hopes and dreams. Was it Fate or some kind of Destiny? Whatever it was, it sucked! And, now that he thought about it, he had actually started to lose time, to forget about days, weeks, months, and even years, at just about the time that Susan had given him that watch. He had never before seen it as a problem, only a minor frustration. But, he now could see that the ever-increasing difficulties with his relationship to time and his fuzzy, Swiss-cheese memory, all tied together back to that new but unpredictable electronic watch.

A lighting flash lit up the horizon and Marty counted the seconds. At four, he heard the distant roll of thunder and concluded that the ever darkening clouds grouped low on the horizon were 4 miles off. *That's funny* he thought.

He rolled to his front and paddled. The waves in the deepening waters were broad and soft, not too high and rolling. Marty rolled in sync with each. He wondered curiously why he hadn't thought to pack. It seemed natural to swim *au naturel.* To him, *au naturel* meant a red speedo, some swimming goggles, and a pair of long red swims fins. Over time, this outfit had become part of him. He kicked slowly. His strokes were easy, long, and extended. He was in no hurry. He had no goal, no intent to arrive. He hadn't given a thought as to whom he might meet or whether his arrival anywhere might require that he be dressed. accordingly. He never intended to finish. Hell, his only real intention was to swim. His only purpose in starting was to swim. What else was there?

Still he thought, didn't the idea of departing from someplace imply an arrival in another place with all of its incumbent circumstances? He was forced to admit that he expected to meet up with someone, just not in the way one might assume. You know, the bus arrives, the plane touches down, the cell phones come out. Arrangements are made for pick up curbside or someone meets you at the dock. We've been expecting you. Your room is ready. Oh boy, have we got the rest of your life planned out for you! Hugs and kisses all around! But he never expected there would be someone out

here to meet him. Solitude had been his companion for so long, he was never sure if those he met along the way were real or Memorex. But this one, in some ways, he had always expected. Here at the reef, under the roar of the breaking surf.

She seemed an angel sent to escort him home; a mermaid from the deep blue whom he had known before, but. before what? Marty wasn't sure just why he expected her. Why this one? Why her? He swam and she accompanied, silently. He would wait for her to speak. He was in no particular hurry, and this pace was truly relaxing. The roar of the surf was not clamorous but gracefully attuned somehow, and peaceful. He felt like he could go on forever.

There it was again: that familiar feeling that Forever was the exact destination toward which he swam. Where was Forever anyway? What was it? There was also a peculiar feeling that he'd promised something, just what and to whom, he could not say; and that it was this promise that kept him from his desired destination. It kept him from Forever. It was also this promise that kept him swimming even though he had literally come to find the bottom of things. He was flummoxed. Didn't his present state of mind presuppose that he just stop, exhaust the last reserves of oxygen and abandon himself to the deep? He didn't know how far he should go. He wasn't sure how far he had come. His arms were weary, but he'd found a rhythm. He barely used his legs. In fact, he'd found a bit of a current so the going was easy. He stroked with the open notes on his acoustic guitar: EADGBE, EADGBE, EADGBE.

Marty approached the passage. He turned over to his back to ponder as he slowly backstroked. He needed to puzzle some on this. Large and dark cumulus clouds appeared now skyward and were lowering. He was in for a bit of a storm. No matter. He was thirsty. Later, he could choose to dive, to get away. Later, he would take the passage. Later, he could escape -for good, as it were - to the unfathomable depths. But for now, he'd just take a break; maybe go to the fridge for a cold one. You see, out here commercials play unimpeded by the unwanted inserted operation of some disagreeable "fast forward" taken to otherwise interrupt the television timeouts. If the players can break for Time, so could Marty.

CHAPTER I

The cry of seagulls awakened Marty to an alternate reality. He opened his eyes to the bright sunlight overhead but quickly squinted to get them closed. Ouch. He lifted the small, red swimmer's goggles from his eyes and set them on his head. He shaded his eyes with his hand and attempted again to open them. The gulls cry continued. Once more, he squinted in an effort to adjust his eyes. He was in the water and found himself clinging to the edge of a swimming pool. There above him on the pool deck, he saw, silhouetted against the blue sky, the outline of three little girls quizzically peering down at him and squawking.

"Hi pops!'" chirped a wiry little blonde girl with eyes of steel blue, "What doin'?" She sported those wicked eyebrows that angled high in the middle.

"Hey, papa, why are you takin a nap in the pool?" said the older one. "Does your big belly help you float? She seemed the most astute, very pretty with long dark hair and wonderful eyes – also deeply blue.

"Yeah, does your big belly help you float?" giggled the third, a very pretty blue-eyed urchin also with blond hair. She giggled again, an infectious laugh. The three ran off.

Marty rolled onto his "big" belly to watch them join a family on the lawn near the larger pool. He reached for the pool deck, where he folded his arms to dangle his legs into the swimmer's lane. Big belly, indeed! It wasn't that big, he thought. Silly little girls!

Yet, each silly girl carried with her a promise: the type of promise that only the future holds. Marty envisioned young coeds, roommates at an upscale university there on scholarship: one athletic, one academic, one in the arts. He saw a CEO; a Corporate President; a U.S. Senator. Mostly, he saw young mothers who loved keenly and cared deeply for their own children who were young men and women of integrity, who recognized the truth as something independent from themselves to which they must appeal to know the right and wrong of things.

Yeah, that was it: the right and wrong of things. He'd been swimming now for decades, maybe. He didn't know. He was still uncertain as to the very right and wrong of things. Conscience whispered often to point the way. Marty listened although he knew that others didn't. Most chose to turn off the voice, to eliminate the guilt. Yet, guilt was good in the proper doses. It kept one balanced.

Marty was more concerned about the larger "truths" that seemed to go begging. For example, why was the world filled with so much suffering? Could anyone truly blame God for the decisions made by the human race? And, did those wholly human decisions negate God's existence? Just because we couldn't hear or otherwise refused to listen, didn't necessarily mean that He didn't speak. Did it?

Why was it that He was credited either for great drama: a burning bush on Sinai; a large part in the Red Sea (Marty laughed suddenly at the thought of God with a bad comb-over); or, with that highly prized, but difficult to ascertain – except by the chosen few-still, small voice that should direct a person's path for good. Marty preferred the drama. At least, you knew who to credit. The idea of personal revelation was too subjective. Did that voice in Marty's head belong to God, making known His will? And, if it was, why did it seem to Marty, to resemble his own. Or, was Marty simply engaged in a silent, but delusional conversation with whom... himself? And, why should he be left to guess? God, is that you or am I just muttering?

Marty felt that if you truly needed, had to have, couldn't do without – let's just say -a block of cheese; you are starving to death; can't get cheese any other way except by divine intervention and it must be cheese-- nothing more, nothing less – then, you should just ask; and, without qualification - none of that: if your faith is sufficient; and, not: only if you attended services, prayed enough, went to catechism, said your "Hail Mary's", or struck the pose like Tebow and say: "I believe". Nope, no pre-conditions, but just: I need a block of cheese, and the next morning, on your front porch, God's Fed Ex has thrown over the gate – yeah, A BLOCK OF CHEESE! Hell, Marty wouldn't even be upset if it was damaged. No need to post the YouTube showing the delivery guy's carelessness. A damaged block of cheese on Marty's porch would be enough of a miracle to make him a believer. Oh, - and to the sign-seekers, Marty isn't one of you; nope, not Marty. If Gideon could leave out the woolen fleece, two nights running –once to get soaked and once to stay bone dry – without catching hell to pay, then Marty should be able to ask for his block of cheese. After all, it's not a sign that Marty wants, it's just cheese.

That was a fair expectation, wasn't it? Marty had always been honest with the Man, (well, maybe not always, but that's one of those pre-conditions we've chosen to dispense with) just, perhaps, not always with himself (and, that is a whole 'nuther thought for a whole 'nuther contemplation).

Anyway, Marty had never really asked for his block of cheese. He knew the rules. He knew that you first must believe – and, wholeheartedly without qualification, or equivocation. Faith was a pre-requisite. You also must repent, change your life, conform, and live by the rules: those "Thou shalt not", not ever, no never....rules - including a passel that you needed to first discover and learn while you sojourned on this planet and if you did learn and discover, then good luck trying to interpret your own delusions. He grew exasperated. He'd never expected nor insisted upon direct intervention. He could live without the cheese. Really, he could. And he did survive on the vagaries. Over the years, he'd become proficient at deciphering the hidden meaning of things. His intuition was well-developed. He could read the gathering storm on his dad's face even behind the smile when he'd had one too many beers. He was willing to read between the lines to find God's hand in the thin and thick of things, and he was even willing to make the proper assignments. You know, be grateful and all glory be for any and all of the good stuff; but masticate, savor, and swallow the full and bitter blame for any of the bad. Marty's exasperation was understandable, wasn't it? If not, justified. He'd always accepted his fate, but fate always seemed more interested in Marty's ruin and rarely in his success.

Why was it that he could never break 80 in a round of golf? No matter how well he started, the end-game was usually the same: 88. Not bad, but never better. Always the same round of golf; the same slice on number three; the same lake on number six; the same occasional par; the same cherished, but infrequent birdie, and always the same score. And, if he did happen to take par on number one right out of the gate instead of the typical bogey, Fate would intervene to make up for it with a triple bogey on number 11-- a hole Marty usually would par, only to arrive at...yep: an **88**.

Then, there were those numerous touchdown opportunities in high school: the interception to win the Regional Championship stolen right from his fingers at the last minute by the opposing tight end who ran it to his own end zone; that catch and subsequent shoestring tackle by the opposing safety that sent Marty head first to the turf just short of the end zone and the winning score; the hard cut up field behind the exceptional crack block by his tight end that culminated with a slip of the cleat on the wet grass and Marty in a heap at his tight end's feet.

And lest we not forget, there was baseball-- that 380-foot loft in the ninth inning that went foul by a foot at the left field foul pole – a shot that if fair would have won the game. But, it wasn't and it didn't. To Marty, it seemed he was always coming up short. Fate – if that is what it was – seemed always to intervene to forestall personal success. He had never expected much. He'd always given God the glory; never expected intervention; never sought his sign; never asked for his block of cheese. Marty never asked for miracles, even in the face of tragedy. He simply expected that because of something that he had done in a time long ago-- a time that he could not now remember or only vaguely recall, if at all that he was not entitled. Others who had lived a better life or who had somehow enjoyed a special place among God's favorites may be, but not Marty.

There it was, again: that vague and disturbing memory of some promise made a long time ago. What was it? What promise?

Marty heard the gulls again: Those three little cuties. So much promise in these little girls, Marty observed. How much would go to waste? How much would they squander? How much would be stolen from them, lost through no fault of their own? Had the three been older, he wouldn't concern himself. Had they been older, they just may have pissed him off with their snide comments about his belly. Their agenda would include – more than likely – a certain mean-spiritedness engendered simply by the longevity of their lives. Such narcissism, as it is so widely celebrated today, would offend and there was plenty of it around the pool today, just not in these silly but adorable little girls. Never mind. They had rejoined their family, and Marty was left to his own devices.

He again grew bored as he clung there at the pool's edge. Once more, he thought to resume his swim and looked about for his mermaid companion. There she sat across the pool deck with her back to Marty on a chaise lounge. He watched as she untied the neck strap on her bikini top. He could swear that she offered a surreptitious glance, even a wink in his direction. He instantly came to attention in more ways than one. He was definitely intrigued. She tapped the shoulder of the giant sleeping next to her and asked him to slather some sunscreen onto her back. As his hands moved over her shoulders, arms, and back, Marty marveled at such a back; so youthful; so taut and supple. Oh, what a back...a canvas for the tattoo that she sported-- a tattoo in the form of large sensuous vine or was it a serpent? The serpent ran from the front of her right shoulder over the top and across her shoulder blades to the other side of her slender torso to where it disappeared around the front side. Marty's heart caught in his throat at the thought of THE FRONT SIDE!! The serpent again emerged, this time lower down on her back only to disappear beneath her bikini bottom. And – oh, what a bottom! There certainly was promise in this beautiful creature: a treasure trove of tan lines. Boy howdy! Marty realized that he was thinking thoughts that he hadn't in a very long time. It seemed like years. When was the last time?

Then again, just about everything that Marty did remember seemed like years since he had done them, seen them, said them, sung them, smelled them, played them, performed them, insisted upon them, argued in favor of or against them, conceded or compromised them, lost or won them, or even simply thought about them. The memories, when they came of late were painful. He didn't know why. He just knew that he couldn't hold onto them for long. At times, he simply discarded them as no longer interesting. Oft times, he flat out rejected them literally because he could not cope with the emotions they engendered. The only thing he could think of these days that gave him any peace was to put one arm ahead of the other to swim and to remember from time to time, to breathe and to kick.

He took one more appreciative glance at the sexy girl with the serpent tattoo and one more curious look at the family and those gorgeously silly little girls. There with them was a striking blonde woman of about 55 who looked to be the matriarch. Marty was shocked to realize that he knew this woman! More surprisingly, he knew that he knew her well. He just could not recall from where. Her apparent family surrounded her as they picnicked on the grass.

And, there was something about the younger, slender mother with long dark hair that disquieted. She exuded confidence and exhibited the same engaging smile as the attractive matriarch. She was herself, very attractive, athletic, and confident. But her attractiveness to Marty wasn't physical; to others, maybe, but not to him. To Marty, this girl was no mermaid. She was...well, bright- almost incandescent, and familiar. He knew her too from somewhere. But he couldn't place it. In fact, he realized now that he somehow knew all of them. A strikingly handsome young man with thick dark hair and designer shades patted the slender woman's butt as she pulled sandwiches from the cooler for the three little girls.

A handsome blond kid was joking with the guy in the designer shades. He was small, compact, and agile. He was jovial and charismatic. His smile ingratiated. A sexy wide eyed young wife and mother accompanied him. A bored teenage girl watched over a batch of younger siblings.

Marty was captivated by each of them, in turn by all of them together. He longed to be with them, to be a part of them. He felt that he belonged and longed to join them on the grass not just for the picnic, but for always. The feelings were powerful and caused him to flounder. He lost his grip on the edge of the pool. The air in his lungs expended. He was no longer buoyant. He sunk like a stone. He gulped a mouthful of air mixed with water, just before he lost the surface and plunged to the depths. He wasn't prepared for this swim. He'd not taken sufficient breath. He dropped interminably. He waited for his end... a time for which he was, of course prepared, just not yet. Then, when ready to abandon the struggle, to give up the swim, Marty felt a strong hand grip the hair of his head and haul him onto the pool deck where he gasped, choked, and spat out chlorinated water for what seemed an eternity.

"Dad, are you alright? How many more laps are you gonna swim?", the handsome blonde guy joked, "Quit playin' around. You'll scare the kids. Hey, by the way...it's nice to have you back from the islands." He chuckled a bit at this one. "Which was it this time? Raivavai, Rurutu, or maybe one of the Marqueses? We're never quite sure whether we'll see you back. You were gone this time a bit longer than usual". He paused and fell silent as he helped Marty sit up. Marty coughed up more water and stayed silent.

"No kiddin' Dad. We've been worried about you. You're okay, right?" he asked. "Anyway...we're headed out. Thanks for the day. We'll come for a visit – maybe this weekend. Sorry about last week, but the kids don't like the smell of that place. They don't like to see you there. We don't like to see you there. We'd have you with us, but...you know" he trickled off. "We'll plan another outing soon, maybe Santa Cruz – Sunset Beach? Think you can handle a tent for a night?" He waved with a backward glance and said "Later". To the young wide- eyed mother, he said. "Hey, grab the kid", as he pointed toward the family pool.

This handsome, blond dad was disturbingly familiar. He reminded Marty of his own young son –but all grown up! What was his name, anyway? His next glance discomfited. He gasped and nearly choked again not from a near drowning, but from utter surprise. There, across the way - just exiting the family pool and wearing goggles- was this guy's son.

He looked to be about 6-years old with long, blond hair – the kind that Marty would want to cut on his own boy so he'd look like a jock. His mom, on the other hand, protected him from the barber's shears because – she said - it made him look so cute.

"You'll thank me one day when you look back for keeping you cool", Marty remembered the kid's mom saying. He could remember the words, just not the time or the place. Besides, Marty had disagreed. The fact is... the kid –at this stage - could care less about curls. It would be a few more years before he'd worry about mermaids and what they might think of his haircut. Marty's own dad had made him wear his hair back –even during the Age of Aquarius when everyone wore it long and down. Marty was a "greaser" in the time of "betas". He still resented it. So will this kid. His mom's got it wrong.

This boy was thin and athletic – a feather merchant, a flyer. Marty remembered his own boy and the days when Marty could not wait to return home from work so they could play. Marty would throw him as far skyward as he could and let gravity bring him back. The boy would tumble fearlessly and fall giggling back into Marty's arms. Marty would whiz throw pillows from the old green couch in their empty living room at the boy's feet as he tried to cross "no man's land"

– the area running from the hall way at the left across the blank wall to the edge of the empty living room, to the right, and the sought after safety of the dining room. The boy would giggle and Marty would laugh like he had never laughed when a well-thrown pillow found the mark to knock the feet from under the dashing boy.

Yes, dashing. He was oh so very handsome! - So, very appealing. He was Marty's dearest and only son. Marty loved him so! The two had been inseparable when Marty was a young father. They were each other's closest and dearest friends. He was the brother that Marty never had.

Suddenly and instinctively, from a place very deep within his soul, Marty knew that his son – this small boy - represented his own redemption. He was the long sought for sign to Marty that he had found forgiveness. Forgiveness for what, he could not say. He only knew that whatever he had said or whatever he had done previously was bad, very bad and he knew that he had made a promise – a promise that he could not now recall. He worried that if he ever did remember, he may not be able to honor it. These days, confusion – like the mermaid – seemed to be Marty's constant companion. Yet, how could this be? His son was not six but was in fact, much older. Marty was sure of that, wasn't he? He puzzled through and tried to focus. He could vaguely recall that his son had a son of his own – very much like the blond dad and his boy. He also remembered something about his boy's name and the name of his boy's boy. They had the same name. It was just that - at this moment - Marty couldn't recall it. He couldn't bring it back. Damn it, anyway! He was sure that, if given time, he could better remember both his boy and his boy's boy. But suddenly, Time was something of which he didn't have much of. He knew that much for sure, didn't he?

Marty obsessed over Time. He'd heard once about Einstein and his theory about a train and a light clock-- the faster the train travelled the slower the light clock worked. He wondered whether he could ever swim fast enough to slow down Time or to even stop it.

And, once stopped, where would that leave him? Could it be restarted? Or, would he just be stuck? To slow Time would be interesting, but of little use to Marty. He might put off the inevitable for a while. But unless he could stop it outright, any attempt to manipulate Time would be useless. He had seen certain sci-fi movies where, with the help of fancy Time machines, folks managed to push time into the future. Interesting, but Marty wasn't sure he'd like the future even if he could figure a way to get there. He didn't have much Time left and unless he could stop it outright the effort might prove useless. Then again, if he succeeded and did stop Time, what would that do? He'd seen an episode of the Twilight Zone where time stopped and when it did, everything stopped-- all the people, the subways, the busses, the cars...everything. He really didn't want to stop Time at all. What he wanted was to escape it. He figured he could run Time backwards to where his Swiss-cheese memory told him that his life had been tough and simply jump over that portion. He knew that 1967 was a particularly bad year. Still, he didn't know why. He knew only that he had absolutely no memory nor insight into any of that year. 1967 was an enigma. He figured that if he was going to jump over 1967, he should know exactly what it was that he would be missing with the jump.

He yawned. This obsession could wait. It wasn't some mental fog or the Swiss-cheese memory that plagued him now. Oh sure, he was bothered by the uncertainty in his thinking and the vague memories of his own boy or was it his boy's boy that he had seen there at the pool? Then, there was 1967 or more specifically, the absence of 1967 in his recollections.

Now however, it wasn't these patched and sketchy thoughts that currently possessed his thinking, but the hard stirring in his loins as were served up by the mermaid with the serpent. Again, his eyes had wandered to the mermaid on the chaise lounge. Yeah, well. He thought that he should swim, to dive deep but instead elected to stay stuck to the side of the pool; mostly, to hide his enjoyment at the stimulation currently caused by the mermaid's tattoo. Although the memory now served up by the boner he bore was embarrassing, it wasn't his first experience with this dilemma. These recollections were entertaining, if nothing more.

When he was a young man, this current circumstance occurred frequently and was all too common, most often related to some mental image brought to mind by a television show - Elizabeth Montgomery from Bewitched or Mary Tyler Moore from the Dick Van Dyke show never failed to rev his engine and, the thought that Barbara Eden's belly button might somehow elude the censors could keep him glued to the set for hours and never failed to raise his flag. Early on, the sensations that he encountered were vague and wholly unfamiliar, almost alarming, but never truly connected to concurrent circumstances. As he matured, he learned how best to control such circumstances so as to better enjoy the overall experience. The feelings, though strange, were pleasant, and the best feelings always related to some "new girl" in his life. These feelings now, though rare, brought an added benefit. They helped to fill in some of his missing memory.

Marty's first real love was a girl named January. She was an older sophisticated woman, , a sixth-grader at Marty's elementary school. He was in third-grade and sex appeal hadn't yet dawned on him. Still, in a masculine display of discretion, Marty would never reveal her last name. In practical reality, he had simply forgotten it. He was intrigued when he had seen her leave her bus to walk up the street to the school. He left his own bus and followed her a few steps behind. He could not recall her face. He had never really seen it, only the long curtain of thick and luxuriant auburn hair that fell down her back to the crease at the back of her knees. What a gorgeous cascade! Marty was smitten! But this romance really went nowhere. After all, January was an older woman and Marty was in third-grade and never did these two worlds meet in any regular elementary school, let alone in the real world. And, third-grade never presented the embarrassing physical reaction more frequently encountered as Marty matured. By the time Marty had arrived in sixth-grade, he had matured.

He had forgotten the older woman, and was now enamored with Alice Jane aka AJ. This was more of a bargaining arrangement with his pal, Rick. Rick was the BMOC. He was the only kid who could kick the soccer ball from home plate that was painted on the asphalt in the corner of the playground and onto the roof of the school that only slightly infringed into the centerfield of the baseball diamond also painted on the asphalt on which they played kick ball. (Despite his own athleticism, Marty never earned the honor that came with kicking a soccer ball on the roof from home plate).

Rick liked Ellen. She was pretty and elegant, but not yet endowed. He also liked AJ. She was freckled and athletic. She enjoyed the slight favor of her budding teenage years and wore a bra.

Ultimately, Ellen held sway and laid claim to Rick. AJ was free. She could also kick the soccer ball with the best of the boys. Marty always chose her first to be on his team and an early romance burgeoned. She bought him a Monkees album for Christmas and gave him a nice card that proclaimed how "neat" she thought he was and that "she liked him very much". Marty was not so suave. He lifted a few bucks from his mom's purse and gave the money to AJ. Sheepishly, he asked her to buy herself something nice. Somehow, Marty's mom discovered her son's regrettable faux pas and moved to smooth the romance. She took him to the local Rexall Drug Store and allowed him to select a nice crystal necklace (made of polished plastic) affixed to a delicate gold chain and a nice card. The effort helped him to continue their love through the summer following 6th grade.

Then, there was a brief infatuation with a girl in junior high school, but her name and image now escaped him. Marty had grown very used to and so much dependent upon his rather exquisite memory that his current inability to recall people and places, which he somehow knew were most important to him, proved troubling to say the least.

And of course, there was Susan-- his high school sweetheart. The ever stiffening memory currently brought on by the sex goddess sunning there at poolside and her dragon tattoo brought home to him this romance. He met her first while in junior high school. He had a few classes with her, but admired her only from afar. She was a beautiful blonde with blue eyes and a stately demeanor. She was already spoken for. She was going "steady" with a high school guy. She wore his ring on her left hand, wrapped with a boat load of ribbon to help size the ring to fit. Late in the spring prior to graduation from junior high school, the school held an afternoon dance in the gymnasium. Susan was confidently flitting about. She knew how to dance and would dance with every boy who would. Marty was entranced. He had been so entranced for the entire year. Needless to say, the crowd was small and the gym was big and Marty couldn't find a way to sidle on up to her as she danced with some schmo on the hardwoods. He was forced to take the direct approach. He timed it discretely. He arrived at her shoulder just as her last dance ended. As Marty had hoped, her partner had not determined how or even whether he would ask her for a second dance and before he could inquire, Marty was there with a glance that said scram. Luck of the draw, it was a slow dance. Marty's memory may falter, but he'd never forget that song. The Beatles. 1970.

♪♪"Something in the way she moves attracts me like no other lover. Something in the way she woos me. And, I don't want to leave her now. I can only believe and how". Ba bump ba daaa daaa daaaaaaaa!"♪♪.

Susan held him close, closer than any "woman" ever had. He was literally locked in her embrace – not only for romantic reasons, but for very practical ones. As the song ended, the bell rang and it was time to go. Marty tried to hold the pose in the hope that his loins might relax. No luck. He awkwardly parted from her close embrace with his hands in the front pockets of his Levi Straus 501 jeans in a rather fruitless effort to hide what –though embarrassing - may be best described as utter enjoyment. Susan took a quick glance downward. She kindly offered her baby blues together with a sweet and understanding smile. The buttons at the front of his jeans bulged further and were set to pop. Marty could do nothing more than pull his hands from his pockets and cross them directly in front to thank her for her gift. His embarrassment notwithstanding, Marty was truly a happy man.

He saw her next at the winter ball at high school. Marty was one of only three sophomores to earn a varsity letter in football. He wore one of only three varsity letter jackets yet to be displayed at the school. He wore it proudly to the dance. He danced with all the most popular girls. He was much more confident with the women. He was out to strut his stuff.

Unbeknownst to Marty, Susan; Collette; and Sandy each had broken up with their upper classman boyfriends. Also unbeknownst to him, each boyfriend was at the dance and grousing. Further unbeknownst to him, each girlfriend likely accepted Marty's invitation to dance not because he was suave, debonair, or sophisticated, but because a dance with Marty might rekindle a slight flame elsewhere to be lit by jealousy.

That night, as he left the dance, he saw Susan at the door. He had a new car and had just earned his driver's license. He held two tickets to see Grand Funk Railroad in concert. He took the chance afforded, but saw it more as destiny. He asked and she answered. After that, they were an item at school through their junior year. They split for a time in the senior year then, reunited only to last see her – and his self-winding jewel of a wristwatch - at the airport.

Yah well, all this reminiscence proved boring. None of it made any sense and Marty could see little import to those things that he could recall. He was more concerned about what he couldn't. The young family that had intrigued him there at the side of the pool would have to wait. He was in no mood to be familial. Oh, sure. He had parents. He had a wife, he knew that. He had kids, he knew that. But these memories danced at the edge, never more definitive, never exact. He had realized sometime back that his memory was best described as Swiss cheese. It was full of holes. He could try to remember. He was always trying to remember. Sometimes, he'd succeed. But the memories were always... always full of holes.

For example, he thought to himself, he knew that he loved his wife. He knew that he had one...a damn good one and that she was very good looking, very much like the blonde at the pool. Somehow, he could not bring her to mind just now. He knew that she would let him off of the hook for such brief indiscretions like his youthful distraction with this mermaid at the pool. She knew that at his age, a mermaid was a brief distraction at best and, as Marty had come to learn, such a very long time ago, "youth" was a fleeting fantasy that could be better enjoyed without the stiff eroticism and outside the rather rigid constraints that frequently accompanied.

So, for now - either for embarrassment, or out of utter exasperation, Marty wanted out-- out of the pool, out of his Swiss cheese memory. He just needed to get out! He wanted to rejoin the young family. He wanted to feel whole again. But in this current fog, he was uncertain whether he belonged there with them. He was not sure whether he had any connection to them, anyway. He was even more uncertain of himself. Who was he anyway? He adjusted himself, adjusted his goggles, and pushed off and -for the moment- he calmly swam the surface to enjoy the soft orange light of the setting sun. Then, with some regret, but in desperate need of something, he dove

CHAPTER II

Marty had been down for some time. He remembered little when he broke the surface to awaken to the cries of gulls. Was he back on his island? He could barely deal with such starts and stops. He looked around expecting to see palm trees and coconuts. Instead, what he saw were those same 3 little girls running around a bed on which he was propped. They chattered wildly. Boy, were they ever happy to be together with each other. He reached a hand to wipe his eyes. His vision was obscured by what seemed to be water spots like those on the windshield of his truck following a brief but hellacious thunderstorm.

"Dad, where did you get those goggles? Why are you wearing those?" an attractive young woman asked him not necessarily expecting a response. "Why is he wearing those?" she looked at the blonde matriarch seated next to her. "Here, let me help." This was the slender and disquietingly familiar young dark haired mother from the poolside earlier. She reached for his head as he rested it on his pillow. She smelled nice and, again, so familiar. He knew one thing for sure. He loved this girl and she loved him. She didn't need to say anything. He knew her thoughts. He knew her strengths. They were many.

Was this one of those new, but fleeting superpowers that Marty seemed to arbitrarily possess? Sometimes he could read minds, but not always and not predictably. There were times he'd give a testicle to know what others were thinking. Hell, there were times he'd give the other testicle just to know what he was thinking. His thoughts were so scrambled these days, he didn't know if he was coming or going. But he knew this! He knew that this sweet smelling girl was exceptionally talented: fluent in I-tal-i-an; an accomplished athlete; a caring, young mother who had experienced her own brand of personal trauma and was stronger for it; a loyal wife and... was she his daughter? He puzzled briefly at this last thought. His mind clicked over as if ranging through a roll-a-dex. Whatever it was that he sought had vanished as quickly as it had appeared. Yes, he knew this girl. He knew her enough to know and understand even her vulnerability and just how very well she masked it. He wasn't sure how he knew. He just did.

She removed the red pair of cheap, plastic swimming goggles from his head. The elastic band pulled at some of the thinning, residual hair at the back of his head. "Ouch", he squawked, and thought to himself, "Hey, girl, don't lose those. I'm gonna need them again very soon".

She seemed to understand: "Sorry Dad. Don't get excited. I'll put them here on the nightstand". She patted his cheek.

Little blondie with the wicked eyebrows chimed in. "But mom, those are my goggles. I need them for the hot tub with Nona". "Hey pops!" she said, looking to Marty, "Those are my goggles. I need them for the hot tub with Nona".

The attractive blonde matriarch rescued him. Marty knew that she'd been taking him off of the hook like this for some time now. He knew that he loved this woman, too. He knew that he had a history with her, a long one. But he'd be damned if he knew what it was. He also wasn't sure just how it was that he knew what he did know.

"Nona, gave those to Papa," she said. "Yours are at home in the drawer, remember? Yours are the yellow ones. Papa's are red. We'll leave these here, then everybody will have a pair. C'mon you girls, give your Papa a kiss. It's time to go. Should we go to the Dollar Store? How 'bout a cupcake?" This woman was busy, Marty noticed.

To the young and slender mom, she said, "As soon as we brought him here, he went back to that island. It's where he goes, where he disappears. He'll mention it from time to time when he is more lucid". She swallowed hard and choked back a sob. "I'm not sure how he got a hold of these. Isn't that funny?"

The older, more astute of the 3 little girls chimed in, "I want A S'more. Can Papa come with us? He has to build us a fire to make S'mores." S'mores. Yeah, Marty knew what they were. He didn't much care for them -way too much sugar. He was on a restricted diet. He was hyperglycemic. When did that happen, anyway? Melted chocolate and toasted marshmallows on a graham cracker meant sticky fingers and insulin shock. They reminded him of Boy Scouts.

He hated scouts. He'd made second-class by spotting three constellations while standing in the front walk of his local church and staring skyward. There's the Big Dipper with the North Star and the handle that points to the Little Dipper. It always bugged Marty that he could only find the "Dipper" constellations, and then only by relying on one to point to the other. Why couldn't he just step up and point to both? The scoutmaster never really followed Marty's finger as he pointed skyward. Yep. There's Orion with his belt and the Dog Stars. Hell. Marty could have taken credit for a few more if he had remembered their names. He'd simply named three of the requisites. That's all that the scout master cared and that's all it took to secure 2nd class. Big deal! It was nothing like the effort it took to make the junior high basketball team. Not even close to the talent required to earn a varsity letter, let alone seven in three years plus two team captain stars and the self-winding watch that went to the Best Senior Athlete.

Tears suddenly welled in the eyes of both women: the smiling eyes of the attractive matriarch and the exotic green eyes of the athletically slender young mom. "Not today. Papa needs to rest," the matriarch protected. He felt bad for these women. He knew that somehow he was to blame for their sadness. He wasn't sure what they wanted. Such uncertainty had become de rigueur, it seemed.

Marty couldn't see the sentiment. Here at the home, he was left with nothin' but stinkin' memories and scout camp was one of the stinkin'est. But this place was worse than scout camp and only his memories could take him away from here. Even the crappiest were better than decaying here in bed. His first experience with scout camp was a day camp with the Guide Patrol. They had told him to bring a tin foil dinner. His mom, resourceful as ever, put a frozen

Mexican TV-dinner into his backpack. It wasn't even a real backpack. It was more of a shoulder bag. Marty felt silly with it on. It felt like some kind of man purse in a day when no one had yet to coin the phrase and even if they had, Marty wouldn't wear one. He just felt silly. But, his dinner was a hit. Probably because it wasn't made of authentic scout stuff: hamburger or Salisbury steak; carrots; peas; potatoes; onions – you know, all the makings of a mid-western stew. Marty ate the enchilada. The other boys ate most of his refried beans and rice. Marty knew that that meal didn't conform. He knew that he didn't conform. He didn't belong here with these boys, with these leaders. He was taller than almost every other boy in the patrol. He'd gotten most, if not all, of his 6 feet and 1 inch in early adolescence. He was a budding athlete and the other boys sensed the threat. Even though Marty never suspected, they seemed to recognize instinctively that he would surpass them, in short order, in the teenage popularity contests that would soon swallow them all. Acne held him back and kept him bashful. Most of these boys were still testosterone-challenged. Many retreated to literal mind games which – in that day – meant chess or calculus.

"What are we doing for scouts tonight?" he had asked at his first meeting with the patrol.

"Chess tournament," Mikey responded. Mikey was the patrol leader and seemed to be the man in charge. Marty knew him. He was a bit of a punk. Couldn't play basketball to save his life; never went swimming with the rest of the troop; always lorded over everyone as if he knew what he was talking about when most always, he didn't know a lick. Marty participated regardless. He held his own well enough with chess, but was soon eliminated. Well, okay...so Mikey knew how to play chess, and Marty spent the rest of the night shooting hoops alone.

He came the following week, hoping to go to the local indoor pool at the junior high school or, even better, to Pingree's pond to skinny dip and steal cherries from their orchard.

"What are we doing for scouts tonight?" he asked when he arrived.

"We're finishing our chess tournament," Mikey responded. Soooo... Marty shot baskets again. He was getting good.

"What are we doing for scouts tonight?" Marty asked the third week running.

Mikey again responded in that dry monotone of those uninterested, "We're starting a new chess tournament".

That was it. Marty was done. He left and, except for a final scout camp over three days of rain that cemented his decision, he never played "scout" again.

In later years, Mikey Morrison – top third academically in the graduating class and President of the High School Chapter of the National Honor Society – would routinely remind Marty that he held the dubious distinction of carrying the lowest GPA – a 3.65 – of any member of that vaunted group. Until one day, when fed up with all the reminders, Marty acknowledged Morrison's snide observations and conceded that in contrast to Morrison's raging intellect, Marty could hold no candle. But Marty did also conclusively confirm to Mr. Morrison that he could and, indeed, he did through the course of high school – kick Morrison's very smart ass clean cross campus.

In large measure, the success that Marty enjoyed as a high school jock masked the insecurities that he felt. Now as he strapped back on the red goggles, he couldn't quite remember why he felt their stares: the stares of his peers; of his neighbors; of the church members and its' leaders; of his very own grandfather. He only knew that they judged him for something that he had done – something that Marty somehow knew was very bad, but that he just could not seem to remember. His mind clicked over again and his eyes fluttered as he tried to access the role-a-dex, but nothing. And if that wasn't enough, they judged him because he was his father's son. Marty was determined to swim through Time, if necessary, to find the answer. The key was speed, but he hadn't yet determined how best to control it. Only recently, he had begun to experiment with his medications.

He remembered his dad as a functional alcoholic. He was a successful auto dealer who squandered most of his income by drinking, gambling, and philandering. Marty puzzled again over the larger truth. How was it that he could legitimately say that his father, though a lousy husband, was a good father? How could he convince people that, though he beat Marty's mother, he never laid a hand on Marty or his siblings? How could his own father ,who was so dishonest in marriage, be the only person to have fired Marty from a job because he insisted on absolute honesty with his employer. Marty had fudged his time card at the dealership and dad, the used car manager at the time, found him out. He fired him on the spot. This same guy who cheated regularly on Marty's mother canned his ass for dishonesty. Was it any wonder that Marty puzzled the complexities?

How was it that although Marty's mom hated the man, Marty loved him? Loved him for his bold character, for his charisma and charm, for his integrity - no matter how compartmentalized. He loved him for his strength, and for just how safe Marty felt in those rare moments when his dad was around and sober. Kids brag that their dad can beat up the other dads. Marty knew it for a fact. He was there on more than one occasion to watch his dad brawl, always out of a sense of honor or chivalry. To Marty, the incongruity was staggering. But it spoke volumes about why Marty swam.

Mom hated dad, not for his infidelities, nor for his physical cruelties. For those, she hated only herself for enduring them. No. She hated dad because he'd killed himself and Marty's younger sister when he fell asleep at the wheel while drinking and driving. Dad was 40. Sister was 19. Marty was 23 and soon to be engaged. That explains that.

Marty realized that this line of thinking was taking him nowhere. He had to get to the water. He needed to swim. But the two women still chatted privately out in the hallway as the three little girls played with their toys around his bed. The tiny brunette dribbled a soccer ball off of her feet, first one foot and then the other: 5233, 5234, 5235....she counted. Impressive! Marty thought. The tall pretty blond gazed into a small compact and carefully put on lipstick over and over again. She was very pretty, he observed. The youngest lay on the bed at Marty's feet, distracted. Yeah, sometimes that's a good way to be, he silently admired. She appeared to be watching some kind of television, but the screen was much too small and Marty could see no antenna. On any other day he would be curious to see this new-fangled gimmick, but not today. Today, he needed to swim.

The two women had moved further into Hallway A intent upon their conversation. They apparently had some business and spoke to each other in whispers. Marty wondered whether the little girls might want to join him.

He wiped the water marks from his goggles, swung his feet over the bed, straightened and smoothed his speedo. He stood weakly, but defiantly. He tied the beach towel around his neck to make a cape to help him fly. Attached to each foot was a red swim fin, color coordinated to match his speedo and goggles. He duck- walked out of the bedroom door with practiced stealth. The fins made little sound against the linoleum floor. He moved deftly, stealthily, instinctively - even in fins. He waved silently for the girls to join him. He held a finger to the side of his nose as a signal to them to be quiet. They smiled back. They were up for the adventure. They followed him out of the doorway and easily crept unnoticed past the two otherwise anxiously engaged women.

Whether it was his red goggles or the pill combination that he had pulled from his speedo and swallowed he couldn't say, but his night vision was enhanced in the darkened convalescent corridors. A blue light from a television streamed from an open bedroom door while the room's withered and overly ripe occupants slept. A stray light from a small night lamp emanated from several rooms on either side of the hallway and further helped to navigate. Marty and the three girls successfully traversed Hallway A, up to and across the front entry and stopped against the darkened wall directly across Hallway B from the nurse's station where sat Ms. Bichette noting in her ledger the nightly medication recap.

The little girls were excited for the adventure and a giggle escaped. Marty quickly put up a fist in a military signal to stand still. The little girls apparently knew military and froze in place. Without turning, he again put a finger alongside his nose to signal quiet. The older girl clamped a hand over the mouths of each of the younger girls. The giggling ceased.

Ms. Bichette was at the front desk. She looked up from her work. She leaned out and over the counter to inspect. She looked down Hallway B. Nothing. She looked over to the front entry. Nothing...except Maggie. She was parked in her chair near the window. As always, she was sound asleep and snoring. Except for her snoring, the hacking cough down Hallway B, and the crickets in the moonlight outside the front entry, all was quiet at Golden Hills. Ms. Bichette sat down at the desk and went back to her books. Marty signaled to move. The three girls silently stepped in line and followed him along the wall to the door, just across the front office where Ms. Bichette was standing guard. This door opened to a length of stairs that led downstairs to the temporary morgue. Marty and the girls took these stairs down to where Golden Hills delivered the old folks who, on any given day, had failed to make the final call.

From the stairs, they stepped into the temporary morgue. The place was dark, empty and sterile. No one was home either living or dead. Three body-sized stone tables with stainless steel tops sat beneath the fluorescent emergency lighting in a single row across the concrete floor. Three stainless steel tables on wheels were parked in the open access to the back room. The place was made of stainless steel. One wall consisted of nothing but drawers: six columns across and four rows high with stainless steel fronts and a chrome handle in the center of each. Opposite the body-drawers was an open access to a darkened storage and receiving area further back. Across from the stairway were a small working desk and a circular adjustable stool. The desk was surrounded by wooden cupboards and drawers that contained supplies. The morgue was not fully functional so the supplies mostly consisted of hoses, detergents and other cleaning supplies, and temporary cloth coverings for the dearly departed; no surgical or other cutting tools were needed. It was not intended to be a preparation station.

To Marty, it was more like a "limbo", or a temporary holding terminal where the departed souls freshened up to wait for assignment. Marty felt that a snack or some kind of lunch counter would have been nice for those patient souls, but then again...why?

"C'mon girls", he waved for them to follow. He led them through the darkened morgue to the exit door into the garage. He reached over the doorway header to retrieve the key. Somehow, he knew there would be one. There always was a key at the header. He unlocked the door and shepherded the girls through. He shut the door and placed the key under the mat. He saw writing on the mat which read: "The course of the Lord is one eternal round (1 Nephi 10:19)."

The effect was immediate. Marty stood stone still, lost in thought. He knew this scripture. He wasn't sure, but it seemed to fit in with a new vision that on which he'd given some thought recently. He called it, his No Time theory. What did the scripture say: "one eternal round"? But how, he wondered.

He had been toying with a theory- his theory- the theory that once a person has attained the speed of light, he finds himself in a place, if you will, that he called: No Time, a place where Time itself was not measured or cut up into little pieces that we call seconds, minutes, hours, days, weeks, months, or years; a place where the past, the present, and the future, are all the same.

Since he had come to the home and adjusted to life in this place, he found himself in a daily battle to reach the speed of light, if only to erase Time, to otherwise stop it so as to capture events, to cement memories. Indeed, he fought each day to stop Time, to somehow arrest its inexorable progress. He wondered sometimes whether the secret was somehow associated with the number and sequence of the pills that he took. On occasion, he had experimented, but so far, nothing had come of it.

To him, No Time would free him from any one time or place. He liked to think that once he got to No Time, he could pick and choose where – or, more realistically – when he wanted to go. He continued to experiment. He saw No Time as some kind of launching platform, or better still, a library where one could be free and without pressure to select from the "Pages of Time" as it were, any specific date and time that one might find intriguing or even needful, and then to enter it. To Marty, No Time was the library from which one could research and select from among the infinities of Time. He had experimented to find No Time, but so far it remained a secret still to discover and yet to explore. Marty sensed that the secret was somehow locked in the year "1967" and was coupled with the random thought, as taken from a physics class that he had dwelled upon for years now.

The class talked about Einstein, his speeding train, and a light clock. Marty wasn't much sure what it all meant - together or alone. He squinted hard and attempted to focus his mind. With a concentrated effort, he recalled learning about a bouncing beam of light between mirrors in a clock set inside a train. The theory, as he vaguely recalled, was to send the train forward along the track at an ever-increasing speed. As the speed increased, the light beam grew longer as it ticked and tocked between the mirrors. As the distance between ticks and tocks lengthened, the time from tick to tock slowed. As the distance continued to lengthen, the beam took longer to reach a tick at one mirror to the tock at the other which caused the measure of Time to take longer and Time to move more and more slowly. So, when the rocket ship finally reached the speed of light to match the speed of the light beam between mirrors, the two would be travelling parallel to each other and Time would...well, not so much stop, but it would no longer be measured; no "tick" no "tock" because it travelled with the train at the same speed. This was No Time.

Marty didn't concern himself with what might happen after No Time. Nor did he worry much about if the train should move faster than the speed of light, in essence faster than a ticking light clock, itself. The theory held that if the clocked ticked and tocked faster than light, Time would move backwards. But – to Marty - if Time was no longer measured, Time would no longer exist. He was sure that it was in No Time where he needed to be. It was this "place", if you will, that he needed to find. He knew that he should ponder this some more, but for now, he remained frozen there at the door. He couldn't move if he wanted to, until...

...the bright little brunette tugged at his Speedo. "Papa, let's go", she urged. "C'mon".

Abruptly, he awakened and shook himself. For a moment, he was unsettled. He shook himself again to clear his head. He bent to straighten the mat and said, "Yeah, okay. Let's go". He left the garage with the girls in tow. "Hey guys, how about a swim today?" he asked. They each nodded to him and smiled. They all headed down the road together. They were going to the high school. It had a pool AND a high dive.

CHAPTER III

The high school was closed for the summer. Of course it was. There were a few landscape personnel cutting the lawns, pulling weeds, stuff like that; and some maintenance folks coming in and out of the main building. But the pool was deserted. The summer hours were posted: 12 pm to 6 pm. Marty figured that it must be early morning. The gate was locked. He popped an orange pill and within minutes his fins were fluttering. He was able to helicopter each of the three girls up and over the six-foot fence. The pool was theirs. Still, he was troubled. Another sign on the gate said "No Life Guard on Duty – Unaccompanied Children under six, Not Permitted without an Accompanying Adult". It was a lap pool with a deep end for diving, and these girls were young. Marty didn't know – or, at least could not now recall – their respective ages. He was worried for them. He had only assumed that they could swim and if they couldn't, he certainly would not qualify as an accompanying adult. He frowned at the thought. He remembered something about pink and blue...pink and blue? He reached into his speedo and found three pills: one pink, two blue. He popped all three into his mouth and swallowed. He waited a moment. The air around him began to buzz with "white noise". The scratchy sound faded in and out, lengthen and slowed, grew short and quickened. His vision blurred and became fuzzy; his horizontal hold began to slip like a TV station with poor reception. He turned to the girls seated expectantly on the lawn next to poolside. He closed his eyes and reached out his hand toward them. Instinctively, almost subconsciously, he began to flip imaginary pages. He flipped to the left and backward through the imaginary book and the girls appeared younger with every turn; forward and to the right, and they became older. He continued to flip the pages to the right until each of the girls appeared to be in their teens: the older brunette – maybe 17; the second and younger blond – possibly 14; and the youngest 12 or 13 maybe. Marty blinked incredulously. He wasn't sure what he had done. He had acted spontaneously and was now baffled by the effect.

Each of these young women was exceptionally beautiful with incredible promise. Each of these girls was familiar. He knew them. They were very much like his granddaughters. They were his granddaughters.

"Hey pops, c'mon" the pretty brunette, tiny in stature, smiled and signaled him to follow.

He smiled and ran to dive with them into the pool. They raced down the parallel lanes to the deep end where Marty pushed himself up and out. He mounted the high dive and jumped onto the springboard. The board shot him skyward. He rocketed upward and glided comfortably into a nicely executed back flip. He stood for a moment in the open air above the pool where he calmly flitted, fluttered, and floated softly downward to slip silently into the pool. The experience was exhilarating. One after another, the girls climbed the high board to hit and bend the board to execute a beautiful swan dive to follow him into the deep end of the pool. They dove together. They laughed together. Their Time together was uproarious.

But within seconds it seemed, as he rose to the surface from his last dive, his mood quickly darkened. His head ached and he began to sink. His mind swirled and thrummed. The spell hit him hard. He wondered whether he had overdosed. Maybe he should have taken TWO pink and only ONE blue; or, maybe – only one of each. He had never tried any combination of pink and blue...or, had he? He might have, but just now, he didn't remember. Still, he must remember! He must know what to do; how to escape.

He mentally scanned his Swiss-cheese mind. He drew blanks. He felt like a jalopy pounding over a speed bump. His mind would bounce and rattle to a brief halt, only to start up again with a jolt. Sometime, just after an exceptionally hard jolt in his thinking with a subsequent rattle in his efforts to remember, he found a place of clarity. He inhaled deeply and exhaled hard to clear his nerves; again, he inhaled and this Time he held it and deep. He dove to escape the light and confusion at the surface. He dove deep into blackness to find peace. Instead he found a library.

It appeared to be ancient building with broad and low lying stone steps and Doric columns that supported large stone eaves, equally as broad as the steps – all covered by a roof. Between the columns, he saw what appeared to a front façade and entry made entirely of glass. The interior was open to view. Marty treaded water as he searched for a door or some way in. He found none. He swam up close and put up a hand to test what appeared to be glass. There was no glass, but rather a clean-cut separation between the water in which he swam and what seemed to be the typically cool, dry interior of a typical library. He was unsure about the interior only because his had could not penetrate to the library's interior ,and the "separation" felt gritty and hard. He attempted to knock. Instead of smooth glass, he felt what seemed to be the roughened surface of cement plaster. Marty realized that he was feeling the wall of the swimming pool. The realization dawned and Marty struggled to keep the vision open. The "white noise" waned. His thinking blurred and bumped. He shook his head vigorously to clear the buzz and extinguish the incredible headache that had seized. He squinted in an effort to bring back the vision, to see through the glass and into the library.

Instinctively, he raised a hand to eyes as if to see better into the brightened interior. He struggled to open even one eye. As he did, the vision opened again, and clarified to where Marty saw a large crystalline chandelier hung from the ceiling. The interior lighting was exquisite. The flooring appeared to be of ancient marble- cream in color, rich and relevant.

In front of him stood a single bookshelf made of what appeared to be Cherrywood. On the wall at either side was a large mirror that virtually filled the wall on which it hung. A third mirror was affixed to the rear wall in a similar fashion. The reflection of the Cherrywood bookshelf in each mirror revealed row after row of what appeared to be identical bookshelves, one after another, after another. These bookshelves seemed to stretch out to,well, to eternity. The label affixed to the outside of this shelf carried some kind of Dewey Decimal mark: **mmm110344.00:01** through **mmm110344+01.01.00:00**. Marty could make no sense of the markings. Marty could see the backs of the first few volumes: **mmm110344+00:01**, **mmm110344+00:02**, **mmm110344+03**. The markings appeared consecutive. Marty speculated that each marked volume represented one second. Interestingly, each of the other shelves that appeared in the mirrors carried what were "different" Dewey Decimal markings. In this way, each shelf was unique and different from the others.

Marty's mind began to scan the vast array of apparently limitless Cherrywood shelves. When he found a shelf, he would scan for a book. When he found a book, he would pull it down and begin to peruse, page by page, one page at a time. When he finished one page, he would systematically lick his thumb and turn another page. Over and over in his mind, he turned the pages, subconsciously licking his thumb as he tried to remember, as he tried to decide what he might do to counteract his reaction to the medications he had taken.

But he couldn't remember and as the library faded from view, he was sinking fast. He reached for the pocket inside his speedo and pulled out a pill. It was blue. He took it and he hoped. He hit bottom and was fading into blackness. Normally, he wouldn't worry. He had been here before and, normally, wouldn't fight. Oft times, he would simply let go, pass out, and ride it out beneath the waves until he came to – typically back in bed or sometimes engaged in a new adventure. He'd done it before. He would surface eventually.

But today was not normal. Nothing about his experience here was normal. More importantly, the girls were somewhere above and he worried for them. He pressed hard to shake the fog from his head. Surprisingly, the pain was now bearable as he stroked upward toward the surface. Each pull upward was stronger than the last. When he broke the surface, he visually scanned the pool for the girls. He could not see them anywhere. He squinted to engage his bionic eyes. His vision magnified and he scanned the back fences, the picnic area, the stands, the pool deck, and the pool. They were nowhere to be found.

He continued to scan and soon realized that, unlike previously, the pool was occupied and busy; kids splashing, families picnicking beneath shaded tables; the Lifeguard blew her whistle at a few boys racing each other to the lunch counter; and young adults flirted with each other as they sunbathed. Marty thought he caught a brief glimpse of the Mermaid with serpent tattoo sunbathing near the back fence. He would have loved to linger. But he must find the girls.

His eyes scanned again the grounds and the pool's edge where he first noticed a familiar young boy about twelve years old, and a familiar young girl about ten. They were seated together at the pool's edge dangling there feet. The young boy saw him and waved.

"Hey Dad" he shouted across the pool. The two swam to Marty's side. "We've been waiting for you. Let's race". The young girl pushed herself up and out of the pool. She stood and took a starter's stance. The young boy followed. "C'mon Dad, let's go."

Marty remained baffled, but he was never one to turn down a challenge. He figured that the little girls couldn't have gone far. He scanned the swimming pool again to make sure they were not with him. His meds must be toying with him, again. He seemed to know instinctively that the little girls were safe and back at Golden Hills. Likely, they never really left. Instinct told him that he was right. He could take a quick turn to appease these kids. He stood at pool's edge, lowered his goggles, and crouched. "Go" the boy shouted. Marty dove. He swam easily with long and slow strokes. He reached the opposite wall, raised his head, and pulled up his goggles. The two kids sat on the edge of the pool. They had been waiting for him. This is not possible, Marty thought. How did these kids beat him?

"Let's race back", the girl shouted. "Go, Dad. We're right behind you". Marty pushed off of the wall and stroked. He pulled strongly this time and he kicked. He figured he'd put in enough effort to beat them by maybe a length. He hit the wall and turned to wait. He remained submerged and scanned the waters: Nobody. He stood up, confused.

"Hey Dad" he heard the young boy from behind. "We won!" Marty spun around in surprise.

"Yeah, Dad", the young girl chimed in. "We beat you again! Not bad, huh Dad?"

Marty's pride was wounded. His meds were messed up. He knew that to be true. They were not working or they worked too well or, maybe – and he knew this also to be the truth - he had taken the wrong combination. He certainly didn't feel like himself. But he very soon realized that, for some strange reason, he actually felt better than himself. He felt young or, at least, younger- more alive. He may as well take the advantage.

He stood up at pool's edge and took the swimmer's stance. The young boy and girl joined him. He looked to the young girl. She smiled and said "Reeaaady...GO!" The three dove and swam. Marty went for all that he was worth. He kicked hard. He stroked long, not so smooth, but fast. He needed to breathe. He touched at the wall and broke the surface hard. He looked up. There sat the young boy and the young girl together at the side of the pool.

"Hi Dad, we won again", the two said in unison as they stood and high-fived each other. "Bye Dad, Mom's calling. It's time to eat". They scurried away and disappeared.

Marty pushed himself out of the pool and sat alone at the edge. His feet dangled in the water. He inhaled hard, held it for a count, and pushed it out. His breathing quickly returned to normal. He felt great. Still, these kids had beaten him. He looked into the water. Only then did he see that he was not wearing flippers. Of course, he thought. No wonder he lost. He'd lost his flippers. It seemed like a good excuse; a great reason to explain the vagaries of age. He'd worn them...well forever to help him swim. His pride was assuaged. He looked at his legs and felt his abdomen. His legs looked and felt strong. His stomach was flat. He felt his pectorals. They were... firm. He looked to each bicep. Whoa! He felt strong like back in the day. He realized that he had indeed grown "younger". On self assessment, he placed himself in his forties.

Then it came to him. The boy and girl who had raced him across the pool were indeed his own kids. He grinned. He remembered the day that they had raced, the day that he first confronted his mortality, the day they forced him to come to grips with aging; and, he knew this pool. The kids joined the swim team here shortly after they had moved as a family to the area. He and his wife had purchased a home and raised the kids in the surrounding bedroom community. On one of the first Saturdays here at the pool, the kids had challenged him to race and....yes, they had won. Marty grinned. The fog in his head was lifting. The effect from his pills had dispersed. He felt like he was 40, and like when he was 40, he was very happy. He moved to the lawn area and lay down beneath a large oak tree. He thought to enjoy this moment a moment longer; how much longer, he could not say. As it was, the Time was very brief.

Once again, he head began to spin. "White noise" came back and buzzed around his ears. He became queasy. He felt faint. He stood up and moved shakily back toward the pool. The air around him vibrated and his vision obscured. His horizontal hold began to flip again and frazzle as he splashed, head first into the pool. He sunk into the deep end where he blacked out. Seconds later it seemed, three little girls swam to him at the bottom of the pool. Each one tagged him and swam away. He knew that he should follow. He swam to the surface to find them: the oldest sat on the chaise, smiled and waved at him, the middle was in the shallow end taunting him, and the youngest was seated in the nearby hot tub preoccupied and currently disengaged. Each was appeared younger than when they had first come to the pool.

"You're 'it' pops", the little brunette called out. She was the oldest. "Good job hiding. How'd you stay down for so long, anyway? We got worried".

"Oh, sorry" Marty offered weakly. "How long was I down?"

"I don't know. But you did a good job holding your breath. Way to go!" she smiled. "Hey, I'm hungry. Can we go find Larry in the cafeteria? He makes great sandwiches".

Re-entry into Golden Hills was uneventful. They arrived at the glass front doors and stood outside. The little girls sat on the edge of the fountain. Marty lined them up from oldest to youngest there on the short wall. He instructed them to make a chain. He took the hand of the oldest; the oldest joined with the middle girl; and, the middle girl then held hands with the youngest on the end. He told them to hold tight and to follow him into the fountain.

"Follow me down, one right after the other. Hold your breath and hang on to each other. Don't let go and don't stop. We'll be out in just a second', he instructed them.

"Coooolll" they all cheered together.

Marty pulled his goggles over his eyes. He looked at his feet and wondered how he had found his flippers. He gave the thumbs up to the girls and stepped into the fountain. As he submerged, he felt the oldest follow him down. He could sense the other two follow suit.

Within seconds it seemed, they emerged, one at a time from the hot tub in PT. He looked at each of them and swore them to secrecy. They smiled and nodded. It was their secret. He pulled some towels from the stack left by the maintenance staff.

Back in Hallway A, just outside of Marty's bedroom door, they found the two women still chattering. The little girls surrounded their mother and asked, as they dried their hair with the towels, if they could take lunch with Larry in the cafeteria. Their mom looked curiously at the towels, but did not ask. She looked at the pretty older woman who Marty figured was Grandma, or Nona, maybe. The pretty woman with long blond hair and a beautiful smile nodded to the three little ones, and they all traipsed off to find Larry. Marty went to bed and sleeping soundly with seconds. It had been an exhausting day.

CHAPTER IV

Sometime later, whether by hours or maybe by days, Marty awoke lying in bed on his back and above the sheets. The air was thick, muggy. He stared at the peeling paint on the ceiling. He could hear the faint din of people out in the corridor and far away down the hallway. He sniffed the air to experiment. The place in which he found himself smelled of old people. This island that seemed to hold him captive was musty and decayed. Death visited here frequently. He sensed it.

Death was a mermaid: sensual and appealing especially to someone of Marty's age, with his Swiss-cheese memory, and a host of other ailments: hypertension; hyperglycemia; acid reflux; sleep deprivation; and, erectile dysfunction - for the most part anyway. He sensed her presence. He felt her dark, but enticing energy. She was a worthy opponent and her presence here explained the barely audible sighs, the moans and groans, the occasional chokes and gasps that reverberated through the otherwise silent hallways, which accompanied the smell of hospital food that wafted through the corridors along with the other disagreeable smells of the old folks' home.

He wondered how it had come to this? How had he gotten himself here? Like an out-of-time Briggs and Stratton, his mind chugged hard to catch up. How had he come to this? His life had held so much promise. His legs were his life, or maybe a better description would be his "ego", his sense of self-worth. He was maybe not the fastest in terms of sprinter's speed, but definitely the quickest on any squad. Yep. He was a pronator; his toes pointed slightly outward as he walked, or even better, as he "stalked" the playing fields and hardwoods. His locomotion originated in the knees and tarsals. It wasn't the preferred method of athletic ambulation, but none of his coaches complained. 4.5-second speed in the 40-yard dash earned him a couple of JC scholarships in football and in baseball. These he rejected for bigger dreams - a walk-on at the University. His first shot never materialized. The second came round, but a blown knee only a month later – like many bad breaks in Marty's storied career – and, his chances fizzled. Yet, in the day, those quick dives from the right half usually earned him five-to-seven-yards. On sweeps and reverses, he'd usually get pinned at the sideline. He didn't have enough flat speed to beat the linebacker to the corner. Fate employed that linebacker. At times, Fate also employed even his own teammates.

Marty could not count the number of kick-offs and punt returns that had been called back: 30, 40, 50 yards - even a touchdown or two - because of penalties (plural). The first thing he looked for, after a long run back, would be the yellow flag on the field. nine times out of 10, there it was like a huge dandelion flower: a weed springing from the turf. The play would come back; the yardage negated. He could jump a route from the right defensive corner better than the best. He averaged an interception in each of nine games, three years running. Marty knew that if the receiver beat the push, it could be six. Could be, but never was. Only one – maybe- was ever fast enough to beat him: an Italian kid from Murray High School. Thank Gawd, the QB overthrew the pass. That was one time that Marty felt he'd beaten Fate. Ironically, the realization came only after he'd nearly been beaten. Yeah, well...one battle won, but a war left to battle.

In baseball, the coaches gave him the green light on the base paths. Whenever he got the itch, he was good to go. A catcher slow out of the crouch or with a weak arm, or a pitcher – even the lefties – who signaled too early their move to home, and Marty was gone; and the outfield...? He owned it! -the whole of it! The rule was that if Marty called for it from centerfield –even if foul to left or to the right - the other fielders gave way. His skill on the diamond had even served him well in his early career as an associate attorney. The biggest bonus he'd ever earned in his seven years at his first firm -comprised almost exclusively of former jocks- was on the softball diamond in the

Barrister's League. In that year, he'd gunned the opposition - the state's top personal injury attorney - from right center field, when the wannabe attempted to go from first to third on an outfield single. The game's etiquette said that second base belonged to the runner even if Marty might have taken him on the quick hop. Marty rarely breached etiquette. But damn it! Trying for third, especially after Marty had given him the nod, was just rude. Marty took it personally. It was an insult that he couldn't abide, so he took him out with a rope to third. The senior partner crowed about it for the rest of the year and the bonus was big! Tres big!

Now days, age dogged him. Success seemed to have let him be, most likely because he was resigned and Success found no more fun in teasing him with brief glimpses of chances otherwise destined to fail. Marty no longer moved with an athlete's grace, but like an old man. Yet his pride would not allow him to concede the fight. He was not prepared to surrender to Fate. Not yet. He moved now like he was washed up, but he was an athlete nevertheless. With rare glimpses of residual grace, he consciously strode the hallways at the senior residence while hearkening back to the glory days to let the memories quicken his stride and give flight to his feet. Memories and medication served to enhance his ambulation. When he strode, he strode with short choppy steps and clipped movements. To the observer with a quick eye the movement was deft, but to most, this movement went undetected.

These days, it was a new found power that Marty had developed to skulk about without being noticed, a flutter of his feet that sometimes lent him flight or an invisibility that he might acquire even as his memories faded. Medication fueled the engine. But he could never outpace Age. Each morning, as he swung his legs from beneath the covers and over the side of his bed, a stranger stared back from his reflection in the closet door mirror – a stranger: grey and balding. The stranger wore veneers on his top front teeth that gave a fake smile. He sported a pot gut that hung- albeit slightly- over his speedo. His muscles felt brittle, no longer supple like in the old days. His skin sagged. His handsome features lapsed. His reflexes had slowed considerably. His youthful strength was long gone. His eyesight was no longer keen, except in what Marty called his "bionic eye". He had undergone cataract surgery at 50-years old. His doctor said to him back then, "My, you're such a young man to need this surgery". Marty thought to thank him with swift kick. Thanks a lot doc.

Marty relied heavily on his meds. Since he had come to the home - whenever he had come he could not now remember – he took 5 pills each morning: one for blood pressure; one for an underactive thyroid; another for acid reflux; a pill for allergies; and one for depression.

ne for depression. Imagine, depressed? Did he seem depressed? His pharmaceutical sales rep daughter told him he was depressed. He couldn't believe that she would say that. So what if he'd snapped at the Taco Time employee who couldn't get his order right at the drive thru?

"No! I did not order, 'three empanadas'. I've never even heard of an empanada. I said -three enchiladas... What do you mean you don't make beef empanadas? I said 'enchiladas. ENCHILADAS', dammit! Don't make me come in there". She touched his arm, leaned toward the speaker, and corrected the order. She kissed his cheek and suggested that he might benefit from Lexapro. Marty couldn't think of anything more depressing than the idea that he needed to take yet another pill, and this one to fight the very depression that the fact that he needed pills to beat back depression created. Yet, the cocktail of pills that he took like clockwork, each morning, not only controlled his blood pressure, stopped the reflux, pushed back the fatigue, and cleared up his sinuses; but, in combination with Lexapro, inexplicably created in him a serendipitous power, that was unpredictable in both its' timing and its application.

Lately, he had begun to experiment with the dosages of his medications, the combination in which they were taken, and the order in which he took them. At times, like hot flashes to a pre-menopausal woman, Marty would be overtaken – sometimes with the power to speak in foreign tongues, sometimes to interpret ancient languages, sometimes to compose orchestral strains, sometimes to hear pins drop, sometimes to solve 1000-piece jigsaw puzzles in under 10-minutes, sometimes to solve the Rubic's cube in 30-seconds or less, sometimes to both knit and pearl, sometimes to move invisibly, sometimes to fly, and sometimes.... Why damn, the list was endless, the powers myriad and unpredictable, both in type and in timing. Here when stalking the hallways at this death center with the artificial lens in his right eye and his swimmer's goggles, Marty's vision was "bionic" – in the one eye, at least. He couldn't say for sure but when he wore the goggles, he not only saw like a cat at night, but he could see – day or night- at 20/10, for up to 10-miles distant. Damn, if he couldn't see, from the glass doors to the lobby at Golden Hills Rest Home, the roaches laying siege at the wastepipe opening in the foundation of the old First Security Bank building across the street, some 4 blocks distant and on a moonless night, no less!

The problem was that Marty never knew exactly what might come, nor when. And, he failed frequently – mostly – to keep track. He never wrote anything down. He never recorded for future reference just which combination of pills that he took would produce what effect on him. His Swiss-cheese memory allowed but a few memorable instances: like when he suddenly knew the right chords and exact syncopation to play the tune: Skateaway by Dire Straits on his acoustic guitar. It was his "acoustic" no less and not the Ibanez electric to which the heretofore unendowed Marty would otherwise have ascribed. The possibilities were endless and the potential for anything to happen was staggering.

To ponder, he needed to swim. To swim, he needed the tub. The tub was that tall, narrow, stainless steel hot tub in Physical Therapy that barely accommodated one body and upon which he had come to rely so heavily like the one he would often use after football practice to work out the kinks; or when necessary - as physical therapy - to heal any one of a number of leg, knee, ankle or other muscular injuries that he had sustained through the years. And, more recently the one he would use to effectuate his escape. Which way was it to Physical Therapy? He had to swim.

He adjusted himself in his speedo, affixed his goggles, and tightened his swim fins. He retrieved the pills he kept secreted in his speedo, popped a few: one red, two blue, and a yellow- and waited for a superpower. He never knew what might develop. He was only now beginning to recognize that any given superpower he might encounter was related in some way to the order in which he swallowed his pills. But, he had yet to experiment. He was more interested, just now, with what might develop. As he flipped and flopped his way to Rehab, those of his neighboring residents, lying fitfully and trying to sleep in their beds on either side of hallway, found a sudden deep and long denied rest rendered by the smell of Elsha cologne that wafted on the flatulence that boosted Marty down the corridor.

CHAPTER V

What Marty found in PT at the end of the hall was puzzling. There at the other side of the room sat an array of exercise equipment: a large exercise ball, mats, a treadmill and some free weights. Over in the corner, he saw the stainless steel tub. The tub was in use. A pretty red-headed technician in scrubs hovered over a bald headed elderly man. She was shapely, even busty, and familiar. There, on her neck he thought he caught a glimpse of a tattoo...a serpent maybe? Curious, he thought. The old guy was thrashing about and seemed to be fighting to get out. At the same time, she was using all of her strength to push him back into the tub. One hand was on his head. In the other, she held an upright electric floor fan. She was working to submerge the fan and the old guy together. The tub water surged over the stainless steel edges where the blowing fan tossed the waves into an angry froth that sprayed everywhere. She and the old man squinted against the eye stinging spray as they struggle together to fight the tempest and each other.

Strangely, Marty remembered a time as a missionary on the island of Tubuai in French Polynesia. A tiny boy named Pero, presented himself for baptism at the waters' edge on the beach where the surf rose and the waves broke at two-four feet in front of the small gathering hall. As Apia, the branch president, immersed Pero into the surf, he lost his grip and Pero disappeared. With a surprised look, Apia stood and began to peer searchingly into the waves. He parted the water with his hands like a golfer looking for a lost ball in the tall weeds. Not moments removed from the tiny boy's salvation, Apia had lost his grip on the poor young soul. Moments later, a half a furlong to the lee, Pero's head broke the surface and Pero bobbed on the waves like a piece of cork in the sacramental wine. On a breaking wave, he body surfed to shore to the applause and congratulations of the entire congregation. Apia looked to Marty to validate the baptism. Marty could see no reason why not and Pero was later confirmed.

But here in Rehab, Marty knew intuitively that this pretty woman would not be losing her iron grip on the old fart. Given the billowing surge, the thrashing, and the desperate strength of the struggle between the two, Marty recognized that the old guy's intended salvation was soon at hand if he didn't act quickly. He waddled – but deftly - into the room where the slap of his flipper-ed feet caught the attention of the two disciples. He raised his eyes and outstretched arms to the heavens (and to the acoustical tiles overhead scheduled for removal under State order as a health risk due to asbestos) and shouted to the waves:

"Peace. Be Still!"

All of a sudden, the struggle ended. The pretty redheaded technician stood awestruck and let go her grip. She tugged at her top. She'd lost a button during her struggle and her uniform fell open at the neck. There on the skin of her shoulder, Marty thought he saw a bit of a tattoo. A serpent, he wondered? She stood up straight to glare. This angel of mercy dropped her fan to the floor. The fan bounced with an echoing clank, the spinning blades rattled and rang slowly to a stop. The storm gradually subsided. The old guy stopped thrashing, blinked the water from his eyes and coughed with a spit. The surge of waters stilled and a deepening hush fell into puddles over the black and yellow, checker board, linoleum tiles. The only sounds to be heard in PT were an occasional electronic beep from one of life monitors down the hall, the old guy's fitful sputtering, and the barely perceptible background sound of "white noise" apparently left over from the Big Bang. Time froze. The redhead and geezer stared curiously at Marty who stood there in his red speedo, matching swim fins, and goggles.

In utter astonishment, the old guy in the tank exclaimed, "WTF" which he thought to mean: well....just that -WTF. He really didn't know what it meant; only that his teen age grandkids usually mouthed it to each other in surprise when he showed up unannounced at one of their teenage parties from the TV room upstairs. Typically, he came to nab a piece of pizza, wearing only briefs, white socks, and a "beater". The TV room had been an accommodation until a spot opened at the facility. He did love pizza and the looks on his grandsons' faces was always priceless. "WTF -whatever the fetch that meant- seemed a propos to this moment here in the hot tub at PT.

"Don't mind me." Marty broke the spell. "Just here for a swim". He asked, "You guys done with the tub?"

To the pretty redhead with the mysterious tattoo, he said, "Please, don't concern yourself with MY soul's salvation. For me, I've been baptized. Yep, by one with God's own authority. Can't enter the kingdom without it, you know? None of that fake religion stuff for me", he smiled.

"Go ahead, if you don't believe me. Check with Nicodemus. I know the old geezer. Tell him Marty sent ya. Yes, ma'am. I've been saved since '62'. And the old boy, there...?" Marty pointed to the guy in the tub. "He seems pretty well pickled. You should probably let him be. If he's not saved by now, well...pretty likely, he won't ever be."

Marty moved to the tub. "C'mon doll. Let him go. It didn't look like he was having much of your testimony, anyway. Why not give the spirit a chance to work on him a bit?" He pointed to the towel rack at the wall next to the tub. "Hey, fetch me a towel on your way out would you? And take a break. I need to be alone to swim".

The redhead peered curiously with suspicion in Marty's direction as she walked slowly to the exit. The old boy remained stone still in the tub, his eyes wide- incredulous.

With some exasperation, Marty said to him, "Dammit, get your ass outta there." He pulled a few pills from the secret pocket in his speedo. He popped a few in no particular order. If asked, he couldn't say just which colors. He watched a few bubbles gurgle and break the surface like a cutthroat rising to a dry fly. He was getting annoyed.

"C'mon, get outta there man, before I call EPA", he hollered at the guy. He figured he couldn't hear. "And, pull the damn plug before you leave! I'll need to refill. Sheesh!". He stood at the edge of the tub and looked in. "You better hope I don't find any floaters or I'll call back our pretty Angel Serpent to bring you to your final salvation, if you know what I mean!"

The old guy bolted from the room fully clothed and dripping.

To the pretty redhead: "Please, ma'am. Better leave the fan". He popped another pill for good measure and smiled. This one was purplish. He reminded himself to remember the color. He had no clue what the purple pill was for. It didn't matter. He wouldn't remember anyway.

The pretty technician continued to watch Marty warily as she stood the fan up from the floor. Without a word, she plugged it back into the wall socket, adjusted the fan's angle and speed, and padded from the room in her water stained scrubs as she towel dried her hair.

A stray thought hit Marty as he watched her shapely form recede. He imagined – there beneath the scrubs, resting nicely in that loin stirring crease where the slim female waistline meets the expanding hips - a sly serpent inked into the alabaster skin that winked at him from time to time from just above the elastic waistline of her scrubs, as her top hiked up slightly with each youthful and strangely alluring movement.

Damn! There he was again strolling Abbey Road at the Jr. High dance on Friday afternoon. "Something in the Way She Moves" brought Marty to strict attention as he absent mindedly hummed it. He could once again pitch a tent at scout camp if he had wanted. That pretty technician, she could move! He pondered whether he should refill the PT tub with cold water. Hell no! This sensation hadn't been around for some time. He may as well enjoy it while it lasts. As it was, it didn't last long. Purposefully, he turned the spigot marked in blue. He spit into his goggles to clear the residue, adjusted them to a snug fit, and perched himself at the tub's edge like a peregrine stalking a salmon. He gulped a bit of fan-refreshed air and took a head first plunge. The cold water braced. The brain freeze that followed granted to Marty a coma-like meditative state. His heart-rate and breathing slowed to a crawl. The mammalian reflex kicked in and he found there at the bottom of the rehab tank that quiet peace that he so much craved.

CHAPTER VI

The warm waters of the South Pacific awakened him. As he swam, he looked around. A few brightly colored and exotic fish were scaling the reefs near an outlying island –maybe Easter Island - for a meal. This appeared to be the South Pacific and, for a while, the water was warm and the view excellent. But more and more as he swam, the water became cold, ice cold. He pushed himself topside to inspect. What he found were waves that were short and steep, and growing larger as he started to swim the water's surface. The cold East Wind gusted more and more powerfully as he continued to stroke and paddle. The cold water suggested that he had moved well past Tahiti. He must be close to Cape Horn. He must be coming into Drake's Passage. Intrigue drove him on. He swam with no real intent to arrive. Still, he thought, Cape Horn presented a challenge.

Some time ago, Marty had stumbled across an interesting read. He found a thin but colorfully illustrated magazine lying on the fireplace mantel and gathering dust in the front sitting area at Golden Hills. A tab on the spine was labelled: **Mar de Hoces.1578.09:12:43**. From this tab, Marty speculated that the magazine formed part of some library inventory, somewhere. Pasted inside the back cover, he found pouch with a card in it. At the top of the card, in the space where one would normally expect to see the words: "Due Date", this card carried a heading entitled: "Drop-In Date". The first date listed was the same as the first set of markings on the spine: **1616.0715.13:32:23**. The name that accompanied was signed: **"WCSchouten – Nlands"**. A little research revealed that Willem Schouten successfully circumnavigated Cape Horn through what was known then as Drake's Passage in the year 1616. Over Schouten's signature was a line that carried the signature: Capn.JCook – GB. The last date listed was **1788.0402.11:23:16**. His research told him that Captain Cook had attempted unsuccessfully to cross through Drake's. To get to the Pacific Ocean, he was forced to sail eastward, around the Cape of Good Hope the southern tip of Africa. Marty was intrigued and kept the magazine tucked into the drawer of his nightstand.

Inside the magazine, Marty read an interesting piece about Drake's Passage. His competitive juices stirred ,and he determined to "Double the Horn". To the first sailors who sailed this trade route, this was considered a badge of honor. From his reading, he knew that he should press south to 56-degrees well into the zone of the fiercest winds. He didn't know his latitudes and had no way to find out. So, he decided that when he hit what he determined to be the "fiercest" of the winds, he'd be in the passage. Once in the Passage, he could "Double the Horn by swimming 930-miles from 50-degrees South on the west coast of South America to 50-degrees South on the east coast, and back. Should be a piece of cake, he figured. He didn't give much thought to encountering the fierce winds that were exacerbated by the funneling effect between the Andes of South America and the Antarctic Peninsula. That would be Drake's Passage. He ticked through his Swiss cheese memory. He had read somewhere that these lower latitudes below 40-degrees are uninterrupted by land around the globe so that the prevailing winds can blow from west to east virtually unimpeded to make the circuit around the world. The strong winds in the shallower waters south and west of the Horn cause the waves to greatly increase in size, to grow shorter, steeper, and more treacherous. The eastward current is strong and when this current encounters an opposing east wind, the waves get even bigger. If the strong eastward current through Drake's encounters an opposing east wind...well, Marty thought, he had better pay attention. This area is particularly notorious for rogue waves which can build to heights approaching 100 feet. Yeah, well. Marty had nothing to lose. He figured he'd give it go.

He was, however, very chilly in these waters. In truth, Marty had never really experienced waters this cold for any length of Time ,and especially not for the time required to cross almost 1000-miles of arctic cold. Typically, he swam unaffected by ocean temperatures. He rethought his earlier expectation; not so much a piece of cake, but more like "a challenge". His speedo offered little protection, but his mindset was strong and though the waters braced, the cold did not intrude upon his meditation. As he swam, he encountered an iceberg or two floating on the current from east to west and soon met up with a raft of penguins- maybe 15 or 20. They swam with purpose and were not inclined to play. But, they honored Marty with an invitation to join. He accepted. They swam hard and fast, close to the surface. They did not stop to play or feed. They swam, gave a nod to Marty to acknowledge his ability to keep up. Marty grinned. The only better compliment that may come would come from dolphins.

In keeping up with the penguins, Marty swam through the 15- to 20-foot waves. About 150 miles in, they turned right to Antarctica. They cackled a quick good bye and told him to take care. He continued east through Drake's Passage and soon hooked up with a large white whale, old and scarred. He was headed Marty's direction.

"Hey", Marty bubbled in an attempt at conversation. "You from around these parts?"

The old boy seemed friendly, but quiet. He gave Marty a sidelong glance and continued to swim. His stroke was long and slow, but propelled him nicely beneath the rough waters.

Marty tried again. He figured that the whale could interpret bubbles. "Pretty tough section of water, you been through here before?"

The old boy again looked at Marty. "Yep", he responded with a whale like trill. "I'm gonna sound". You comin'?" He signaled to Marty to latch on anywhere.

"Yeah, thanks!!" Marty bubbled back his gratitude. He was thrilled to take the invite, happy for the company. He latched onto the whale's hump and signaled his readiness to roll. This boy was huge, but seemed to hearor better, to interpret well enough Marty's bubbling from back here at the hump; and the big boy's trills, squeaks, and squeals literally echoed through the surrounding waters. The two soon gained an audience of other grey whales.

Marty looked at the crowd of greys. He noticed the large white. This boy somehow seemed...well, familiar. Somehow it seemed that he had seen this big boy before, but where? He had never been through Drake's Passage previously. He didn't recall this big boy in the waters around Tahiti, maybe the North Atlantic? Yeah, maybe there. This boy seemed to like the cold.

Say", Marty bubbled. "Do I know you? Ever been to the North Atlantic?"

The great white whale offered a quick, literary trill, "Been around a long time; been around the globe too many times to count. Moby....Moby Dick's the name. And you?"

"Oh, yeah", Marty gurgled back a quick mumble in recognition. "I read about you". He quickly fell silent. He knew this story. He figure he better not ask about Captain Ahab. It's probably not a good idea, he bubbled silently to himself.

Marty left Moby at the Fortieth parallel somewhere east of Brazil. He thanked him for the ride; told him that he knew somewhat of his history, but didn't mention Ahab. Moby trilled a short "umm huh" as if he knew, and bid Marty farewell. He was headed north to visit royalty: Harry, Meghan and their little kid, Archie...was it? Marty had figured right: the North Atlantic.

Marty headed back to the Fifty Sixth parallel and started west. The going here was fast, the current strong. As he headed back through Drake's into the shallower waters of the passage, he encountered a waves ranging in height from 70-, 80-, even 90-feet. He body-surfed these rogues nicely. He hadn't lost his touch. But, the weather had turned exceptionally cold. Typically, he enjoyed the ocean temperatures and swam unaffected by sea waters that ranged from maybe 72 degrees on the warm side to 50 or 55 in the colder waters. But, he was pretty sure that the waters here in Drake's passage approached freezing. The air temperatures in this area were even colder, and the large icebergs that roamed just south of here virtually assured him of that. Never mind Antarctica a bit further south - not so much a tropical venue this place.

He had taken an exceptionally high wave, swimming back and forth across the face. The weather had turned very cold and blustery. The skies darkened and lightening flashed. Thunder crashed almost in sync with each jagged bolt, and he tumbled. Here, as a mere spec on the deep blue ocean, struggling against the rising swells, the cresting and crashing waves, the poisonous jelly fish, the paralyzing fear of sharks, the baking sun and bitterly cold rains, thunderstorms and lightning, icebergs and howling winds, the parch, the hunger, the thirst, and the crushing and ever present potential for drowning; here amidst the everyday challenges to his very survival meted to him as some purported blessing, either as a gift to bring him comfort, or- if not a gift, then a challenge to make him strong, Marty had what he deemed his epiphany.

In the moonless sky on the deepest and broadest of ocean, he beheld his Southern Cross, he seemed to have found his North Star, and he came to find that they were all an illusion. The thunder crashed as a jagged bolt tore open the lowering sky. The rogue smacked him senseless and he tumbled down the face to the cold, deep, and black water far below. He went deep and couldn't tell which way was up. The dark waters cleared and he coughed, sputtered, and almost drowned again as he tumbled uncontrollably. He reached the trough and the wave broke on him just to spit him out once more. He was tossed and shaken but found a lull between waves. He rolled to his back to find a breath. He opened his mouth widely and sucked back the heightening wind. The sky -now black - broke and the storm waters poured on him.

For the first time since Marty could remember, which- admittedly was not so long ago - he was scared. But no sooner had he thought to dive deep into safety, then another rogue wave raised him up and he was suddenly swept from its face. The rogue spit him high into the frigid skies into blackness. The darkened skies held him imprisoned. The strong winds gusted to hurl him high and let him fall, only to toss him again even higher and to fall. As he bounced through the turbulent air, ice formed around him, layer after layer, until he fell like the hail back into the ocean far below. He crashed into the sea, the encrusted ice broke on impact, and he sunk deep. He was frazzled. He felt beat up, weak, and uncertain of who or where he was; and he was tired. He drifted aimlessly and succumbed.

CHAPTER VII

Marty awoke lying face up on fresh waters. He was confused. Where was he and how did he get here? He didn't float so much as he was driven by the wind, pushed up quickly, and left to fall back on the waters. The waves here were choppy and not as tall as at Drake's. But they were nasty and mean. The water was not salty, but fresh, clean, and icy cold. It reminded him of the stream at Dimple Dell, but it was not. When young and stumped about what to do, he could always click through his memory, a catalog of information, a catalog of things he'd read, or otherwise learned on the way to "learning other things" as the saying went. In those days his mind clicked rapidly through the catalog and, almost always, he would land on the information that he needed. Nowadays however, with his Swiss-cheese memory, his mind slipped and stalled, missed a beat and sped forward, coughed, and chattered to where Marty could either never find, or if he did, could never be sure of the information seized upon. The effect made him appear to be a bit of dimwit whereas – he knew – that he was not. In any event, he still had to think. The pill combination prior to Drake's – whatever he had taken he could not now remember - had worked, alright. In fact, it had worked almost too well. He had managed to keep up with the penguins and he had conversed rather intelligently with a famous white whale. Who'd a thunk? More importantly, even now he could still recall these events. The fact that he could recall was itself, a miracle. The problem remained. He could not remember the pill combination that accounted for this current ability. He wondered whether Time itself had moved, sped up, advanced perhaps a tad faster than normal. He could not remember futzing with Time. He still wasn't even sure just how that was done. But he was beginning to find evidence. And, he told himself, he should find a good way to keep track of his medications, the order in which he took them, and the superpower that the order of pills produced. That would help.

But for now, he was beat and needed to rest. Drake's Passage had taken its toll, and this water here was not helpful. It was cold and windblown and though not as frightening, was just as much work as had been Drake's. Marty looked around. The sky above was crystal clear and blue. Snowcapped mountains surrounded the waters. The air was thin and dry; clean and fresh. It felt like Dimple Dell, but different. Yeah, well. He best pondered at the depths. He adjusted his goggles to submerge and inhaled a lungful of mountain air ever so slowly so as to cherish the serenity that it brought; and dove through the clear mountain waters of what he came to recognize as Lake Tahoe- the beautiful, crystalline lake, upslope from his more recent home in California.

He swam through these cold waters into what was the American River that cascaded down the western slope of the Sierra Nevada Mountains to join the Sacramento River. He enjoyed the ride. From the Sacramento, he swam on through the Delta and into the San Francisco Bay where he passed under the Golden Gate Bridge and back into the northern Pacific Ocean. The waters were chilly, but tolerable. They felt a bit like the waters of the North Sea- cold and different from the South Pacific where he had started this adventure, and where he now sought to return. South from the Bay, the waters began to warm. The further south, the warmer they got. It felt as if someone had turned up a dial. It felt good.

Initially, Marty had left his island without a purpose. Nothing much had changed. Following what had been a rather arduous trip, the only purpose he could bring to mind was to cruise these warm ocean waters for no better reason than to stop shivering. Granted, he was very much accustomed to the icy waters at Dimple Dell and, he enjoyed the ride down the American River. In large measure, he preferred these colder waters and the cool freshness; particularly those found in the mountain, rivers and streams. He slept without blankets and showered solely in water taken from the tap at the right side of the spigot. He enjoyed the invigoration: cold, clear, and clean! Before he had come to reside in the warm waters of the South Pacific, he had lived and played in waters that flowed as melted snow.

The waters that he sought here in PT were cold like melted snow and could carry him away to the waters of Bell's Canyon that crossed the front pasture at his childhood home in an irrigation ditch that flowed along a 300-foot frontage on the front pasture where he played. The ditch ran three-feet wide, three-feet deep. The waters came from the glaciers in the steep cut canyons of the Rocky Mountains that stood guard over the three-acre home and property where Marty grew up. He could stretch full out on his belly atop the small stream. He could coast intent on reaching one end from the other across the pasture's width. The challenge was to endure the icy cold for the entire 300-feet. Marty could endure and he did every time. He had done it daily every summer until he grew up and left home. But after Drake's Passage, he wasn't so much interested in cold water. Right now, he needed warmth, and Marty had come to love the warmer waters of the South Pacific and so he swam to return.

"Hold on!" he thought and sat up quickly. He lifted his goggles and wiped his face and eyes. He looked around. He was in luck. He found an attendant there in PT. "Hey, while you're here, would you turn up the dial on this tub? It's a bit chilly".

Curly had been watching quietly from the doorway. He was surprised when Marty called out. He didn't think the man knew he was here. "Uh, sure," he said as he tiptoed back through the darkened room and turned the dial on the side of the tub as high as it would go. The temperature read: 104 degrees Fahrenheit. "Enjoy", he said as walked back to the doorway. This Marty guy was an enigma- a bit strange, but intriguing, Curly thought. He flipped the switch and turned out the lights.

Marty's descent played out through the fathoms. The further removed from the icy mountain waters, the more peaceful became the experience. The further south he swam, the warmer the waters became. It felt as if someone had turned up the dial. It felt good. He felt no bursting desire to breathe. He felt no urgent need to surface. Drake's Passage had been frightening, but fun in an unnerving sort of way. Lake Tahoe was beautiful; the surroundings fresh and elegant. Yet even now, these experiences were starting to dwindle and fade.

As he swam, he continued to experiment with his medications, the order and dosages. Mostly, he just picked a few colors and downed them. These seemed to help, but he never could remember when, what color, or if he had even taken them. Regardless, the exhilaration that he felt with each new superpower never got him any closer to 1967. He could never associate the events or the accompanying exhilaration that he felt with any specific time, day, month or year. Surprisingly, this last revelation seemed most significant. He pondered on it for a long moment and wondered again about No Time. He tried hard to cement it. Then...Oh well the thought was gone. He figured the revelation would come back in short order. Of course, if it ever did, who would know?

He resurfaced somewhere back in the warm waters of what he assumed to be the South Pacific. He went topside to investigate. He broke the surface and breathed in deeply. It was early evening. The sky was bright orange at the seemingly endless horizon. The water was calm, the waves broad and rolling, oh so gently. This was not as fun or as exciting as had been Drake's passage, but it was much more soothing. Marty's breathing calmed and he relaxed lying on his back in the ocean's water, the most recent events slowly fading with both the setting sun and his short term memory. He relaxed at rest on the concurrently swelling and receding waves of the deepest blue ocean. He relaxed to the distant sound of the quietly crashing surf that signaled some forgotten island, an island that Marty remained disinclined to visit. Afloat in these peaceful waters, he began calmly, more determinedly, to mentally catalog all of those "faces" that now disturbed him so much – disturbed him for the buried acquaintance; for the now familiar unfamiliarity of them all; and for the very distinct understanding that he loved these people. Or, at least, he thought that he did.

There were those three little girls at pool side including "little blondie" who had commented on his big belly; the striking blond matriarch; the slender, young, and very attractive mother (he smiled at the dude in the designer shades who affectionately patted her backside pockets); the wildly sexy and wide-eyed beauty with her bold and exceptionally beautiful blond beau. (Of all of them, this one, this handsome young man was the most familiar, the most disturbing in his unfamiliarity). Who were these people? And were the others just passengers on this train through time? Were they just figments, fantasies, or pure memories – someone who might once have existed but then again, perhaps not? He focused now, trying hard to remember their faces.

Some, Marty thought he may have invented for his own amusement: there was Moby Dick. Had he really chatted with the famous White Whale? There was the mermaid – his swimming companion; and the girl at the pool - both with the same tattoo. Had he conjured them? Maybe, but he wasn't sure, although he was certain that the mermaid's tattoo was real! He knew for certain he had seen it somewhere. Maybe he had built the mermaid and the pool girl around it. If he had, all he could say was, "What a piece of magnificent construction!"

Others ... he was not so sure about. There was the redheaded Angel of Mercy in her scrubs with the electric fan in hand in Physical Therapy. She was real ,and she had a strangely familiar tattoo, one very similar to the mermaid's. He did enjoy the thought of the naked skin at the Angel's waist peeking from beneath her scrubs. Still, he remained skeptical.

Then, there was Curly in PT. PT was a puzzle. Marty was uncertain whether he'd ever been there, yet it was a place to which he seemingly returned Time after Time. When he wasn't swimming he slept...in a bed, in a room, with a hallway just outside and a cafeteria down at the end, just past PT. Trudy, Maggie, Mo, and Larry were all part of this place. What was this place anyway and was it even real?

Some of the other folks that strolled through his memories he knew were real but they belonged to the past: Susan was very real, and lustfully sexy,-a wonderful part of his reminiscence. Marty knew her. The memory was real, but she was – after all – just a memory. His dad, his mom, cousins, aunts, uncles, boyhood friends, team mates – all of these were firmly ensconced as real, but now just memories comfortably relegated to the past - "comfortably", because Marty was certain that, if called upon, he could recall both their names and their faces albeit with some effort. And, if he couldn't, they were part of something that could not now be changed: his past. Still he wondered. Why was that anyway? Why couldn't the past be changed? If he could get back in Time, why was it that he couldn't change the game? He wasn't sure, but it just seemed that whatever he had said to them, done to them or for them, could not now be undone. Or, could it? Briefly, his thoughts returned to the light clock in the train, and he wondered.

He thought of his recent introduction to his own kids at ages 10 and 12. He knew them to be his kids. He was aware of the Time in which their swimming race had occurred. He knew that pool and the places that surrounded it; and, he knew that he had been back. How was that anyway?

He realized that he must have - somehow - gone back into Time. He would need to figure this one out so he could do it again. His No Time theory didn't account specifically for either backward or forward time travel. Rather, as far as Marty could determine, when he hit No Time, the future and the present did not exist within that place. This was, of course, if No Time were such a thing.

In essence, he saw No Time as a switch, a junction, a place without restrictions on Time itself; restrictions like past, present, and future. But he surmised that to get to a specific Time – whether past, present, or future – he first needed to get into No Time by well... by riding Einstein's Train. The goal was to reach the speed of light. Once there, where Time is not measured, he could then drop instantaneously back into Time. But a problem remained. Absent any measured Time within that place called No Time, how could Marty know just when he would drop from No Time and back into Time and just where might he touch down? How could he know where his jump would take him? Would he land in the future or would he land in the past? In No Time, there may be no sign posts to designate just where he might jump back into a past, a present, or a future. Any jump back out of No Time may be wholly capricious. He could not know until he landed back what Time he had reentered. That would not be good, he feared.

Marty figured that he should study some more on No Time assuming that he could find such a book or even a periodical. He presumed to set out for the library just down from the park on M Street, but this presented him with a problem very similar to the one that he intended to study. For the first Time in Marty's life of adventure, he knew exactly where he intended to go. But he had no true idea as to how to get there. Never before had he strapped on his goggles, hiked up his speedo, and tightened up his fins with the specific intention of going to one specific place, previously identified to, and known by him. In all of his experience with swimming, he had never set as a goal such a goal. Always, he just swam.

Marty grinned. He couldn't say why. He didn't know. He could not really explain it but for the first time in a long while, his mind was open and clear like it had been yesterday, or perhaps he should say, like maybe 15-to 20-years ago. Whatever it was, it was working.

As he swam, he continued to ponder. Suddenly, a stray thought struck him: "like the pages of time". That was it: the "PAGES of Time". Why hadn't he thought of it sooner!? Time itself, or at least the events that were incorporated by Time could easily be written on a page and printed in some kind of a book, a book consisting of...of other pages.

Assuming he could ride Einstein's Train into No Time, he should be able to find there some way while still on the train to lock onto any one year, month, day, hour, minute, or even second in a manner similar to flipping through the pages in a book! He vaguely recalled a recent visit to a marvelous library filled with wall-sized mirrors, cream colored marble tile floors, Cherrywood shelves, and exquisite lighting from crystal chandeliers. If he could wander the library to sift the pages of the seemingly infinite number of books kept there on the vast array of shelves spread between the wall sized mirrors hung there in the Library, he could find the answer. If only he could visit, he figured that he might be able to jump from one Time to another simply by turning pages in a book; either slowly, one at a Time to better explore, or in chunks depending upon where specifically in Time he might want to go. When finished with his Timely exploration or research, as it were, he should then be able to close the book and set it back onto the shelf – without ever leaving No Time. Marty was not exactly sure whether he could explore Time while still stationed in No Time, but he was willing to chance it. He figured that since he would be in a Library that was already part of the moving train, he should find it rather easy to step back into the library car that was coupled to the No Time train. Marty grinned again. It seemed so simple, so easy, and so elegant.

Of course, there was the sticky question of just which Time he might enter. Marty remembered a dog that he had once: Skye. Skye was a beautiful black Labrador. She loved to swim and he had taken her out daily, sometimes twice a day to swim with him in Folsom Lake. He loved that dog and he often wondered just how long she might stay with him, how long she would live. She was very much like another favorite dog: Gus, whom Marty had also adored. Gus lived 10 years. He wondered how long he and Skye would last.

The veterinarian estimated for him that Skye lived seven years of her lifetime for every one year that he lived his own. Then of course there was his seventh-grade science project that complicated the matter. He had undertaken a presentation on house flies. He recalled nothing except that a housefly could live somewhere between 15 and 30 days. This told Marty, as he cogitated, that a housefly might see him as almost immortal, given his own 70-year life expectancy as contrasted to a brief 30 days.

Then there was the biblical claim that the earth was built in six "days" and on the seventh, God rested. This was confusing, at best. The claim was that to God, one day equaled 1000 years. On this assessment, the earth should be 7000 years-old. Marty didn't put much trust in this thought, but whether true or not, this estimate together with Time as measured for the dog and the fly – led Marty to wonder whether the very differences in the measurement of Time might further complicate his theory. In searching through the Library for the Book of Time, might he encounter even a variety of Books that dealt with Time – each with a different print on its pages, or even a different language for Time; each page printed with a different measure: one for the flea another for a Philistine; one for an aphid, another for Apollo; one for a rosebud, another for a stone. Marty got the picture. He could envision a Library with an infinite set books and of volumes, to be shelved in an infinite number of different and varying sections of the Library of Time; and, the only available access to the Library itself was via a ride on Einstein's Train.

Marty wondered as he bobbed up and down in the rolling waves of the South Pacific: if he dropped from No Time into Time, just whose Time would he enter? He had to trust that whatever book he selected would come with instructions. Still the theory troubled him: Would he drop into a fly's future and find only moments left before his own demise; or maybe into a dog's Time and find perhaps 7- or 8-more of his own years until he died. Or might he drop into God's Time and live for well...over 1000 years or more? And, of course, none of this answered the larger question: What would happen if he died while in a Time measurement different from his own? Marty had yet to figure just what may happen should he die in his own Time, let alone to die in the Time of a fly. He shuddered at the thought.

And of course, he had no clue as how Time itself, may be measured for him should he land in another's Time. Would he move according to his own Time? When he exists in his own Time, how might he behave after stepping into a fly's Time or likewise into a dog's? Would he move very rapidly and speak in a high squeaky voice, so high as to be unintelligible? If he could enter God's Time, would he move so slowly that his intended movements would be imperceptible so that he would appear to stand still? Who knew? The options were infinite even within his own Time frame and equally as numerous if he could even consider the infinite number of volumes of Time, each with an infinite number of pages, placed there on the infinite number of shelves in the Library that were contained within a boxcar there on Einstein's Train.

Marty grew weary. He lay back and pondered. He would need to assume that whatever Time he entered, he would always remain on Einstein's Train and so, therefore, his speed and movement would be measured by No Time with whatever Page of Time he selected or, in other words, in whatever Time frame that he operated.

He lay back to let the waves rock him gently to sleep. He'd done enough thinking for today. As he lay there on the deep blue swell of the next wave and, for a brief moment as he crested, he was bathed in the light of a lighter blue horizon, tinged with orange.

It brought to mind an old, sailor's saying:

"Red sky at night- a sailor's delight; Red sky at morn, sailors take warning".

He wasn't sure whether to feel delight or trepidation. He knew that he had arrived in the beautiful morning. But now....he was uncertain whether he was swimming into a morning or into an evening sky. The sound of the far away surf was silent and he lost all bearing. He continued to swim, searching, contemplating, struggling to find himself, struggling to find, not just an explanation for his current difficulties; pains; and circumstance, but to discover a...raison d'etre, a purpose for his life; an answer for his own existence and answers to the questions of Time and No Time. And so... he dove.

Today, his "descent" felt more akin to an "ascent" ,and the measure of Time seemed different. He could feel it. He was sure that he was being drawn downward at about 30 degrees through a tunnel towards what looked to be a pin-dot of bright light. Perhaps ironically, as Marty moved with increasing velocity to an ever expanding light, for reasons still unknown, his mind was darkened to just what awaited him at the other end of that tunnel. He did not know what lie beyond the light, and he feared.

He thought again about 1967. If only he could better remember that one fall afternoon, October, he seemed to recall... October 1967. He again found disconcerting this more and more frequent inability to remember. Not minutes before, his mind cogitated likely a finely oiled machine. Here again, he was keenly aware that there were people whose names and faces he should know and yet he did not; people and things that should hold precious meaning to him, but they did not; and places with which he must be, or at one time was, familiar, but now was not. And he wondered: "Why"? The answer seemed oh...so...close. But Marty came back around. He was too tired to think anymore. He told himself that he could wait to remember. He was confident that he could discover all of it, again.

He knew that he would come to know all of it, again. Of that he was sure. Only quiet desperation whispered that he might just leave well enough alone and shivered.

For now, the water temperature here was not seasonal. It was just plain hot and seemed to be getting hotter. He pushed out with one hand as he pulled back with the other hoping to move south for cooler waters; stroke after stroke, reach after reach, he swam harder: four strokes and breathe; two strokes and breathe; four strokes and breathe; Kick and kick and kick and kick. He headed south. He must find the colder waters. These waters were becoming unbearable, and...whoa...ugguhh...owwWWAA...Caliente!

His reverie was broken. The waters here approached scalding! He surfaced seeking an escape. His head broke the top waters just as a hot pot of oatmeal passed like a missile through the skies overhead. How had he come to this place? He quickly looked around to see oak cabinets, a linoleum floor, rough sawn rafters overlaid with tongue and groove finished pine. This was the kitchen in his childhood home on Dimple Dell Road. He was here in a sink full of hot dishwater and at this moment, he could not be bothered with details. The water was hot and getting hotter. He jumped out of the sink and down from the counter, his red flippers splatted on the linoleum. Someone had left on the hot water faucet. He quickly switched the tap from hot-to-cold in an effort to temper the steaming hot water already in the sink. He needed this avenue to escape quickly. He had been here before, many times. His mom and dad were engaged in a classic battle.

Pre-occupied though she was, mom recognized that she had left the water running. She reached back without looking and shut off the valve. Marty could not be caught in the middle of this classic battle. He couldn't risk having them see him. Who knew what cataclysm might ensue should Mom or Dad find him here? Quickly, he jumped back in. The home waters were still hot, but tolerable. He stayed submerged as he waited for the "All Clear".

From beneath the agitated kitchen waves, he watched through the water as a spoon full of oatmeal first launched. Dad counter by breaking a bottle of ketchup on the tile counter top. Marty ventured again topside but was forced to duck when oatmeal plastered the ceiling. Payback, Marty thought. Dad had deserved it. He knew that he had been here before. He specifically remembered this episode. Dad's first indiscretion had been to come home drunk at zero–dark thirty. Mom confronted him at breakfast with the oatmeal. He responded in kind and exploded a ketchup bottle on the tile counter in one smooth, but demonstrative motion seizing the bottle neck as it sat on the counter, raising it skyward over his head and slamming the butt onto the hard tile. Ka Blewey ! Oh! The humanity! Ketchup rocketed across the room and etched out Rorschach in high speed splatter patterns across the kitchen's interior.

In rapid succession, a volley of oatmeal flew in response, slung first by a wooden spoon and followed by the stainless steel pot that had - until very recently - occupied the burner on top of the stove. Mom lost her grip and the pot flew high like a sailing fast ball intended as chin music. The spoon was heavy with oatmeal that splattered across the kitchen. Marty kept his head down as he watched the pot hit the wall over Dad's head then fall to the floor and spin to a stop.

Usually, Marty would awaken in the morning to the sounds of Buck Owens and the Buckaroos:

♪♪"I've got a tiger by the tail it's plain to see. I won't be much when you get through with me. It's getting late and I'm feelin' mighty pale. Looks like I've got a tiger by the tail!"♪♪

A propos for these Times, he supposed. This relationship was a tiger and Marty grew weary of trying to grapple with it. Mom and Dad usually reserved their personal business for the wee hours when he was only indirectly made aware by the thumps and bumps from upstairs while he was in bed downstairs. In the morning, Dad would be gone. Drawers would be fully opened, toppled, and overturned onto the floor. Kitchen chairs would be turned over. And, of course, remnants of last night's dinner – once heated, but cold by the time dad came home- would be scattered over every part of the kitchen or living room. Sometimes Marty would awaken to find the little boy next to him in bed. The boy would be crying and Marty would comfort him; tell him to go back to sleep. Marty was determined to remember. But, for now he was hot and uncomfortable. The water in the kitchen sink was still much too warm, hot even. He had found no relief in this journey further south. Something was not right.

He surfaced again to find himself in the therapy tub there in PT, and the water was hot and getting hotter! He put a hand at the top of either side of the tub and quickly hoisted himself out. He plopped onto the checkered tiles wearing his fins and speedo. He lifted the goggles from his eyes and placed them on his forehead. He was beet-red from head to toe. He checked the thermometer at the back of the tub. It read: 104 degrees Fahrenheit. That should be warm, but nothing near boiling seemed normal for a hot tub. He tapped the glass on the front of the thermometer. The needle jumped up to 114 degrees, the highest on the dial. Whoa! He really should get maintenance in here! But for now, he was exhausted. He had been swimming the world's oceans for a long time. Tomorrow, he thought. Tomorrow, he would ask Maintenance to check the gauge. He skipped dinner and headed off to bed.

CHAPTER VIII

Missouri "Mo" Johansen, Lawrence "Larry" Finklestein, and William "Curly" Stone crept silently down the darkened corridor from the couch in the front living room. Following completion of his yogurt count, Larry found Mo and Curly in early morning. Typically, they were there in the kitchen at first light: Larry to count yogurt and take inventory; Mo for some bacon; and Curly to gossip. "Forget breakfast," Curly told them. He was still troubled by the strange actions undertaken by Mr. Markham. "Let's go". He led out without turning back. Out of pure curiosity, they followed Curly to the room in Hallway A - the Ahlzeimer's Wing, the room that held Bed 13 and its' current occupant: Mark Mark Markham. Marty lay on his back in the elevated and inclined bed, his trademark red goggles on his head. He was sleeping soundly and snoring loudly, oblivious to the curious looks from these silent onlookers peering through the open door and into his room from the darkened hallway. Had they looked closer, they would have seen that the sheet beneath him was wet – but not from intemperance.

Next to the bed sat a small dresser –Victorian style - with a single drawer. It was painted in faux antique white. The drawer was partially open. Curly was curious. He opened the drawer quietly. Inside were a Gideon Bible, a Book of Mormon, a personal diary, and a pair of reading glasses. All were sitting on top of a travel magazine. Curly was most curious about the personal journal, but circumspection got the best of him. Instead in the bible, Curly found a dog eared page in the Old Testament. He recognized the story. It was about Moses escaping Egypt with the Israelites and taking them across the Red Sea on dry ground. A paperback version of an old story called: The Time Machine lay open inside the drawer and was pushed to the back. A thick hard back book sat open, face down on top of the dresser. The cover was blue. The title on the front was white. It read: Moby Dick by Herman Melville. A drawing of a large White Whale filled the cover from top to bottom.

Curly glanced at the open book and shrugged. He moved the bible off of the magazine and pulled the magazine from the drawer. He was more curious about "Patagonia" as advertised on the splashy cover:

Why Go To Chilean Patagonia

> With its aura of remote romance, wind-whipped Chilean Patagonia attracts those travelers with an eye for beauty and a zest for adventure. Icy glaciers plunge into emerald lakes; wild fjords snake through hardwood forests; and the Andes' dramatic peaks ascend into swirling clouds and mist. Patagonia's fabled lands have lured Magellan, Darwin, and even Butch Cassidy and the Sundance

Kid. Spend a day getting acquainted with the quirky Magellanic penguins congregating on Isla Magdalena. Then, continue south for jaw-dropping views of Tierra del Fuego's sky-high mountains, pristine glaciers, and verdant forests. When you're ready for some R&R, retreat to your cozy lodge to get energized with some fresh Patagonian air and a hearty supply of seafood and wine.

Curly quickly thumbed through the remaining pages. He stopped briefly at some cool photographs of penguins sitting on icebergs. He checked out another photo that depicted a large "rogue" wave breaking onto an iceberg; another showed a pod of whales spouting.

An article more to the back of the magazine together with some slick photos of the Great Barrier Reef caught his attention. The lead paragraph read:

The Great Barrier Reef is Being Eaten Alive by Killer Starfish.

The starfish were responsible for the significant loss of coral cover between 1985 and 2012, when an average of 50 percent of the live polyps disappeared. Since then, protectors of the reef instituted a culling program which has resulted in the removal of more than 600,000 starfish.

This articled included a brief history of the discovery of the Great Barrier Reef by Captain James Cook in 1717. He put the magazine back and shut the drawer. He looked over at the bed's occupant. Marty continued to snooze.

Curly looked around. In the corner of the bedroom was a small "black and white" television set, sitting on an old oak chair that bumped against the white painted cinder block wall that bordered the room. The plain red oak chair was faded and worn. The seat was bare, no cushion. A single antenna extended 45 degrees from the TV to the white cinderblock wall, a recognized aid to clear reception. The end was covered with a wad of tin foil. The television set was turned on and blathering. A Starkist commercial suddenly came onto the small black and white screen. "Hey Charlie..." Curly popped off the set with a quick slap of the palm.

"I'm telling you", he said. "I just left him in PT. I saw him earlier. He was there all day. He was there for a swim...or so he said", Curly whispered loudly. His hearing had deserted him years ago. The batteries in his aids had died and his kids weren't set to visit with replacements for another month or two. Regardless, Curly always spoke loudly just so he could hear himself speak. "Le Biche tried to kill me and would have if those goggles and flippers hadn't a waltzed into the room at the just the right time. I ain't never seen anything like it".

By "Le Biche", he meant – of course - Ms. Lauren Bichette, the dark red haired and sensually but dangerously attractive head nurse who stalked the halls nightly herding home the care facility's occupants to their temporary beds, while she schemed up some new and nefarious plan to open up bed space for another of the recently applied. These Medicare still recognized. These came in exchange for the old and stale residents whose insurance had lapsed and whose family had pretty much abandoned to be quietly euthanized by neglect. What the families failed to recognize and what the residents knew for certain was that the neglect that Ms. Bichette would dish out was so very much more than benign. Talk to any one of the residents who had spent any time there and each one, without exception, would tell you that Ms. Bichette was hell bent on vanquishing the Baby Boomers, the increasingly infirm, and the irrelevant.

But then again, in more lucid moments, Ms. Bichette's serpent tattoo was the talk of the place. The boys all wanted to admire it, the curious intoxication of it; and fantasized just to get a chance to trace the soft outline with a bony finger on her tanned and toned torso.

The ladies outwardly disdained it, but inwardly all wondered how the damn thing would have held up with time and drooping skin had they had the temerity to go under the ink needle when they were younger. Each of the girls dreamed of days long past when they were once admired for the softness and curve of their own hills and dales, their majestic peaks and verdant valleys. Each of the boys struggled to retrieve and to treasure those ever more vanishing memories – enhanced by Time- of glory days now gone when they were taken seriously. Oh, gawd! How each of them longed for youth.

In response to Curly's outburst, inappropriate for the serious intensity of their current off-limits investigative wanderings into the Alzhiemer's wing, Mo reacted reflexively and quickly struck Curly on the forehead with the knuckle of his right index finger to silence him. At the same time, he ssshh'd with a left index to his nose and whispered emphatically, "So why did you bring us here?"

"Look", Curly shot back. He turned his head away and pointed with his eyes further down the hallway as if someone were there – all in an effort to distract Mo. It worked. Mo turned his head to follow Curly's eyes. Curly was waiting. He reached out to pinch Mo's nose between his thumb and forefinger. With the nose secured, he quickly slapped the pinch away – nose and all - with his other hand. Mo was unfazed. He was trained in the art of boxing. He responded with a left hook to Curly's right ear. Curly anticipated the attempted blow and ducked. Instead of Curly, Mo caught Larry in the throat which caused Larry to choke back the Luden's cherry cough drop he'd been nursing. He gagged and began to cough. His face reddened and tears filled his eyes.

The sound of rubber soles on the bottom of white hospital shoes swiftly padding on the checkered-tile floor outside the door silenced the trio. The footsteps stopped Larry in mid gag. Mo covered Larry's throat to prevent an inadvertent gag. His face grew more and more red in color as he fought valiantly – with Mo's help - to stifle his cough reflex. Mo gave one hard and fast swat to Larry's mid-back. The red cough drop ejected and bounced across the floor into Hallway A. Larry sucked back a big breath and began to exhale. Mo clamped a large hand over his mouth and held it there awaiting some kind of "all clear".

Curly – unhearing - was oblivious. He reacted to the others' sudden silence. Their wide eyes and furtive glances were directed down the darkened corridor in the direction of Physical Therapy. He exclaimed perhaps a bit more loudly than was kosher for the moment, "W-T-F?" Ever the stickler for propriety, he enunciated each letter to ensure clarity and understanding. Mo offered a couple of quick nods sideways toward the hallway outside. Curly's eyes followed. They looked back at each other and dropped to the floor where they scrambled over and around each other to hide under the bed. The foot of the bed rode atop Mo's bulk raising Marty's feet at one end above his head at the other.

Then she appeared, just outside the door: Le Biche - Ms. Lauren Bichette - the new Head Nurse at Golden Hills, their new boss-lady standing at the intersection of Hallways A and B, just up from the cafeteria. She was headed to the kitchen - likely to the refrigerator – to retrieve a cup of contraband Tapioca that she had confiscated earlier in the day from one of the resident's private stash. She stopped in the quiet hallway intersection, her head up and turned to listen. She thought that she had sensed some commotion in the darkened corridor of the adjoining wing. She bent to listen more closely. Evidently, she decided it was nothing. She hadn't yet ventured into the A-wing. Instead, she continued to the kitchen.

Ms. Bichette was relatively new to this gig. In prior occupations, she'd been a fitness instructor, a lifeguard, and a golf-cart hostess. She knew the effect that she had on men and frequently used it to her advantage. She smiled to recall the fake accent she adopted when stationed at the intersection of holes 12, 13, and 14 on a bright summer day while employed at the golf course just down the road. Her summer attire and that accent had helped her earn mucho dolores in tips that day. It was somehow British – but neither the King's English, nor was it Cockney. To those assembled it didn't matter. It was not American, just English. She had successfully drawn 14 different golf carts including occupants away from 3 different holes all in the name of needed refreshment. The accent was intriguing, but this was not the reason for the gathered crowd. The entire male assemblage would agree. The primary influence, by far, was the sun bleached, light auburn hair - long but gathered at the back of her head -together with the tanned arms projecting from a sleeveless white cotton top, unbuttoned two buttons down to a tan and expansive cleavage, and the long legs – also lightly tanned -riding nicely beneath a short, bright yellow, golf skirt. The crowd of men was wholly mesmerized. She held them bound. A feat she had managed often at various times and places. She held the power and she knew it.

She was just ready to celebrate when one at the edge of the crowd asked, "Where'd you get that accent? I can't quite place it."

She turned to see a skinny, older man, dressed all in red: red shorts, red golf-shirt, and wearing a red hat and red rimmed sunglasses. Normally, she didn't pay attention to any one person. She never turned to acknowledge such singular attention. She was deaf to the sound of a single voice. She was smitten less by the one and more by the many. But that day at the course had been unusual. Who was this guy she wondered. What did he want? She couldn't help but feel that he was calling her out. But, again... why? A furrow creased her brow when she thought that she somehow knew this dude...no, wait...! It was not that she "knew but rather that she would come to know him. Yes, she expected to meet this dude, again. Where that might be, she was unsure. She was disquieted, but no matter. At present she was curious as to what he wanted here at the golf course. She would have carried the pretense further, but she was astute enough to know that she may have met her match and that the jig might just be up. Still, she was not one to be intimidated. She straightened to smooth her skirt, brushed her blouse with both hands, and tucked back a few stray hairs, fallen from those that were gathered behind her ears. Once composed, she said to the crowd at large, without hesitation or pretense and in classic, straightforward, and accent-less "California – style" English: "Grass Valley, California". She offered a cute and sexy smile, hopped into the beverage cart, waved to the slightly bemused crowd of admirers there assembled, and rode into the sunset. She was not one to continue a gig if there were any chance that she might be revealed.

Ms. Bichette smiled at the memory. She wasn't sure just how she'd come to apply to this old folks' home. The money was lousy; the benefits the same. The place smelled like old people despite the covering stench of bleach and disinfectant. Even in the Commons Area where the families came to visit; the old blue hairs applied make up and flowery perfumes; and the old geezers liberally applied their after shave and colognes ranging from Aqua Velva and Skin Bracer to Hai Karate, English Leather and British Sterling. (What was it about these Brits and cologne?).

One of the newer boys had a penchant for an old brand called Elsha that she recognized from who knows where. This silly fact vaguely disturbed her at some deeper level as did the fact that she had even taken this gig. Usually, she was certain of her mission and the requisite actions to be taken. But like that old boy who called her out on the golf course that day, this Elsha dude troubled her. He seemed to sense her insecurities. He seemed to know her mind and purpose. He was a figure with whom to be reckoned and she would take all necessary precaution in dealing with him. For some deep seated reason, only known to her at a yet to be plumbed subconscious level, she felt a sense of mission here, a mission that she shared, in some yet to be revealed fashion, with this sweet smelling new guy.

She had stopped there at the head of Hallway A on her way to the kitchen. She wandered a bit further down. Yes, she thought. Here in Hallway A, she had found a potential nemesis right here in Bed 13. She stopped just outside Marty's bedroom doorway. All was quiet except for the slight murmur of shallow breathing from the sleeping occupant. The faint smell of Elsha as it wafted from inside the bedroom, out the doorway past her and on up Hallway A toward the front lobby, confirmed her suspicions. She read the chart posted outside the door. The bed belonged, at least for the time being, to one: Mark Mark Markham– newly admitted. She inhaled deeply to catch the familiar fragrance: Elsha. Yeesss, she remembered. She knew this guy. She recognized him from the golf course and again – for the first time yesterday in Physical Therapy. That was some performance. Something about that crazy confident dude in PT had been familiar, and she remembered. He had called her out years back at the golf course. She remembered his fragrance. The other residents called him "Marty".

Yes she knew him now. Marty was it? Okay Marty. Why don't we try to get along, shall we? Marty seemed to have made a raft of friends already here at the home. She took note. She would need to watch this one and closely.

The squeal of rubber on polished linoleum caught her attention to the activities in B-Wing. Damn! Those two blue hairs: Margaret Lassiter and her pal, Trudy Chapman. They were drag racing with their wheelchairs, again. It might be time to strap them into bed. She would need to get the goods. Admin here is careful about discipline. Without solid proof, she'd never get them to go for it. But to Ms. Bichette, total control over the residence was only a matter of time.

"I'll get you my pretties. I'll get you and your little dog too", she grinned as the movie scene came to mind. She quickly padded back toward B-wing. She would bide her time and treasure her moments here. But for now, she remembered the plundered Peach Yogurt and headed for the kitchen. She had plenty of time and was in no particular hurry.

What the young Ms. Bichette did not know was that Time was a luxury afforded to, abused, and taken for granted by the young. Ms. Bichette didn't know that Time to the elderly was a beast to be tamed; an enemy to be befriended; and- as Marty would come to understand – was to the Hubris of Youth, an Achilles Heel to be bruised or even cut, if necessary.

CHAPTER IX

Later that same afternoon, Curly was headed down Hallway B to PT to hang up his broom and put away his mop and bucket. He stepped into the darkened room and flipped on the light. Broken chunks of ice in differing sizes were strewn and melting across the floor. He looked to the PT tub. He was surprised to see the dude who'd saved him from Le Biche earlier in the afternoon. That was hours ago. Last he knew, the old boy was asleep in his own bed. How long had he been here, Curly wondered? The old guy must be pickled by now. His bald head was down, his face in the water. He appeared to be blowing bubbles. The water was turbulent and Curly could hear a few low pops and a rumble. Ice surrounded the old boy in the water; and, then there were the chunks of ice on the checkered tile floor that surrounded the tub. Where had this ice come from, he wondered again? He hadn't seen any ice earlier in the day and the skinny dude certainly didn't carry any with him into Physical Therapy.

Curly walked over to the tub and tapped the skinny dude on the shoulder. Marty sat up and wiped his face and eyes. He looked around the room oblivious to Curly standing above and behind him next to the tub.

"Hey", Curly stepped back and to the side of the tub. He waved. He didn't want to scare the old boy. "I'm Curly. Remember me? I've been meaning to thank you for...you know, this afternoon when you saved me from Le Biche...Ms. Bichette I mean". This guy was a patron and Curly figured he better respect the line of authority: Bichette to patrons. He could save the informality for himself and his crew. Still, something about this dude told Curly that he was no regular patron.

Marty stayed seated in the ice cold tub. Frost had gathered on the outside of the steel sides up to the water level. He turned his head to see Curly. "Do you mind? Last I remember, I was visiting with Moby and riding the curl. I should really get back."

Yeah, Curly thought. I bet.

"No, I don't mind", he said as he gave an easy but uncertain wave and moved to the doorway, his hand on the light switch. "You'd better get out of there soon though. Dinner's done. It'll be lights out in an hour. You don't want Ms. Bichette to find you here. Then as he turned to leave, he muttered to himself, "Come to think of it, I don't want her to find me here". He stepped lively to find Mo and Larry.

Initially, he figured that they might be in the cafeteria, but he remembered that dinnertime was over and he didn't want to be conscripted to help wash dishes. Larry may be overseeing that task already. Both would want to hear about this, but he knew it could wait until morning. Still, he had to tell someone. No way could he hold onto a story like this one.

He intercepted Mo in the front living area off of the foyer. He had just punched out on the clock in the front entry office and was now enjoying some Perry Mason reruns on the black and white. As usual, Maggie was parked up front near the window, deeply asleep and snoring. A cool evening breezed wafted through the open window panels beneath the large picture windows that dominated the exterior wall at either side of the brick fireplace and chimney that acted as centerpiece to the front office, front entry, and front living area. As usual, the front desk was empty. Curly figured Le Biche was maybe catching some zzzz's. The night sky was ablaze with a full moon and a myriad of stars strewn across the celestial landscape. Crickets played an orchestra that resounded on the breeze. Bullfrogs accompanied at the edge of the pond just outside the front entry.

Mo was watching television in the front living area. The couches were comfortable, but still strong enough to bolster his broad frame. The TV was a color set with decent reception. Mo watched intently. On the TV, he could hear the dialogue:

HAMILTON BURGER: "Objection, your honor. As counsel must most assuredly know, the Rule Against Perpetuities is a common law rule that prevents people from using legal instruments to exert control over the ownership of property for a time long beyond the lives of people living at the time the instrument was written. Specifically, the rule forbids a person from creating future interests in property that would vest beyond 21 years after the lifetimes of those living at the time of creation of that interest."

THE COURT: "Weelllll... let me think on this a moment. If I am not mistaken the Rule Against Perpetuties provides that certain future interests must vest, if at all, within 21 years after the death of a life in being at the time that the interest is created. That's true isn't it, Mr. Burger?"

HAMILTON BURGER: "Yes, you honor. That is true."

THE COURT: "And, as I understand it, of all the rules that have developed with regard to limiting the ability to transfer property, the one with the strongest ramifications today is the Rule Against Perpetuities, is that not also correct, Mr. Burger?"

HAMILTON BURGER: "Yes, your honor, I believe that you have accurately stated. I would only note that the Rule Against Perpetuities was designed to ensure that some person would actually own the land within a reasonable period of time after the death of the transferor."

THE COURT: "Hmmm, huhh. I do recall that. Mr. Mason, do you concur?"

PERRY MASON: "Yes, your honor. But may it please the court?" Mr. Mason holds up an index finger as if to make a point.

THE COURT: The Judge holds up his hand to Mr. Mason and looks again to Mr. Burger. "Please, Mr. Burger, you may finish".

Now interrupted by the Court, Mr. Mason sets his index finger to his lips and looks to be a bit befuddled.

HAMILTON BURGER: "Thank you, your honor. I was just going to say that to accomplish that result, the rule states that no interest in property can be valid unless it is shown that the interest would vest, if at all, no later than twenty one years after some life in being at the creation of that interest".

THE COURT: "Yes. I see. That is well stated, Mr. Burger. Thank you. What say you Mr. Mason?"

PERRY MASON: "Your honor, I am simply trying to show that my client did not commit the murder."

THE COURT: The murder? Oh, oh yes, the murder. Very well, I suppose that the objection is overruled. Anything more gentlemen?" the judge asks. At his point, Curly steps up intent upon speaking with Mo.

PERRY MASON: "Yes. In fact, your Honor, if you would grant me some leeway, I believe I can shed some light on these proceedings by pointing to the murderer who is here in this very courtroom, but uh,...only... after the commercial break, of course.

THE COURT: "Any objection, Mr. Burger?"

HAMILTON BURGER: "Why no, your honor. Given that we are only 5 minutes from the top of the hour, I should think that there would be no more an appropriate time to reveal just how wrong I have been throughout these proceedings. (Mr. Burger smiles obsequiously).

The TV briefly fades to black and then emerges on screen a cartoon depicting Charlie Tuna wearing dark horn rimmed glasses and red beret sitting in the balcony of an underwater opera house. An octopus is on stage draped in a Roman toga and a gold crown of laurel leaves around its large head. Seated next to the Charlie in the balcony is a small hermit crab wearing an opera cloak around her shoulders and peering at the stage through some opera glasses.

CRAB while peering through her glasses: "Charlie what are you doing at the opera?"

OCTOPUS is in background and on stage is singing inaudibly and gesticulating.

CHARLIE standing in balcony at the forefront and responds to the Hermit Crab: "I came to the opera to show Starkist that I've got good taste" as he smiles and winks at the camera.

CRAB drops her glasses and looks at Charlie: "But Charlie, Starkist doesn't want tuna with good taste. They want tuna that tastes good." (A fishing line drops into the picture with a large fishing hook on the end. A note is affixed to the hook that reads: "Sorry Charlie".

ANNOUNCER over reads: "Sorry, Charlie" The commercial fades to black. Within seconds, Perry Mason returns. Mason is standing in front of the bench. Hamilton Burger is seated at his table. A janitor is standing next to the bailiff at the back of the courtroom in front of the closed courtroom doors. Mason turns from the bench and peruses the courtroom. His eyes find the janitor at the rear.

JANITOR: "Okay. Okay... I did it. I DID IT, ALLRIGHT". He holds out both hands to accept handcuffs from the bailiff. The bailiff looks at him a bit astonished. Those present in the courtroom gasp in surprise. As if by permission from the crowd, the bailiff reaches to his belt, brings out the handcuffs, clips them on the janitor and leads him away.

MR. MASON: "Nice try, Mr....umm.... Mr. Janitor. But, not so fast. May I borrow..."

Curly steps in front of the tube and pops-in the volume button to turn off the set. "Hey Mo, we need to talk?"

Mo sat staring at the tube, mesmerized, his hand to his chin. He was thinking. Charlie looked healthy enough. Why wouldn't Starkist take him? That fish had class; nice glasses; nice hat. He was a one cool dude.

"MO!" Curly snapped his fingers in front of Mo to break the trance. "Mo. I need to talk to you about the new guy. You know, Marty...I mean, Mr. Markham".

"Whoa, whoa, now wait a minute". Mo was on TV time. No one interrupted Mo when he was on TV time. "Let me see if I can get this straight", he investigated. 'You want to talk to me about the new guy?"

"Yeah, the new guy: Marty Markham".

"Mr. Markham, is he in some kind of trouble?"

"Well, no".

"Is he trying to escape?"

"No."

"Is there any reason that I should be concerned RIGHT NOW?"

"Wellll....no, but..."

"Is there any reason that I need to be concerned, at all?" Mo asked impatiently, a bit frustrated.

"Well, no. I suppose not. But, I..."

"Then c'mon man" Mo complained loudly. "You turned off the tube for nothing right in the middle of Mason. I was waiting to see what was coming on later. The earlier commercial said something about JAWS. I saw that at the movies a while back. Man, was it ever intense. This big ole bad ass shark shows up at a resort and..."

"Mo, MO, MO...hold on, HOLD ON! You know...the new guy?" He circled his fingers on both hands and held them to his eyes, "The guy with the goggles, the speedo, fins?"

Mo inhaled deeply, blew it out with a deep sigh, "Yeah, okay. What about him?"

"Well, I mean...he is just...well, I mean he is unusual, odd maybe. I can't figure. I just saw him back at the tub in PT. The sides were covered in frost and chunks of ice were scattered across the tile floor". He looked at Mo, wide eyed, hands out, inquiring.

Mo shrugged his shoulders back at him.

"Gentlemen, if I may?" Maggie had heard the commotion. Glad to find an audience, she rolled her chair on over. She had been thinking and needed somebody off of whom she could bounce her thoughts.

Mo and Curly nearly jumped out of their respective skins. Both fell back and sat onto the couch. Curly held and hand over his pounding heart and panted.

"Ms. Maggie, you're awake?" Mo observed for no better reason that to regain his balance.

"Of course, I'm awake", she shot back. "Don't be an idiot. I think more of you than that, Mr. Mo. You should know that by now. Now listen to me. Mr. Markham – Marty as you call him – is a on to something intriguing...although I'm not sure that he knows it yet".

Mo and Curly looked at each other quizzically.

Maggie continued, "I was able to visit with him...don't ask me how...a few years back. I mean, I didn't really 'visit', more like 'observe'. But I was there with him. I mean, we were here, but it was there. Anyway, he was younger then; quite handsome, if I do say so myself. I was younger, slimmer...I was well...I was pretty". She set her hands on her hips, set her jaw, and dared their sarcasm.

Curly interrupted, "Look Maggie, I don't want to be a drag, but so what? You knew this dude some time back. Have you spoken with him lately? Does he even remember you?"

"No you dolt, I just told you. I 'observed' him only yesterday when he was asleep in his room. I was here really, but somehow I was there. Don't ask me how. All I saw was him, like...lick his thumb and flip it as if he was turning a page in a big book. He did it kind of slowly; page by page, forward a little, then back some, searching".

Mo took a chance, "So where is 'here' and where is 'there'?" He smiled sardonically.

Maggie continued unfazed. "It was a bit of a first. He wasn't wearing his standard swimming gear – you know: no goggle, no speedo, and no fins. He had on a pair of long trunks with the word: 'OHURE' across the butt. Like I said, he was handsome. He was, well...younger. Anyway, it seemed that he had somehow messed with 'Time' itself. He talks a lot about 'No Time'...you know...when he is dreaming. I've heard him at night when I can't sleep..."

Oh really, Mo thought as he began to doze off. YOU can't sleep? Puhleeze!

"Like I said", she repeated. "He moved it forward then moved it back...Time that is. I couldn't really see how he did it. It looked like he was turning pages ,you know, the pages of a large book, maybe. I sorta knew by watching". She turned to look at each of them for needed affirmation. The boys were yawning.

"And besides" she went on stubbornly, "I've seen his daughter. She came to visit just yesterday. She brought her little girls. She's gotta be 30 plus, maybe a bit older by now. But yesterday..." Maggie became confused with the telling. "Well...no way was she the little girl...uh the same girl that I also....uh...that I also saw uhhh... yesterday". She paused again to puzzle this one through. "Yet somehow, both were the same girl – only one was little...and one was, uh... big, and I saw them both yesterday". She insisted. She was talking to herself.

She couldn't really press this one. Trudy might understand, but Maggie wasn't sure that even she, herself, understood. She had better stay quiet. Folks around here might think that she's was nuts. "Nuts" was a ticket out. Management didn't keep crazy folks here. Still, she felt as if she had somehow fiddled with Time ,and this was important. She had seen Marty's wife and daughter sign in yesterday at the front office with Ms. Bichette. They had come with three little girls- his granddaughters - to visit Marty. She had met these ladies previously. They visited Marty quite regularly. It was sad that he rarely remembered their visits. But he certainly enjoyed their company when they came. In the moments immediately following their visits, he would speak adoringly of his pretty blonde wife. He'd say that she was gorgeous, that she was both sweet and kind to everyone that she encountered. Maggie had to agree. The woman was adorable. Marty would say that where his wife cares for the world, he cares for his wife.

His daughter was both beautiful and tremendously bright; a successful business woman in her own right whose priority was the three little girls. She loved them tremendously, individually - her care for each was occasioned by the attitudes and temperaments of each. It was easy to see that she knew them and loved them uniquely.

These women had come with the girls to visit Marty, and she saw the girls with him yesterday – the three little girls. They were walking Hallway A at Golden Hills. She watched as they took the stairs to the basement morgue while the women continued to visit in the hallway. Why would he take them down there, she wondered?

A few minutes later, she had seen them from the front picture window as they played in the outer fountain. She put two and two together. Marty had found an escape from this place through the garage to the downstairs morgue. Her intuition told her that these three little girls were Marty's granddaughters ,and that the pretty blond older lady and the gorgeous young woman must be Marty's wife and daughter. Marty often bragged about his tremendously bright daughter who was, at that very moment, chattering with her mom outside of Marty's room.

Maggie wheeled herself over to the top of Hallway A. She rolled cautiously so as not to alert Ms. Bichette. A brief glance down the hallway confirmed that Marty's wife and daughter were still busily engaged in conversation just outside of Marty's room. Maggie trundled back to the picture window. Marty and the girls were still outside playing in the fountain. She watched them form a human chain with Marty in the lead. She watched as he dove into the fountain and each followed in turn. Maggie's head began to spin. She blinked and rubbed her eyes. She looked again. She remained for a Time there at the picture window, but soon conceded: Marty and his granddaughters were gone.

She quickly trundled herself back over to Hallway A. The hallway was empty. Marty's wife and daughter were gone. Outside the front entry and headed to the parking area, she heard the faint echoes of three little girls:

"Mom, when can we come back to play with Papa. He does fun stuff", one of them said as they all disappeared.

Maggie slowly wheeled herself back to the front window. She set the brake on her wheelchair. The breeze outside played with leaves as the shadows danced across the picture window as Maggie fell fast asleep in her chair.

As for Mo and Curly, they, too, were both fast asleep. Mo had leaned back, his arms up on the back of the red leather couch. He snored loudly. Curly snuggled against Mo's large frame. He contentedly purred. The two rested peacefully until morning there on the couch in the front entry of Golden Hills Convalescent Center. The nighttime serenade brought by the bullfrogs and crickets, as highlighted by the fireworks display offered up by the full moon and star filled skies brought peace, and the two smiled contentedly.

CHAPTER X

The next day found the "Tres Amigos" peering from beneath the inclined bed of the newest resident in the Golden Hills Convalescent Center - one, Mr. "double M" Markham who was now officially recognized by Ms. Bichette as Marty - where he lay on top of the sheets, snoring loudly. The bed was inclined because Mo had crawled beneath it. Had anyone pulled back the sheets to investigate, they would have seen the red goggles lying up near the pillow, the red speed-o apparently suspended in air at mid-bed, and the pair of red swim-fins stacked and neatly balanced vertically, side-by-side, near the foot of the bed. Had they not been so intent on listening to Ms. Bichette's receding footfalls, they would have remarked at the annoying tinnitus that each seemed to experience simultaneously, a "white noise" of sorts. Had they re-directed their auditory focus, they would have discovered that it emanated from the vaguely visible outline of a bony form lying in the bed. They, like Ms. Bichette, would have noted the faint smell of familiar cologne. But in testament to Marty's always surprising, oft times frustrating, and too-often annoying ability to "fly under the radar" -as it were-, they did not.

"Let's git!" Mo whispered. "She's gone." The trio scrambled quietly from beneath the bed. Curly banged his head on the bottom of the moveable safety rail, "Oww"! Now, it was Larry's turn. He clamped a hand over Curly's mouth.

Even Marty took a turn, that is to say, a turn in bed. Reflux had sent a spout of gastric juices into his throat and he snorted loudly to capture it before it moved into his lungs. He woke with a start. He sat up gasping for breath. He'd had the affliction for decades now, so he no longer became alarmed as he stood there at the brink of death, drowning in his own bodily fluids. He waited for the spasm to clear. He pulled a deep breath, coughed and choked, in an effort to find normalcy. He reached to drop the safety rail and dropped it onto Larry's neck pinning him to the floor. The trio was trapped beneath the bed and behind –or in Larry's case, under -the aging iron grates of the rail. They watched as an out-of-focus and skinny pair of feet, ankles and legs – colored "fish belly white"- dropped from atop the bed to the floor in front of them. The bed's most recent occupant stood and draped a bath robe over his form. To the occupants under the bed, he appeared to lose control of his horizontal hold, to fade in and out, and to trail with him the sound of "white noise". The trio watched him walk out the door, clicking and buzzing all the while, and turn down Hallway A toward the kitchen.

Mo quickly exited from beneath the bed at the back, nearest the wall. He came around front to free the trapped Larry, who for the second time tonight had faced death by suffocation. He and Curly scrambled to their feet from under the bed. They stuck their heads out the door way and into the hall: Mo first and up high; Larry second directly beneath Mo; and Curly came third at the bottom. The corridor was empty. The morning light was breaking. They could hear some commotion from the direction of the cafeteria. The still sleeping residents began to stir. They smelled newly brewed coffee. Of course, per usual, last night's reheated and rancid brew would go to the residents. Only the staff tasted the new stuff.

They treaded toward the kitchen where they expected no real surprises: Oatmeal, scrambled eggs, and some tasteless fruit not in season. What they wouldn't give for one slice of smokehouse bacon or a fresh banana. But the staff dietician had ruled bacon: "Verboten - packed with Nitrates; too much Sodium". The bananas caused constipation, never mind that the potassium was good for the heart, bacon and bananas were not good for the old and dying. Who were they kidding?

Nitrates and Sodium, as delectable vices, weren't really good or healthy for anyone. Yet, the young justified it all because they were young, indestructible, and had years to spare, years to recover if their health took a turn, years to indulge. The old and dying were...well, old and dying. What harm would sodium, or nitrates, even nicotine or alcohol, or a host of fun prescription drugs do to them: three very old and fading duffers who only felt old because they were told that they couldn't eat bacon? ...Really? You can't break something that is already broken. Why not let them try to live again? "W-T-F" as Curly would say.

Better yet what was almost incomprehensible to those at Golden Hills was the dearth of peach yogurt? What possibly could be the health consequence of eating yogurt? Hadn't they hated it as kids? Wouldn't they rather have eaten ice cream loaded with carbs? After all, when they were kids, wasn't Oleo Margarine made from saturated fat, considered the "healthy" choice? Wasn't butter considered unhealthy and fattening? And, wasn't bacon -yes, bacon with nitrates and sodium- to be a requisite part of a healthy breakfast?

The amigos entered the cafeteria. Muzak drizzled from the home's overhead intercom. Without warning, the smell of Smokehouse bacon hit them broadside. The sound of sizzles oscillated from a distant grill hidden somewhere behind the serving counter where the staff dolloped over-cooked oatmeal and scrambled eggs, cafeteria style, onto the trays of the barely lucid residents as they passed each station.

Ms. Bichette was there at a side table apparently lecturing to an audience of two residents: Trudy stood with a walker next to Maggie whom she had parked – on demand by Ms. Bichette – directly in front of the table to best accept the anticipated lecture. Maggie had adopted her usual air of catatonia as she drooped in her chair. She gripped the wheels as if ready for the starting gun. Despite the fact that she had left her full set of dentures in the glass next to her bed, her toothless mouth was sternly set. She stared past Ms. Bichette lost in the thought of her own plans for rebellion. Trudy, too, was lost in thought, her attention drawn to a table in the back where Marty had taken up residence.

Curly, Mo, and Larry hurried over to dutifully attend. They followed Trudy's gaze to see that the occupant of Bed 13 had awakened and beat them –somehow- to the cafeteria for breakfast. Curly elbowed Larry in the ribs, pointed to Marty and nodded. Marty sat alone, silent and motionless at a table in the back. He wore what appeared to be only a bathrobe, but there on his head sat a pair of red goggles; on his feet – red swim fins. A few residents of Golden Hills began to gather around Marty's table in expectation of some action. Rumors were that with this new resident, there was always a good chance. They were chatting enjoying the day, not usual for Golden Hills. They had slept as well as old age would allow ,and it seemed that Marty's recent arrival had administered a level of "calm" to the Golden Hills' residents. For once in a long while, the residents were smiling at morning breakfast, ready to welcome the new day and whatever new adventure was in store.

As the Tres Amigos entered the cafeteria, Curly nudged Mo. He needed some acknowledgement. He pointed across the way to distract Mo. He directed Mo's attention to the old guy in the red goggles seated at the table in the back. "Hey, how'd he get here so fast?" The question was not part of the ruse. He was legitimately curious.

Still, Curly couldn't be trusted and Mo reacted reflexively. He raised a hand to cuff Curly upside the back of the head. But Curly was a quick learner and recovered quickly. He anticipated the move and instinctively ducked. Mo missed his mark and, once more, caught Larry directly in the Adams Apple. Larry reached for his throat with both hands in what appeared to be a signal for the Heimlich. His face reddened as he began to choke. He teared up. Curly patted him distractedly with another swat, this time to the back of the head. Larry coughed loudly into an explosive exhale then sucked back with a huge wheeze to catch his breath. He coughed and hacked and soon bent over with his hands on his knees to keep from falling over. He continued to wheeze until his chest loosened and the spasms calmed.

Curly looked to the back of the cafeteria where he spotted the occupant of Bed 13 seated at what the residents had come to know as "Marty's Table" where he was surrounded by a host of octogenarian admirers and said again to no one in particular, "C'mon how'd he get here so fast? We just left him in his room?"

In exasperation, Mo took another errant swipe at Curly, this time from the opposite direction with his left hand. Curly again dodged the blow. Mo missed and once more caught Larry, this time in the back of his head. Splat! Larry went down face first. He was out like a light. Both Mo and Curly felt guilty. Unintentionally, as it were, they had inflicted a beating on Larry. They reached down together and hoisted him up. He was dazed and murmuring. They looked at each other and shrugged. Both felt badly, maybe even bit guilty; then again – Naahhhh! They dragged him across the checkerboard tile floor to meet with the crowd assembled at Ms. Bichette's table where they joined her together with Trudy, Maggie, and a couple of junior attendants. Nods, handshakes and smiles were passed all around.

"Los Tres Amigos" participated in this impromptu meeting with a degree of anxiety. They sensed a coming onslaught from the residents generally, now altogether in the cafeteria - their "leader" seated quietly at his table in the back with a growing number of supporters there to bolster and encourage him in whatever may be his next move. He was calm for now, but this boy's reputation had preceded him. The attendants were worried. Word in the halls was that Marty had been evicted from a previous senior home for belligerence with staff. The write-up done to justify eviction stated that he had refused to take his meds; slept for days without showering; and argued that the food served in the cafeteria was both inadequate and unhealthy.

Curly couldn't imagine how this guy was that much different from any other resident here at Golden Hills with whom they dealt every day. "W-T-F?" he thought as he shrugged and looked again to Mo and to Larry.

Trudy and Maggie were stationed at Ms. Bichette's table only because they formed part of the staff here at Golden Hills.

Trudy helped sort and dispense medications to the residents. Maggie kept track of all incoming and outgoing residents; mostly outgoing. She made journal entries in a ledger kept by Ms. Bichette at the front desk for both incoming and outgoing residents. Mostly, she dealt with the deaths. Ms. Bichette typically handled the marketing aspects at intake. To listen to her, Golden Hills was Heaven. Sheesh, Maggie whispered to herself. When one of the residents died, her job was to enter the date and time of death. Mostly she would guess. Some of the dear departed, long since removed, had spent days in bed, stiff as a board, before The Death Squad were summoned to assume the removal efforts. Almost always, Ms. Bichette notified her to initiate removal and enter a new vacancy into the company books. Larry took care of and managed the kitchen and foodstuffs. He had come across this assignment quite ingeniously. Curly took on custodial duties – a big job, but he seemed okay with it. It gave him access to almost the entire facility, and plenty of time alone to smoke pot. Mo was a kitten, but looked so big and bad that he administered discipline, took lost and wayward residents back to bed and generally laid down Ms. Bichette's law.

Ms. Bichette dictated the day's assignments. From day to day, the "daily" assignments remained wholly unchanged. Repetition seemed unnecessary. But Le Biche enjoyed the focus of attention, so the daily meetings continued...daily. Thankfully even her need for attention was on a clock. Typically, the meetings lasted no more than 30 minutes. This one was no different. She thanked them for their attendance; called them into a huddle where each put in a hand and signaled: on three – one, two, three, "Bich-ETTE!" She waved and turned away with a huge smile on her face. It was the same, every day. Those left at the table shrugged and breathed a collective sigh. This, too, was the same, every day.

Trudy, Maggie, and the junior attendants took off. Curly, too, was set to leave until Mo put his large paw onto Curly's chest and whispered, "Hold up a minute". He reached inside his shirt and pulled out a manila folder. The label on the tab read: "Mark, Mark, Markham".

"Whoa...wait! What is that?" Curly bent to look. He grabbed the edge of the file folder there in Mo's hands and pulled it to him. Mo thumped him, he let go, and Mo pulled it back.

"This boy was evicted from Greenhaven a few months back", he read from the file, his finger on the page. He glanced back over his shoulder as if in some conspiracy, licked his thumb and speculated out loud that the old boy's threat to cold cock a staff member at his former place of residence may have justified his eviction; never mind that the former staff member matched Mo in height, just not in bulk and had been fired months' earlier from Golden Hills by Le Biche just after she had taken over.

"Hey", Mo noted in surprise as he read further. "Markham and Jamison were together at Greenhaven? That's it! This dude must have some stones to take on Jamison. Either that or he's plain nuts". Mo was beginning to like this old boy already.

Mo knew the Jamison's history with Golden Hills. Just after leaving Greenhaven, Jamison took a post here. He came on board about the same time that Le Biche was hired. A power struggle ensued. One day, Le Biche caught Jamison stealing from her secret stash of Tapioca pudding kept in the kitchen refrigerator and hidden on the lower shelf behind the milk.

She was new to the gig in general and to Golden Hills specifically. Jamison had been around the block at various nursing homes and with several head nurses. He figured he had her number. He figured wrong.

Mo, Curly, and Larry had been there at breakfast when Le Biche entered the cafeteria and spotted the old boy bent over with his head and shoulders in the refrigerator. He was scrummaging around in the back. Le Biche immediately conscripted Mo, just for his size alone, and called him to follow her to the kitchen. Larry and Curly traipsed behind if only to appease their own curiosity. Le Biche marched into the kitchen with the boys in tow and camped herself a few feet back from the open door.

She could have remedied the problem herself with a good swift kick into the Jamison's backside. But the residents knew, even then, that Le Biche never sullied herself with physical attempts to convince. She left that to the lower minions. She had conscripted Mo for just such a purpose. She threw a look at Larry and Curly, and they retreated. Confrontation was not in their nature.

"Mr. Jamison", Le Biche raised her voice to command attention. Jamison lurched up in surprise and bumped his head on the underside of the freezer. The fridge jumped and rocked back and forth as Jamison backed out, his hand rubbing the new found lump on his head. He turned to see Le Biche standing directly in front of him, her arms crossed with a stern look on her face. He continued to rub the back of his head with one hand as he grimaced. In the other hand, he held a cup of Tapioca pudding. "What the hell?" he whimpered.

"As you have been apprised, that refrigerator is off limits to members of the staff", she said. Curly was enjoying this show. Never mind, he thought, that the Tapioca there in the fridge was hers and that she was also considered a member of the staff.

Jamison appeared confused.

"You have been instructed in that regard, both in writing and by me, on numerous occasions", she noted officiously.

She turned to Mo and said, "You shall escort this former employee (she emphasized the word: "former") to his locker where you shall monitor his removal of his personal things. Then, ensure that he exits the building, please".

Escorting Jamison out of the residence was Mo's first call to serve. He was happy to abide. Le Biche needed it done to help ensure both his loyalty and the loyalty of all of the residents. This was her chance to send the message that she was in charge, and she took it. The effort succeeded; her reputation virtually cemented. But, Mo was astute. As much as he wanted to take Jamison by the scruff and boot him from the home, he was beginning to learn that one spoke only when spoken to, and one moved only when commanded. Mo stood still and looked to Le Biche. She nodded to him and pointed to Jamison. Mo looked to Jamison as if to say: "You wanna go easy, or you wanna go hard?"

Jamison's hackles were up and he bunched his fists as if to fight. Mo paused, sighed heavily, and then reached suddenly with his own overly large right hand for Jamison's right arm. He caught him by the right wrist and pulled it to himself. While keeping hold of his wrist, he pulled Jamison through to where he locked Jamison's arm behind his own back. Mo's height helped him leverage the arm lock to where Jamison was bent over forward and squalling. With his left hand, Mo latched onto Jamison's belt at the back of his waist and duck-walked him up Hallway B, out the front doors, to deposit him onto the front porch.

"Wait..." Jamison argued as Mo started to pull the doors closed. "What about my stuff?"

Mo held the door patiently for a moment longer and said, "What stuff?"

Jamison paused to give this some thought. Mo was not a violent man, but he could be impatient. So okay, he figured. He may not be violent but he was big, much bigger than Jamison. Usually, his own size convinced others to circumvent violence. Jamison silently took stock. He worried that if he pushed Mo, there could be mayhem. He also figured that the mayhem would probably be him. He thought a moment longer, then smartly chose to see Mo as wholly sincere. For his own sake, he would trust Mo's earlier representations. He suspected that he had pushed Mo a tad too far, and he hoped that Mo would do what he had said.

"Never mind", he said with a wave of his hand. "Just drop it by my home. Or better still, just mail it". He smiled uncomfortably. "Thanks", he muttered as he quickly turned to save grace and walk away. Mo let the glass door close softly and returned to the cafeteria.

Ms. Bichette had conscripted Mo – together with Larry and Curly - from among the residents at Golden Hills ostensibly to help put down an uprising that seemed to be brewing among some of the residents. The uprising was not so much a rumor nor even a suspicion, but more of an expectation by Ms. Bichette. She knew that some of the changes that she would require there at the home would not be well received. She had been here before: breakfast between 6am and 10am with lunch from noon to 1 pm, and dinner sharply at 5 pm; social hour from 7pm and 8:30 pm; and lights out at nine pm (most were in bed and few rarely stayed up past 7 pm) with visitors allowed between 7 am and 1 pm for breakfast and lunch and then again from 5pm to 8:30 pm for dinner and social hour. (This four hour stretch from 1pm to 5 pm was designated as time for physical therapy, swim exercise, and cognitive therapy. But the residents referred to this four hour stretch as either nap time or Canasta).

When she appointed Mo to serve as her enforcer, Larry and Curly had come along for the ride. Mo had insisted. From his perspective, this package agreement was not negotiable. It was one of very few agreements to which Ms. Bichette had succumbed. Besides, it proved useful. Mo was the enforcer. Larry managed the affairs, kept the accounts receivables, and ordered supplies. Curly cleaned the restrooms. Why he had volunteered to take that job was an open question. Their employment with her – well, with Golden Hills, really - served as a "treaty" of sorts that required them to work for "her" in exchange for some part-time pay and a modicum of protection that only she could provide. But as Mo reasoned, the only protection they seemed to need was from Le Biche, herself. Still, the protection afforded allowed for certain privileges. They were given access to the cafeteria and to the refrigerator, an extra hour at bedtime to 10 pm., and freedom to leave the residence without accompaniment by a relative or responsible friend. But the protection afforded to them and the privileges allowed did not, in their view, appoint even a rare offering of the Smokehouse bacon kept there in the fridge with Le Biche's tapioca. Today, she claimed victory.

CHAPTER XI

While sitting there, at the table, listening to Le Biche's overused and over-hyped pep talk, Larry was contemplating; barely half hearing her chatter. He, too, was thinking of the "treaty". It had advantages. But in many respects, the treaty proved deficient. Bacon was a deserved nutrient, wasn't it? He was thinking about cafeteria management. He was thinking about Smokehouse bacon. Most of all, he was thinking about peach yogurt and how to get that onto the daily menus. In their own way, each one at the table with Ms. Bichette was formenting some kind of rebellion.

Larry contemplated how best he might find an advantage. He had already challenged her accounting of foodstuffs purchased for the residents at Golden Hills. He, himself, was fond of peach yogurt as were most of the old folks. Yet, they were frequently shortchanged of this popular commodity. Larry had taken it upon himself to check the delivery order. He intercepted the delivery ticket. The "white" ticket detailed the number of cases delivered. The accompanying yellow ticket confirmed the order. He learned that this was kept by the staff to keep track of expiration dates on earlier deliveries. As expiration approached, the accompanying yogurt delivery was supposed to be moved from the back of the cafeteria fridge to the front for more immediate consumption. The pink was kept on file to track the relative few deliveries that had expired and which required removal by the cafeteria staff.

The "white" read four cases containing one hundred ½ cup containers each. Assuming twenty ½ cup containers consumed weekly, the yogurt supply at Golden Hills should last through 16 weeks of lunches, or if you counted a pilfered container or two during night visits to the cafeteria fridge to curb insomnia, – maybe 12 to 14 weeks. (Good luck with this. Le Biche typically posted two guards in the kitchen at night specifically to watch the refrigerator. No one person who had taken on Le Biche for the sake of peach yogurt ever remained for long at the home after that). By Larry's accounting, the peach yogurt supply typically lasted no more than eight weeks, and Larry thought to bring this matter to Ms. Bichette's attention.

Later that day at lunch, he asked her about it as she passed his table. Trudy, Maggie, Curly, and Mo sat with him. They were all curious about the apparent discrepancy in the delivery of peach yogurt. They were all concerned that the cafeteria staff was splurging on their own richly deserved supply. His inquiry was innocent enough.

"Ms. Bichette?" he said as he raised his hand to catch her attention. "Excuse the interruption, but may I ask?, as he pulled the yellow ticket from his pants pocket and extended it to her, "I noted from this ticket that that there should be plenty of peach yogurt left for at least another month. Shouldn't there be some left for us today? We'd really like to have a treat?" he asked as innocently as he could muster and smiled sweetly.

Ms. Bichette paused. She looked at him with a prolonged stare. Her gaze was discomfiting. She gazed at each of her crew there at the table: Mo, Curly, Trudy, Maggie. Here at lunch, Eldon and the removal crew aka The Death Squad had joined the crowd for lunch. These last were employed by the temporary morgue downstairs. It was their duty to deal with those residents who had taken their leave as it were. In other words, they managed the dead.

Each one on whom her gaze landed lowered their eyes as she silently acknowledged with her stare the interruption into the tight schedule that SHE had set for herself. In response to Larry's intrusive inquiry, she abruptly pulled her own accounting sheet from beneath the collar of her uniform and showed it to Larry. It was "yellow". As Larry knew, the "yellow" sheet detailed both the newer cases delivered and the older cases that were moved forward inside the fridge.

As she read, she noted smugly, "This 'pink' copy that I hold here in my hand confirms that 198 containers, almost two full cases had expired and were removed by the cafeteria staff", she proclaimed. "I have received this 'pink' copy every month now for the past six months, and the removal rate of approximately two cases monthly has been consistent. You folks don't seem to like the peach yogurt that much and we are contemplating a change. You will be informed".

"But Le Biche...umm, Ms....I mean, Ms. Bichette", Curly blurted. "That ticket is..." – Larry quickly interrupted Curly with a cuff to the back of his head. "Owww", he pouted. "Why'd ya do that?"

For sure, Curly had seen her "weakness" and sought to press his advantage – mostly for the simple satisfaction it would give to call out her screw up. Curly's reaction was instinctual, neither contemplated nor planned. Larry's reaction – on the other hand -was well planned.

Ms. Bichette eyed them both suspiciously. Usually, it was Mo who clipped Curly like that. That was the main reason she had chosen Mo as the home's "enforcer". Larry was usually more circumspect, more gentlemanly. This was somehow out of character. Something was up.

Larry read the tea leaves. He needed to do something quickly. He looked at Curly sternly and chided, "Yes, Curly. It's 'Bichette', pronounced: 'BiSH – ETT' accent on the second syllable, Ms. 'BiSH-ETTE', Curly...and you know that".

Curly began to retort. But Larry was deductive, reason driven, and now it was his turn. Curly had barely opened his mouth when... BAM!! Larry smacked him again upside the head and gave him a look that said, "Not another word!"

Ms. Bichette's officious look turned to surprise. What was going on? Why this sudden turn of events? Her suspicions were raised; her hackles up.

"Now, please apologize to the lady", Larry looked at Curly with a side long glance as he bowed slightly and nodded to Ms.Bichette.

Curly looked at Larry quizzically as he adjusted his jaw, "Yeah, right... 'Ms. BiSH-ETTE'", he emphasized, more for Larry's benefit, still not sure just what was going on. "I'm sorry MAAA'AM", he purposefully lengthened the appellation to emphasize solely for her benefit. He knew that she didn't like to be called "ma'am". It made her feel like an old lady. She had said as much. Still, he couldn't resist. He eyed Larry with a pretended innocence and spoke quietly to him, "What? Wassup?"

Ms. Bichette was pissed but kept her composure. She still wasn't sure what was going on.

As for Larry, he had seen her Achille's Heel. She was color blind; at least when it came to the difference between "pink" and "yellow". The copy that she held was not "pink", it was "yellow"!!!

The cases she had been returning as expired were the older cases to be moved forward for more immediate consumption and not the expired cases to be returned. It was also apparent that since she saw the "yellow" copy as "pink", she had paid no real attention to the details. Otherwise, she could read for herself the difference between those to be moved forward and those to be thrown out. Since she was seeing this as a "pink" copy, she was rejecting peach yogurt that was still good! Larry was unsure whether she knew this, whether her monthly rejection of peach yogurt was purposeful or accidental.

Curly's sarcasm had saved them. His retort had distracted her, but only somewhat. Total distraction was requisite. He nodded to Ms. Bichette to quickly confirm, for her and to the crowd at large.

"Thank you, Ms. Bish-ETTE" he deferred to her. "If I could just take a look at your 'pink' copy, I'm sure I can help to convince these unruly residents. Please, just let me see your 'pink' copy." With that he offered a surreptitious wink to each in the assembled crowd. Each nodded, somewhat uncertain, but enough to echo agreement as if to say, "yeah, please, take a look at the 'pink' copy and we'll all be satisfied". The wink had convinced them that they knew what was happening when really, they did not.

Under normal circumstances, Ms. Bichette should have seen this subterfuge for what it was and reject the invitation out of hand. Normally, she offered assurances to no one. In part, she was confused. In part, she was curious. The juxtaposition left her flummoxed. She could only nod.

Larry, himself, would be wholly surprised should she offer him the slip. After all, he didn't expect it. He didn't need it. His communication to the crowd was understood and that was all he needed. His job here was done...for now. That is why he was surprised when she timidly offered the yellow slip forward. Curly's outburst had upset her. For the first time, she was discombobulated in front of the residents and crew. Larry would not risk that she might learn that they knew her weakness.

"Please", he entreated and all eyes turned. "If you would be so kind, peach... yes, peach yogurt will suit us fine. And thank you, again for your kindness", Larry uttered quickly as he corralled his table mates and shuffled them off to their rooms.

Ms. Lauren Bichette was taken aback. The feeling was disconcerting. Initially suspicious, she now had to wonder: Had she just been bested? What was Larry up to? Was this a scam? Was Curly in on it? For now, she couldn't say.

She would need to rethink this little tete-a-tete that she had just played with Mr. Lawrence Finkelstein. She would need to make some sense of it. She could feel the residents rising and she didn't like it. For the time being, they were dispersing and she would let it rest – but only for now.

Just then, the "Warden" came in for his morning repast. He glanced and waved in their direction, "Good morning. As you were". He grinned as his own joke. The tension broke. The assembled crowd dispersed including Maggie and Trudy. Ms. Bichette was perturbed. She hadn't completed her agenda.

The Tres Amigos gratefully started back to work to take up their assigned duties. But they moved too soon. Ms. Bichette had not signaled for them to resume their duties: Curly to the mop and bucket; Mo to stand watch and to offer discipline when directed; and Larry, to get back to kitchen accounting. (Larry was one of her assignments that she would definitely need to re-think). Each knew that, although the Warden's authority offered some protection from Ms. Bichette, it did not supersede her own rules of discipline. Each knew – including both Maggie and Trudy – that there would come another day. No one figured that this skirmish was the last. Au contraire! It was just the beginning and was soon to burgeon into full scale rebellion. Each knew there would be hell to pay for the events of this day ,and each knew that Ms. Bichette would rely on this premature break in ranks without the requisite nod from her to justify her response.

The Warden was in an expansive mood, and she must let it ride. "Let them eat bacon!" he called out to no one in particular as he took another piece for himself. The cooks were puzzled. They directed an inquisitive glance at Ms. Bichette. Silently, she seethed. Yet for now, she would cede the battle, just not the war. That could wait for another day. She stood up slowly, straightened her uniform with a brush of her hand, brushed back a stray hair from her face and adjusted her cap. Once composed, she looked to the cooks. With a quick circle of her raised index finger, she gave the go ahead to serve up the bacon. The residents cheered. The cooks went to work. Ms. Bichette, smiled weakly and waved to the assembled cafeteria as she exited. Silently, she was livid. Her so-called staff was worried.

CHAPTER XII

The Battle of Smokehouse Bacon, as it would come to be remembered, was still fresh in the minds of all of the residents at Golden Hills. Each would relive this day if only to remember the taste of bacon, a taste that all who were present in the cafeteria on that day would never taste again. It would be a long time coming, and many would go to the great beyond before the treat would be offered again in this earthly realm. Many trusted that they would get to the great beyond and would receive all of the Smokehouse Bacon that Heaven could present.Mo headed for the TV in the front reception area. Mason reruns ran from 1 pm to 5 pm. He needed a nap anyway. Larry went to the kitchen for further machinations involving peach yogurt.

As for Curly, he decided that such a delectable memory of bacon was worthy of a smoke. He took a bathroom break, as it were, from his cleaning assignment. Joints, like bacon, were prohibited. But Mary Jane was his legacy – or so he thought - and the day's events had stifled caution. He convinced himself that he could risk a toke. Bacon and a joint: what could be better?

The truth was that Curly was no weed cowboy. He had simply found a joint, a few weeks back, when he vacuumed the couch in the front reception. This assignment did have advantages. Although Curly thought himself a man of the 60's, this was his first joint.

He perched himself on the toilet seat in the end stall, closest to the exit, like a falcon perched on a wire awaiting a mouse on the field below. He licked the paper along the side to reseal it like he'd seen Dennis Hopper do in Easy Rider and struck a match. The flare died down and he lit the joint. He put it to his lips and closed his eyes to first taste and then to tenderly suck the tip to inhale. The smoke immediately seized his lungs and he gasped. His eyes bulged and he teared up. He broke into a loud and wracking cough, over and over and over. He grasped the tops of the stall at both sides with either hand to steady himself on the toilet seat. He continued to wrack. Eventually, the cough subsided and he calmed. His lungs relaxed and he could breathe again. After a time, he tried again. This time, his next toke was less eventful and more rewarding. Curly was getting the hang of this. A dull haze enveloped him as life became simpler and easier to grasp. As he relaxed, he pulled Marty's personnel file from inside his jacket. He conscripted it when it fell from inside Mo's jacket as he escorted Jamison out of the home. Curly figured that he was entitled to know more about the man who had saved his own life.

"Curiosity killed the cat", a voiced stated matter-of-factly. Curly fell off of the toilet seat. He landed with thump on the ceramic tile floor. He peered under the door from inside the stall to see Mr. Mark, Mark, Markham positioned there on the second sink down from the stall he was in.

Curly opened the stall door so he could stand. He brushed himself and asked "Man, you scared me. What is up with you? Are you some kind of wizard?"

"You dropped your smoke" Marty pointed to the joint, burnt out prematurely and lying on the floor next to Curly. Curly picked it up and stood to face Marty, seated on the sink next to the door. Marty snapped his fingers and a flame appeared at the tip of his index. Curly's eyebrows lifted in surprise. As he watched the flame, he put the joint back into his mouth and bent to inhale against it. He took a drag, lit the joint, pressed out his chest, and stood up straight. He paused to hold his breath a moment longer and exhaled. He looked at Marty closely

"You want to know about me?" Marty asked. Curly inhaled deeply and held it. He nodded as a small cough with a puff of smoke escaped.

"Relax...and listen", Marty said. He reached into his speedo and pulled a rather large orange pill. He popped it and swallowed hard. He held up his hand as if to signal, "Wait a moment". Curly was in no hurry. He nodded as he exhaled.

As if on cue, Marty pulled out two six-inch film reels to an 8mm projector from the back of his speedo. He affixed one to his pinky finger on his right hand and put his hand up with his pinky to the ceiling. This reel was fully wound with 8mm exposed film. He took that film and proceeded deftly to thread it between the back molars on either side of his mouth from right to left. He, then, affixed the second and empty reel onto his left pinky and held it up in the same fashion. He threaded the end of the film onto this reel. He gave a quick nod. His mouth opened as if caught in mid-yawn. He winked at Curly then closed his eyes. His face became drooped and deadpan. Within moments, a woman's voice -sweet, almost girlish -began a monologue which surprised Curly. An 8mm usually didn't project sound with the pictures.

The Priest stuttered when he christened Marty. The new
Markham boy entered the public record as: "MMMark, MMMark,
Markham. His dad was 17. He chose the name. He wanted his first
born son to be named after his own stepfather: Mark aka "Tiny" who
had raised him. (Curious, Marty thought, why is it that everyone who
named their kid "Mark" would later change the name).

Dad was young and had never been a church goer. With the
priest's erroneous pronouncement, he was stumped as to how best to
raise a challenge to priestly authority. Was there some procedure?
Was it appropriate to correct a man of the cloth or was his word law?
Dad could only appear puzzled. He never corrected the Priest. His
mom was 18. She ,too, was herself a baby. She looked to her husband
to take the lead. He did not and so, in the school years that followed,
Marty suffered the slings and arrows of countless, mean spirited jokes
about "hair-lipped" dogs as were levelled by the less mature
classmates all competing to scratch their way past Marty on up the
school's social ladder.

Each time he entered a room or joined up with a group of
friends, he'd hear some dimwit retort: "MMMark, MMMark"
followed by giggles and a snicker or two from those of lesser merit.
Those of his vaunted society saw the joke as crude. Either that, or they
were unsure of Marty's limits. Regardless, Marty had grown used to
the recognition and accepted the good natured teasing from his
friends. As for those lesser beings, his athletic prowess and academic

accomplishment kept his own social status free from open assault. But at present, Marty questioned that athletic prowess. The glory that he had achieved, as he would tout to others some years later, was well exaggerated and overblown.

But he could still submit, with full credibility, his academic accomplishments from those early years. Yes, it was true that John Dominquez, a member of Marty's senior class and head of the school's Honors Society, outranked him in GPA. Dominquez got his kicks from doing Calculus homework while on the bus home from school. Of course, he saw Marty as less than academically qualified to enter. Mister Dominguez continually sought to remind Marty that his 3.65 grade point average was the lowest GPA of all the other members in that society. Marty truthfully admitted to it. He also admitted to and further reminded Dominquez of the one given: that despite his relative low GPA, he was more than qualified to kick John Dominquez's ass and was willing to be tested. Dominquez declined and the topic was never mentioned again.

It is also true that Janet Lansen- she, too, a member of the Honor Society - was – at least to Marty – more than pleasantly surprised to learn the results of the Honor's English exam. 21 kids had earned a spot in Honor's English. The purpose of the class was to prepare the students for the college exam to be taken at the end of the semester. Success on the exam meant a waiver for incoming college freshman on the 1st year English requirement. The possible scoring for the exam ranged from one to five. Five was the highest, but any score between three and five would earn the sought for credit. The results were in, and the last day in class Janet was cruising among her classmates.

"What did you get on the exam?" she would ask smiling, peering through her thick glasses, her formless dress hanging from her thin shoulders.

"I got a three", a classmate would respond.

"I got a four", she would say with a snarky grin.

And, again to another: "What did you get on the exam?"

"I got a three".

"Oh. I got a four" she said, still smiling. Up and down the rows she would go.

She stopped at Marty's desk. "What did you get on the exam?"

"I got a four", Marty said.

She tossed her hair, raised her bright eyes and thick glasses to the ceiling and said: "Oh, well. I got a fou... a what? You gotta a four?" she exclaimed as she lengthened the word "fourrrr" with incredulity.

Marty enjoyed being underestimated. Game. Set. Match. He would say.

Honors English first introduced him to James Clavell as required reading. He'd chosen "King Rat" because the book itself was short by contrast to the others and paperbacked. The cover itself was intriguing and the number of pages –particularly for a book by Clavell - was minimal. Although he enjoyed the challenge later occasioned by those much longer Clavell novels like Shogun or The Covenant, he was not inclined at this point in his senior year to take on such a monstrously long read.

For Marty, Clavell's, King Rat best characterized his high school experience. In that day and in those times, Marty – like the King - ruled his world. Yet, reality catches up and in later years, with what Marty wished desperately to see now as remote, the experiences were fraught with insecurity and danger; the danger presented by unhinged emotion and doubt. The places he had built for himself were always unstable; never secure. His hard-won reputation from decades passed was even now unreal and threatened. He didn't know just how – or even whether – he should be proud of the accomplishments he made in those early years or try to forget them altogether.

Regardless, from what he did know now at his current age, these memories of accomplishment long since passed, held no value; not even in the "bragging rights". The times were gone. The seasons passed. His memories were fading and few; and they were getting fewer.

****

"Whoa, wait, wait, wait", Curly held up his hand, the joint he was holding burned to ash that sprinkled to his feet. The 8mm film kept clickety-clacking, the sweet voice continued to narrate. Curly pressed loudly, "Hey, hold on, would ya? Hold on, hold on..."

The sound emanating droned slowly to a stop as both spools stopped. The first spool was about three quarters full on his right finger. The second spool had begun to fill on his left finger. Marty closed his mouth, opened his eyes, and blinked. Curly reached over and waved a hand in front of his face - nothing. He pushed him on the shoulder – nothing. He pushed again, this time harder. Marty shivered and pulled out of the daze, his face placid. He sat stone still.

"Hey", Curly shouted and snapped his finger in front of Marty's eyes. "You there? Anybody home?"

Marty shook his head, blinked, and appeared to wake up. "I'm here," he said. "How can I help?"

"Well...this is interesting stuff and all, but could you just give me... you know...the high points?" he asked hopefully.

"I can't" Marty responded. Following a more directed inquiry from Curly, Marty explained that he didn't know what was on the 8mm film. Someone had created the film some time ago, maybe years.

He had lost or misplaced virtually all of the reels. He had found these in the Library. He had only a few left.

"It doesn't matter anyway" he explained. I don't know any of the information on this one and have no way to find out. I can play it" – he opened his mouth and pointed inside – "but I can't see it when I do. Like I said, I can only play it" – he again opened his mouth and pointed inside.

Curly impatiently waved him off and muttered, "Yeah, yeah, no need to repeat it. I get it".

Marty shrugged. "Soooo.... I was hoping you could tell me what it is that's on there?" He looked at Curly as if to inquire. "Maybe you would write it down for me?" He seemed almost desperate. By Curly's assessment, desperation was unusual for Mr. Markham.

"Hold on a minute...'Marty is it?" Curly said. "I mean, you're a cool dude and all, but...this is 8mm film you say? With 'no sound', that's what you said right?"

Marty nodded and smirked, "Yeah, of course, its' film, what d'ya think? And yeah, there's no sound. Everybody knows that".

"Now wait a min..." Curly thought twice about debating. "Listen", he said, "I'm not the guy to...I mean... I can't help you out. Not that I don't want to, but I'm just no good at, uh... writing. You know...bad penmanship. And, I mean uhh, well, truth be told, I... uhh..." Curly fell quiet.

"You can't write", Marty finished for him glumly.

"Well yeah" he said. "But look, we'll get Trudy. She's a great writer. She helps me with my Time cards", he said enthusiastically. "And, look... if you don't mind, we can pull the crowd together: Mo, Larry, Trudy...maybe even Maggie, if we can wake her up. We'll help you remember what we can...what you can, I mean", he looked to Marty and smiled. But Marty was blank...again. He was zoned and couldn't respond.

He had known this would happen. The few times that he had used the big orange pill previously, he had gone zombie within an hour or so. This was the only pill in his collection about which he could predict the outcome. He knew what it could do. He knew its' narrow parameters and very limited effects and ,of course, he knew the side effects, those were that he couldn't remember a lick of what was on the film after he played it.

Curly figured it was time to get Marty back to his bed. He pulled the film reels off of Marty's fingers and placed them together in the back waist band of Marty's speedo. He trusted that Marty could take care of them from there. He stepped to the door and opened it into the hallway. He checked the nurses' station and front desk. He checked Hallway B. He was in luck. Larry was at the other end. He appeared headed to the cafeteria. Curly gave a loud whistle. He kept it short with the hope that he'd only need it once and that only Larry was there to hear it. Larry looked up and waved to Curly inquisitively. Curly waved back. He gave Marty a push and waved to Curly. Marty walked, zombie-like, down the hallway toward his bedroom and Bed 13 headed in Larry's direction. Curly signaled for Larry to get him to his room.

Larry really had no clue what Curly was gesticulating about. He surmised that he was high. But when he saw Mr. Markham stepping clumsily down Hallway B, he felt that he should help the poor man. He intercepted him and tried to speak with him, but Marty gave no response. Given that he was ambulatory and appeared healthy otherwise, Larry decided to help him back to bed.

Curly returned to the men's room. He hadn't finished his joint. He figured he'd light up another bong, take a few more tokes, and then get the restroom smelling clean and fresh. He had bought this stuff called: "Fabuloso"...and boy, was it! He stepped into a stall and perched himself comfortably on the seat so that his feet did not show beneath the stall, never mind that smoke billowed above the stall and gathered across the entire ceiling. He had just about decided that this job here at Golden Hills was true "rocket science" and the he was, indeed, a true "rocket scientist. He released his grip on the sides of the stall, took a better balance on the seat as he squatted, and sat back on his haunches to enjoy. Just then, he heard a knock on the outside stall partition. Curious, he thought.

He raised himself up enough to peer over the edge where his eyes met disaster. It was Le Biche. She stood there looking up with arms folded, right foot tapping. She wore those high heels that only enhanced her imposing nature – and, of course, they made her legs look great. She also wore an overly stern expression that she adopted when she was pissed. She shot into the stall and grabbed Curly by the ear. She pulled him out and immediately instituted a new work assignment. Curly was now in permanent possession of the "mop and bucket" and he assumed apparently what would be forever his newfound assignment. Le Biche insisted on full redemption. Curly's repentance was requisite. She required him to thoroughly clean and scrub – to "spit shine" as it were – all of the restrooms in the old folks' home – 9 total: the one up front aka "Curly's Lair"; two in the front hallway; two at each end of A-wing; two at each end of B-wing; and, two in the Cafeteria. As usual, his luck was adverse. But he didn't mind much. After all, he had wished for the prestige that came with the "mop and bucket", even if the prestige was short lived. Mostly the job was boring. Restroom duty was an almost daily chore. Then of course, there was his new found "friendship" with Mr. Markham – Marty, as it was - and his interesting history. He had agreed to help and he would.

CHAPTER XIII

T he corridors were now dark in A-wing. Curfew was hours ago. The usual sounds travelled the hallway: snoring, a loud sigh, a few gasps and a choke or two, perhaps a chortle at the late night program with closed caption, or the quiet sound of speed dial as an "infomercial" snagged another customer.

Trudy stood with her cane just outside of Marty's door. He was lying in bed; virtually comatose; his red-goggles on his head; his red speedo around his skinny hips. He seemed to generate an almost imperceptible "white" noise that went mostly unnoticed.

Yes, she knew Marty. She had recognized him when he first came to the home; not so much from his boyish good looks (Yeah, right. At this age how could anyone recognize a junior high school classmate from decades back?), but more from the way he moved. The deft and still coordinated motion of his hands when he insisted on taking directly from Ms. Bich the cup full of his medicines that she tried to foist on him each morning. She'd tell him to open wide. He'd simply reach quickly and before she could react, he'd snatch the small cup from her hand almost before she could lift it from the cart that she pushed from room to room. The rule was that Golden Hills offer the medication. The responsibility to take the pills rested with the resident. What was that old song by Steppenwolf? – Goddam the Pusher Man.

Marty never allowed Ms. Bichette to foist medicines on him as she did with the others. He knew the rule. He never opened his mouth to stick out his tongue to accept the handful of pills that the doctors had dictated. Every morning the "dance" was the same and even though Bich knew Marty's game, she could never anticipate his quickness. Before she could say, "Open wide and swallow", Marty had the pills in hand. He'd pop and gulp the handful without the water chaser leaving Ms Bichette speechless. And, as always with Trudy at her side, she could not force the pills down his throat. She was determined to find a way. She began to wonder whether Trudy had outlived the political expediency of serving as her assistant.

As for Trudy, she recognized the light that now rested somewhere behind Marty's eyes, a light that went hidden periodically, as now. But a light that Trudy knew from her days with him at junior high school. She first saw that light when Marty, a starter on the 9th grade basketball team, noticed her with her friend Shelly at her locker next to Marty's. He had nodded to them and smiled as he headed to his next class. In his eyes, she saw with crystal clarity, there in the depths, a burning light that held purpose and ambition. It was a light that reflected hurt and hinted at a haunted search for redemption; a lonely light that required meaning; sustenance without which the light would dim and die. As for Shelly, she was in love.

Trudy smiled wryly now as she recalled watching one of Marty's games from the top row bleachers. He took an elbow to the midsection while chasing after a loose ball. The blow sent him to the floor and apparently knocked him cold. He lay motionless on his back. His teammates tried to lift him to his feet. He was dead weight. His eyes were open. They slapped him as if to wake him up. He didn't revive, but stared blankly at the ceiling. His chest heaved, but he took no air. The coach peered into his eyes, thinking that he was concussed, "What's your name?....What's my name?....What day is it?...Whose your mama?"

When satisfied that Marty only had his wind knocked from him, the coach snarled impatiently, "Get him off of the court" and signaled Anderson to substitute. The game resumed. Marty lay beneath the bench while the team manager waived a white towel in a show of surrender ,and the assistant coach wafted smelling salts under Marty's nose.

Trudy crept from the top row of bleachers to behind the teams' bench. She knew, but instinctively, how to revive Marty. She reached for a water bottle. She tested the water temperature by drizzling some onto her forearm as if testing a baby's bottle filled with warmed milk. She rejected the first bottle and reached for another. The water in this she found to be ice cold; only recently refreshed. It belonged to the coach. Never mind. She removed the lid and threw the contents into Marty's face. He revived with a sputter. He gasped and quickly tried to sit. He smacked his head on the underside of the bench. He fell back with a groan, but not before he looked to Trudy with gratitude and kinship.

How it was that Trudy knew these things from what was just a quick and friendly glance into the eyes of one whom – until that moment – had been just another good looking but silly boy, she couldn't say. It was a testament to the insight and intuition held by this very young girl whose friendship for Shelly had run deep and who, she could see, had fallen deeply and madly in love that day, two locker's down from Marty Markham's. Trudy thought he was cute. Shelly had loved him instantly. She had seen what others could not fathom. She had seen his pain. Trudy loved Shelly and so she loved them both. Then, like now, she watched Marty. You might say she watched over him. Then, like now, she cared for Shelly. She missed her. The instincts, the insight - and indeed the love that she knew back then for both of them. These were awakened the very moment she first saw his hand reach for the medicine cup to snatch the pills from Le Biche's grasp to tip the balance of power there at the home.

Trudy knew - yes, instinctively -that all of them at the home were "in for a bumpy ride". She also knew that the love that she felt was, and would always be, unrequited.

As for Ms. Bichette, almost from the day she started as Head Nurse, she recognized Trudy as one of the more lucid of the home's residents and had tagged Trudy as her assistant. Trudy was no dummy. She knew that Ms. Bichette knew, and that Ms. Bichette knew that she knew that Ms. Bichette was capable enough of her own accord to hand out and to record the daily medications. She didn't need an assistant. She did need Trudy. By the same token, Bichette knew and Trudy knew that she knew that beneath Marty's rather shy and catatonically demur façade, lived a formidable foe. Bichette had tagged Trudy to keep her close: "Keep friends close and enemies closer" as it were.

No doubt, she understood Trudy to be her enemy. By allowing Trudy to record the daily administration of medicines, the names, dosages, and expiration dates, she had crafted a perfect scapegoat for the moment when she might find it necessary to send Marty into the light. Ms. Bichette's own refined instincts whispered to her that such a time was coming for both the occupant of Bed 13 and perhaps for her able assistant, Trudy.

As for Trudy, her own razor sharp instincts told her that Le Biche had unwittingly miscalculated the power play between them. Yes, indeed. Trudy knew and was quickly calculating, how best to harness the power that was, one Marty Markham.

As she watched Marty, she saw him stir. He sat up, but did not awaken. He seemed in a trance. He reached into his speedo to retrieve a single pill – big and orange. He popped it into his mouth, tilted back his head and swallowed. A few moments elapsed. His face was empty, unfamiliar. He reached around to his back and pulled two 8mm film reels from his speedo. Trudy watched as he set up his projector system with reels placed onto each pinky finger and the exposed film running through his mouth from molar to molar. The "projector" fired up. A sweet female voice- girlish but not, began to narrate.

****

Mark, Mark, "Marty" Markham was three months away from graduation. He would earn his Bachelor's degree from the University of Utah. But, at present, his future was uncertain. That is to say, he had no idea concerning job prospects. Journalism was his major; French his minor. Neither offered much opportunity. For a time, he had worked as a "stringer" for the local evening daily. He covered the local municipalities; specifically the council meetings held one time weekly at night. He enjoyed the work. His editor told him that he was the only reporter that he knew that could make interesting to the reader, the formal approval by South Jordan for a sewer line to be installed down 10400 South.

South Jordan's mayor didn't like Marty or at least did not like what Marty represented: the free press. The council met to discuss a hush hush deal between South Jordan and Draper to bring disputed water rights from Draper to South Jordan. Typically, at the weekly meeting Marty found in attendance an elderly widowed woman who would sit and knit as the council conducted its business. She reminded Marty of the woman at the guillotine in Les Miserables. But on this night, a good five- to twenty- people attended to witness and participate in the City's business. Rather than write about another sewer line or the local dog attack on the neighbor's chickens, Marty chose to write about the attendance at the meeting. That was newsworthy. He wrote about why they had chosen to come to a meeting they had never before attended. He wrote about their view on the council's apparent skullduggery. Mostly, his decision was pragmatic. These citizens had arrived at the beginning of the meeting – seven pm. Usually, to find a "story" worth printing, Marty would need to attend sometimes to midnight and sometimes beyond. Rarely, did he find a good story. Mostly, he needed to choose between various mediocre versions of various local events. In this case, he was home by eight pm; his story submitted by ten pm.

He often thought about his decision to choose this "story". Did he have a keen awareness or some insight into human interest? In reality, the best that he could conclude was that this story would put him home with his wife and kids, some three hours earlier than usual. He was nothing if not pragmatic.

His story was published the next day. The effects came a week later when, at the outset of that next week's meeting, the mayor informed Marty that he was not welcome and must leave. Marty was befuddled. He had no idea what consequences the mayor or the city had suffered from his story's publication. He never did learn. But as he stood to leave, still confused by the apparent hostility, it occurred to Marty that what he represented was the free press. He was and had been protected by the First Amendment. He turned back and stood with a modicum of conviction and quietly reminded the mayor of the Sunshine Laws about the constitutional entitlement afforded to those who reported the news. For a brief moment, he endured a silent standoff with the mayor until one of the councilmen reminded the mayor that Marty was right. The mayor backed down and sat down. Mostly as a matter of principal, Marty remained at the meeting for a time to hear the Council's business. The best the City could do that night, by way of a story, was to approve an extension to the sewer line previously authorized to extend down 10400 South. Marty left, not for fear of arrest, but for the boredom of it all.

As rewarding as was this journalistic endeavor, the practical results added up to $1.65 an hour. In essence, Marty spent a good seven- to twelve- hours in securing, writing, and presenting the story for publication. As a "stringer", he was paid by the line. A sewer line approval, no matter how dramatic Marty might make it sound, did not have the legs to get past even eight column inches. The last stringer to be hired by the newspaper and the junior reporter had been on the job for ten years. An opening was not anticipated for another ten years. Needless to say, Marty's chances at a job in journalism were remote at best. Most of his friends chose to prolong the inevitable job search by changing their major or they otherwise submitted to law or some other graduate school to stay ensconced within the protections of the ivory tower. For now, Marty needed to work. As it was, he found himself on the bus daily, riding to and from the University, and reading the want ads. He was newly married with a baby on the way. He had never before experienced this type of pressure.

To make real money, he worked afternoons and weekends for a local home builder, a guy named...Gary, Gary something or other. Marty remembered his first day, a Saturday. In a call the night before, Gary told him to bring a nail apron, a hammer, and a measuring tape. Marty had never before worked at any type of construction. He grabbed from his Dad's tool bench, a cloth apron with a large pocket on the front, a 12-ounce hammer, and a 12-foot measuring tape. He showed up the next morning with a group of about 10 other guys. He carried his 12-ounce hammer wrapped in the cloth nail apron together with his 12-foot tape in hand. The others each held a large, leather "belt" ranging from well-worn to brand new with pockets, pouches, and loops necessary to carry their 20- to 25- ounce hammers, a 25-foot measuring tape, a pouch full of 16- penny framing nails, a razor knife, and a variety of other specialized tools.

Gary looked at him and said, "Where did you get those, from your mother's sewing kit?" In later years, Marty realized that Gary knew what to expect and had planned the joke.

In the part-time days that followed, Marty would sometimes string lights at night with Big Mike so they could nail asphalt shingles to the roofs of the new homes under construction. Marty learned early on that he was favored. He was the only one of a full time crew who had earned a Bachelor's Degree. The rest of the permanent crew were talented, but most did not possess the insight that Marty exhibited. Marty recalled the day when Big Mike had just finished placing plywood forms at either side of the garage door opening to hold the concrete for it to solidify inside the two- foot wide returns; one at either side of what would be the garage door opening. Marty had been picking up trash from various sites nearby. As the cement truck came on down the road, Marty could see from the set of the forms that the opening would be off center. One form was set to accommodate a pour only 1-foot wide. The other was set at three-feet wide. Marty told Mike not to pour and that the forms needed to be reset. But Mike was insistent. The job needed to get done. He feared to tell Gary and he was worried that Gary may require him to pay for the mud that came that day if he didn't use it. Marty told him that he would take whatever consequences, but that he should send the truck back and correct the forms. Gary came to Marty later that day and thanked him. The error could have been more costly had the pour been made. It was Marty's first summer at work, but from that day forward, he became the general superintendent responsible to monitor the job progress on each of the semi-custom homes built.

Marty smiled to himself. Gary knew Marty from his days at church with the young men and the never ending chess tournaments. He was a church leader and a good guy. Years later, he had volunteered to lead another group of young men in a successful effort to replace the leaking roof on Marty's mom's home at Dimple Dell while Marty was away serving his mission in Tahiti. With these recollections, Marty's thoughts turned to Dimple Dell.

Dimple Dell was a great place to grow up. Marty first learned to shoot baskets at the hoop Dad had nailed to the front of the carport and horse stalls. Donny lived across the street. He was 4 years older than Marty, a senior in high school. Marty was a freshman in 9th grade at Junior High. Donny's dad was rich and needed some yard work done. Each day in the summer, Marty would report across the street from his home to would weed the large strawberry patch, pull rocks and boulders from the lower pasture and paint the wood framed windows at the barn. Every day, Marty would take his lunch at home. Every day, before lunch as he left work, he would stop at the stream across the 300-foot frontage to the front pasture as this own home, to plunge into the icy cold waters and float the entire length. Every day after work ended, he would take the time to float. The float braced, but still relaxed Marty. It opened his mind to a grander scheme of things. Here it was that he first began to consider, to cogitate, and to even experiment with Time. More practically, during the hot summer days that could somedays exceed one hundred degrees Fahrenheit the trip refreshed and cooled Marty.

Donny was on the golf team at the High School. His dad had created a short fairway and putting green running out about 60 yards from his front porch where Donny would practice his pitch shots from the front porch. He was good. On Saturdays, he would take Marty golfing with him. The two would play 18 holes. Donny taught Marty to be a better golfer. Marty reciprocated by helping Donny play better basketball.

Frequently, Donny would come over to shoot baskets at the hoop affixed to the front of the barn. The court covered a space between the driveway from the home to the road and the front of the carport. The driveway curved down the hill from the back of the court which rested approximately six- to eight- feet higher next to the drive way that ran past and down to the road, then at the basket. The north eastern corner of the court rested at about 45-feet out and next to the drive. The back line then ran west approximately 60-feet along the edge of the driveway to approximately 25-feet out from the front line to what was the back north western corner. The west line and court itself petered away at the back line with the driveway as the driveway dropped to the road. A lodge pole fence bounded the western line about another 35-feet out from the basket. The front line ran straight from west to east. The front eastern corner rested deep in a corner formed by the front line and a five-foot retaining wall that cut back sharply from the western line to the northwest. The western line then continued back at a lesser angle to north and east to join with the drive way at the longest 45-foot line and eight- foot up the hill from the basket. There at the front east corner was room enough to launch a shot, but no room to enter when guarded. Donny never shot from there. Marty never let him. He was adept at using the wall to double team.

But Donny was an ace while on the gravel court with no defense to confront, especially from the smoother and more level front west corner. He had no reflexes to speak of, and those that he did have, were exceptionally slow. But, the arch to his shot from the well extended corner of the court, just there in front of the carport, was both high and resplendent, and from deep in the corner, Donny was a dead eye. He sank virtually every shot straight through the netting with a swish and no iron.

The arch came of necessity. When Marty's dad installed the backboard and hoop atop the carport, he placed it at an additional 3-inches" in height – 10 foot and three inches - so as to accommodate a planned for, but later addition of asphalt to the hard packed road base that was applied years earlier. The "later addition" never came. His dad never added the asphalt. So, both Marty and Donny developed high arching shots to accommodate entry. The arch served Marty well in high school. He played at forward. He wasn't too adept at the dribble. At all of six-feet, he needed to shoot high to get over the outstretched arm of the taller forwards who defended. He and Donny would shoot hoop all summer long.

But the winter at Dimple Dell was unsurpassed. At night, when it snowed hard and deep, Dad would drive home a Chevy Blazer with a plow on the front. He would first plow the long drives into both the Jone's home next door and at Donny's home across the street. When he finished with the neighbors' drives, he would plow his own long and serpentine asphalt driveway. The plow would leave a slight skiff of snow pack, maybe a quarter inch thick along the length of the asphalt pavement. Marty's job was to spread salt to melt the remaining quarter inch. But before he did to come in for the night, his Dad would let him and his brother sled.

The driveway was S-shaped and ran a good 350 feet from the front door, down the sloped sidewalk entry, onto the asphalt parking area at the front of the home, down and around the first sharp left hand turn, down the steeper slope past the basketball court and barn to a right hand turn, and then straight down from there to Dimple Dell Road. The ride was a blast and he and... he and...???

Funny, the memories had been wide open. Why the glitch just now, Marty wondered? He paused and shook his head to refocus. To keep the memory alive, he speculated that it was the "bed wetter" who rode the other sled down the long drive and into the wee hours of the morning. Even after Mom called the "bed wetter" inside to go to bed, she allowed Marty to stay out as long as he wanted.

She would only say, "Be sure to spread the salt before you come in".

"I will", Marty would respond.

On these still and peaceful nights Marty would spread the salt, he would chop the firewood, and – before he could think of ever coming in – he would pull the hood on his woolen sweatshirt, tight around his head and face. He would grab his football, and he would pound his was up and over, around and through the piles of snow that Dad's plow left at the side of the parking area, next to the front lawn. This became the defensive line through which Marty was obliged to run in order to score the game winning touchdown. Marty scored every time.

On other days, on those mornings when the cold and clear blue sky highlighted Lone Peak at the back of his home, without any evidence of a contrail stretching from the very top, Marty always faced a dilemma. Should he ski Alta, just ten minutes from home at a cost to him of $10 bucks? Or, should he drive 45 minutes around the snow covered Wasatch Range to ski Park City West for free? His Dad had a business arrangement with the resort. Marty could ski any day for nothing. Whatever his choice that day, the snow would be very light, very deep and very soft. The day would be "cool" in every way. He would simply tell his mom that he decided not to go to school today; that he was going skiing. Mom never challenged his choice. She never told him "no". Later, she would say that she never worried for him; and that she felt badly for it. She was just too busy worrying for herself and for Dad. She was grateful that Marty was so responsible; so grown up. He never gave her a moment of concern. He never caused trouble. He had wondered: Why didn't he? Why didn't he give her any trouble? Why didn't she need to worry? What made him so "responsible"? He would think why when he would ski and ski fast, why he never flew. Why was that?

He would ski the moguls and enjoy the powder, but he never really pushed himself to take any real chances. Come to think of it, he never pressed his Dad for a "fast" car or -gawd knows-for a motorcycle. "Speed" and "Danger" were not high priorities in Marty's life. His first cars were good examples.

Dad was in the car business, a used car manager. His various offerings were pragmatic; and Marty simply abided.

Marty's first car was a hot '63' Chevrolet Impala with a '69', 350-engine, an overhead "cam", and dual exhaust. Dad found it for him. It had all the look and sound of one fast roadster. It also had a three-speed transmission that could not handle the powerful engine. The result was that the car sounded large when standing still. But it could do 0-60 no better than the straight six-cylinder engine that it had been born with due to the transmission. Dad knew and Marty learned quickly that his first car was solely for show; not for go.

His second car was a clean "one-owner" - really... a '62' four-door Mercury sedan. An elderly lady pushing 80 gave it up with her driver's license at her son's insistence. His concern was well overblown. She bought it new and only drove it to church. When Marty bought it in 1972, with his dad's blessing (and insistence) the odometer showed only 18,000 miles. The seat upholstery, carpeting, and headliners were all like new. The tires were original with plenty of tread. Here the engine was a straight-six. And again, the transmission of choice for Marty – or to better say, Marty's dad - was a three-speed on the tree. His dad didn't offer more and Marty didn't ask. He never pressed for speed. He often wondered why.

In these moments his thoughts would shift to somebody's son. Was it the "bed wetter", or somebody else? Curious, he thought. Whose son...his son?

Marty remembered a day beneath Lone Peak when he skied alongside a guy on a snowboard, a real flier, a kid really. Marty never learned to snow board. He already knew how to ski. He didn't think it worthwhile to spend the day on his butt trying to learn to board when he could spend the entire day upright on his own skies. Still, who was this kid? Was it his brother? Did he have a brother? Was this kid his son? Did he even have a son?

He remembered the day as special. The kid had been away for a while. The two of them took a day together. The kid spent most of his time on his board, skyward, upside down and flipping while Marty skied alongside, but always close to the ground. He remembered when the kid missed a flip. Marty watched as he turned, sized up, and then leaped from a large mogul at the edge of the run. He watch him uncharacteristically pause in mid-air, slow motion, and indecisive. He failed to flip fully, a perfect picture in mid-air, but upside down. Then, from 12 feet up, he fell and landed headfirst onto the packed snow. His head appeared to stick and Marty waited. He waited through the awful silence. He waited for what seemed like eternity. The kid was surely dead. But then he screamed, an awful heart wrenching scream, and time sped up. Marty breathed a heavy sigh. The kid was alive, but shaken! Marty helped him to his feet. He could walk on his own. His face was scraped, but nothing was broken. Marty was so very grateful. But again, why? Who was this boy and why was he so special? Somehow, he was the key to Marty's ability to recapture his memories. Marty knew that if he could recapture this kid, he could recapture it all.

He concentrated further and recalled more of Dimple Dell, the barn, the horses, and the trail to the upper pasture. He remembered the trail from the barn to that pasture. He was curious about what he might find. He saw the familiar ground and the backyard behind the home. Still, he wondered. The backyard was blurry. He knew it in a general sense. He knew the outline. But his memory would not focus here. The home sat uphill from the barn, downhill from the pasture. His memory skirted around the home along the southern property line marked by a rusted barbed wire fence. He remembered. He had cut his back on this barbed wire. He'd been riding a horse.

Toro was a large quarter horse that Dad had bought to take deer hunting. He was slow, but sure footed, great in the mountains, not so great in a barrel race. He had grown bored one day as Marty rode him up in that upper pasture. He decided to go back to the barn. With Marty aboard, he headed for the trail down and pulled his usual trick. He ran under some low-lying scrub oak to scrape little Marty off of his back. Marty got him stopped and dismounted. His dad had been watching from over by the incinerator – a 50-gallon steel drum, shot full of bullet holes. Marty recalled the barrel only vaguely. It was part of the backyard, not so much a part of Marty's memory. Marty would burn the household garbage in this barrel. The holes in the steel barrel allowed air to help the fire burn. But something was still missing. Marty was always troubled, but would continue to swim through the memories.

Dad came to the rescue; more angry with Toro than concerned for Marty. He brandished a quirt, and gave Toro a swat. The horse turned his backside away from the quirt and directly into Marty. The movement knocked Marty backwards into the rusted barbed wire fence. The wire cut into his lower back, a wide gash just above the belt. It didn't hurt. The barbs were sharp. But his shirt filled with blood. Dad helped him up, but otherwise proved useless. Uncle Dean was visiting. He was a coach and knew first aid. He tended to Marty. No one mentioned stitches. No one worried about infection. Marty still bears a jagged scar across his lower back.

Marty remembered more horses: Princess, a beautiful dark brown quarter horse. Princess accompanied Toro. Two others rode with them. Lady was a mare -"Pony of America"; Polly, her 1-year-old filly. There was a day or was it two? On one day, Marty rode Lady. Mom was on Princess. Dad rode Toro. For some reason, they left Polly back at the barn. They were trying to "wean" her away. Dad told Marty that if Lady should bolt, he should single rein her. He instructed him to pull a single rein back and hold it against her side to lead her in a circle, to make her spin, and that he should hold the rein there until she stops. Not one-half mile up the road, she turned back and started to run. Marty did as instructed. He pulled hard on the right rein to put it against her side. He held firm with his right hand and held firm to the saddle horn with his left. Lady was determined, but so was Marty. She finally tired. The instruction worked; they continued their ride. One would think that Marty would be pleased with this memory. But he was more troubled by the part that included a little brother sitting astride Toro at Dad's back. Marty had forgotten, and it seemed as if he had intentionally chosen to forget about this little brother. He realized now that of the memories that he could recover, only a rare few included....this little brother.

There was a second memory of a different day. Marty was now behind Dad on the back of Toro and little brother was riding Lady. Polly again whinnied from the barn approximately one mile distant.

Lady again bolted. She ran hard and little brother didn't' know or Marty had never taught him to single rein. Why was that? Dad kicked Toro to follow hard. Toro was a horse opposed. Marty, on back, was baggage. With a hard boot heel, Dad called on Toro to serve. Toro bucked to show his attitude and Marty landed in a heap on a large sage brush. He had been holding onto the saddle blanket during the bumpy ride and it came with him as Toro loped away with Dad to rescue little brother.

Marty was only beginning to realize that of the memories that he could recover, very few included this little brother. Why was this? And why were the memories of the backyard so unclear? Everything that he could recover wasn't much, but what was there was crystal... except for the back yard and incinerator. Why were these "recovered" memories so...well, so... "fuzzy"? He didn't know.

Marty also remembered his Grandfather. To him, these memories were strange simply because Marty had no fond memories for the man. This Grandpa was his mom's dad. He rarely visited, hardly ever spoke. But one day, he had made what seemed to be a "special" visit to the home on Dimple Dell. He rarely spoke to Marty, never really communicated at all.

Harold was a giant of a man at 6'5" and 230 lbs. He made his living as a machinist. He was strong and taciturn. Marty had never seen him smile. Marty's mother was Harold's youngest daughter and the 6th of 7 children. She reinforced Marty's memories. She didn't like him either. Marty didn't know the source of his grandfather's disapprobation. He had never really thought about it, but it just now occurred to him that his own illicit conception was indeed the reason. After all, his mother was 17 and just out of high school. Marty's dad was 16, and though he claimed he had graduated high school, Marty suspected differently.

His parents married saving Marty from that disgrace, but only because Emma, - Marty's grandmother – had insisted. Harold gave his dad a job sweeping floors at his foundry. It would not be surprising that when dad showed little gratitude by leaving within the year to take a milk route that he failed to ingratiate Harold to all things Richard – and to Marty's view, that included Marty, his bastard firstborn. Harold's disappointment on his daughter's behalf exacerbated the resentment.

Marty had assumed – because he was taught so- that grandfathers love their grandsons. But that was not Marty's own experience. Harold certainly never told him so. He never held him when he was a small child in the rocking chair and rubbed his ears like Marty's great grandfather had done. He never took him for a ride in the cab of his pick-up truck. He never took him anywhere. Sure, Marty participated in all of the family gatherings: Pioneer Days and Thanksgiving. He loved being with the cousins – all 18 of them, but his dad never felt welcome at these gatherings and they often left early or sometimes never arrived. Mom and Dad would argue. Dad would unilaterally veto the day's plans ,and Marty wouldn't see his cousins until next year – maybe. The fact that Harold had 18 grandkids likely didn't help Marty's cause. He was fifth in order of age. But by the time he arrived, the newness of grandchildren – if it ever did grab Harold – had likely worn off. Marty wasn't sure, but that might explain the distance. And, yet...Marty felt that there was another reason, specific and real.

****

The right hand reel ran empty as the last of the film passed on through Marty's mouth to empty onto the left hand reel. The left hand reel continued to spin with the film strip passing over the top again and again, lop, lop, lop. Marty had gone zombie and once more Trudy grew concerned. She waited for him to awaken. He closed his mouth and opened his eyes. His stare was vacant. He stayed stock still. Trudy pulled the reels off of his hands. She tried to hand them back. He was incoherent. Not so much like he was here, but disconnected; rather, it was more like he was just not here at all; like he had left for another place, or even – another Time. Trudy was confused. She held the film reels and thought to keep them safe. He might remember them one day and want them back.

"Marty? Hey... Marty?" she jostled his shoulder and wondered, "Are you in there?"

No response. Instead, still disconnected, he reached into his speedo. This time he pulled out an entire handful of pills. He popped three into his mouth and put back the rest. The "white noise" -initially almost imperceptible - was now enhanced; a blue glow emanated and grew to surround this resident of Bed 13. He dropped his fins over the edge of the bed and stepped out. Trudy jumped to steady him, but his feet never reached the floor. Rather, the blue light buzzed loudly around him, enveloped him, and carried him out.

As he floated, the blue light snapped and sparked as flying insects pressed for what was an unexpected execution. Marty appeared to float cloudlike a few inches above the floor. The blue light, inside of which he rode, buzzed and snapped at the touch of each housefly, mosquito, or other insect that it sent to its death. Fwap!, Zzzt!, Poppp! Trudy watched, mystified as Marty crackled and snapped above the floor, past her through the door, into and down the hallway - back to PT.

She tucked the film reels inside his desk drawer, beneath the travel magazine advertising "Patagonia" and behind the Gideon's bible.

CHAPTER XIV

After Marty left, Trudy puzzled. She took a seat on his bed. Had she asked, assuming Marty could answer, she may have learned that he was planning to plunge again into the warm waters of the South Pacific or maybe the icy cold waters below Tierra Del Fuego. Of course, the source of all of these waters emanated no further away than at, and flowed freely from the water faucet at the "hot tub" in PT. But she didn't inquire. Instead, she sat alone on Marty's bed. She wasn't quite sure what she had just witnessed. Some of what she had seen in the film clip was familiar to her; much appeared to be afterthought. Of course, she knew nothing about "Donny". She had never met Marty's dad. But she knew that he helped Marty get some of the hot cars that he drove during school. She also knew that the family lived on Dimple Dell, and that they had horses.

But even more intriguing were the secondary memories: those that suggested that Marty was striving to remember something important, almost vital. She knew about the open stream in front of his home. When she and Shelly were young and Shelly was in love, they had ridden their bicycles to his home. During the afternoon, they visited with him beneath the shade of a huge Cottonwood tree that bordered his driveway and sat next to the stream. She remembered Marty's home on Dimple Dell and recognized his description. She knew also about his current struggles with his memory. She was surprised to hear from the recording that he recognized his own struggles. The rooms off of Hallway A were for the Alzheimer's crowd. The fact that he held on to the 8mm film suggested that he was searching for something, something that he had lost, or maybe something that he had stashed away for safekeeping but had now forgotten. Trudy realized that though he may have forgotten, he knew that he had forgotten it. It was something very important to him and he was struggling to recover it. From his recording, he seemed to know that he had difficulties with his memory...What did he call it, A "Swiss-cheese" memory? As for the Alzheimer's crowd, they had no clue about what they were missing. That wasn't Marty. He certainly did not belong in A-Wing.

Trudy had been in the cafeteria earlier. She had overheard Curly singing the new guy's praises, something about saving his life in Physical Therapy. He knew something. The two of them should commiserate. Maybe they could figure out just what Marty was doing here and what he seemed to be searching for. She quickly jumped from the bed and exited. As she ran through the door and into the hallway, she ran smack dab into Curly coming to find her. The two bounced off of each other and fell splat across from one another into the middle of the Alzheimer's wing.

"Owwwwwwaaa!" Curly wailed rubbing his head. (This action was becoming habitual.) "Where are you going in such a hurry?" He scrambled to his feet to pick up Trudy's cane. He reached down to help her up.

"I might ask you the same thing", Trudy responded. She grabbed his arm with both hands and stood as he pulled her up and handed back her cane.

"Hey" Curly announced. "I was looking for you. What do you know about this guy Marty, you know, the new guy? Do you know him?" he asked with some urgency. "I just met him this morning in PT. He saved my life. Can you believe it?

"No, I can't. Why would anybody?" she muttered under her breath as she brushed herself off.

Curly was oblivious and continued. "He's an interesting dude; seems like a bit of a magician or wizard maybe".

Trudy interrupted impatiently, "Yes, I know him. Meet me in the cafeteria at lunch. Bring Mo and Larry. I'll get Maggie. Go!" She waved him on down the hallway. Curly looked puzzled, but saluted. He took off down Hallway A with a hard right at the intersection with Hallway B. He had to finish his restroom cleaning before lunch.

Trudy headed to the living room to find Maggie. In the winter, she would be close to the gas fireplace where it was warm. In the summer, she sat near the large picture window where outside it was shady and cool, and the dappled sunlight played on the glass. For Golden Hills, the front living area was the perfect sales pitch, the best advertisement. It helped to assuage the guilt of those who came to say "good-bye". Today, Maggie was parked by the window. She was cogitating, lost in thought.

Maggie?" Trudy called out. "Are you in there?" The question was well intended and legitimate for literally all of the people here. On most occasions, many of the elderly residents enrolled were gone. To where, Heaven only knew. Sometimes, if you asked with the proper tenor, the right attitude – who could ever know what was proper or right to these folks – they might just answer... maybe. No promises that the answer would make any sense but when successful, the effort could be wholly entertaining.

"Oh hey, Trudy", Maggie replied. "It's you. Say, did you ever feel that this place was Heaven?" she asked seemingly out of nowhere.

Trudy thought that she was prepared to answer anything. But this one shook her. "This place...? What place is that?" she asked, confused.

"You know...this place – Golden Hills" Maggie repeated.

"Trudy realized that she was serious. She immediately considered the query. Initially, she might have responded sarcastically; something like: Perish the thought. But about all she could muster was a subdued, "Uhh, well..."

"I mean, think about it..." Maggie continued. "I heard somewhere that 'the course of the Lord is one eternal round'. I'm not sure what that means, but I think it means that the past, present, and the future are all the same. You know, something like: don't worry about whom you'll marry because you're already married; don't worry about where you should go to school or whether you'll graduate because you've already graduated; don't worry about whether you get a job or what that might be, because you're already employed, retired, and now seated in a wheelchair taking sun in the front visitor's center here at Golden Hills...", she trailed off.

Trudy nudged her chair. "Hey, you're not going religious on me are you?" She tried to joke. She needed to find her friend, to bring her back. She was worried.

Maggie took a deep breath and continued right on past the intended interruption, "...don't worry about fatigue, illness, or even death because...well, you'll get better or you'll come back to Me. We worry only because there's a curtain of sort or maybe a veil that is drawn over us...you and me...that keeps us from seeing....everything; you know, the past, the present, and the future – all at once...I think that's what that means...." She dwindled again back into her own thoughts. But now she had Trudy's attention.

"Wait...Maggie. What do you mean, 'one eternal round'? How does that make this place 'Heaven'? Maggie? Maggie!" Trudy snapped her fingers in front of Maggie's eyes. Maggie had gone back to sleep. Like Marty, she slept a lot. Trudy wouldn't get her back now, not for a while. Never mind, she thought. She had a meeting to attend. She headed to the cafeteria.

CHAPTER XV

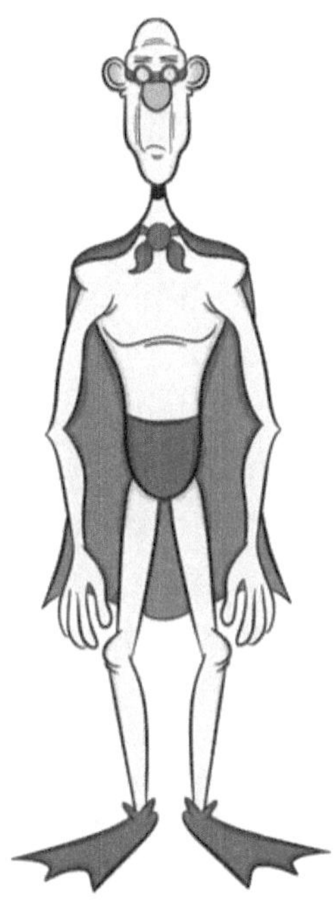

Marty dove into the therapy tub there in PT and returned to the crystal clear waters that ran the frontage at his home on Dimple Dell. Something was bothering him. He was determined to discover what it was so he floated cloud-like through this mountain stream. He stopped for a moment and knelt there on the sandy bottom to adjust his goggles. He knew that he must revisit his memories, but he was stumped as to whether he could ever recover a single one. He had to figure out how best to remember. Damn the Swiss-cheese! He must find what was here. He had to find it and he was pressed by Time. It was running short. Recent memories confirmed that this stream eventually would be piped. Access to the waters would end. And, in fact, this entire "place" would disappear as if in a dream. Progress would remove this small dell altogether. Urban sprawl would erase forever the memories that were here, that are here. And, Marty knew that he must find each memory that surrounds this place. He also knew that he would need to endure these cooling waters for a Time longer. He could only hope that his wind would endure, that he could hold his breath during his descent. He must go deep, deeper than he'd ever been, and he didn't know how or whether he could stay down. But he was sure that he needed answers, and he was determined not to ascend until he found what he was sent there to find; until he remembered what was lost.

He returned together with his thoughts and memories to the tall granite peaks that rested behind the home where he grew up. He meditated on these granite mountains that offered so much security and peace and on this stretch of mountain stream in which he now found himself; this place that had always been a place of refuge to which Marty would retreat frequently throughout the summers. He had oft times ached for a reprieve from the winter months if only to get back to this stretch of water. It was in this cold and crystal clear stream of mountain fresh waters that flowed from Bell's Canyon that set Marty's mind right. His frequent plunges here were contemplative and healing. Here, there was a memory; vague, but real. It touched upon his relationship ... With whom? With his little brother; the brother on horseback bolting home to a filly; the brother on the other sled who raced with him down the drive on the snowy winter nights; the brother smoking cigarettes in the tree where its leaves could suck up the smoke; the brother who...? Ohh...he didn't know. The brother who...what?

The memories ranged further, he knew it. They must. Marty set his feet into the sandy bottom and laid back into the oncoming current. The rushing waters pushed at his back and bubbled around his shoulders and ears. His body churned and vibrated under the flowing current. His mind cleared and he found better recall. Still, it wasn't a recall on which he could focus. His Swiss cheese memory didn't work like that. The memories came randomly and were frequently scattered.

Right now, he remembered a sister: Deanne was her name; Dee Dee. He had lost her early. She passed with his Dad when the two were in a car accident together. Marty only vaguely recalled this moment and either could not or perhaps he chose not to remember this episode of his life. But he did remember Dee Dee. She was a lonely child, a bit awkward, and socially clumsy. Animals loved her; kittens and puppies especially. Marty remembered how sad she was when Mom ran over her puppy Petunia, a tiny Maltese poodle, while trying to get up the driveway in the snow. Petunia had run out the door to greet Mom and Dee Dee who had just arrived home. Marty recalled how she had loved that little dog and how Petunia had loved her.

Adults, too, loved Deanne. She was very sweet. But kids her own age antagonized her ruthlessly. The Clark boys lived up the street about a half mile. They lived in a house on a hill with a long driveway very similar to Marty's home layout. Their driveway crossed over the same stream that flowed one-half mile down the road across Marty's 300 foot frontage. The stream crossed under the Clark's long driveway through a concrete pipe about 5 feet in diameter. The force of the water at the downstream side as it exited the pipe created a small pond into which the waters gathered before continuing south toward Marty's home and beyond. The small pond ran about three to five feet deep with a circumference of about 10 to 12 feet.

Dee Dee came home one day from school. She was crying. Brian and Scott, the two Clark brothers had teased her without mercy on the bus ride home. Marty had tried to toughen her up by giving her examples of how she could respond to these two bullies to deflect their mean spiritedness, and if necessary, how she could further discourage them with a kick to the shins or testicles. But Marty should have known better. That wasn't Dee Dee. She was incapable of even considering such justified revenge. Now, Marty was fed up. He hopped into his car and drove the half mile up the road. He parked on the street. The Clark boys were expecting him. They knew they had gone too far this time. Marty could hear them at the top of their drive near the front of their home – a good place to spy on anyone coming up to the house; a good place from which to lob rocks down upon anyone trying to come up the drive. But Marty had been called upon in times past to babysit these younger boys – Brian was 11, Scott was 9. Their parents astutely recognized that a teenage boy, Marty's age, was the perfect babysitter for their own hellions. They had already tried the local teenage girls who advertised to babysit. The Clark boys had run off all of them. Marty took the job on a whim and for 2 years was fully employed every "bowling night" for Mr. and Mrs. Clark. By now, he knew how to deal with these turds. He took the back way around their home and up the hill. He moved up the heavily wooded side yard to emerge from the backyard and on to the front porch. From there, he watched the two Clark boys as they watched their front drive and tossed a few rocks in expectation of Marty's anticipated frontal approach. Silly boys! By the time they grew bored and turned to enter their home, Marty was there at the front entry to grab ahold of both. He wrestled them together on down to the driveway bridge and dropped each one - butt first - into the pond at the downside of the culvert that ran beneath the driveway. Then, he issued his instructions:

"If Dee Dee has any more trouble with anyone, and I mean anyone, whether on the bus or at school - anyplace where you are there together with her, I will come looking for you. I would advise Mr. Brian Clark that you take it upon yourself to ensure that she is never bothered again by anybody. From today forward, if I were you, I would become her staunchest defender. Are we clear?"

Brian and Scott stood scared while dripping wet. Both nodded sheepishly. Marty hopped into his car, conveniently left there on the road and headed home. Dee Dee remained awkward and continued to struggle socially, but she was never again picked on at school or on the bus. She had Brian and Scott to thank for that.

Memories of Dee Dee took him to Shanna. She was the family's youngest, Marty's baby sister. Yeah, Marty remembered her. She needed no introduction nor did she need his protection. She was tough as nails. No one gave her trouble at Junior High or High School and, at least while young, she was very manipulative. Like any younger child, she could readily place the blame with the best of them on anyone but herself. Marty recalled the day when she was maybe three years old, a day when she was playing in the toilet in the upstairs bath. She had placed a handful of Marty's plastic toys: army men and dinosaurs in the toilet. Mom came in to find her. She saw the drowned plastic combatants and the molded early Mesozoic lizards and asked knowing full well who had done it:

"Who threw those toys into the toilet?"

3-year old Shanna did not miss a beat. She responded as she continued to splash and play in the toilet, "P-, P-, Pwoobbabbly, P-, Pwwoobbly Mawkie did it".

Mom could only smile. She scooted Shanna out of the bathroom and rescued the drowning toys.

Marty and his baby sister were two peas in a pod; except that Marty held the advantage. He smiled now as he remembered. He was 7 years her senior and Mom trusted him. He had never given his mother a reason to distrust him. He always kissed her goodnight to let her know he was home safe; and, when he didn't come home, he would call her to let her know where he was and what he was up to.

When they got older, the one thing that Marty could do to piss off his baby sister was to remind her that Mom loved him the best. Of course, Mom never said as much. The fact was that Mom and Shanna remained in close proximity throughout their lives. They lived within one to two miles from each other always. The relationship was such that if one of them needed a cup of sugar or a stick of butter, either would call upon the other before even considering the equally short drive to the nearby grocery store to make a purchase.

"Hey, Shan, I need a pair of socks. Bring some by when you come over, please." Mom would ask her instead of buying a cheap pair for herself.

"Hey, Mom, I need some laundry detergent. I'll come over and grab a cup of soap from ya. I'm leaving now. See you in a few", Shanna would ask finding it easier to turn right to go to Mom's instead of left and go to the grocery store, even though the grocery store was closer.

Marty had a mean streak and loved to tease. Whenever he could, he would remind Shanna that Mom loved him best. Typically, her response was testy, but she had no appropriate come back. If she tried, Marty would remind her that Mom had never caught him out on the driveway at 16 years old, late at night, drinking beer with an ex-convict ten years her senior. Marty could only smile at the thought. The truth was that Shanna had turned into a very fine and responsible woman, wife, and mother; and she remained to this day, a loving, loyal and protective daughter whom Marty trusted explicitly to take care of their Mom. Marty loved both of these women deeply. Strangely, Marty remembered these women, and he knew that they knew about "little brother". But neither of them ever spoke of him to Marty. Why? He wondered.

He lay back into the current, took his feet off of the sand and again began to float. The wind came up. A small twister made of swirling dust flecked with dried alfalfa from the barn and small chunks of manure grew larger as it passed across the pasture. The blue sky quickly began to grey. The sun hid its' face behind the imposing cumulus clouds. The clouds grew until they conquered the skies. Jagged bolts of lightning tore open the heavens. Loud and clamorous thunder poured out, and Marty thought that he smelled rain in the air. He was wrong. Rather than rain, the skies unleashed marble sized hail that pounded the barn and covered the pasture, bounced off of the driveway, and ricocheted off of the stones and fences. For the first time ever, Marty failed to float the full 300 foot length of the icy mountain waters that flowed across the frontage of his pasture. Of this he knew. He had never before failed to complete the refreshing ice water blast. Never! But he found no refreshment here. Instead, he was troubled. Not so much by the thunder and lightning. Not so much by the hail itself. The Cottonwood tree overhead sheltered him from much of the ruckus. Still, he couldn't help but wonder. Why now?

A brief, but incomplete memory accompanied another jagged bolt that flashed suddenly to tear open the skies. It was this memory that caused him to flounder. He recalled his little brother, the "bed wetter". He recalled how much this little brother had begged Mom to let him play little league football with Marty when Marty brought home an advertising flyer for a new team being formed in town. Marty had no plans to include his little brother who always sought to tag along. In fact, he had decided to insist with Mom that he go this one alone, that his little brother could not play, never mind that the Hayes brothers were themselves, teammates. Still, this was Marty's chance to break free, to legitimately ditch his clingy little brother because he – Marty- was "grown up".

But here and now, there was something specific that he could not remember; a memory that he could not recapture; a memory that had come back to him recently, but one that he had failed to hold onto. This failure was disconcerting to say the least. Why did this one bother him so deeply? The memories of this place were mostly pleasant and peaceful. The memories of his family were mixed – some fun and happy; others, even frightening. Still, overall, the memories were kind. More importantly, he had memories of his family; all except this brother, the "bed wetter", and these were minimal to non-existent, and those that touched even remotely on him were better described as empty and woefully incomplete.

Like the skies, Marty was troubled. His memory of sign-ups for little league football was one of the last that Marty could resurrect of this little "bed wetter" and, for some reason unexplained, Marty felt guilty. The feeling was poignant and Marty needed to swim. He stood up in the stream bed to hoist his suit. He fixed his goggles and tightened his fins. He filled his lungs with the crisp and crystal clear night air and he dove, both fast and deep. His temptation was to go back to the island. But that would reveal nothing. Rather, he dove now to confirm the truth not to hide from it. He dove to ponder the speeding "light clock" that moved quickly to light speed. He dove to ponder if only to see "but through the glass darkly".

CHAPTER XVI

Maggie was stationed partway down Hallway A, just down from the TV room where she was usually parked. The weather outside had been windy with dark grey clouds. Hail had begun to pelt the circular drive outside Golden Hills. Lightning tore open the skies. The booming thunder that accompanied rattled the picture window. For safety, she thought to go back to her room. For company, she chose to head to the cafeteria. She found neither. She had started down Hallway A, but thoughts had overtaken her and she fell asleep in mid-sojourn. She cogitated as she snoozed. She believed that she was on to something.

Marty exited Physical Therapy. He had just returned from a lengthy swim to Dimple Dell and onto the South Pacific. The swim was refreshing. He had thought a lot about things, some of which he could remember. He stepped out of the tub and waddled from PT into the Hallway A. He was dripping wet. He pushed what little hair he had left back up onto his head and trapped it there with his goggles. He wiped his nose and eyes. He was working his way up Hallway A and back to his room when he saw Maggie parked in the middle of the hallway. He took a quick look up and down Hallway A. It was always hard to say whether Ms. Bichette was on the prowl; and, her boys: Curly, Mo, and Larry owed an allegiance of sorts. Marty liked them, but one could never be too careful in this place. Marty knew that Maggie was at risk.

As usual, she was sleeping. Generally, Mo kept her parked in the living room up front. Normally on a day like today, she would be found near the fireplace for warmth. If Ms. Bichette found her stationed here in the hallway, she would restrict her to her room. Marty was at risk outside of his own room. Ms. Bichette would restrict him as well. As he thought about it, he wasn't quite sure just how she could accomplish that. But never mind. He had some thinking to do and couldn't do it with Le Biche's bad vibes muddling the reception.

On any other day, he would take Maggie to the cafeteria. Most likely, Trudy would be there playing solitaire; pinochle if she was lucky to find someone to play it with her. Normally, Marty could get from the living room to the cafeteria in No Time. (No pun intended, he thought as he smiled as his own joke.) But he couldn't risk it taking her there now.

He grabbed her chair and tried to push. His initial efforts were fruitless. His flippers slipped and slid as if on ice. He turned and put his back into it. He dug in and pressed from his heels through his back and into the backside of Maggie's wheelchair. Slowly, she began to roll. Marty turned quickly and pushed. She rolled faster. Physics had taught him that once an object is placed into motion it will remain in motion unless acted upon by some outside force. He smiled when he remembered that he and Mo had talked about this only recently; just when, he couldn't recall. No matter, he knew that both gravity and friction would come into play, but he also knew that Maggie's mass gave her an express advantage for which he should be prepared.

She was a just a few doors up the hallway from his room. Marty let her coast and she wheeled toward the open door to the room where Bed 13 is found. Marty ran ahead and posted himself to intercept. At that moment, he heard Le Biche coming from the cafeteria and giving directions to Trudy. They were dispensing the afternoon medications. "C'mon, c'mon", he muttered as he waited. "C'mon darlin'" he urged. Maggie slowed as she rolled up to him and he easily turned her into his room just as Ms. Bichette and Trudy entered Hallway A. Marty was standing in the open doorway, his back to the hallway and ready to enter.

"Oh, Mr. Markham, we've got your medications ready" Ms. Bichette announced to no one in particular. "We'll be right in".

Marty let Maggie roll on into his room. Then, rather than wait, he turned quickly to intercept both Trudy and Ms. Bichette outside of his doorway in the middle of Hallway A. He walked straight up to Trudy who held the medication tray. Across the tray was an array of paper cups, each cup was filled with a different assortment of a variety of colored pills. Both women were a bit surprised to see him awake, let alone so lively and out in the hallway.

A sudden thump inside Marty's room distracted them. Marty had miscalculated either Maggie's speed at entry as he rolled her into his room, or her weight – likely the latter. She had rolled a bit too quickly through the door, past his bed, and into the rear wall where she banged her knees into the room's air conditioning unit. The entire episode unrolled as she slept...soundly.

Trudy's remained frozen, her eyes fixed as she tried to see who might be inside. Could be anybody, she worried.

Ms. Bichette took a step toward the room. The thump had distracted her. She intended to investigate until Marty stepped into her path and held out is hand to Trudy without saying a word. Both she and Trudy looked at him quizzically. Never before now, had he put out his hand to accept his medications so willingly. Never before now, had he swallowed his pills so readily in front of Ms. Bichette. Generally, he swiped the cup from the tray and stashed them under his pillow. Golden Hills had no mandatory medication order for Marty. Regardless, even if they had, he was always too quick for Ms. Bichette to medicate him herself.

Trudy saw his outstretched hand. She put two and two together. She took the cup of pills marked for Bed 13 from the tray and held them out to Marty. She dumped the assembled medications into his open palm. He popped them into his mouth and swallowed. He opened his mouth wide and moved his tongue from side to side, up and down, to show them both that he had swallowed. He offered a handsome smile to both women. Trudy almost blushed. Ms. Bichette watched him with wary eyes, but said nothing. She was prepared to argue, but he swallowed his pills so quickly that she could form no debate. She looked to Trudy, snapped her fingers to secure her attention, and nodded to the room across the hallway. They both crossed the hall as Marty turned to walk opposite into his room. He stumbled over Maggie in her wheelchair stationed at the door's threshold. She was still asleep. She had bounced off of the in-room, metal AC unit with enough momentum to where she had rolled back to the open doorway to stop across the door threshold, part way into his room and part way into Hallway A. Marty hastily rolled her back into the room and parked her in the corner. He stuck his head outside the door and took one more surreptitious glance up and down Hallway A. Nothing – all clear. Then, he climbed into bed.

Sometime later, Maggie awoke. At first, she was confused. She thought she had heard Marty talking in his sleep. She looked around and recognized that she was in his room although how she had come to be here, she wasn't sure. Anymore, this was a routine occurrence. She took it in stride. Marty was flat on his back in bed and mumbling something about No Time. She could see that he was awake – which was unusual for most of the folks here. She waved at him. He waved back, but seemed lost in his own thoughts. He was mumbling to himself about some new pet theory.

"Marty, it's me, Maggie". She introduced herself. He didn't seem to recognize her. But he was willing to visit. As they visited, he mentioned his "No Time" thing about which she had been so intrigued. At the time, it sounded like only so much nonsense. But now...well, it made some sense or at least those portions that she could interpret. She didn't know why she was suddenly so intrigued. She didn't know why "now" was so important.

Initially, she had thought that Time was linear, a teacher that took us to a nice home and to a life that we had somehow earned. Time gave us opportunities to learn, to discover, to acquire. Then Time gave us our reward at the end. A part of that reward was to let us continue learning lineally through eternity. The problem with the lineal theory was with the "Beginning". Not so much of a dilemma if you allowed that you never had one; that you were somehow always here. But the lineal theory begs the question: Where and what were we in that "Beginning"? How'd we get started, or did we? Were we even people, men or women or, were we some kind of spirit, maybe even some kind of fog, haze, or better still...energy? She had focused when Marty mumbled, and she felt that he was on the right road. Maybe he had it figured out. He had said something about a Library; either that he had visited or intended to visit. But Golden Hills had no Library and besides, with his description of this Library, she was certain that it had to be downtown in one of the big office buildings. To spout some of the things he spouted, she figured he must have been studying, but where?

She had had spoken with him when he first arrived. Marty had mumbled something about how we got here. At first, she thought he was talking about Golden Hills. He said something about how we were put her or somehow dropped in. He spoke of how we lived, worked, breathed and accomplished while here. Maggie never understood. To her, it was jibberish. The best she could figure, when anyone arrived at Golden Hills, they were already way past working and accomplishing anything; breathing-maybe and oft times with the help of a machine; and living?... Well, even that was an open question.

Suddenly Marty snorted as he rolled over in bed, his monologue interrupted momentarily. He remained asleep as he reached a hand up to rub and scratch his face and push his red goggles askew. He coughed a bit and snorted. He reached a hand down his speedo to readjust himself before he settled back down into sleep; and after a moment, he renewed.

The more he spoke, the more she came to realize that he was speaking almost metaphysically. He wasn't speaking of Golden Hills at all. He was speaking about The Library- about a place where Time does not exist or, at least, where Time is not measured, a place where No Time governs. The best she understood, this was a place from which we can see and be part of the past, present, and future – but all at once. In this Library, we should be able to find any number of volumes that rested there on Cherrywood shelves. These volumes measured Time in any number of seconds, minutes, hours, days, weeks, months, even years – either in consecutive handfuls, or singularly. In making a selection, we drop from No Time into any given sleeve- or better still – any given "Page" of Time so as to live, work, breathe and accomplish; and then - as he droned on through occasional snorts and chortles, coughs and hacks, – at some point (and, Maggie didn't know quite when), we would step back out of Time with all that we had learned to return with it into No Time. Maggie smiled. She had been here already: "a Page of Time". She was intrigued and wheeled her chair closer to his bed.

If Maggie understood him correctly, we were born into and lived through Time so we can learn how to reach No Time which was well... like a Library of sorts- a Library that held books filled with pages that accounted for, kept track of, or otherwise measured every second, minute, hour, day, and year of Time. This made perfect sense. Still, Marty himself seemed stymied by the thought that life was "one eternal round"; a thought that he had picked up somewhere; a thought that he had shared with her in these late night mumblings. She'd read about it too...somewhere. She'd need to find just where and do some research. It somehow sounded religious. She would check with her Bible, the Adventists had a Bible of their own, the Mormons owned some kind of book, or maybe the Koran, or the Talmud, who knew?

If she guessed correctly and this "eternal round" thing was true, then she figured that we had already lived, breathed, worked, and accomplished everything in one fell swoop called "past, present, and future"; that to us ,while in Time, took a lifetime to accomplish.

Yet, somehow on the metaphysical plane, we already loved; we already lost; we already married, had kids, grandkids, and we already died. "Wwwhhoooa", she breathed as she tried to muddle through. What did all of this mean? She didn't know, but she was intrigued. She knew that she must look further into this No Time thing with its "eternal round" component.

"Hey". Marty said as he sat up and blinked. "Maggie? Is that you?"

Maggie was startled, but she recovered and smiled.

"Why yes Marty, it's me. It is nice to see you; so nice to have you here with us now".

Like Trudy, Maggie had also known Marty back in the day. It was hard to say just "when" they had first met. To some, he was the "new guy". But to her and to Trudy, he was Marty. She really couldn't say how long they had known him. Sometime back in junior high school, but it seemed like forever.

She had been present the first day that they checked Mr. Mark Mark Markham into Golden Hills. A beautiful blonde woman, her stunning daughter and three cute and very expressive little girls had accompanied him; or better, they delivered him here. He was incommunicado at the time. Maggie helped to check him in. Ms. Bichette had been busy with the Death Squad. They were removing the occupant from what would become Marty's room there in Hallway A and delivered him to the temporary morgue downstairs. In the words of Ms. Bichette: "One in; one out. It's hard to keep the rigor out". Maggie knew that although crass, the saying was true. That was just how things went around here. The turnover was quick and dirty; and always consistent.

She looked around his room. It was nothing much, or so it seemed: a fluorescent light at the ceiling; 4 walls, cinderblock and painted white; a water cooler just beneath the small 5010 window high on the wall; an old fashioned, single iron bed with a safety railing that sat high off of the tile floor; an antique end table painted faux white with a small lamp on top; a separate toilet and shower; and an open doorway with access to and from the hallway with no door to keep out intruders. The staff required immediate access if the need arose; typically the need arose daily somewhere in the halls of this place. It was a small private room much like any motel room, only smaller.

"I need to swim" he announced. He jumped up off of the bed. He pulled a pair of red swimmer's goggles from his head, smoothed his thinning hair, and adjusted the goggles to fit snuggly over his eyes. He straightened a rather ill-fitting red speedo, and tightened the straps of the large red swim fins at his ankles.

"But you just woke up, or...I mean, you just came back from, uhh.." she muttered, unsure of what to say exactly.

"Look before I go, can you take some dictation? He asked. He reached into his speedo and pulled out a large orange pill. "This should only take a moment. You should find my journal and pen there in the drawer next to the bed".

Maggie was a bit bewildered, but she searched the drawer and found the pen and journal. She sat on the wooden chair next to the bed and nodded to Marty. She wasn't prepared for what came next. Marty quickly noted how his medications gave him a variety of different superpowers. The problem was that he never could remember which combination of pills produced which superpower. Generally, he would pop a few pills, wait a few minutes, sometimes hours and take whatever superpower came his way; except, he did know what the orange pill could do. He showed her the large orange pill. He tilted his head far back, opened wide his mouth, and dropped the single orange pill straight into his gullet. He held up a single finger and smiled at Maggie, as if to say: Wait. After a few minutes, he dropped into what appeared to be catatonia. Maggie became alarmed and thought to call for staff. But then, he pulled the 8mm reels from beneath his mattress and set up his "projector". Now, Maggie was curious. But Marty was in no condition to answer questions. The reels began to spin, the projector to click as a bright light hit the white paint on the cinderblock wall across from his bed. There on the wall Maggie watched as a sweet, almost childlike female voice narrated:

****

Marty remembered a girl. Was she the one? He wondered. He met Shelly when he was in the 9th grade. She was in the 8th. Marty played basketball. He was popular. Shelly was in love. She was intent and pursued him. He enjoyed the attention.

Marty floated peacefully as his vision narrowed. He squinted in a valiant attempt to see through the enveloping fog; the thick fog that was his memory. His memories focused not on tall buildings, or residences. Rather, he pressed his attention to a single abandoned home in White City.

Shelly lived in White City in a small brick home, single story with a flat roof covered in tar and pea gravel. He recalled a 6-foot chain-link fence that surrounded this small home and yard. "No Trespassing" and "Keep Out" signs were posted on each of 4 sides of the fence placed temporarily at the lot lines. The old and pre existing wooden fence had fallen and been removed long ago. The windows to the home were boarded shut. High weeds at the front had supplanted the front lawn. The surrounding trees, shrubs, and former landscaping that once decorated the property were dead. The backyard bordered on and was visible from 7th East with its extensive flow of traffic. The home and yard were only 4 lots south of the last school bus stop, the last stop on the same route where the bus had stopped earlier to pick up Marty, there at the entrance to White City. The entrance sat on the south side of a large, dry gully naturally landscaped with sagebrush. Marty suddenly remembered, and he knew now that these memories were real!

Each day on the way to school, as the bus slowed to pick up kids from the last stop there in White City, the bus would roll past the backyard of the small home made of red brick and topped with tar and gravel on a flat roof; the fourth home down from the bus stop there at the southern entrance to White city on 7th East. The fourth home down where Shelly lived with her family. She had loved Marty, and he was flattered.

Marty's memory was sharpened. He clearly recalled her now.

As an 8th grader, she was the younger woman to Marty who was in the 9th. She set her sights on Marty early. He was on the basketball team and popular. He was tall, handsome, and very skinny. She was his match - tall, skinny, and very pretty. Her strawberry blond hair was long. Her smile was beautiful and entrancing. Marty didn't know it at the time, but he, too, was in love. She was his "first".

Lagoon Day– a celebration for the last day of school before summer recess– was coming. Lagoon was an amusement park approximately 50 miles north in Farmington. Lagoon Day was a good excuse for newly star-crossed lovers, fresh out of junior high school to begin a relationship. Marty asked Shelly if she would spend the day with him. They rode the bus together. Marty paid for her day. He took her on the roller coaster. He shot baskets and won for her a stuffed animal. At day's end, he stole a kiss. She smiled, and Marty was happy.

Once during that summer, Shelly and her best friend, Trudy rode their bikes to Marty's home. Marty was impressed with their forbearance in the long and strenuous ride up to visit. He was even more impressed with the continuing interest that she showed in him over the following summer months when the buses no longer ran and significant effort was required to reinforce a friendship. He regretted now, more than ever, that he did not try to steal a second kiss from Shelly on that summer day. He could have ridden with her on her bike. He would have liked that. These recollections stunned, and he began to cry. A single tear first stained his cheek. He wiped it from his face and puzzled. What was happening? He was bewildered. He had never before felt to cry like this. Then he saw and he remembered, and huge waves began to roll as if Marty swam in the deepest of oceans. Thunderheads gathered, the wind howled, and an opaque darkness swallowed him. The black rain poured down and Marty drank deeply from the deluge. He fell to his knees in the stream bed, the clear mountain waters rushing around his hips and chest. At once, he remembered, and he saw.

His vision clarified further, and his memories became more full and acute. The tears now ran in torrents and Marty felt....what? He felt pain– a pain that he had long since buried, a pain from hurtful recollections past. He began to sob uncontrollably, irreconcilably, inconsolably. He cried because he had loved her so very much. He was ashamed. Why had he forgotten her? He cried because he had lost her. He cried now because he missed her so very much. Why had he not remembered her?

Darkening clouds continued to trouble, but the memories remained clear and vivid. He was 15. It was the first day of school. Although he had been driving since he was 13, he had yet to buy his first car. More realistically, he didn't yet have a licensed to drive. He was riding the bus to school. As the bus reached that last stop on the route, Marty looked for her. He had not seen her that summer since her last bike ride up to his home. Emails, text messaging, Instagram: none of that was even invented. Neither Shelly nor Marty were sufficiently sophisticated to get a phone number. Somehow, for both, the memories and the dreams they engendered together with the anticipation of their next expected meeting at that last bus stop served better to fuel the excitement. But she was not there at that stop on that first day of school, nor was she there on any of the days subsequent. Marty was disappointed but remained expectant. He was then a sophomore in high school. She was in 9th grade back at the junior high. This was a tough arrangement. He would stay after school for sports. He didn't take the usual bus home but took a later bus after practice. This later bus didn't stop at the junior high to pick up passengers. This later bus didn't pass by the White City stop. After an interminable number of days when he returned home from practice, he searched the phone book for her last name. He found the prefix he knew to belong to those "White City" numbers. The address listed was hers. He called. The phone was disconnected. At the stop the next day again, she was not there. Over the next several days and weeks, Marty tried over and over to reach her.

He even took one Saturday and rode his bike from his home to hers. No one answered at the front door. He rang the bell several times. It echoed audibly, but no one came. He tried the back door. It was locked; so, were the doors to the garage. He knocked at each, but no one answered. Dark drapes covered the windows. He could not see inside. He called out, but no one came. He saw no cars in the driveway. He could not see into the garage. He found remnants of "yellow" warning tape in the trash can - the kind you see on police movies that show car wrecks or murder investigations. The place was deserted. Marty was "concerned".

Days later, as he sat on the lawn outside the front of the school to wait for the activity bus, the senior QB and his buddy Jeff came by the stop. They were headed to the Circle Drive Inn across the street. Jeff was with his girlfriend, Trudy. Marty recognized her. He was surprised to see her, but hopeful. Normal protocol would be that Marty would not speak to the first string varsity players unless they spoke to him, but his intended inquiry fell well outside the normal protocols. He stood. He nodded to the varsity players, but asked Trudy directly if she had seen Shelly lately. The agitated seniors approached to step in, but Trudy held up her hand. They sensed the import. They somehow knew that the usual protocols didn't hold and backed away.

Clumsily, he sought to explain, "I haven't seen her since summer when you guys rode up. Thanks, by the way. I didn't get a chance to tell her...well... you know, to say... well... that I like her...a lot. I didn't get to say thanks that you guys came all that way on your bikes to see me". He smiled weakly. Trudy began to tear up. She couldn't speak. Jeff saw her distress and again started to come over. She held up her hand as if to say, "Stay. I can do this. I must do this".

She looked Marty in the eyes. Tears filled her own. She held him by his shoulders then, she drew him close. She put her head onto his skinny, sophomore chest. She choked back the tears and whispered.

"Shelly is dead. Her whole family is dead. Her dad murdered them. He shot her. He shot the whole family- her mom, her younger brother, and her two little sisters. Shelly tried to run, but he followed her from room to room. He shot her last and then killed himself. Nobody knows why. I don't know much more. My mom told me, and... I didn't know how to tell you. Marty, she loved you!" she sobbed. "She told me so. She told me she would marry you someday! She dreamed of it! And, I knew, just from seeing the look in your eye when we were around you, that you loved her too! Marty, I am so sorry that I didn't tell you sooner. I am so sorry for it all!" She sobbed uncontrollably. Marty was in shock. He could not speak. He searched for the proper emotion. He had loved her. He still did. For a moment, the feelings were sweet. But the taste was soon replaced with anger and bitterness. He began to think of the unfairness of it all. Shelly was a sweet kid and innocent.

His thoughts turned to the world at large. Why was there so much suffering? Why did God allow it? What was the sense of it?

Soon his thoughts turned personal. It was all crap! It was scuttah to think that God loved him; scuttah that He cared; scuttah that destiny was anything more than arbitrary circumstance that men scrambled together to find some purpose; a purpose that Marty was just now coming to believe did not exist.

He thought some more and tried to find sense of it. Somehow he had never doubted that God existed. In fact, throughout his life, Marty had placed more than a fair share of trust in Him. But what Marty now realized was that his trust was misplaced; not because God did not exist, but because He did. He did. He just didn't care for Marty. And now, Marty realized that he would not care for God. He grew bored.

Huge waves rolled larger. The wind howled a mournful dirge. The black rain poured down and Marty drank deeply from the deluge. At his age with all that he had encountered in his young life, he could only conclude that this type of supposed retribution was... mundane. Yeah sure, he had blasphemed and the heavens unleashed a dreadful retort. So what, he thought.

He yawned to find his breath and another deafening thunderclap rolled over mountainous waves and across the void. Another white hot saw-cut tore a jagged wound in the firmament as Marty floated and gazed deeply into the blackness. He figured that if God wanted to take him home, He was welcome. Marty pillowed his head in his hands as he rolled on the waves. But God didn't take him home. Instead, Trudy reached to touch his cheek. She looked into his eyes. He looked into hers to remember. Trudy had been with Shelly when they came to visit him. They were friends. His memories were full and complete, and he fought now to hold back tears. The dam burst and he cried in concert with the wind. He cried as the waters calmed. He cried as the rain fell down in torrents to wash the skies clean of all his bitterness. He and Trudy remembered as they held each other, and the two friends wept together.

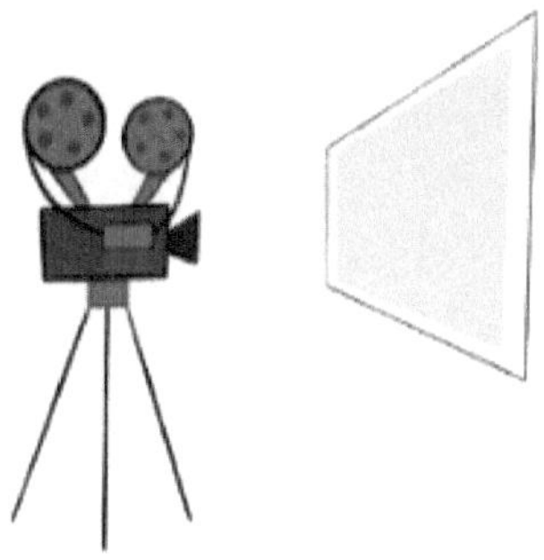

When the memories ended, Marty lay back. The sobs continued to ebb. For a long while, he cried quietly. His mind was blank. After a while, his vision cleared, and he felt lucid for the first time in many years. The right spool emptied onto the left spool and Marty awoke. But he did not retreat as usual into a virtual coma. Instead as his recall clarified, he found himself kneeling on his bed. He looked up. Maggie was seated in her wheel chair across from him. She watched him closely. There was a calm and sweet peacefulness on her face and in her eyes.

"Hey", he waved briefly in recognition and smiled.

"Hey", she smiled back.

He wiped the tears from his cheeks and from the grey hairs on his skinny chest. He wiped his eyes with the back of his hand and sighed. His pot belly expanded and contracted with each receding and soulful sob. Gradually, his sobbing ended. His belly calmed. The frequency of each rumination lessened in concert with each dying sob. For a moment, he sat silent.

"Thanks for taking notes", he said to Maggie.

"No problem, Marty. It was my pleasure" she smiled sweetly.

He put his right hand to his forehead and removed his red goggles. His red speedo hung loosely at his skinny hips. He pulled and straightened it to fit. He turned and sat at the bed's edge. These feelings had been intense; the bittersweet pain surpassed all other emotion. He had never before felt this way. The peace that he had craved found its way back to him; a peace that replaced the thunder storm and lightning that had engulfed him; a peace that replaced the boredom; a peace that tasted so very sweet. Never had he known such an experience. He was...happy. A load had been lifted.

"Thank you Ms. Maggie. I am truly grateful", he said as he held her and kissed the top of her head. "Now please, what may I do for you?"

CHAPTER XVII

Marty cruised topside on the South Pacific. He had ridden backstroke most of the way. The sky was azure, the ocean bright blue. The two tended to blend so that Marty felt suspended. He had no way to measure either time or distance. He didn't know either how long or how far he had travelled. In many ways, this was very much like when he first left the island; except that he was in much better spirits now. For what reasons, he didn't know exactly. Currently, he seemed to have a purpose. Ironically, it was Time that he needed both to figure and to figure out.

He flipped over to try the breaststroke for a while. In the distance, he could see what might be considered one of the seven natural wonders of the world. This he wanted to see. He stopped to tread water when he was joined by a flashy tuna fish wearing glasses and a red cap.

Marty puzzled to himself, what is this fish doing wearing a beret? He looks familiar.

The fish doffed his cap to introduce himself. "They call me Charlie, Charlie Tuna at your service".

"Hey. I'm Marty. Say, don't I know you?"

"Don't think so. You may have seen me on TV. I represent Starfish"

"Heyyyy, yah...." Marty was beginning to recognize this fish. "Don't you mean, Starkist...as in Starkist Tuna?

"Starkist, Starfish. What's the difference?" he shrugged. "I'm down here chasin' a sweet yellow tail, know what I mean?". He slapped a fast fin onto Marty's back.

Marty coughed, but recovered quickly. "Huh...what?..."

"C'mon. I'll give ya a tour while I'm waitin'. Damn women. Takes them forever to get ready. Besides, I've got to breathe 'ya know. What are you anyway? Some kind of topside breather...?" He didn't wait for an answer. "Sayyy, nice suit ,and I like the eyewear. Is that some kind of brand name?" He pointed to Marty's head where he wore his goggles. He removed his own eyeglasses to show them to Marty for comparison.

"Mine are goggles", Marty said.

"Yeah, right" Charlie shrugged, "goggles, huh. Mine are designer: Warby Parker Hardy, Tortoise Shell frames, chic huh?" Then he sidled up close, put a fin to his mouth, and whispered. "Not real 'tortoise shell' of course. Artificial, you know". Then rather proudly, he said, "Made from shells abandoned by the hermit crabs from Fiji; high quality stuff, right? I'm pro-environment all the way", he said as he pointed a fin to his chest.

He looked at Marty and with a wave of his fin, from head to foot as if to introduce Marty for display, he commented, "Nice matching affair. Red goggles, red suit, red fins. Tres Chic. Then he interrupted, "Hey, d'ya mind? I need to go below. Like I said, I need o breather". He smiled and dove. Marty followed as Charlie slowly drifted with the current along the expanse of the Great Barrier Reef. Like an experienced tour guide on an ocean cruise, Charlie began:

"The Great Barrier Reef is the world's largest coral reef system composed of over 2,900 individual reefs and 900 islands, did you know that?" he asked to no one in particular.

"It's southern end rests off of the coast of Queensland and stretches northward more than 1,600 miles - a little more than the distance from Boston to Miami". Charlie paused and looked to Marty. "Boston to Miami? What is that, do you know?" He looked at Marty. Marty nodded.

Charlie continued. "Overall, it covers an area of 133,000 square miles and can be seen from outer space". Again he paused with a quizzical look to Marty "Outer space?" Marty had yet to go into space. He didn't have much use for it. Swimming wasn't an option in outer space. He thought for a moment and again nodded to Charlie together with a twirl of his finger as if to say, 'yeah, keep goin'.'

Charlie smiled back, "The Reef is the world's biggest single structure made by living organisms, billions of them known as coral polyps..." frustrated, Charlie paused as Marty tried to engage a few of these little guys along the way. Mostly, they chittered and chattered amongst themselves in a language indecipherable. Like ants, they were anxiously engaged carpenters and good ones. Marty leaned in to see if he could hear what they were chittering about.

"Uhhh, Umm", Charlie cleared his throat. "D' you mind?" Marty looked up. "Oh Sorry", he mumbled and backed up. Charlie gave a brief smile and continued.

"The coral polyps are animals in the jellyfish family. They team-up with an algae called zooxanthellae to build the reef structure. In return for a cozy safe place to live, these algae provide the building blocks to make the limestone that the polyps use to build the vast reef structures that they need to survive. This Great Barrier Reef is about 500,000 years old, but it hasn't always looked like this. Reefs on Australia's continental shelf have taken on many forms, depending on the sea level. The current formation is about 6,000 to 8,000 years old. Crescentic reefs are shaped like crescents as the name implies. These are the most common shape of reef in the middle of the system; Ribbon reefs - which are narrow and winding - and Deltaic reefs as the name implies, resemble river deltas. These are found in the northern part, ,and,Flat reefs known as planar reefs are found in both the northern and southern parts. The land that forms the base of the Great Barrier Reef is the remains of the sediments of the Great Dividing Range, Australia's largest mountain range. About 13,000 years ago, the sea level was 200 feet lower than the current level, and corals began to grow around the hills of the coastal plain, which had become continental islands.

The sea level continued to rise during a warming period as glaciers melted. Most of the continental islands were submerged, and the coral remained to form the reefs and the low-elevation sandy islands or cays of today", Charlie looked at Marty with a proud smile. Much of this information, Marty could take from an encyclopedia, but it was worth the entertainment value to watch Charlie take on the role. Marty gave him an encouraging smile.

Charlie went on, "The Great Barrier Reef supports a vast array of life forms. Thirty species of whales, dolphins, and porpoises have been recorded in the Great Barrier Reef, including the dwarf minke whale, the Indo-Pacific humpback dolphin, and the humpback whale. Large populations of dugongs, large marine mammals that are relatives of the manatees, also make their home here. More than 1500 fish species live on the reef including clown fish, red bass, red-throat emperor, and several species of snapper and coral trout together with about 5,000 species of mollusks; seventeen species of sea snake which live in the warmer waters up 160 feet deep and are more common in the south than in the northern section; six species of sea turtles which include: the green sea turtle, leatherback sea turtle, hawksbill turtle, loggerhead sea turtle, flat back turtle, and the olive Ridley - all come to the reef to breed".

Charlie's gills were moving in hyper-drive. He paused, bent over, and held a fin up in a signal to Marty to hold on. Marty waited patiently for Charlie to catch a breath of sea-water as it were, his gills were pumping madly. Then with a sigh – of sorts - he continued:

"The Great Barrier Reef is also home to 215 species of birds – both seabirds and shorebirds that visit the reef or a nest or roost on the nearby islands. The white-bellied sea eagle and roseate tern are frequently sighted", and with a grand wave of his fin and a theatrical bow to Marty, he finished triumphantly, "The reefs are vital to the survival of several endangered species".

Although Marty could not hear himself as he brought his hands together to applaud, still he gave a silent clap knowing that the whales and the dolphins, and perhaps a wide array of other sea creatures from miles away could readily appreciate the vibration offered through the sea water by the performance; and for a moment, Marty thought that he may have heard, or somehow sensed back through the currents there in the South Pacific, the faint echo of a "Bravo" or "Bravissimo"... – or so he assumed.

But Marty knew because he could read. The Library magazine that he kept in his nightstand drawer had an article in it about the Reef. The Reef had been discovered by Captain James Cook in 1717. At present, the Reef was in trouble. It was first in trouble from a predatory starfish that ate the coral cover that housed the polyps. The starfish had eaten so much that protectors instituted a culling program to eliminate them. The Reef was also in trouble from human use such as fishing, tourism, and dredging sludge; and from environmental pressures including runoff and climate change with warming ocean temperatures contributing to coral bleaching. The low birth of new corals is thought to be the death of the mature breeding adults with the failure to reproduce in consequence of these bleaching events; and the types of corals that do reproduce have changed as well.

He read a paper published by Nature which showed that huge sections of a 500 mile stretch in the northern part of the Reef have died due to high water temperatures. The paper reported that some attribute the warming temperatures to climate change due to which the percentage of baby corals being born on the Great Barrier Reef has dropped drastically. Scientists describe this as the early stages of a "huge natural selection event unfolding"; and note that this points to a potentially long-term reorganization of the reef ecosystem overall should this trend continue.

Marty looked at Charlie. Charlie shrugged, "Sad, huh? Fish can't do much about it".

Just then, a cute little yellow tail emerged from the reef. Charlie introduced her. She smiled a greeting at Marty and snuggled up to Charlie. Charlie tipped his cap and saluted. The two were set to leave when Marty remembered why he had come.

"Heeyy, before you go. Can you tell me where the Library is?"He looked back and forth at both fish. They looked at each other, then back at Marty and shrugged.

"Never heard of a Library, not in these waters anyway", Charlie smiled and the two disappeared together into the Great Barrier Reef. Marty waved back. He was disappointed. He surfaced to catch a breath and then dove deep. Maybe he could catch a pod of whales for ride back to cooler climes. He'd need to explore some more. So far, no one in any of the oceans of the world had heard of the Library. He worried.

CHAPTER XVIII

The room was dark. The door was open, the hallway dimly lit. Patrons could be heard sometimes rustling with an occasional cough or dry hack. A couple of residents in charge could be heard visiting at the check-in station down A-wing at the front entry. Curly, Mo, and Larry suddenly poked their heads into the room with bed 13 from the side of the door at the jamb – Mo on top; Larry in the middle; and Curly at the bottom. They had come to inform Marty to watch out for Biche. She was on the warpath and set for vengeance. They thought to ask for Marty to intercede on their behalf. He seemed to be the only one around who could stand up to her. They had fallen from her graces; their alliance was uncertain. Would Marty take them in?

Marty was dripping wet and rummaging through his closet to find a towel. The Tres Amigos were too preoccupied to notice. Marty listened as he toweled off. He knew these jokers as three of the residents at the Golden Hills Senior Center, residents along with himself. He knew that they had worked out some type of arrangement with Ms. Bichette that gave them special privileges in exchange for work around the home. Typically, they wandered the halls at night, pressing back into bed a variety of rambling residents who had gone unknowingly absent from their rooms. Where Le Biche was the "law", they were the "order". But they had broken Le Biche's "law" and their "order" was now in disarray. Bichette saw them as untrustworthy and their lives were uncertain. Curly reminded Marty that she had already tried to drown him in the tub at PT.

"You were there! You know she is the Angel of Death! Man, if not for you, I'd be a gonner". Marty was puzzled but said nothing. "She already made one attempt to send me to the great beyond. You intimidated her. You're the only one that can stand up to her! You're the only one that can save me....save us! Absent you, what will become of us? Please, protect us....protect ME!"

Marty hoisted himself into bed. He lifted his legs and lay back onto the pillow. For once, he was unable to help Curly with his appeal. The speedo that he wore was becoming uncomfortable. He fidgeted to adjust it. He longed for a nice pair of long cotton boxer shorts. He lifted his legs up and tucked himself back into bed. He sat up, punched the pillow to prop it up and pulled up his sheet. He adjusted his goggles to the top of his head and lay back. With arms up, elbows out, and both hands behind his head, he stared up at the ceiling and wondered. He could remember the day he had first arrived. His wife and daughter brought him here. The sweet blonde with whom he was married now, going on... what was it...50 years? His exceptionally beautiful and exceptionally bright daughter had accompanied them. She was there to help her mom get through it. They were admitting Marty to Golden Hills, the Alzheimer's center. He had been having trouble remembering things. The Center was at the north end of town. Marty knew this part of town. His memory was better today.

As his wife and daughter completed paperwork, Marty had taken a walk. In those days, it was easy to slip away. They weren't used to watching him so closely. He had wandered east to the Avenues – a rich neighborhood of smaller, older homes, some inherited maybe twice or three times over and remodeled just as many times. Most of the current residents were older, some living alone. Some were young families with small kids.

The Avenues rested against the southern slope of a small mountain range that dominated the north end of the city. At "M" street, Marty found a park. The park was approximately 1-acre of fenced lawn on the steeply sloped southern exposure. Large oak trees guarded the entire perimeter at every side. A small pond with lily pads surrounded by flowers anchored the slope at the bottom. A few picnic tables were scattered miscellaneously at the pond's edge to invite area residents to rest and relax. Students from the nearby University occasionally stopped by to study or to play chess with the local wise ones who seemed to inhabit the place.

Marty's thoughts returned to the "here" and the "now". Today, the sky was blue. Large white cumulus clouds signaled a possible thunderstorm but for now, the day was warm and peaceful. He knew that he should get back to the water. He needed the peace that he felt while swimming. He knew now that a clear and full recollection could bring back the happiness associated with forgotten times, people, and places. He also knew that a life fully forgotten could bring peace...of a sort. A peace brought by a life without pain. Recollection may bring back happiness, but happiness brings with it the pain that accompanies. Yet was a peace without pain, really peace?

At present, Marty's mind was clear; and he knew what he had always known, but that he had forgotten yet again: that the therapy tub was too small to accommodate the swim that he needed. He also learned – again, with an absolute clarity that otherwise rarely came around - that the Senior Resident Center had no pool. His life here had been an illusion, perhaps a delusion- a type of delusion that accompanied old age. He knew that the closest thing to a pool here at the old folks' home was the large decorative fountain just outside the front entry. Kids would throw coins in the fountain to wish that grandma or grandpa would get better and come home. On good days, their moms and dads would wish for their own moms or dads to pass peacefully. On other days, they would just wish for them to pass. Marty was, for once, fully lucid and he must know, he must discover: Was anyone wishing for him?

Most nights, he would lay in bed hoping to find deep ocean waves or the cool mountain waters of home in which to swim. Instead, he found a crusty mattress in need of a change of sheets and a tired old pillow. The clarity that currently gave him such peace was also heavy and difficult to bear. Nevertheless, this moment of clarity had produced a plan. With age came religion, perhaps as a last hope to the ancients for a rescue, a rescue from the old folks' home if nothing more. Marty had picked up a Gideon's Bible that someone had left in his nightstand. Most likely it was Gideon, he smiled a bit at his own wit. He had been reading the Bible and was intrigued by the Red Sea, mostly by Moses' miraculous command over water. He wasn't sure, but he hoped that with his current clarity and with a nudge of the faith that seemed requisite for this type of endeavor, he may just be able to direct his search: no pills, no thrills, and arrive directly at the Red Sea, no fuss, no muss. His mind was open, but he knew that the tub in rehab was too small, too slow to accommodate but one. Marty also could not be sure, but the fountain out front may just attract too much attention. He couldn't risk it. The park and pond, just a few blocks away at "M" Street, should work out well and should allow for an appropriate moment of celebration.

"Hang in there boys! Hope is on the way!" he spoke to the ceiling. The boys looked at each other in puzzlement. Then Larry thought that he heard some steps in the hallway. He lifted his finger to signal quiet. Curly – always on alert – moved to avert what he thought to be another attack from Larry. He swung his mop out and behind to forestall the expected onslaught. Instead, he caught Mo in the knee. "Owww"!

Mo jumped to grab his knee and stomped on Curly's toe. "Ohhhh!"

Curly poked his outstretched finger into Larry's eye. "Ouucchh"!

Mo then grabbed both Curly and Larry by their respective collars and the wounded three began to exit. Marty figured that he could at last settle down to rest comfortably. He had some cogitating to do.

But Ms. Bichette surprised them all. "Well, well, well, if it isn't Mr. Markham and my very own three amigos". She had found them in Marty's room while on her nightly rounds. "Gentlemen, I presume that you do have some work to do? Don't you suppose that you should be at it, hmmmm? She asked with more than a touch of sarcasm.

"And you, Mr. Markham, what might you be doing up and out of bed at this early morning hour?" she asked with snit. "You know, I really must write you up for this incident. This will mean no tapioca for you at lunch today." With that, she quickly turned on Marty to gloat, but prematurely, "And, for good measure, I'll just confiscate the peanut butter that you're holding there beneath your pillow". Suddenly, and without warning, with one swift and synchronous movement of her left hand, she reached beneath Marty's pillow on the empty bed. Then, just as swiftly, she froze. She reached further into the void. She patted and patted, but came up short. Her smirk was gone, washed away. Where was the peanut butter? She had seen him, jar of Jiffy in hand and licking from a spoon, not 30 minutes past supper. She had watched him close the lid. She followed silently, tip toeing after him down the hall to see him stash it beneath his pillow. She was waiting for this very moment to confront him, for this chance to demean, for this opportunity to dismiss, for this moment to control the erstwhile "Keeper of the Flame" here at Golden Hills Senior Resident Center. Yet once more, he had out foxed her.

She steamed but fought to retain her self-control.

In a delightful surprise to boys there in the room, the top button on her tightly fit uniform popped off. Each ignored the flying button. Each instead stood transfixed by the tan-line at the cleavage inadvertently offered up by Le Biche as she bent there at the bedside. The line that divided the "tan" from the previously unexposed "white" skin there at swell over the top of her lacy white brassiere took away their respective breath. Each choked, their chests heaving, hearts pounding.

Larry gasped. Mo gulped. Curly glazed over... and Marty, who was now fully lucid, not only remembered the glory days of youth but recalled them with gusto. For these amigos, each was hugely surprised by the ever so slight rise pressing there, low and beneath their belts (in Marty's case – his speedo). This kind of experience had been most recently viewed as but a "dinosaur" from days long ago, hardly remembered and now extinct. But in this "here and now", the reptiles reigned; and Marty's was a raptor.

Curly swallowed hard and gurgled, "There. The dragon! Do you see it? See? There. At the left, at the collar bone and then down to her...her, ummm, yeah...and, then it hides under her ...yeah, well...it hides again". He coughed and wiped a bead of sweat from his forehead. Each stared admiringly, smitten and unable to move. To Marty, the confirmation was clear: Ms. Bichette was the mermaid that swam with him. She was the girl at the pool on the chaise lounge there at the pool. Boy, howdy! Some things were well worth remembering, the greater the detail the better.

Ms. Bichette seemed to know that she again had the upper hand. She stayed bent for a moment to let their eyes linger. Marty may have prevailed. But she was still in charge. She pulled her left hand from beneath the pillow and slowly straightened. She smoothed her dress, brushed back a few stray hairs from her face and calmed her features to compose herself. The boys remained transfixed. Their eyes had moved from her cleavage to her hemline three inches above her tan and very sexy knees.

She dictated officiously, "Gentlemen, I would recommend that each of you return to your rooms. I will be around shortly with your medications. Breakfast will be served at 8:00 a.m. sharp. Mr. Curly, as you know, you will receive no tapioca today. I will inform the kitchen". She narrowed her eyes at Curly. She turned to offer a stern look at Marty, but the best she could muster was a worried glance. She must deal with him on separate terms and quickly. The rubber on the soles of her shoes squeaked as she turned abruptly and disappeared into the hallway.

The sigh of relief was unanimous from the amigos. Each exhaled slowly. Their respective blood pressures declined in unison. Each grinned ever so slightly. Each fixed himself to avoid injury with movement; and as they exited the room for breakfast in the kitchen, each patted the other on the back for the memories that each had enjoyed in that singular and most glorious moment. From that day forward, each would bequeath a modicum of respect to Ms. Bichette for the Dragon that she bore and for the grace with which she had occasioned the lift in their ....well, shall we say: in their day. The Tres Amigos exited with a wave to Marty. Marty lay back to catch some rays from days long past. Sky – oh, so cloudless and so azure blue.

CHAPTER XIX

Marty had a sudden thought and sat up. For the first time in a long time he wondered, just what was the Time? Following this morning's eventful encounter with Ms. Bichette and the help she had offered to better clarify some of the confusion with his memory, he finished off with a deep and restful sleep, and it felt good. But for the first Time in a long Time, he had some work to do. He threw off the top sheet and jumped out of bed. Under the bed, he found his flippers. He must have slept for a short time. Likely, Maggie took off his flippers so he could rest. On his pillow at the top of his head, he found his goggles. He adjusted his speedo, affixed the flippers to his feet, and pulled the goggles over his eyes. Swiftly, he waddled from the room, headed straight for the front entry with his intentions set on the lake at M Street.

Breakfast had been served and the kitchen was cleaned and scrubbed, ready for the evening meal. Marty wasn't hungry. Various guests and visitors had arrived. Residents wandered the halls or spoke with friends inside their rooms. Marty was in no mood to talk, even if he could. At present, he wasn't sure that he remembered how to speak. The pretty blonde and her daughter who had brought the little girls to visit were registering at the front desk. They stood there as Ms. Bichette held out "Visitor" tags and a Magic Marker with which to write their names.

Marty marched, goggles affixed, eyes ahead with flippers angled outward at 45 degrees, and flopping. He recognized no one because he saw none. He did not direct his route to Physical Therapy. He knew that the whirlpool bath, for today, was irrelevant. His gaze was locked rather on the front yard fountain that was centered there in the circular drive at the entrance to the Golden Hills Senior Center, just outside the sliding glass door entry. The fountain was safety in the event that he couldn't elude the anticipated posse and had to abort. In truth, M Street was his goal.

Then without warning, Le Biche whistled. She was there again and had been watching. Larry, Mo, and Curly appeared and stood at attention at the front desk. Larry reached for the bronchio-dilator in his shirt pocket. His bronchial tubes restricted whenever he sensed confrontation. His lungs really could not handle the agitated air there in the foyer. Per usual, he was worthless in these types of encounters. His job was to spy for Le Biche. Typically, she would give him silent nod or a raised eyebrow to indicate whom she wanted him to surveil. She never gave specifics. He would simply observe and report back.

Marty remained oblivious and continued to march, his flippers flopping.

With some irony, Le Biche directed Mo and Curly with her arms like a ground crewman positioning a plane for take-off. Clearly, she did not expect what would come next.

As much as the Tres Amigos had come to like Marty, they had themselves to consider. Mo took center and behind Marty's line of travel. He was the "muscle" should Marty prove aggressive. He was large and black, and took the job by default as was assigned by Ms. Bichette. He was older than most of the staff there in the home. He'd been across the ages as measured by whether people called him "colored", "black" or "African- American" as opposed to "Mo" or the "big guy with two left feet". He had heard and experienced most of the racism over the course of his years. He didn't much like to remember.

In a high school that was "all-white" except for Mo and likely due to his size, but certainly influenced by his color, he was recruited to play football, never mind that he was no good. At 6'3" and 300 plus pounds, the coaches could not pass him up. They had recruited him from high school biology to 7th period athletics. Again, never mind that they never asked him. But, never mind the trade was worth it. He didn't like the life sciences so much. He preferred geology. When they could find no helmet to fit him and came to realize that he couldn't play a lick, he settled in nicely to 7th period study class. Somehow the fact that his uncle had played professionally at defensive tackle for the Green Bay Packers never translated to Mo. The coaches had heard the rumor and decided to make a run at it. The season was dismal at best. Mo had grown used to the perception rendered by both his size and his race. He accepted it and generally forgave peoples' ignorance. In these more supposedly "progressive" times, people could generally blame his size for whatever rejection they intended to render. No, you can't be a pilot. You're too big to fly planes. You won't fit into the cockpit. No, fine art won't work for you. Your hands are just too big to handle the tools. Computer science is no good either. Your fingers don't fit the keys.

Mo had come to like Marty who saw past these prejudices. He was a good man, but now there was trouble, and Mo had a job to do. He wasn't happy, but it was his job.

Curly moved to head off Marty at the sliding glass entry doors. He didn't like this business. He, too, liked Marty. Marty had saved his life. But, he was more afraid of Ms. Biche. With arm and hand movements, she directed him to post guard at the front entry to keep Marty from escaping to the outside. Reluctantly, he steered his mop and bucket-on-wheels toward the entry doors on a direct line to intercept.

Marty was fixed, even catatonic in his thrust for the door. His senses were primed. As he reached the foyer to first see Ms. Bichette and to give a nod to the two very pretty and very familiar pretty lady visitors getting badges at the desk, he anticipated trouble. He reached inside the pocket at the waist band of his speedo to retrieve a plastic pouch that carried his medications. These he had hidden from Ms. Bichette during bed check. Although uncertain as to which super power he might create, he knew, at this moment, that any power was better than none. He pulled three pills from the pouch. But then, he thought twice. He was clear -headed now. He knew as clear as day where he wanted to go. He could see the image of the Red Sea as taken from the quick perusal that he made of the Encyclopedia Britannica, letters "Q" through "T". Thankfully, this volume was on the shelf. Volumes E-G and X-Z were missing. He gambled and chose not to swallow his pills. He slipped them back into his speedo pouch.

Marty hadn't tried something like this without his pills for a long time. But again, this was the first Time in a long Time that he had been so clear -headed. The gamble was worth it. There is always a first Time, and this first Time gave back to Marty the foot speed that he had once known as a young man. His flippered feet swiftly began to paddle with almost invisible speed. Swiftly, quickly, back and forth, he padded toward the door. His arms swung in synchronicity like the wheel arms on a locomotive. Faster and faster, his speed increased exponentially. It appeared to most there in the foyer – including to the two pretty visitors there at the front desk and to Ms. Bichette (although she would not admit this publicly) - that Marty had taken flight. Others would say that he simply vanished, disappeared. No matter the perception. Curly failed to contain him at the door way. (Ms. Bichette would later accuse him of being purposefully lax – all the more reason to rid herself of this worthless "mope").

The automatic doors flew open and a "wind" blew from the foyer through the opening to the outside circular drive. The power of the wind messed with visitors' hair and clothing, pulled at the residents' robes, and dragged the hardwood furniture – chairs and tables - across the polished tile floor. People crashed into each other and tumbled. Artificial plants were blown over. A large waste basket, near the entry counter, upended. Litter, blown through the open door, was elevated into a small whirlwind. The whirlwind followed Marty's invisible exit as he marched toward the entry doors where Curly stood stationed, leaning on the mop stuck there inside his bucket. The passing whirlwind pulled water from the bucket to create a water spout. The spout pulled the bucket on wheels from beneath Curly's balanced stance. He fell flat on his face onto the polished floor tile. The automatic doors closed. The water spout collapsed bathing Curly in dirty soapy water and soggy litter. He had failed. Marty had exited. But had he really? Curly could not swear that he had seen Marty exit. Still perplexed, he sat up, wiped the water from his face and eyes with one of the wet tissues that he wore on his head, and looked to see Ms. Bichette staring sternly in his direction. It was clear, she had had enough. Painfully, that much was apparent.

Curly could see his life now, as if on "winged" feet, fiercely rush past his sputtering eyes. If Marty was gone, Curly had lost a true protector. If Marty was gone, Curly would be blamed. He knew it. He stood up, trying not to slip, and quickly retrieved the "Caution: Wet Floor" signs from the janitor's closet. He hastily placed them around the entry and began mopping up the spilt water. He was nothing, if not both careful and efficient. He worked and tried to act as if nothing had happened. For now, nothing had.

It was the evening hours. Too many visitors had come to see the residents at the "old folks' home". Ms. Biche would wait until "her time" later that night to take care of Mr. Curly,once and for all. With the fuss over Marty temporarily out of the way, she should be able to finish the task only recently interrupted by that pesky Mr. Thorskelsen. Her chance for him would come soon enough. We shall see "my pretty", she thought. Yes, we shall see.

CHAPTER XX

His getaway was "clean". Once he flew through the front entry, he forgot entirely about the fountain. Instead he headed, on "winged feet" as it were, straight to M street and the small lake. Rather than take M street and climb the hill to the main entrance to the park, he took the direct route along Front Street that ran parallel to the front end of the park at the bottom of the hill. This more secluded and less used part of the lake was separated from Front Street first by a large copse of aspen trees that ran along the side of Front Street and then by a deep layer of tall pine trees that bordered the lake.

Marty was on a mission, intent on finding what the Red Sea was set to offer him. Still, he felt a new found freedom, a freedom that he had not enjoyed for quite some Time, years maybe or even decades. He felt the excitement of an escapee, unjustly imprisoned for a long, long Time; and was now out and free to explore but with nervous excitement, the exhilaration, and the fear of getting caught that accompanies. He needed to take it in, to explore it, to embrace it before he was recaptured. The going was tough. Walking the city streets and sidewalks in his flippers was awkward, even difficult. But he couldn't submerge, not just yet. He was too excited to be out!

He clambered and clunked his way down the sidewalk on Front Street. He crossed Main, careful to go with the green Walk sign. He waved to other pedestrians along the way on the sidewalk with him, many of whom could only stare in amazement as he passed. A few in cars would whistle and point at him; some good naturedly, some in derision.

He was both amazed and confused at the number of people he saw, both walking the City streets and driving in their cars with what appeared to be a small television set or a streamlined "walkie talkies" that they held to their ears and sometimes spoke into or sometimes just watched. If they were TV's, they had no antennas. How could they get any reception? If they were phones, they had no dial, nor any slot in which to put a coin to make a call. Marty looked around. He was surprised that he could find no phone booth on any of the street corners, nor affixed to any of the walls at the nearby grocery store or across the street at the bank. But he was delightedly curious to see people pulling cash money out of the walls of the bank at place identified as an ATM. Who'd a thunk it? Money straight from the walls of a bank!

Another one-half block and he stumbled into a familiar place. It was an old elementary school converted to a boarding house. Marty had spent 5 days here some time back. He could not now recall just why nor exactly when, but he did remember it. He remembered preparing for bed and settling down to sleep in room filled with maybe 40 bunk beds and maybe 80 young men – all of whom held the same goal – a worthy goal - but in different parts of the world where they would be sent to serve for a period of two years. Marty remembered now, it was a church "mission"- dedicated service, wholly volunteer and unpaid.

"We were just 'boys'", Marty thought.

He recalled a young man named Kincaid, another, Olsen. They were bunkmates. Olsen was from Panquitch, Utah. Kincaid was from New York City. The five-day introductory sessions at the converted elementary school sought to teach each of these unique and uniquely postured young men to treat each other with respect, to love one another, as the preaching goes. Marty smiled as he recalled the second night. The indoctrination had been steady and ongoing. The young men tried hard to learn and to incorporate. Olsen was the room monitor. His job was to turn off the lights exactly at 10 pm at which time the entire room was asked to settle in, to go to sleep, to be refreshed for tomorrow's next day wake-up at six am. Kincaid was a stranger to the local culture. The preaching touched him, but he was uncertain as to how best to take it in, to utilize it, to best express his positive feelings.

Olsen had just finished polishing his shoes. Kincaid had just won a contest for the number of push-ups that he could do between the back rails of bunk beds placed end to end. Showers were over. Teeth were brushed. The young men were ready for bed and had just settled in. All were bedded down in their individual bunks. Several engaged in light- hearted gossip; some shared stories, recollections, even worries for what the next two years should reveal. All were filled with optimism and excitement. Marty remembered these days. They were good Times. He had participated.

Olsen finished his shoes. He stood up, walked to the light switch on the wall next to the door, and flipped the switch. The roomed darken. The whispers and murmuring began to settle. And, then...

Kincaid felt it somehow appropriate to share his "feelings" with his assigned companion: Olsen. The person with whom he should spend the next several days; the person who shared the same "testimony" of the truth, the same faith, the same doctrines, the same religion as did he. Surely, Kincaid must have thought, and legitimately so, that Olsen was a person whom he should love, as his Savior had loved him as was written in his Scriptures. He couldn't contain himself.

"Elder Olsen?" he inquired.

The entire room heard the query. Whatever agitation was left in the room was quelled. The room fell quiet, no sound, not a rustle of a sheet, not a slight cough or a sneeze, nothing. The entire room bent to hear the reply.

"Yes, Elder Kincaid?" Olsen too was curious.

Then, following a lengthy pause, undoubtedly intended to help Kincaid screw up his courage, Kincaid pronounced.

"I love you".

The silence thereafter was deafening. And then, the in one corner despite best efforts to an escape:

"Pffftt, PPFF..."

With the dike broken, the dam ruptured, the explosion was ominous and loud:

"BUWAHHH, HHHHHHAAAAAA, HAAAA, HAAAAAA. BAAHAAAA, BUWWAAAAHHHAA. AAAAHHAAAAHHHAA, BUUWAHHAAAHAAA, UUHH....HAAWWWW, HAWWWW, HAWWWW..."

And over the intercom, far beneath rollicking peals of laughter, a voice could be heard but barely entertained.

"Brethren, Brethren....calm down! Go to sleep! Your day comes early. Now get to sleep!"

For a Time, the roar of laughter continued but eventually, the intercom held sway and the room calmed. The next day, Kincaid had arisen early and taken breakfast by the time the others came in. For most of the day, he stayed ensconced in a small classroom doing "independent study". Some would grin and wave to him through the small glass window in the door. Others would snicker, but Time heals all and in large measure, the tough guy from New York City overcame his own embarrassment; and, to their respective credits, the other young men let him of the hook. "But for the grace of God, go I..." Marty guessed that this was the thinking. Still, he had to smile.

CHAPTER XXI

He should waste no more time. Marty flip flopped his way back down Front Street in the direction he had come and silently slipped between the Aspen trees and pines. The lake was beautiful this time of year. He inhaled deeply, held it, and dove. He was set to explore, determined to find answers. But to what, he didn't know. All he did know was that he had actually escaped and through the front entry doors, no less. He was in untested waters. There was no telling what he might find in this beautiful lake. Who could say what he might find at these depths.

He had never been to the lake previously, and if he had, he didn't remember. Typically, he avoided the smaller waters: too little to explore, and he hadn't yet gotten a good enough grip on time management to make it worthwhile. But soon after entering, his attention was drawn to a small dot of light that seemed to mark the bottom of the lake. The lake was much deeper than he had expected. As he drew downward, the light grew. The brightness expanded until he came to recognize...The Library! It was The Library that Marty visited in his dream at the swimming pool that day with the three little girls. On that day, he had somehow flirted with Time travel. No, he corrected himself, not Time "travel', but rather Time "management".

He smiled to recall just how pretty had been those three little girls on the day they got older. He recalled that, when at the pool that day, he had not been allowed inside the beautiful Library; maybe because it was only a dream.

Today, he swam up to what appeared to be a front glass façade. In fact, the entire front was glass. He could see no knobs, handles, or hinges. He reached to touch the glass, but felt nothing. He tried to feel around the glass façade, but felt nothing. Still, as he moved his hands over the apparent surface of the glass, the façade suddenly slid open at the center. Interestingly, when the façade opened, water from the lake did not spill through the opening and into The Library. He tried again to touch the glass. His hand passed through into the Library's interior and what felt to be the cool dry air inside. He pulled his hand back in surprise. He hadn't expected to nothing between himself and the interior. Today, it seemed, The Library was open for business. Tentatively, Marty stepped through what had appeared to be glass.

Once through, Marty heard a glass door of sorts slide close behind him. But when he turned to look, he again found no glass. He put a hand out to feel for the door, but his hand dipped directly into water. He felt around some more to find "glass" at either side of the door, but found none. In fact, although The Library seemed to be housed in walls of glass, in his exploration of the entire Library, Marty found no glass nor walls of any sort. Once inside, and upon closer examination, he found nothing at any of the four sides, to separate the lake water from the cool dry interior. The water simply stood to allow Marty to step through and into the welcome dry interior.

With that first step, a sign lit up in front of his eyes: "Please, remove your footwear. Our Library is a clean Library. Thank you". Marty bent to pull the flippers from his feet. He removed his goggles from off of his forehead and placed them together with the flippers in the small box provided. After placing his flippers, both the box and sign disappeared. Hmmm, Marty thought. He was anxious, but impressed.

With that accomplished, he took another step. Another sign lit up: "Take the robe made available for your comfort; place the socks on your feet to protect The Library floor".

Marty looked around. On a small and elaborately cushioned bench, he found a white, silken robe together with a pair of fluffy white cotton socks. Along the soles of the cotton socks, he found an array of rubberized dots placed there for safety to aid with traction on the polished floors exquisitely comprised of shiny crème colored marble tiles in large 3' x 3' squares.

He put on the robe. As he wrapped it around himself, he felt the soft silk with his thumb and forefinger. Never had he felt anything so smooth, so aesthetically warm and pleasing. He sat on the bench to put on his socks. His feet were old and aching, but the socks seemed to remove both the age and the ache. He stood and immediately, the bench disappeared.

As in his dream, The Library held two bookshelves, aligned parallel to each other. Both were identical in appearance, rich and red, large and long – made of a Cherrywood. The one to his left carried an identifying sign that read: "Self-Help: Access Restricted to the Speed of Light"; the sign on the one to the right read: "Observation Only". Marty puzzled. He wasn't sure what the signs meant. Large mirrors on the walls at either side reflected an infinite number of similar bookshelves. Marty stepped up to the bookshelf to his right and ran his hand along the smooth and polished surface. The wood was exquisite; the Cherrywood – a beautiful compliment to refinement in this educational facility. Chandeliers overhead cast a glorious light. The crystalline chips quietly chimed in the circulating breeze that kept the temperature delightful.

He turned to examine one of the mirrors and the bookshelf reflected there. As he reached for the glass, his hand instead encountered the same smoothly polished Cherrywood. It was not the expected reflection, but another shelf; this one with a different array of books than the set found on the first shelf that he examined. He stepped to the edge of the first shelf in the mirror to see behind the first shelf and into the mirror. He was nothing if not logical. He expected to find nothing. Instead, he encountered yet another

Cherrywood shelf. This, too, carried an entirely different and unique set of books: periodicals, magazines, newspapers – an entire history of Time in various and differing segments as may be requested. But the signs at the top of every set of two were the same for each set: Self Help: Access Restricted to the Speed of Light and Observation Only.

Marty grew even more curious. He wondered whether this enchanting Library might hold in reserve, any books or references for 1967. No sooner had he thought that than the schedule of books on the shelf in front of him quickly rolled and stopped, rolled again and stopped. Each book on the shelf carried the Dewey Decimal tab on its spine: "mlh1967". Individual tabs on each book carried different tabs that followed the "mlh1967" tabulation. Those presented to Marty, apparently at his request, carried the tab: "mlh1967.????" Marty was unsure as to the reason for the question marks that followed the general tab.

He had some familiarity and concluded that the question marks dealt with the unknown "month", "week", "day", "minute", and "second". Apparently, these remained questioned since Marty had only wondered about the year 1967 in general. In fact, he never really made a request, but only thought about the year, 1967, and he'd given no thought to any of the smaller increments which had remained blank to his mindset.

Marty needed to test out this new Library. His curiosity overwhelmed. Still, he stayed cautious. He figured he'd give it a try on something not so significant as 1967. He stepped up to the Cherrywood and opened his mind to the first thought he could muster. He was always curious about which representation of the parting of the Red Sea was the most, if not accurate, then at least the most entertaining. Immediately the shelves began to roll up in sets of two, each with the same listings at the head: Self-Help: Access Restricted to the Speed of Light and Observation Only. Just as quickly, the books began to slide across the shelves and within seconds, if that, the shelves stopped. At the first shelf – Observation Only - two volumes were set in front of him. Dewey Decimal listed the first as: 1956???-Heston. The second was listed as: 2005???-Bales. Marty grabbed both from the shelf. He began to peruse first one, flipping the pages, and speed reading the text; then the other. He was not sure exactly what he would find, but generally he knew what he was after. He marked pages in each and set them aside onto the small pull-out table at the center of the grand set of Cherrywood shelves.

Far away, as if in the distance, he heard what he thought to be "white noise"; his head began to spin, and his vision began to flip like an unchecked horizontal hold on a black and white TV. The "white noise" grew louder and faded, and grew louder again. The buzz increased and Marty grew dizzy. He held his head as if to stop the symptoms. He reached into his speedo and pulled out a large vitamin pill with an iron supplement. He tried to avoid the hard meds. He pressed his temples in an effort to quell the "white noise". He set his feet wide to postpone the dizziness. The effort was worth it. Silence prevailed, as Marty held himself steady to qualm his nerves.

Then almost instantly he was transported up from the depths. His trip had become a voyage. Somehow, the Lake at M Street was unfathomable. His ascent went on for what seemed like minutes, even hours through the waters to what he figured would be the surface of the Lake at M Street. But when he finally broke the surface, if for no better reason than to breath, things had changed. The sun was high overhead. The trees that once bordered M Street and shaded the lake were gone. The ever present and ever expanding ripples from a variety of gnats, mites, mosquitoes, and flies on the water had disappeared. The splash of a trout taking an evening meal was gone. The surrounding lawn and upper parking lot were also gone.

The hot sun here had baked both insect and animal traffic into submission. Noise from the auto traffic on M Street had ceased. All traffic here was done by camel. Marty's feet found purchase in a sandy bottom. He treaded in a turquoise sea in water to his chest. As he looked about, he found sand everywhere. Large dunes along the shoreline moved easily with the gentle breeze like a serpent headed home. He saw nothing but blue skies extending far away into the distance. He swam closer to the beach until his feet found purchase ,and he stood up in water to his waist.

Instead of the fresh water at M Street, he tasted heavy salt on his lips. He lifted the goggles from his eyes and wiped his face to look about. The long view was sparse, but beautiful: barren sand and rock surrounded the waters and contrasted with the sea of beautiful turquoise. He was definitely not in the Lake at M Street.

Wherever he was, Time seemed irrelevant. He could not say just "when" he had arrived. He had supposed either 1956 or 2005 and had selected them together for his own convenience more or less. Given Time, he knew he could develop a much more precise search methodology so that perhaps he might even find Moses escaping the Egyptians to better know just how he had done it. In any event, he was here. He thought a moment. He pretty much knew that he had found the Red Sea. His request had determined as much, observation had confirmed. After all, his question had related to two Hollywood epics in which a character called Moses sought to cross yeah...the Red Sea from Egypt. He looked around some more. Yeah, he thought, I got that right!

He wondered why they called it that: the "Red" Sea. The exquisite color appeared almost turquoise. He checked the sun and figured he was on the western shoreline, Egypt for sure and likely across from Saudi Arabia and well north of the Tropic of Cancer. Yikes, he thought. Given the topography, he figured this may be considered –from a climactic standpoint- to be a "temperate" zone; but from a political point of view, the climate in this location would be better described as "torrid". Yeoowwee.

Marty treaded the sandy bottom in water up to his chest. As he walked to the beach, he looked more closely and could see the "red" in the Red Sea. He guessed that this was the "cyanobacteria" that he had read about in the encyclopedia. The shoreline, itself, was barren.

Across the water, in the distance, he saw what he thought to be some kind of luxury hotel or apartments, maybe. People, like tiny ants, were bustling about, swimming, tanning and otherwise recreating. In the skies overhead, Marty could hear the vague roar of passenger jet and his eyes found the contrail. On these beautiful waters, also in the distance, he saw what looked like huge tankers passing one another. These spoke of a more modern era, but to Marty, it may as well have been 1600 years B.C. As far as anyone could say, he might be back with Moses.

He affixed his goggles and dove back into the warm and shallow waters. Exploration was fun. He found a wide variety of brightly colored coral, an array of invertebrates and 200 different species of hard and soft corals. The reefs extend along more than 1200 miles of shoreline. The coastal reefs are visited by a fish unique to the Red Sea and by 44 different species of shark. Marty's Britannica told him that the Red Sea is a rich and diverse ecosystem. A variety of volcanic islands rise from the center of the sea. Most are dormant. But one recent eruption was violent with the formation of 2 new islands.

As he snorkeled, his fin came loose and he swam back to the beach to relax a moment. Again, the landscape was desolate but beautiful, especially in contrast to the gorgeous waters. As he sat there, he heard a commotion. Just up the shoreline, he saw two men dressed like a couple of ancient Egyptian pharaohs. Each wore a Nemes, a royal headdress. Each had on a Shendyt, a royal loin cloth that was covered in accordion pleating. One looked an awful lot like Charlton Heston; the other, like Christian Bale. Marty smiled. He had seen both movies about Moses. This was more like it. The Library had put him in what seemed to be the right place.

A film crew surrounded both Heston and Bales together with large cameras, spotlights, a boom, a dolly and slider, a director's chair and a clapper board, and other miscellaneous items found with a film crew. The guy seated in the director's chair was frustrated. He sat as if bored while he waited for an argument to clear between the two

Hollywood superstars – one more a superstar than the other; the determination as to which rested with which generation of moviegoer one would more naturally associate. A large blue screen was placed behind them. From what Marty could tell, the debate was about how the parting of the Red Sea should be displayed.

HESTON: "How many times do I have to say it, the Miracle of the Red Sea was just that, a miracle. Moses raised his staff and the waters parted, simple as that?"

BALE: "Oh, c'mon you old duffer. Today's audiences are much more sophisticated and, if I don't miss my guess, so is today's technology. You can't fool the folks with a few magic tricks. You've got to explain it so a six-year old can understand."

HESTON: "What...a six-year old, huh? Sophisticated, really? Look, it's easy. I'll show you. He stood at the shoreline and while holding a broomstick, he raised his arms, spread them high and wide, and began to emote at the Sea. "Stand still (pregnant pause as he turned to see the reaction of Bale and film crew) and see the Salvation of the Lor...duh..."

The director interrupted and stifled Heston. His irritation was clearly evident.

DIRECTOR: "Gentlemen, please. Did we really need to fly all the way to Egypt to film this scene? Did we really need to bring along the "blue screen" to capture what could have been easily filmed back in Burbank? Did we really need to bring along nearly 100 extras dressed in full costumes and driving chariots to make this work here....in Egypt... really?

Bales suppressed a grin. The assembled crew and extras nodded their agreement. Okay, sure. They all had voted to come along. But the hope was that they could convince the two blowhard actors to avoid the Red Sea altogether and to part the Mediterranean instead, somewhere near the South of France if they had planned it correctly. But no such luck.

Marty had hoped to catch a glimpse of Hollywood magic, but he grew bored with the two prima donnas. This battle of egos was set to endure. He repaired the strap on the loose fin and tightened both. He replaced the goggles and adjusted them against his eyes. He hiked up his speedo and launched back into the Red Sea. Interestingly, the Red Sea was relatively shallow, at least in so far as seas go. He hadn't stroked out more than 100 yards when he spotted what appeared to be an interesting artifact on the bottom about 25 feet down. It some sort of stick or staff. It was lodged tightly in the sandy layers with one end sticking out. At first, he had thought to ignore it. It seemed to be nothing but a bloated chunk of wood stuck to the bottom. But the wooden staff intrigued him. Carefully, he went about scraping away the sand and hard packed clay that surrounded it. As he worked cautiously so as not to bruise it, he could see that it was a good six to seven feet in length and about two inches in circumference. The exposed end, the end that was intriguing was curved over and downward; the other end appeared worn as if it had been used as walking cane of sorts. He successfully freed the staff, rose with it to the surface, and swam back to shore.

Bales and Heston continued to squabble. Bales was more for the subtle approach to the parting of the Red Sea in which he portrays a more confused, less confident Moses while posed there at the waters' edge, where he is simply trying to wrangle nearly 500 thousand Israelites out of Egypt and across – or rather – through the waters to the promised land. Upon arrival there at the shoreline of the Red Sea, the billowing surge blockading their passage with not a Hebrew in sight who could swim or knew squat about how to build a boat, and the Pharoah accompanied by his soldiers in hot pursuit, Moses (Bales) becomes flummoxed as just what to do next. He is looking for escape, but – unlike Heston – he has no thought that the Red Sea will provide an answer. Bales snaps his fingers to get the Director's attention.

BALES: "Look! I see it this way. Moses is flummoxed. He walks up to the water's edge and emotes". He smiled and nodded to the director, to the assembled crew and extras. "Now watch", he says as he stands at the shoreline and stares at the waters, screws up his face, and with subtlety and good acting; he emotes frustration, anxiety, uncertainty, even some confusion maybe. In exasperation, he throws his staff into the waters and falls down on the beach with the rest of 500 thousand or so Israelites and...well he, uh...he goes to sleep.

The Director sits in his chair thoroughly bored, his elbow on the chair arm, his chin in his hand, but he curiously opens one eye to better ensure that he had heard right. The extras too, have stretched out.

Yep, Bales explains that Moses has concluded that the best way to deal with the hard charging Egyptians pounding their Chariots in pursuit is to sleep on the beach and when he awakens, the waters have miraculously diminished and deep within himself, he finds a new resolution and the wherewithal to lead his 500 thousand across on... well, not so much "dry", but rather "wet" and "soggy" ground, maybe even... "spongey".

Marty listened to the two varying versions of the crossing of the Red Sea. Hell, he thought. I could swim it in the time it takes these jokers to expound. The sun was high, the wooden staff was sunbaked and dried out, and Marty's shoulders had taken a slight burn. It was time for him to head out. He had some swimming that needed doing. He waddled back to the shoreline and lightly stirred the edge water with the tip of the staff. The ripples began to spread wider and wider. Suddenly, the waters began to divide, to pile up at each side. The division spread to expose dry ground. The division grew wider. The walls of water on either side piled higher and higher. A relative few fish, apparently caught unawares, began to fall from what had been water but which was now the sky. A few tourists on inner tubes fell from the sky, as well, and bounced away as they landed. The director stirred in his chair and again opened one eye. He sat up quickly, looked around, and shouted to wake up the crew and extras.

DIRECTOR: "Let's go! Let's go!, Let's go! Move, move, move! ...and Action! Move, move, move! No, no, only the Israelites! You, he says pointing at the Egyptian extras, you're supposed to follow.... FOLLOW...as in after or behind Moses and his crowd. Gottit? Charles, we're rolling!"

Heston looked at Bales and saluted as he took the lead of the 40 or so extras dressed as recently enslaved "Israelites".

HESTON: "Hey! You there with the crew, be sure to bring the "blue" screen. Be sure to up the count to 500 or more. It's got to look big, really big!"

BALES: "The 'blue screen'. Heston never had such a thing back in his day. There was no such thing when he was 'acting' if you could call it that. Sheesh!" he muttered under his breath.

As Heston led the chosen folks to the Promised Land, Bales put his face into his hands. He shook his head. Resignedly, he grabbed an Egyptian nemes and put it on his head. He strapped a shendyt around his waist.

Marty had studied "fashion" back in the day. He recognized these as respective pieces of Egyptian haute couture. The shendyt was a kilt-like garment worn by most folks that reached just above the knee. The nemes, however, was a striped head dress highly fashionable and worn exclusively by the Pharoahs. Bales must have figured that if he had to go out, he was going out as Egyptian royalty.

He looked around to find an Egyptian chariot set to follow the Israelites. He jumped in and directed the current occupant with a quick jab of his thumb to get out. He was a bit nervous about crossing through the Red Sea on dry ground. He had read his Bible. He knew what the end would be for the Egyptians. Damn, he thought. This would be over for him soon enough. He'd better call his agent. Maybe he could get another gig somewhere near the south of France. Meanwhile, Heston was hard charging, high stepping with broomstick in hand and headed for the Promised Land.

Marty held onto the staff. He was intrigued. He was tempted to take it with him back to Golden Hills, but he knew that the staff belonged to its own Time. Besides, in No Time, he knew that he could find the staff again, that is of course, should he need it.

And, he was satisfied with himself. He had learned quite accidently how to divide the Red Sea. He returned to his earlier "dig" from which he had taken the staff. At present, the ground around it was now perfectly dry, the soils easy to excavate manually. He re-buried the staff and left it as he had found it. He walked to the wall of water to his immediate right. He cinched up his speedo, replaced the goggles over his eyes, and stuck his head inside the Red Sea to check his route. The wall roiled around him, but he stood on dry ground. He popped his head back out and instead, put his hand into the wall. He pulled it out to expose his index finger which he stuck into his mouth and pulled it out quickly with a loud "POP". He held it up to the wind to assess the wind direction. He made his assessment, reached forward with both hands and arms, and pulled himself in. The wall swallowed him. This swim had been memorable, he thought with a smile.

What was so satisfying about the experience was that he felt that he belonged and that he could stay for as long as he liked. In No Time, Time, itself, is irrelevant. He somehow knew that he could stay as long as he wished and that however long he stayed could be but a moment or light years. He also knew that he was welcome back to No Time at any Time that he may need to step out.

CHAPTER XXII

Time was irrelevant to the patrons of the old folks' home. In the months, days, and hours that followed Marty's exit, a relative calm returned to Golden Hills. A temporary peace had descended. He was gone. No one really knew for how long. No one was even certain whether he would be back. In fact, no one was certain whether he was even gone, at all. Rumors were rife about just what had happened. Some said he never made it out the front entry and was back in bed. Some said that he never had escaped, that he never tried to escape, and the he had passed on and was dead and gone. In any event, with his profound "presence" now missing at the residence, throughout the facility, up and down the hallways, in and out of the rooms, the closets, the corridors, the kitchen, and even the basement morgue, Ms. Bichette had restored a semblance of order – her order.

Maggie spent her days ensconced in her wheel chair in front of the TV, there in the front reception area to ponder the Days of Our Lives. That was the best description one could find. Mostly, she sat slumped over in the chair, television on, and staring- staring long and hard into the blue light as if waiting for someone (or for it: the blue light) to take her home. Tonight was no different.

She missed Marty. She couldn't believe that he was gone. She liked to flirt with him. He was cute and easy to talk to. She was thin as a rail back then with long brown hair and a sexy smile. Yeah well, she thought. That Time is long gone. They had been in high school together. Marty and his crowd had decided to take Home Economics or "Home Ec" their senior year. He and his five buddies were the only boys in the otherwise all girl class. They formed their own "kitchen" – one of five. Each consisted of a table with six occupants, a stove, and the requisite cooking utensils and a sink for doing dishes at clean up.

Maggie took the sixth chair at Marty's table. The team worked well. Maggie mixed all the recipes and cooked the food. Marty and his buddies ate and cleaned up. Maggie earned an "A" for them all.

One afternoon, just before class started, the two were talking. He was riding on the back legs of his chair while seated there at kitchen table number six in Home Ec. He was sympathetic to yet another issue presented to her by her boyfriend. Whether it was his kindness, his new cologne, or the slick new shirt made of brown corduroy that he wore, she kissed him. The kiss was long and, at least to Marty, seemed intentionally so. What was not intentional or otherwise wholly unexpected was Marty's return kiss. He slipped his tongue into her mouth. She stood up straight, stunned. The kiss was nice and for a moment, she thought to return it. But she had her principles and her boyfriend was still her boyfriend. She rose up, reared back her hand, and slapped Marty a hard lick on his cheek. He pitched backwards, chair and all. For a moment, he lay on the floor in a daze then struggled to get up. Maggie reached to help him. He stood as she steadied him and brushed him off. Marty apologized. He should not have kissed her like that. But with her, he attempted explain, he couldn't help himself. He hoped she would understand. Of course, she did. The truth was, she still remembered that kiss and enjoyed the memory almost as much as the day it happened. She smiled wryly as she faded back to sleep. She missed Marty. He had taught her much while he was here.

Mo was on night duty at his usual station there at the front desk. Ms. Bichette was with him, just finishing her nightly duties. She saw Maggie silhouetted in the television's blue light, asleep in her chair. She instructed Mo to turn of the television set, tuck Maggie in, and cover her up. She slept well in her chair and she could stay there for the night. He was to "keep an eye on her". As he moved to the front reception, he looked for the remote to turn off the set, the set suddenly went dark. It was a wall set and had no switch. The reception area descended into blackness. At first, silence prevailed and in this place, silence was golden. Generally, the hallways reverberated through the night with the grunts and groans of the residents caused by nightmares, indigestion, and a host of other age related ailments. Maggie added her fair share. Tonight was no different. Mo didn't know why or how, but the set was off. His job done, he contemplated the silence a moment longer. He moved to the closet to recover a blanket and approached Maggie to tuck her in. As he placed the blanket over her and patted her kindly, she began to moan uncomfortably, at first almost imperceptibly: oww, ohh, uhhhnn, uhhnn, owww, mmm, ohhh, ohhh, uhhhnn uhnnn, mmm, mmm, ohhh, ohhh, - ever so slightly. On and on, she droned. Then, within minutes, the moans turned to a wail: Aiiee, Aaahhh, Aiiieee, Eeee, Aiiee, Ohhh, Aiiee, Ahhhe. Like Johnny Weismiller in a Tarzan movie, she pounded her chest. Unlike Tarzan, she did not stand, but instead pounded her feet on the floor as if trying to put out a grass fire. And, boy did she wail!

Mo stood dumbfounded. To him it was obvious that Maggie needed comfort and that the only comfort available to her there at Golden Hills was the blue light from the television set. She need the TV set to be on. She needed the blue light!

Maggie continued to wail. Mo plugged his ears. He looked to Biche for instruction. He wasn't about to turn the set back on in violation of her last order. She was watching from the front desk. She was watching, not curiously, but intently as if trying to assess the level of discomfort. Mo could swear she was taking notes. He squinted to better signal that he needed some help, some signal for him to turn off the noise. Seeing none, he looked around for the remote. Biche saw his intention. She held up her right hand and nodded for him to wait. She was studying. She wetted the tip of her pencil with her tongue, jotted a few more notes, slapped her notepad closed and put the pencil back behind her right ear. She straightened her hair, smoothed her uniform, and only then did she look at Mo. Her notes now complete and her posture at the home reconfirmed, she would now restore calm to the residence. With an up flip of her finger, she gave the okay for Mo to turn the set back on.

In the interim, Maggie's wail had become a screech. AAHHH... AAAH...AHHIIIIEEE!!!! Mo needed to move quickly. Where the hell was that remote? Upon first glance around, he could not see it anywhere. He began a frantic search. It was not on top of the televisions set, on the nearby table, nor anywhere on, in, or around the couch. Mo pulled the entire couch apart. It was not on the fireplace mantel or on the upper ledge. Maggie screamed and screamed again and again. Mo grew even more frantic. He broadened his search.

He approached Ms. Biche at the desk with a pitiable glance to beg for her help. The remote was not at the front desk with Ms. Biche. She smiled and shrugged. Maggie had calmed back to a moan. The moan turned to a mindless babble. She now fought wildly to get out of the wheelchair in which she was restrained. As she squirmed and fought the wheelchair, there beneath her voluminous bottom, Mo spotted his deliverance. There, trapped beneath her left buttock and the seat of the wheelchair was the remote. This would take some doing.

Maggie was stuck firmly in the wheelchairand Mo was not inclined to again approach Ms. Bichette for an authorization to release her. He would need to figure a way to remove the remote that was bound tightly between the large left buttock and the leather on which the buttock sat. Strategic analysis confirmed. The safest approach would be low and from the rear. Mo decoyed as if to leave. He rubbed his hands and whistled as he spoke to Maggie, "Good night, Maggie. Sweet dreams. I'll see ya in the morning. Night, night", he said as he extravagantly strode away as if to return to go to work.

Once out of Maggie's direct line of sight, he quickly dropped to his knees and crawled back to the rear of the wildly gyrating Maggie. Her chair continued to rattle, to shake, and to bounce erratically. But the brakes held firm and the chair stayed, pretty much, in place. Maggie continued to caterwaul.

Mo peeked through the space left between the short leather back rest and the top of the leather seat; a space of about six inches. Maggie's large bottom continued to bounce and every now and then,

Mo could catch a glimpse of the remote, there under her overly large, left buttock. He waited, trying to assess the timing of Maggie's bouncing and the violent bum drop that could very well take his relatively short life should his attempt to reach the remote prove either a dash too early or a smidgen too late. He was only 52. These geezers at the home were pushing 90 and some even 100 years, or more. Granted, they weren't worth much here. Golden Hills was nothing more than a warehouse for the decrepit.

Families came and went. But the residents stayed, and eventually died. Some earlier than others, some later, but the only way out was in the undertaker's carriage. Whether to the soil, to the sea, or to the flames was most often uncertain, unless one had served in the military: the Army meant soil; the Navy meant sea; and, well --- the flames meant the easiest and cheapest way out.

Mo could sense that Ms. Bichette grew impatient. She wanted order restored. He must move now and quickly, or otherwise face the music. By his assessment, Maggie's bounce lasted and the space between buttock and remote remained open for between .5 and 1.2 second; the reach was approximately the length from his fingertips to his elbow. (Mo never really dealt in such precision, but he always liked to think that he could).

The buttock came up. Mo reached quickly with his right hand and diagonally across the vast expanse of white cotton undies to the left sided buttock to grasp for the television remote. Almost immediately, he knew that he had miscalculated. He should have reached with his left. The 45 degree angle across both buttocks required at least twice the reach. Now, Mo knew only that he needed to dive, all in, to reach the prize. The diagonal measure across was at least an arm's length or more. He did not hesitate. Fate would take him, or not. But, he was committed.

Then the bottom did not so much fall but, simply floated down. It descended more that it dropped. It was more of a transition than a collapse. For Mo, it seemed a transition from life into an after-life, of sorts. He was trapped there beneath two burgeoning buttocks, which held him firmly yet – he must admit – very comfortably bound. Maggie quieted and sighed as she continued to settle. She calmed, was soon asleep, and lightly snoring. For a moment, Mo felt comforted. The white cotton above was clean and soft. He nuzzled his left cheek against the cushiony pillows. He closed his eyes to sleep. But thoughts invaded.

The air here was fresh, but Mo worried. Maggie -he knew - was prone to putter, and he did not want to take the measure. He had been successful in his dive for the remote, never mind his miscalculation. But he was now trapped, unable to move. In his right hand he squeezed the remote, but his right arm was trapped beneath Maggie although, he was capable of some movement. Maggie was big and soft, almost light and fluffy. And, Mo could wiggle some.

His right cheek pressed against leather, and when he moved he could feel the squeeze between leather and cheek. It would burn if he moved or was dragged too quickly. Ms. Bichette could not save him without some pain. This much was true.

Maggie relaxed further, apparently enjoying her rest. She fell more deeply asleep and Mo was further ensconced. He knew that he needed to act fast otherwise,he would likely suffocate in the Downey softness of what were two very soft and seductive pillows. In essence, Mo knew that he could die here. He also knew that unlike many others at the home, he was not ready.

Lying there directly below, Mo held an advantage of sorts. He could hear Maggie's bowels rumble. He had an early precursor of events to come. Yet, he was powerless and feared the worst. He continued to struggle, but his movements were minimal and he found no purchase. In this contest of size, he came up short; and his most herculean efforts accounted for nothing. Time was running out. He knew he was doomed. He abandoned hope and awaited his fate –to die beneath the crush of a fat woman's ass.

On the other hand, he thought, he needed to rest. A quick nap might do him some good.

CHAPTER XXIII

Ms. Bichette sat stationed at the front desk. She was not only the facility's head, but the entire medical staff. From where she sat, she could oversee the entire front section. Visiting hours were over and Golden Hills was getting back to its normal routines. Dinner would be in a few hours. Most of the residents were napping. Visits had gone well except for a brief interruption by Mr. Thorskelsen. The poor man was talented, but very troubled. He had left his bed again and tried to exit the facility. He seemed intent on gaining the exterior fountain at the front entry.

"Funny", she thought, "What was with him and water?" At various times, she had intercepted him trying to get outside to that fountain. But for Curly, who managed to curtail him before he fled... again, he may have made it. No telling what might have happened.

Yes, she hated to admit that he routinely "disappeared" in and around the home. One of his favorite hiding spots was the hot tub in the Physical Therapy room. She kept a close watch on PT. The staff at Golden Hills was growing weary, and she was charged with devising a plan to keep him under control. She did not like to lose "Marty". When lucid, he was a joy to be around. He could keep the residents happy. He was a true leader, very personable; both talkative and thought- provoking. Aside from a few idiosyncrasies, he could be truly inspiring.

For example, it seemed that no matter how hard the staff had tried, they could not get him to wear pajamas. Golden Hills' policy required residents, at minimum, to wear pajamas. His beautiful and friendly wife and daughter had brought several, very stylish pairs to the home. Mr. Thorskelsen would be quite striking in a handsome pair of pajamas, but he refused to wear them. He chose instead to wear a red speedo with matching swim goggles and fins. Frequently, staff would catch him trying to swim in the hot tub. They almost lost him once when he snuck away without the requisite supervision to the private bath reserved for residents. The private bath was rarely used. Most of these seniors preferred a sponge bath, if they accepted any bath at all. This was unfortunate and Ms. Bichette made many unhappy with her insistence that they bathe, at least once per week, for the sake of their own personal hygiene and for other more "olfactory" concerns of both the residents and staff. Often, she could convince them to "bathe" by suggesting that they take to the hot tub to receive some needed physical therapy. Curly was particularly fond of bath time in PT.

Mr. Thorskelsen could be very inspiring to both residents and staff. He led the effort to modify the cafeteria menu. Larry had taken up the cause with a vengeance. Although, she didn't agree with the changes, the dieticians saw no real issues in providing both Smokehouse bacon and peach yogurt to the elderly residents. Apparently, the reasoning was that if it doesn't kill them out right, what's the harm? The rationale was faulty but with the dietician's blessing, they had convinced the headmaster, who himself, graciously endorsed menu changes.

Marty also had a troubling habit of hiding his medications. He had lost his thyroid several years back to cancer surgery, and he was left with a handful of pill requirements. Quite frankly, he was more aware of the requirements than any of the staff. Despite some apparent issues with his fading memory, he managed to take all of his pills in a timely manner, both day and night. Ms. Bichette had enlisted Trudy Bagley, a resident with no family, but who was both intelligent and still in possession of faculties, remarkable for those in Golden Hills, to help monitor. If he forgot, she would remind him.

Ms. Bichette had noted some correlation between the order in which he took his medications, and some of his more eccentric behaviors but nothing that raised concern. She monitored closely and reported to his wife on a regular basis.

The other residents and some of her staff, Curly, Mo, and Larry, fawned over Mr. Thorskelsen. She knew that they all saw her as an enemy. She needed to be strict. Didn't she? She wondered. Discipline was requisite to keep them all safe. It hurt her sometimes to be this way, but that could not be helped. She had taken this job with a sincere desire to bring positive change, and to serve the elderly. She cared for these people especially when they could not care for themselves. Seemingly, no one else did. At least, that is what she told herself.

Mr. Thorskelsen was truly lucky. His wife and daughter came regularly to visit. His son would stop by frequently; his son-in-law when Time would allow. His grandkids clamored for him when their parents brought them to the home on birthdays and holidays. They adored their PaPa and, it was wholly obvious – especially in his moments of lucidity - that he adored them. Others here had no such luck. Yes. He was one of the few lucky ones. He had a family. They loved him and he loved them, dearly.

Ms.Bichette's attention was drawn to the front reception area. Margaret "Maggie" Larson had been dozing in her wheelchair following breakfast. She was awaiting a family. She would wait a long Time. Ms. Bichette expected as much. Maggie had no family. Ms. Bichette allowed her to wait in reception. It wouldn't hurt. Maggie took pleasure to think that her family would come. She would forget soon thereafter. No harm. No foul. But she had been stationed for a while now in front reception. Ms. Bichette felt that Maggie would find better rest back in her room and had asked Mo to take her back. Now, something was amiss. Ms. Bichette left the front entry desk to check out the situation. What she found was puzzling. Maggie was fast asleep in her wheelchair wholly relaxed and dozing. Her smile showed contentment. Her dearth overwhelmed the chair. She spilled out in every direction.

Initially, Ms. Bichette could not find Mo. She called out to him down both hallways. She opened the door to the men's restroom and call inside to him, nothing. She opened the door to the downstairs morgue and called out again, again nothing. She was disconcerted. He was huge and should be easy to find. So, where the hell was he? He had been here just a moment ago. She carefully scanned the entire room beginning at the help desk, across the front entry, past the fireplace and back, once more, nothing. She paced, and as she paced, she tripped and nearly stumbled. She picked herself up and looked to find what she had tripped over. She looked to find Mo – or at least the lower half of Mo - protruding from the back of Maggie's chair. Maggie was seated in her chair, fast asleep, and apparently right on top of Mo. From the depth of her sleep, as confirmed by her contented grin, Mo served as a very restful cushion in support of Maggie's girth. Her girth was the only thing of sufficient size and weight to directly challenge the girth that Mo brought to bear. Maggie was winning.

What in the hell?

"Mo, get out from there!" Ms. Bichette barked.

He kicked his feet, up and down on the floor – bam, bam, bam, -to show that he had heard, but he was ensconced.

She tried to arouse Maggie who only settled further into her very deep sleep. Mo, once again, lay motionless. Ms. Bichette's nursing instincts kicked in and she moved into action. She lifted both of his legs, as if hoisting a wheelbarrow, and pulled. His legs were heavy and difficult to handle. No luck. She took a breath and pulled again. Maggie stretched a bit, adjusted somewhat, but quickly moved to resettle. Ms. Bichette was trim, much smaller than Mo, but strong. She pulled a third time for all that she was worth. Mo popped from beneath Maggie. Ms. Bichette fell back onto the carpet. Mo followed in brief succession. He, like Maggie, was soundly asleep.

Ms.Bichette arose, straightened her cap, fixed her hair, and smoothed her dress. She looked upon Mo and Maggie with exasperation. She was frustrated but quickly regained composure. She chose to let them sleep. This would be a story that they both could share. Mo slept with Maggie. Maggie slept with Mo. For sure, Mr. Thorskelsen would get a kick out it; and they would all hardly wait to embellish the details.

She pulled blankets from the closet; placed one over Mo there on the floor; and the other, she put on Maggie who remained peacefully asleep and snoring. She dimmed the lights in the front reception area and called Larry to the front desk. She assigned him to keep an eye on both for when they should awaken. He was good at watching over the others in this way. She trusted that he would alert her to any trouble, or if either of them stirred. For now, dinner was over and she needed to make her scheduled rounds.

Larry took the post at the front desk. As soon as Ms. Bichette left for her rounds, he lightly snoozed. The divine Ms.Bichette had assigned him to watch over Maggie and Mo. He only half knew what had transpired. Something about Ms. Bichette had sent Mo to help Maggie to bed. Of course, Maggie – all 400 pounds of her – was asleep in her chair. Mo struggled to wake her and to get her out of her chair. According to Mo, she needed exercise. He tried to convince her to take a walk. Of course, she was fast asleep and wholly unlikely to wake up for anything, let alone for exercise. According to Ms. Bichette, Mo was too lazy to push her in her chair. In any event, she heard a bit of commotion; and, apparently Mo and Maggie argued and some kind of wrestling match ensued. Something like that, anyway...the usual stuff.

Larry's mind wandered. He thought of the events of this past week. Had Marty really exited the home? Had he literally "flown the coop" as it were? Had he truly used those silly flippers that he wore constantly – for no good reason that anyone could really see - as "propellers", to lift him past Curly and escape from Golden Hills? He didn't know what to think. He wanted to believe that. He wanted to believe his own eyes. He wanted to believe that when it came to Marty, anything was possible. As an aged octogenarian resident there at the home, Marty showed remarkable dexterity – that is to say – when he was awake and lucid. Larry refused to believe that Time had deserted Marty. He could not believe that Marty was gone.

On occasions, when Marty lay savagely ensconced in his bed like some King Tut, it was impossible to rouse him. Not dynamite, not earthquakes, not even a volcanic eruption could raise him from the dead, as it were. If Larry had not seen Marty literally "helicopter" his way up and over Curly and through the exit at Golden Hills, he would not have believed it. Even now he was uncertain of what exactly he had witnessed. He refused to accept the rumors that Marty had passed away.

Ms. Bichette only added to the confusion. She held firm that Marty was safely tucked into bed and snoozing – just like always. She had seen to it herself. She claimed that he never came to the front entry. That he was never there. But if this was the case, why had his wife and daughter come to visit? A 24-hour notification of a pending visit was required. The visitor would have called ahead to inquire. Marty would be bathed dressed appropriately and led to the front reception, typically, in a wheelchair. For the more physically active (aka relatively healthy) like Marty, they were allowed to walk up the hallway from their room and to the front desk to greet their visitors. Family members and/or visitors would "check out" the resident for release. A relative few families took the resident back home or with them for some extended stay outside Golden Hills. Most times, Marty's family took him to the pool at their private exercise club. He did like to swim and enjoyed the Time away with family. He often commented on how very much he was entertained by a woman in a bikini with a serpent tattoo. Whenever he told this story, he couldn't help but smile. Larry smiled to himself as he thought about it.

Most family members who came to visit those less mobile residents would be there for no more than an hour or so. These visits typically took place in the front foyer, near the fireplace where the Golden Hills Senior Residence made available a nice couch, some overstuffed chairs, a television set, lamps, wall hangings, and other decorative furnishings. Golden Hills' management made every effort to make the visitors feel at home, even if for the most part, none of them did.

A very small number of family and/or visitors could go back with the resident to the room for more privacy. These types of visits typically occurred on holiday occasions – Christmas, Thanksgiving, and birthdays. An attendee would be posted outside the door to help, if needed.

The idea that some "special" help might be required at any time was distressing enough. Most families chose simply to visit out front in the reception area. Let's just say that it made everybody's lives much less "complicated".

Of late, Larry – like Curly and Mo – had come to doubt Ms. Bichette. Oh, they liked her well enough. They certainly respected her. She was a good administrator, sometimes difficult to please, and even harder to assess. But mostly, she was fair. She had hired Larry at Curly's recommendation. Larry, then had recommended Mo. These three had worked previously together at a local Burger King. Curly's job was clean-up the fast-food giant. Spic and Span beat McDonalds down the street. He was adept with a bucket and mop. He kept the place clean and tidy. Larry considered himself to be "intuitive", but mostly he was good at numbers. He could always balance the cash drawer at closing. If, at night, they encountered difficulty – usually with a raucous crowd of teenagers on gamenight or sometimes later at night with the homeless crowd seeking a handout – he would call on Mo who was an enforcer. Mo kept the teenage crowd to a low thrum together with any late night riff-raff from pushing their way into Burger King. He was soft hearted and did hand out, at closing Time, any of the burgers and other foodstuffs not yet purchased. But, those interested were steered to the rear doors and only after closing time.

The three of them typically took the late shift. They were up at night, mopped spills, corrected errors, and kept the peace. These were Ms. Bichette's reasons for taking them on at Golden Hills. Each one had come clean, polished, and with a resume that screamed "okay with minimum wage". This made them acceptable to management. Ms. Bichette was management.

As Larry cogitated, Curly rolled past Marty's darkened room on his way to the men's room near the front desk. He would check on Marty before he took another toke. He didn't notice anyone in Bed 13. Then, again, he didn't make any real effort to look. He couldn't say for sure if anyone was in bed and, of course, Marty was difficult to read when he was awake. It was always difficult to say whether Marty was anywhere, let alone in bed.

Larry would swear and continually reiterated that there were Times when Marty was literally "invisible". Sure, Larry had seen with his own eyes, Marty's goggles there on his pillow, his speedo on the bed, and his flippers plopped at the foot of the bed. He just couldn't see Marty.

Mo and Curly would further attest that if anyone listened at the door they could hear him snoring, coughing, and chortling, as if he was there in his sleep. They could even hear him break wind and smell the pungency of last night's supper, even if he couldn't be seen.

Then there was the most recent miracle witnessed by each of them. If asked, Larry could say for sure- or almost for sure - that he had seen Marty "fly" out of the old folks home, that he had escaped, that he had indeed "helicoptered" his way on out. Still, he remained skeptical. Really, the only thing that he could say for sure about Marty and his "miracles" was that Marty was a "mystery". Curly, of course, had no doubt about that. He would witness to his dying day that Marty was a god. As for Mo, well...he accepted the obvious.

Oh, sure. Larry had seen and heard enough to know that Marty could work miracles but not always; and when he did do something crazy, it was not always when needed. When needed, his workings and cogitations seemed utterly miraculous like the one tonight. But more often, he would unknowingly create, as if by accident, just some crazy event that seemed stupid or even loony – like out of some cartoon. There was the time, shortly after he'd arrived, when he popped a handful of pills only recently delivered by Ms. Bichette and Trudy at medication Time. Surprisingly, unlike more recently when he was being selective, he just popped all of them at once. Trudy was a witness. She relayed the history; and, it has now been repeated numerous times over.

No sooner had Marty popped his pills than he claimed to have gone blind. He jumped from his bed, knocked over the small food table at his bedside, and bumped squarely into Ms. Bichette. He reached around her waist, with both arms, to help his balance. He then stumbled – some say, "accidently" (as reported by the staff), and some say "purposefully" (as reported by the residents) to fall at her feet where he then reached out to goose her on each of her nicely rounded buttocks. Startled, she jumped. Marty held on and Ms. Bichette successfully pulled him again to his feet. He smiled, saluted, kissed her on her cheek, and moved into the corridor where – some say - he headed down the hall to the cafeteria; others say that he went up the hall to the front reception area. In these early days, Ms. Bichette would make great efforts to keep track of Marty. She loudly directed Trudy to find him and bring him under control. She instructed Larry, Mo, and Curly – only recently arrived to investigate the clamor – to help with the search and to bring him back to bed. The fact that he disappeared there for hours is now looked upon as a rather routine affair, particularly, for Marty. Back then, any "disappearance" was viewed by staff and residents alike, as miraculous.

Then there was today -boy, howdy! Today! His flapping flippered feet were flying fast through the fog of those there at the old folks' home. As Larry puzzled, he could not frankly believe that he had ever seen anything like it. Today, he had seen Marty swallow the handful of pills that he usually kept hidden in a secret pocket in his speedo or otherwise tucked into his flipper and literally breach the main gate or fly out the front door, as it were. He had watched previously as Marty swallowed these medications, as if to muster courage in preparation for a food fight with Ms. Bichette in the cafeteria, or to otherwise confront her at bed Time when she tried to steal his peanut butter. If he found no medications in his speedo, he could always find meds available that he kept stashed under his pillow or inside one or the other lenses to his goggles.

Larry recognized that, at least to Marty if not to Ms. Bichette or to the staff, his pills offered some kind of protection, some kind of extra skill or talent, perhaps even some kind of "superpower". Larry had watched- sometimes by accident, sometimes openly but always with Marty unaware- how Marty took his pills. He would hold a handful. Sometimes he would take all, sometimes only 3 at any one time. It appeared that he selected them by color and would place them into a particular order. It appeared that the order in which he took them differed at each time taken. It also appeared to Larry that Marty would puzzle, at each time taken, as if uncertain as to which order and/or the number to be taken. He kept no records and Larry concluded that Marty never remembered any of the prior occasions, the order of the medications, or the resultant "superpower". It was as if he was experimenting each time anew. It would appear that he could not remember from dosage to dosage. Each time, he would stare at his hand ,as if in some contemplation, before selecting color; sometimes, putting back one selected to replace with another there in his hand. One might think that this process would be Time consuming but even with this uncertainty - that Larry had virtually studied over Time- Marty managed to take his medications swiftly, surreptitiously, and with aplomb. Yet, it was still unclear to Larry- and still uncertain to Marty – which particular order and when taken would produce which particular "miracle" or "superpower", as it were. What was clear was that Marty studied that which he knew would produce some kind of result with the timing and order of the taking. What was unclear was what might result from such timing and order.

Tonight's history was anything but clear. Mo had seen him fly on out of here, but remained just as firm that he had seen Marty in bed. He chose not to engage the controversy. Curly was adamant that Marty had helicoptered right out the front door. He embraced the controversy. Larry knew full well that a quick check of Marty's bed could end the controversy. Yet, for some reason he felt the need to continue it. Each was willing to accept that Marty would resurface. Rumors of his death were exaggerated.

CHAPTER XXIV

Marty had learned much from the Library in the Lake at M Street. The pills he had taken – if he remembered correctly - were: one blue, one red, and one half yellow and half white – these had enlivened him; awakened him from what had previously seemed like Death. His feet were light and lively. He felt agile again. He had longed for a swim and looked forward to his return to the hot tub in PT from where he routinely managed to swim in ...well, let's just say the seas and oceans of the world. But today, he was about a more serious work. Today he had gone, not to the open seas, but just a block away to where a recent discovery challenged even the Seven Wonders of the World. Just now, he helicoptered a few inches above the concrete entry outside the glass front doors. He was still dripping from return trip to the outside fountain. He wasn't sure how he had missed the hot tub in PT where he had started and where he typically ended his swim.

This last trip had taken him back through Time, maybe not to 1600 B.C to find Moses and the Israelites, but he was smart enough to know that he had gone back maybe 70 or 80 years to find Moses... uhh, that is to say, to find Charlton Heston who played Moses in the movie, The Ten Commandments. That movie was made 1956. He surmised that he had taken a bit of a Time jump to join up with Heston. But he was confused as to how he had come to find both Heston and Christian Bale together at the same place, or rather, the same Time. Bale's movie, Exodus: Gods and Kings had been filmed in 2014, nearly 60 years after Heston's movie. That was significant and Marty had no answer as to how he managed both.

Suddenly, Marty awakened to the fact that he had lost elevation. He currently glowed with a fuzzy "blue" as he hovered in front of the large windows and glass entry doors to Golden Hills Senior Residence. As his feet helicoptered, he emanated "white noise" like a TV left on in the early hours. He was still unused to the effect generated, and he wobbled as he sought to return skyward. For a moment, he lost his balance and tipped forward into the glass entry door with a thump. He quickly recovered.

Athleticism was still residual in his aging frame. It put him upright and he soon caught the hang of his helicoptering. He looked upward to the tree tops and climbed a few hundred feet. His blue light lit up the surrounding area giving an eerie glow. The scratchy "white noise" predominated. There, just atop the trees, he turned to hover for a grand view of the front drive, the fountain, and the surrounding landscape. The lawns were neatly trimmed. The trees were tall and stately. The shrubbery was bountiful. The flowers had been exchanged by landscape maintenance, the colors selected for this special time of the year. Currently, all was a televised blue. The entry offered peace and security to those families who would lodge their loved ones here to await their passing; peace to know that they had done the right thing; security to know that someone else now owned their problem.

Then again, with no realistic explanation, the seasons had jumped. Time continued to march and it was springtime. Marty was sure of it. Temperatures were cool and soothing. The trees were awakening and beginning to bud. Flowers were blossoming. The jump was from what...October to maybe... April? Unfortunate, he thought. But only from the standpoint that he didn't really care to know much about any given day, any month, or any year.

He always chose actively not to remember the year of any season past. Somehow by tagging a number to the back of a season detracted from that season. It took away from the glory of the Time of the year, as if to say: It's Time to put it away, to catalogue it, to put it on the back shelf and look again at it only if the future should lose its' luster, or if the present should somehow escape requisite attention. A year identified was a hole cut in the fabric of eternity; a place into which one might drop for a while, either for better or for worse; a place to rest and to reside...but more often, to stay chained. In his travels, Marty had learned that much, at least. His birth year gave to him a starting time. A place came with it. But did he really start there? He wondered.

High school snuck up and sometimes attacked. The years were labeled: freshman, sophomore, junior, and senior. But, lying behind these class distinctions were the actual years which culminated in the year of your graduation from high school, from college, and from law school with a Master's or PhD. Marty was very much pleased to remember that he had never before cared to remember any of those years. This wasn't a moment of failing. This was not a hole in his Swiss-cheese mind. This was a viable act of consciousness. That he had consciously selected this moment, this Time was indeed gratifying, but for what purpose?

To remember Time was itself problematic. Time is man's creation. He posits it by creating supposed segments: seconds, minutes, hours, days, years, decades, centuries, millennia and more. According to the brainiacs, even the Universe is supposed to have had a "beginning" – a "big bang", as it were - and will have an "end". But a "beginning" and an "end" are segments of what exactly? Marty assumed that these were "assigned" so that Time could govern and be immutable. But what if there were neither a beginning nor an end, but only "one eternal round"; eternity in other words and he thought about No Time.

Marty had taken "Physics 100" his first year in college. He was captivated by a small cartoon set up to describe Einstein's light clock, placed on a rocket ship. In this cartoon, Time is measured by a beam of light that is set bouncing between mirrors positioned – one, up on the top side or ceiling, the other, down on the bottom side or floor of the rocket ship as it flies horizontally. As the rocket approaches the speed of light, the beam's path between the upper and lower mirrors lengthens. The path of travel for the beam gets longer. The measure of the Time necessary for the beam to reach from one mirror to the other, lengthens; Time, itself, lengthens and slows. As the speed of the rocket ship reaches the speed of light and thereby travels at the same speed as the once bouncing beam, that beam no longer bounces but travels horizontally with the rocket ship and is no longer measured by a bounce on one or the other mirrors. In fact, it is no longer "measured" at all. At this moment, at the speed of light, the rocket ship is in a place where Time is no longer measured. This, to Marty, is No Time - a place where Time is not cut up into seconds, minutes, hours, or days, and therefore cannot be defined by virtue of these divided segments.

This sounded pretty much like Eternity, a place where he might come, at least on occasion, to rest. When he chose not to measure Time by any stated "year", Time would move in on itself to have neither a beginning nor and end, but would be one eternal round. As Time moved in on itself, all was one. Past, present, and future were the same. Arguably, space moved in on itself, as well. To Marty, both Time and Space were one. He naively concluded that if it took No Time to cross Space, either because at the speed of light Time could not be measured or because Space had collapsed, it might be asked: Is there really a Space there at all? Is there really a Time? If never measured, are they even real? It was sort of like the question: If a tree falls in the forest and no one is around to hear, does it make a sound? To date, no one had supplied an answer for that one.

For Marty, the No Time theory was workable. There were moments when he could erase both Time and Space; except for 1967. Except for 1967, he had learned to fully navigate through places and events that represented his past and present. He had initially discovered this "ability" through an effective use of his prescribed drugs. This had taken some Time- as it were. Later, following his discovery of The Library, he would find much greater access and resources.

But in Time, he learned to effectively "swim" through his past, present, and his future as if on a vast pond of crystal clear water. He never crossed this Lake of Time. Rather, he would just swim, in place as it were. Yet, he could envision the vast expanse of both Time and Space; and he could readily speculate about No Time.

Somehow, No Time was a place where one lived in the present, but held the advantage of knowing the past and seeing the future – all at once. The scripture that he had read that described the course of the Lord as "one eternal round" said it best. To Marty's limited understanding, this meant that the past, present, and future somehow folded back onto each other; or better still, that they each existed in the same "round" of things. He figured that they were all the same thing. Well... at least according to the scripture, they were the same, and that was good enough for Marty. That seemed to fit nicely with his No Time theory. Either the past, present, and future were one and the same thing; or they simply were not measured so they did not exist and so, there is No Time.

Yeah, it was true that Marty existed in Time and tracked lineally from the past to the present and through into the future. But on God's side of things, He saw it all at once. When He had a work to do here on earth, He'd show up in a burning bush on one day, sent His soldiers to battle for Elijah and Elisha on another, and even sent a whale to swallow Jonah to bring him back on still another. Yet to God, it was all the same "day", as it were. Marty figured that if He wanted, He could send his angels from No Time to step both in and back out of Time at any given place in History.

Still, this was problematic for Marty. He believed in agency. He believed that he would be judged according to his works; that it somehow paid to be a good guy. But when he tried to see things from the Lord's side of the ledger – from the Library of No Time – there was no agency. This was difficult for Marty to swallow. From the standpoint of No Time, his choices appeared to have no consequences. Or, to better state it: he had no real choices because the consequences were fixed. From the moment that he met her, already, he had loved Shelly. Already, she was lost to him. From before he attended kindergarten, already, he had graduated from law school. Already, he was married, had kids, and had both succeeded and failed in a variety of life's contests. Already, he had died. Already...To Marty, it may seem that he had choices while here. But from the perspective of No Time and from the standpoint of "one eternal round", these choices were already made, they were fixed and the consequences concluded. His life was set in stone.

Marty dwelt on this for a Time. The logic was bothersome. Still, while he lived, he was on Time's side of the ledger. He must live by Time's rules. He must make his choices, not knowing whether they will pay or not because ultimately "payment", he figured, should not be the goal. Should it? If payment was the goal, if payment was the one reward, well then...that was somehow like building the Tower of Babel. Men built the tower to reach Heaven, to reach God, as if they could do it on their own. Marty wasn't stupid enough to think that he could reach Heaven by building a tower. He'd read about the Tower of Babel when he was a kid. Even back then, the idea was silly; the story hard to take seriously.

Marty thought some more about his pills and wondered if, maybe, his pills were only helping him to build a worthless tower. Yes, his pills had helped and, for a Time while at Golden Hills, he had figured that his pills could take him to places where he could not go otherwise. But now, he'd come to the conclusion that the pills had nothing to do with his adventures. It was more his willingness to search, to push, to discover new places and things about which he knew little or nothing. It was the search that took him out of the home, away from his boredom, and into worlds of excitement and wonder.

Some Time back, he had engaged in some rather serious research. He couldn't say exactly when. But he had found a book: The Book of Mormon in which he read about a dude named Alma who had a wayward son. He told his son: "(W)hosoever will come may partake of the waters of life freely; and, whosoever will not come the same is not compelled to come; but in the last day it shall be restored unto him according to his deeds"...Alma 42:27

Marty puzzled on this. He could agree that he was free to "partake of the waters of life" even though he wasn't quite sure what they were. He figured that "truth" was a good equivalent. He came to the conclusion that he could either pursue the "truth" or not. He could at least try to "partake of the waters of life". But if it wasn't truth, then whatever he could come up with during his search, whatever he had found during his sojourn here -whether that was truth or falsity, whatever it was- would come back to him for either good or bad; and right then and there, Marty committed himself to push for truth...always.

From a practical standpoint, he also committed to go "cold turkey" with unnecessary meds. He would avoid the pills. He may not always find truth without his pills, but he believed that it was the "push" that mattered most. If it was the "push" that was restored to him then when he arrived in No Time, the results from that "push" should be restored to him as well. At minimum, he figured that he should be allowed to continue the "push". That seemed only fair. The Truth had to be that Heaven was fair at least.

So far what he had discovered about "truth" was that it must be shared. Nobody can find the truth all on their own. Marty knew that people often spoke of truth as "relative" as if they could possess some specialized version, applicable only to themselves and to their particularized frame of reference. Marty saw this as selfish and misinformed. He looked to the old Indian parable about the seven blind men and the elephant: The leg of the elephant is not the elephant, nor alone is the trunk, the tusk, the tail, or the ear. Each forms only part of a greater whole that awaits discovery. Marty figured that folks must compare notes with each other so that the truth might be unveiled, discovered, and even worshipped.

Unfortunately for Marty, he had yet to discover how best he might share with those still bound by Time and Space; how he might share with those who still saw the truth as "relative" and peculiar to their own perspective. On his own, he could visit glorious places, see marvelous things, but where he was unable to participate in any meaningful way with others, to compare notes, as it were; he could only catch a particle. Whatever truth he could discover remained relative and, in large measure, hidden by the unknown that surrounded it. Still, truth was discoverable, knowable to all. This told Marty that whatever portion that he could discover and know to be true should give him some hint – at least a glimpse – of the truth that remains hidden. The way Marty saw it, truth attracted truth like iron particles to a magnet. The way he figured it, he and the other blind men on the elephant should be able to compare notes. But at present, he had no familiar point to fix upon; no familiar Time or Space on which to concentrate to help prepare him for arrival; no single person from whom he might gain perspective – that is, no other blind man with whom to compare his notes.

And suddenly, Marty's eyes opened. He needed Time. He needed people. Time gave him the chance to compare notes. People gave him perspective. No one person could come to know and understand truth without other people and perspective. Time was a necessary thing.

The sun was high and bright. The early afternoon sky had reached a deep, jet blue. Marty's blue glow was absorbed into the sky. What few clouds cruised the atmosphere were soft and enticing. The fountain below offered refreshment that could slake Marty's thirst. He would nap there later with the remains of this day. It seemed that he had much to do. Hero stuff mostly. He closed his eyes and took a deep breath. He breathed slowly in and out. He relaxed and emptied his mind. E-A-B-D-G-E, E-A-B-D-G-E, E-A-B-D-G-E, he counted as he meditated to swim laps. He cleared his mind of the darkness and he felt good! He could hardly believe his luck. He was here and hovering over the grounds. His control was back; stability returned. With little effort, his flippers propelled him. He drew back his arms and angled his flight path higher. He increased the twitch of his feet to increase the speed of his flippers: 200, 300, 400 feet and higher to catch a larger, more expansive view. There, high above the valley floor with the snow-capped mountains surrounding and the cumulus parading the way, he leveled off and leaned back. He perched there in the air, his back elevated at a good one-thousand feet above the fountain. He was lying on an invisible chaise lounge, his feet continuing to twitch, and his fins to helicopter. He folded his arms over his chest, his right hand across his chin with the thumb to his left cheek, the index to the other, and a quizzical look on his face as he pondered. The "white noise" was now calmed, but continued to adjust, louder, and softer with his movements.

Who was there for him to save today? What catastrophe should he seek to avert? How best could he use this gift of flight? Better still, what must he do to best utilize this extended moment of clarity that emboldened him; this clarity that stunned and enlivened him; this clarity which had been so far removed 'til now? What miracle might he make to save humanity? What truth may he discover? What darkness might he dispel? He smiled at the thought. Could this be No Time? He was not sure. But if it wasn't, it was close to it.

Marty knew that he should continue to puzzle, but he was tired and distracted. He finally gave up and with that his swim fins sputtered. He struggled to control his flight. His balance was off. He faltered, if only for a second.

He recalled his recent swim in the icy waters of Tierra Del Fuego and his visit with Moby Dick; his easy cruise along the Great Barrier Reef, north of Australia and the lesson he learned from Charlie Tuna; and his most recent nautical trek to the Red Sea where he had well, to be modest shall we say, he "participated" in the "parting" – these adventures had enlivened him. For a moment, his flippers continued to flutter and he remained aloft. Miracles did occur, and he had taken part. He had found his freedom, and his mind had been clear; his recollections were vivid.

But his mind had presented him with that one year for which he had no memory at all, not even "Swiss cheese", a year he knew to be labeled and permanently affixed, but a year that would not allow him to drop in and visit. He recalled the year only as 1967. It was blank and it was dark. He now realized that he had no frame of reference to help him penetrate that year. 1967 was a complete blank. He had no memory on which to affix and no perspective to give him direction. It seemed that every Time he tried to enter 1967, he could never say whether he had succeeded. In his memory, that year was a Time that was just as empty as was the future. He didn't know why or how 1967 remained an enigma. He could always arrive there and knew clearly when he was in it. Even if he had arrived in 1967 to pay a visit, he didn't remember any of even the most general events or happenings of that year. For all intents and purposes, he may as well have never gone there. Why was it that he had so much difficulty in attempting to penetrate this year? Was this a mystery that even mandated an answer? Was this a puzzle that required a solution? Who knew? Regardless, this was the reason for which he swam.

Knowing now what he did about Time and No Time had at least given him a purpose. He was still learning. He would find someone to help. He would get perspective. It wasn't always pretty, but he continued to hope; continued to discover, bit by bit, a means by which he might intervene on behalf of those still locked into Time and Space; some way to become and to remain involved -especially in the year 1967. He knew that he had much to do in that year. He was confident of that.

Marty had not tracked his Time in the air, and his flippers continued to miss. The thought of falling brought fear and trepidation. It scared him and caused his mind to darken. He began to lose altitude. His feet stopped twitching. His flippers stopped buzzing. The "white noise" stopped abruptly. Marty began to fall headfirst into a dive directly for the fountain. In desperation and against his only recent resolve, he pondered his medications. He hadn't memorized the pill combination nor had he measured the Time it took for the combination to kick in. Nope. Flying now was out of the question. He eyed the fountain. Forget medications. He would rely on instinct, on skill, on talent – perhaps slowed, but not forgotten. He would rely on the "push". The answer was clear. Someone tell him. Someone else advise. Someone help him to find "perspective".

Marty's swim fins sputtered again and finally failed. He set his target for the center of the drain, shifted his goggles from his head to cover his eyes, and dove straight down and hard. The water exploded on entry. If he had miscalculated, he would instantaneously form part of the coin collection atop the concrete plaster at the pool's bottom. He did not miscalculate. He entered the fountain with arrow-like precision. The water was crystal and cold, much like waters from Bell's Canyon. He was on target. He shot through the sublime waters, straight and true, into the center drain. The waters quickly calmed and Marty was at peace.

In what was a moment, he watchfully broke the surface there in the whirlpool tub in PT, his goggles level at the waterline. He paused, up periscope. He slowly rotated 360 degrees. He saw nothing out of the ordinary there in the darkened room. He silently exhaled as he stood. He pushed what was left of his thinning hair back across his balding head. He lifted the goggles from his eyes. He wiped his face with his right hand. He smoothly lifted his right leg from the tub and planted it on the floor. The left followed in swift succession. He paused again to listen. He heard nothing except for some heavy snoring down "B" wing and a few fitful murmurs from those who struggled to sleep. He stood there dripping onto the tile floor but with a renewed determination and sense of purpose recently rediscovered. He had flown or, better perhaps, he had fluttered outside the old folks' home. He had not been outside for a long time although it seemed that he had.

Yeah, there it was again – Time. Who could really say just how long he had been outside, how long it had taken him to visit Egypt and swim the Red Sea to help make a movie? It seemed to Marty that he only ever chose to measure Time so as to highlight moments in the extreme; moments that approached either pure peace and ecstasy or total boredom and misery. So what, he thought. This had been a moment as close to ecstasy as he had been in a long time. But now, he was fatigued; his earlier resolve weakened.

The effect taken from the particular combination of pills that he had swallowed was shortlived; and, anyway, he could not now remember exactly which pills he had swallowed. Whatever they were, they had left him with a hangover. He shook his head to clear the fog. He resolved again to stay away from "pills". He pulled a couple of vitamins from his speedo and popped them into his mouth. He retrieved from his goggles, a large pink pill made from jellyfish. He justified this one. By advertisement, it was intended to sharpen his mind. It was not a prescription med. This he also popped and swallowed.

Within moments, as he walked back to Bed 13 in Hallway A, he started to float awkwardly as if lighter than air – first upward slowly a few feet, then downward just as slowly. In this manner, he made his way to his bed. As he tried to sleep; he continued, for a Time, to float slowly up and down. The action was peaceful but discombobulating. Typically, he would sleep with no covers on top of both the top and bottom sheets. His blanket had been folded away into the small closet in his room. This night, he chose to sleep beneath the top sheet to add ballast, but under which he continued to float slowly up and down, up and down. The sheet kept him from floating away, but periodically he would bump off of the ceiling and return to his bed much like a helium balloon captured by the varying air currents in a ventilated bedroom.

CHAPTER XXV

Larry was returning to the kitchen from his meeting with Ms. Bichette. He had delivered his count. Weekly, he made sure to update her concerning the delivery and removal of foodstuffs, especially as related to Smokehouse Bacon and Peach Yogurt. So far, he had regularly managed to keep both on the menu: Bacon every Sunday morning, and Yogurt was a daily affair. Larry had become quite popular with the residents and, in this regard, he was quite proud of himself. He had expressly taken the "A" wing to check on Marty. He stopped outside the door and poked his head inside to check the occupant of Bed 13. He was stunned. Marty was gone, again; Larry had not seen him all day. He stepped into the room and looked under the bed - Nothing. He threw back the sheets, both the top and the bottom. He rustled through them. Again - nothing. He stopped to think. What should he do now? Should he report this to Ms. Bichette? She would send out a search party. If they found Marty, he'd be written up. Who knew how many "demerits" he had notched already? This disappearance might tip the scales and give her reason to send him packing.

Just then, he heard footsteps coming from the front office. For a moment, the footsteps stopped and he heard Ms. Bichette call out some needed direction to a member of the staff.

"Say what? She was responding to someone back up Hallway A. Someone repeated something and Ms. Bichette answered back, "Tell them I'll be right there. I've got to check on Mr. Markham. He's gotten to be a bit...shall we saaayy..." She lengthened the pronunciation as she curled to pounce.

Damn! Larry thought. He was worried for Marty, but more worried for himself though he didn't know why. He fell flat to his belly and rolled under the bed. At that same moment, Ms. Bichette launched herself into the room and triumphantly finished her thought..."a bit elusive".

She shouted as if at some surprise party hoping to catch Marty unaware. But her triumph was shortlived. Marty was not surprised. Instead, he slept. He had come down from the ceiling and was floating just above the mattress. The sheet was spread over him. His flippers poked from beneath the sheet there at the foot of the bed. He snorted once loudly as if to say, "Leave me alone. I need my rest".

Ms. Bichette frowned. She was disappointed. It was a good plan. She should try it again sometime. She exited back up Hallway A. When her footfalls fell silent, Larry came out from under the bed. He brushed himself off. He was flummoxed. He had expected a three alarm fire, all hands on deck, and an all-out search for one missing Marty Markham. Instead... nothing happened. He looked to the mattress. No Marty. He was flummoxed. What was Le Biche up to? He puzzled this one. What was going on here? He left the room and headed to the kitchen. He needed answers. Mo would know what to do.

In the meantime, Marty floated slowly up and down, up and down. Not tethered to the bed, he drifted up and down, out the bedroom door, and into Hallway A. Life went on at Golden Hills as Marty drifted with the ventilation up near the ceiling toward the front entry. Below, in the front conference room, Ms. Bichette met with a family, ascribed to them the benefits of living at the Golden Hills Senior Residence. A spot had opened with the untimely passing of yet another one of Golden Hills' seniors. That made three in one week. The Death Squad had been busy.

He circulated through the front reception area. Mo was busy watching television; courtroom drama. Larry was in the downstairs receiving area checking on the recent delivery of Smokehouse bacon.

He had phoned Curly for help. Curly was in the men's room conducting his business as usual.

Marty continued to drift. He travelled with the ventilation and was soon to pass down Hallway B, but Ms. Bichette's afternoon appointment arrived early. An elderly widow opened the front entry and a breeze blew in. The breeze interrupted Marty's graceful excursion and bounced him like an errant balloon back into Hallway A. The breeze pushed him downward to eye level as Curly exited the men's room. The two may have engaged, but Curly dropped his newly rolled joint just as he exited and bent in an effort to pick up and pocket it before Le Biche could find it. Marty slept soundly as he drifted back up to the ceiling just as Curly stood up to peer both up and down Hallway A. He took a good long look into the conference room to ensure that Le Biche remained preoccupied. He smiled to see that she was busy. He crossed the hallway to take the stairs down to the temporary morgue to help Larry with inventory in the receiving area.

In the concrete basement, beneath Golden Hills, was a temporary mortuary – of sorts. It was under contract with Heavenly Rest, the local morgue. Like most, this basement morgue carried several rows of refrigerated lockers with chrome doors and slide out shelves. Approximately ten, four-feet by six feet steel tables on wheels occupied the floor space. Here in the morgue, the bodies were kept until the families could arrange with Heavenly Rest for pick-up to remove grandma or grandpa so as to better prepare for his or her last, good rest. The mood in the temporary mortuary was dampened and subdued, per usual. Death lived here. What else was new? A call had gone out. One of the upstairs residents had graduated. It was time to make preparations for passage.

The delivery truck with a load of Smokehouse had arrived. The roll-up door was open as Larry took delivery in the rear. The outside air and temperature pulled the interior breezes down the stairway to the morgue where they typically circulated for a time until they trailed through to the loading dock. Marty drifted with the breeze. From the stairs, he blew into the morgue and circulated around the ceiling a few times as the breeze fought to move to the loading dock.

Eldon Jones was on duty in the morgue. Despite the somber attitude that pervaded, he was in a good mood. Golden Hills was a good gig, lots of folks moving on. He had been around for a while. He knew how best to turn a dollar, especially during the late night. He was strictly "transport". He didn't have to deal with the more, shall we say, unseemly aspects associated with death. He had come to take one home; one of the old folks there at Golden Hills had gone belly up. As Marty passed skyward, Eldon bent to pull open drawer 13 in preparation to receive a newly cooled occupant. As he pulled the drawer open, the large drawer pulled in Marty from the ceiling.

Then, Larry called from the rear, "Hey, Eldon...you seen Curly? I need to get this stuff offloaded. The driver is behind schedule"

Helpful as always, Eldon started immediately to the back, "I'll give you a hand. I'm still waiting on my customer". As Marty entered the drawer 13 still sound asleep and floating, Eldon reached back without looking and pushed the drawer closed. He heard a loud click and remembered the catch in drawer 13.

"Damn", he thought. That will be tough to get back open.

Usually, any poor beloved who passed on in the nighttime was left to "sleep" his or her remaining hours there in bed until the morning crew could take him or her on home. After all, these folks were – in Eldon's words – "gawd awful old". Not one of them, whether dead or alive, would care much to be pulled from beneath the covers during bedtime. For a few, bedtime could be most of the day, but the morning crew did have a job to do, so the morning shift led by Ms. Bichette would make a morning bed check and dispense vitamins. If Time had finally stopped for the blessed soul, Ms. Bichette would sign the proper form, the morning crew would be summoned, and the dear deceased would be shuffled off. Eldon would catch up to them the next day.

The morning crew – known to the residents as "The Death Squad" - consisted of three persons of unknown gender;each dressed in a drab grey one-piece uniform and a grey baseball cap without insignia. Their hair was short, cropped, and hidden beneath the cap. Each wore dark sunglasses. The style was the same for each. Those residents who retained a pulse chose to ignore the morning crew. Word spread rapidly when a brother or sister passed. Even the comatose, if questioned, would know the name, age, and bed number of the dearly beloved who had set his sail for the River Styx. To them, the Death Squad was ghostlike and haunted. Their pending arrival was not so much known but intuited, The residents can sense it. The Squad would come in quietly when a resident had set sail. The patron's passing was sufficient notice. Death was the invitation, as it were. Should hope prevail, they were gone in much the same way they had arrived- invisibly. As is typical of most mortuaries, those who had passed were ferried from the home, placed in the downstairs morgue on a steel slab, naked and nicely tagged, and shut within a stainless steel drawer to wait for pick-up.

As Eldon walked back to the temporary morgue from the loading dock, he couldn't help but smile. His job was to confirm delivery to the basement, match the toe-tag against his own transport order, prepare and bag the deceased for removal to Heavenly Rest to be prepped for interment or cremation. He wasn't involved in the finalities. He was just the pick-up and delivery guy. Dominoes in five minutes or the pizza was free. He chuckled.

He never knew just how these old folks died. But it was pretty much a no brainer. The clientele was pushing "ancient". It was easy to conclude that age had taken them home. The call came for pick-up at 6:42 pm. Golden Hills was an easy 15 minute jaunt. He drove a large hearse for carry out. The hearse was a gaudy gold color with large chrome bumpers, chrome rails around the top deck and a large HR-Heavenly Rest decorating each side. Might as well advertise, he thought. He parked in the garage at the backside of the mortuary. From there, he walked directly into the basement morgue. He reported his arrival time as 7 pm. The order called for two individuals to make the transport. The fee was listed at $350 plus mileage. But Eldon was an average to sizeable guy. He could easily handle these bodies himself. Most were emaciated. Death had called them home a long time ago. Why they hesitated to sail, he didn't know, but who was he to question? He had learned a long time ago that he could easily bag any one of these boys or girls by himself ,and he was nothing if not efficient. After all, $350 was $350.

According to his most recent transport notice, he would find one "Dear Departed" in drawer 13. The boy's toe-tag confirmed the old guy's age as 93. His height was list as six-foot and weight as 134 lbs; and his cause of death as...yeah well: "natural causes". The tag also provided contact information for the next of kin with directions as to which funeral home or crematorium the body should be delivered. For anyone who, while at Golden Hills, elected to step into the great beyond, The Death Squad would remove the poor soul and make delivery to the morgue. Normally, Eldon would find those delivered to be naked. This job always brought something new.

Ultimately, Eldon didn't sweat the details. Yet with every pick-up, Eldon couldn't help but wonder: When Time conquered and Age finally took control, he expected that he would prefer to move on, to cross over the river Styx, to give up the ghost, whatever. Why fight Time?

He had heard about a scuba diver taken out to sea in a party boat and mistakenly abandoned, who had floated around for three days and survived sharks until the folks in charge realized he was missing and returned to scoop him up. The guy kept swimming, waiting for help for the entire 3 days. He also knew an old-dog, long passed now, who was blown off an aircraft carrier during WWII – the Battle of Midway - and into the water where he floated with other crew members in a front row seat to the ongoing air battle in the skies above. They had bobbed and drifted there for three days until they were rescued. Again, Eldon thought, why fight it? Why not just stop swimming and ease on into the ever after? Life was sure to be easier on the other side...assuming of course that there was another side. With this gig, he often pondered the mysteries. Tonight was no different.

Eldon pulled up a small swivel stool on wheels that was used by the morticians under contract. They dealt with those patrons who lay unclaimed at the home. These would be delivered by the Death Squad, appropriately tagged, to the basement morgue, and when so directed by proper instructions on the transport order as matched by the instructions on the commensurate toe-tag, the Death Squad would dress these in an inexpensive cotton robe, move them from the metal table, and place them into the refrigerated drawer, again, as was designated on the corresponding transport order and toe-tag, to await final transport directly to the crematoria. The ashes would be identified, properly recorded, and interred temporarily to await final resolution by proper authorities.

Thankfully, Eldon did not deal with these poor souls. Anyway, tonight there were none so designated lying out on the slabs to haunt his meditations. He sat and absent-mindedly pushed, wheeled, and swiveled around the metal tables there in basement. He pulled an apple from his jacket, a jar of peanut butter from the other. He pulled a large table spoon from his pants pocket and set about reviewing his evening repast. He spooned a large scoop of Jiffy, spread it on the apple, and took a bite. He retrieved his Apple cell phone from the other back pocket and played solitaire on a new app as he loudly chewed his lunch. With each successive bite, he spooned another dollop of peanut butter and munched away. As he munched, he began to ponder.

He had often wondered whether Time was a friend or an enemy. His visits to the morgue only enhanced his curiosity. When a person died, did he "pass on" to something or somewhere? Or, did Time just run out? Was the term "passed on" just a euphemism used by the living to better deal with the end that was death? Did folks "pass on" only to arrive, what,...nowhere? Was there someplace to go? He came back full circle. If there was a place to go – and people did believe that – then why didn't they just go when Time was up? Why did they struggle so hard to stay? After all, to most folks this world could be a wretched place,and he could point to an entire upstairs clientele for whom Time had run out. And, if there was a place to go, what kind of place was it? Was it all puffy white and cumulus clouds with pearly gates and a comedian who stood guard and told jokes to those who would pass through. Or, was it more like reincarnation? If Eldon lived a good life, would he become an elephant or some other entitled creature better or more highly prized than a man? Some things required prolonged reflection.

He took another spoon of peanut butter and bit into his apple. He chewed contentedly and as he had promised to himself, he pondered. Tonight, Eldon had Time. Time reminded him of a scripture. Or, was it that song, a song his mom used to sing to him.

*****

♪♪ To everything there is a season, and a time
to every purpose under the heaven:
A time to be born, and a time to die; a time to plant,
and a time to pluck up that which is planted;

A time to kill, and a time to heal; a time to
break down, and a time to build up;
A time to weep, and a time to laugh; a time
to mourn, and a time to dance;
A time to cast away stones, and a time to gather stones together;
a time to embrace, and a time to refrain from embracing;

A time to get, and a time to lose; a time to
keep, and a time to cast away;
A time to rend, and a time to sew; a time to
keep silence, and a time to speak;
A time to love, and a time to hate; a time
of war, and a time of peace. ♪♪

Ecclesiastes 3:1

*****

As he munched and mused, his meal was suddenly interrupted.

BAM, BAM, BAM", three loud metallic thuds from the inside of Drawer 13 jarred Eldon to wakefulness. He came to swift attention as he lifted his head off of his arms there folded across the edge of one of the tables. The wheels on his swivel chair moved and the chair itself escaped from beneath him. The fall slowly sucked his top half from the table and left him splat there with his bottom half on the checkered tiles of the floor in the temporary morgue.

"Owwww-uhh", he exclaimed loudly as he landed – Kerthunk!.

"BAM, BAM, BAM", the loud hammering continued on the square chrome door that had a refrigerator handle. The steel door on Drawer 13 vibrated with each thud. The handle bounced with each bump, but held firm. A muffled yell accompanied from inside the drawer. Eldon slowly came to his feet. He had heard a voice of sorts, but couldn't make out the words. Or had he? He pushed himself up from the floor stood on the checkered tiles, and steadied himself with both hands on the metal table top. He looked in the direction of Drawer 13.

Did he hear 'words'? A dead man speaks? He was confused. Was this an answer? He'd been pondering the depths. Had the depths arisen in response? He adjusted his jaw and massaged his chin as he puzzled.

"BAM, BAM, BAM. Let me out of here, damn it! LET ME OUT OF HERRREE!" a muffled but audible demand accompanied,

Eldon marveled, "A voice!"–"Who is it? Who is in there?" He spoke to Drawer 13.

A voice shouted back, "Markham dammit! It's Markham! Now GET ME OUT NOW!"

Eldon had never met Mr. Mark Mark Markham, but he would bet that Mr. Markham had just spoken from the dead. But wait...he wasn't dead. How could he be? He had spoken. Maybe...he thought. Maybe, he was -Eldon sought for his Sunday school **vernacular-**

maybe he was...resurrected! Hooolly Cow! A dead man had risen and had spoken,and Eldon realized incredulously that the voice had spoken to him!

He reverently approached the front of Drawer 13 and fell to his knees. He remembered those Sunday school lessons: The story of Eli and Samuel. Samuel had heard a voice. He went to Eli. Eli told him to go back to bed. Eli was an old dude-prophet. His hearing wasn't so good. They didn't make hearing aids in those days– and Eli was out of practice in hearing the voice of God. Three times the voice spoke to Samuel. Three times Samuel went to Eli to ask "Sup, Dude". Finally, when the kid wouldn't go back to sleep, Eli told him to say the magic words: "Speak Lord, thy servant heareth".

Eldon gave it a try, "Speak Lord, thy servant heareth".

"Open the damn door and let me out!" the voice thundered.

To Eldon, it sounded more like yelling, but the voice of God either "thundered" or was "still and small". In this case it was not "still and small", and whether it simply "yelled" or more eloquently "thundered", Eldon wasn't going to challenge God. He removed his shoes and approached Drawer 13 reverently. His head bowed. He reached up to the refrigerator handle, pulled it open, and quickly backed away several steps where he kneeled like a knight waiting to be knighted.

"BANG". The door flew open and out popped Marty, naked as a jay bird. He stood there on the checkered tile in all of his glorious regalia.

"Thanks man" he said to Eldon. "It was getting stuffy in there". He finished unzipping the bag and sat up. He saluted Eldon and jumped to the floor. Some thoughtful soul had left his red speedo, fins, and goggles there inside the bag. He slipped on his speedo, stepped into the fins, and donned the red goggles. He turned and offered a salute to Eldon. Eldon looked up and stared but stood mute.

"I'm hungry", Marty said. "Think I'll grab some peach yogurt and a donut at the cafeteria. Which way?" he asked Eldon, crossing his arms and pointing in either direction. "Which way to the cafeteria"?

Eldon, still kneeling for knighthood, looked over and pointed in silence to the back set of stairs. Marty pulled the tablespoon from the peanut butter jar left there on the slab and licked the peanut butter from the spoon to clean it. He reached into his speedo, grabbed a few pills, checked them for color, and popped them into his mouth. He paused for a moment. Then, a quick shiver shook his entire frame. He shrugged and turned to Eldon.

He held high the empty peanut butter spoon and loudly pronounced, "With the authority present in me, I do hereby dub thee Sir...uh, what's your full name?"

"Eldon Smith and Jones", Eldon mumbled sheepishly.

"Say, WHAT!" Marty almost shouted with his hand cupped to his ear.

"ELDON SMITH AND JONES, Eldon carefully pronounced with all the necessary emphasis.

"Sir Eldon ..., he paused. "Really?" he asked with a quick aside. "Smith AND Jones, you say?"

Eldon nodded, "Yeah, Smith and Jones!"

Marty took one last lick from the tablespoon, tapped it first to one of Eldon's shoulder, then to the other, and then tapped Eldon's head and said majestically, "I do hereby dub thee, Sir Eldon Smith and Jones – Knight of the Crematoria, Keeper of the Ancient Ones, and Gleaner of Pieces of Otherwise Irrelevant Information". He nodded to Eldon, gave him a quick smile, jammed the tablespoon back into the Jif Jar and flew up the stairs.

To Eldon, it seemed that his flight was literal. He pondered briefly, as he put his hands over his ears to block out what sounded like "white noise". A blue light surrounded Mr. Markham as flew to the stairs. He was enveloped by it. His flippers seemed to flutter, propelling him forward, moving him through the air and up the stairway. *Zowie*, thought Eldon. *That boy can swim!*

In a miraculous turn of events, Eldon would remain mute until the day when he would testify to Ms. Bichette that Marty was a god - of sorts – who should be spared a space at Golden Hills and should not be removed from that facility as she would otherwise direct. If he was to be a permanent fixture, only Time would tell.

CHAPTER XXVI

It was Mother's Day. The employees at the old folks' home thought that a dance would be nice. They would invite the residents' families to come for the day. They decorated the cafeteria with crepe paper ribbons – pink and white. They moved out the buffet table used at lunch time and put down a small fold out dance floor made of Masonite. Someone borrowed it from the local bar. Peach punch and sugar cookies were the treats. They played music by CD put on a boom box and placed on a fold out table next to the dance floor. The only available CD played the Beatles' classics – 1965 to 1970, a bit after most of the residents' time. The piece de resistance was a large rotating ball hung from the ceiling with small mirrored pieces of glass glued to the ball's exterior. A small electric motor was affixed, and a large yellow extension cord supplied power from a nearby outlet to make the large ball slowly turn. A small spotlight was placed on the floor and directed at the ball. A circular cardboard cut-out, divided into 3 pie-like shapes and colored with plastic: pink, yellow, and light blue, was set to spin slowly on another small motor.

At intervals, the spinning cut-out changed the color of the light directed by spotlight at the ball. The effect was to cast small points of light that routinely changed color in various directions, across the expanse of the cafeteria. When the room was darkened, the effect was contrived but dramatic. Few people danced, and the refreshments were boring, but the evening proved enjoyable enough for the families. The grandkids that came particularly liked the sugar cookies, the peach punch not so much. The grandmas and grandpas felt "at home" with the kids there. The evening proved memorable.

Marty was there dressed in a nice pair of slacks and a sweater. He wore his speedo underneath. He found it difficult to move without his flippers. He wore a clumsy pair of sneakers to better meet the dress code for the evening. He was lucid and surrounded by family. He was not wholly clear on just who was there with him. He did not recognize his wife who was there with their son and daughter and their respective families. His young granddaughters had found a box of new syringes in the closet in the back - sans needles. They pulled peach punch from the large crystal bowl and set about squirting each other. They managed to squirt a few of the patrons along way. His daughter and daughter-in-law apologized profusely, chased down the girls, and herded them off to the lavatory to clean up. The older two grandkids were playing ping pong on the patio outside. They were bored by the whole old folks' thing and couldn't wait to leave.

Marty's son and son-in-law were there and had found the television in the front reception. They were watching BYU football re-runs from ages past. His son-in-law came from a football family. His dad had played at BYU as a wide receiver and had gone on to the pros. His son-in-law had played at BYU as a wide receiver and had gone onto the pros. His son-in-law's little brother had played at BYU as a wide receiver and had gone onto the pros. Marty walked-on to the football team at the University of Utah as a defensive back, never played a lick, and gave no thought to the pros. The rivalry between these two in-state schools was well recognized. At his daughter's wedding reception, Marty had toasted the in-law family. The toast went something like this: "I never thought, in a million years, that a defensive back from the University of Utah would give his daughter away to three wide receivers from Brigham Young". Marty did not recall all of those present, but the toast was a hit, at least in Marty's view. He recalled the toast, but did not recall just how much it had helped to cement the two families.

Toward seven pm, the end of a late night for the seniors, the song "Something" by the Beatles came on. This song was special to

Marty and always triggered favorable memories. The song triggered long forgotten feelings. These feeling were much more real than just old memories; only nowadays, to Marty, the difference between feelings and memories was often indistinguishable. Surprising to the crowd still present, Marty got up to dance. There, seated alone, was a beautiful blonde girl- a girl who looked an awful lot like the one who had stolen his heart years ago. He had trouble sometimes remembering this girl, but he knew that she was important to him. The beautiful blonde seated alone did visit often. She would say "hi" and was always sweet. Marty had taken note. With his favorite song now playing, he knew that there was no better time than the present. He walked over to her. He reached for her hand, raised it to his lips, and kissed it.

"Please miss, would you favor me with this dance", he asked gallantly. She looked up at him and smiled.

"Well, Marty", she breathed. "I never thought that you would ask"

♪♪ "Something in the way she moves attracts me like no other lover. Something in the way she woos me. I don't want to leave her now. You know I believe and how" ♪♪

The Beatles serenaded. Marty and his girl moved slowly, caught in the moment, close and sweet. The music continued. The verses spoke volumes; and, the then to the end...

♪♪ Something in the way she knows that all I have to do is think of her. Something in the things she shows me. I don't want to leave her now. You know I believe and how". Bah, bump, bah, dah dah dahhhhhhhhh..... ♪♪.

The music stopped. The spinning lights continued to turn slowly, silently. Starlight spanned the night sky, changing colors: pink, yellow, light blue, and Marty pressed for a kiss- a long and pleasantly wet kiss that brought him to an attention that, until now, had been long forgotten. The lights came on. Ms.Bichette came into the cafeteria. She had been stunned to find Marty back in bed after finding him "dead" in bed. He never ceased to amaze. She was just glad that she had not yet submitted her paperwork. Otherwise, she would have some explaining to do.

Here in the cafeteria her hair was neatly pinned, her cap at attention – much like Marty at this moment. Her uniform was white and neatly pressed, her bosoms straining at the buttons. She announced that it was seven pm and that visitor's hours were over. She immediately set the staff to cleaning up. The leftover cookies were put into pouches and placed in the back cupboard. The remaining peach punch was dumped down the sink drain. The staff didn't like it either. Besides, there was plenty of powder to last through the 21st century. Marty and his girl remained in their embrace. Just like long ago, Marty now needed Time, Time to...well, to remember. But this Time, he wished that this long forgotten feeling could last. He was deserving of it, wasn't he? He loved this girl, didn't he?

The staff cleaned up around them. They unplugged the revolving globe light. They removed the spinning color wheel. They put away the motors and extension cords. The boom box was stored, to be taken back to the bar and to this day, no one knows just what happened to the magical CD. Marty and his girl remained in their sweet embrace. He standing proud and erect; she with her head on his chest. It was sweet, peaceful. He loved her. She loved him. That was clear. At this moment, he remembered and sobbed. For some time, his tears fell silently down his cheeks. The staff remained patient. They were not inclined to interfere. They left the temporary dance floor in place. They would put it back behind the bar tomorrow. The large revolving magical ball, they left abandoned at the ceiling. Again, later would be soon enough to take it down. For now, it was out of the way. The staff finished and took one more long and silent notice of the couple on the dance floor. They smiled at each other. The last one out turned off the lights and closed the cafeteria doors behind him for the lovebirds to be alone.

At 7:00 am the next morning, Ms. Bichette wheeled her pill cart into room 13. On a daily basis, she expected to find Marty comatose, close to death. The bed sheets were rumpled as if slept in. Last night, she was assured that he was in bed. The staff reported that he had gone back to his room following last night's dance. Still, she was not so sure. The gossip had taken its toll. The residents continued to speak of a blue phantom that had floated out the front door and disappeared into the night sky. While at the desk, she had heard what could be described as "white noise". She investigated to find that the television set that Maggie was watching had been left on. She switched it off, puzzled. Sometime later, she heard a scratchy, continuous noise and checked the set again. It was on...again! She tracked down Curly. He wasn't difficult to find. She burst through the door of the men's room next to the front office.

"Hey! Curly!" she called out. Her voice bounced off of the tiles.

Curly was stationed on the toilet seat in the first stall. A cloud of smoke hovered over him near the ceiling. He had just settled into what he believed was a well-deserved break. He choked back the doobie he was smoking and coughed out a clipped response, "Uhh. Uhh. Yeah. I mean, yes... ma'am?"

She asked whether he had seen Marty recently. He hadn't. She asked about the television. Did he know whether it was working properly? Was it on the fritz? No. It was working fine. He and Mo had flipped it on. They were trying to find the TV ad for triple action cleansing.

Ms. Bichette didn't understand why he was searching for cleaning materials. The home furnished all that he needed. "You're looking for what?" she asked.

"You know" he quoted the commercial "'scrubbing bubbles for your intestine'".

She could only look at him perplexed.

He tried again, "C'mon...Do You Poop Enough"? He pushed open the stall door and looked at her like she was a ninny. They'd been after it for the past few days. She had heard them talking at lunch. They'd seen the television ads.

"Sheesh" she impatiently changed the subject. "Did you leave the set on when you, uh, took your break?"

"Uh, no", he lied.

But of course, she knew that he lied. She knew Curly better than he knew himself. She exited the men's room and stepped back into her station. She thought a moment. She was tempted to check Marty's bed for reassurance but checked herself instead. Self-doubt could be crippling. She chose to remain firm. She put her little finger into ear and rattled it around. The scratch felt good. She dismissed the "white noise" as nothing and returned to her books. Her books served to preoccupy her for a short time. But she couldn't concentrate. For her own sanity, she needed to find Marty. She signaled to the male housekeeping attendant turning mattresses in the bedrooms nearest the front desk to take her pill cart back to the infirmary. She went looking for Mo. Each of the residents had apparently taken an oath to Marty to help him preserve his privacy. Curly was the easiest to break. He didn't know. She would check the cafeteria first. If harsher methods were required, she would corner Mo. If that failed, she would stand them up together in a firing squad, as it were, and confront all three of them, together, and one at a time. They would break. They always did.

As it turned out, harsher methods were not required. She was surprised to find Marty in the cafeteria. He was standing on a dining table surrounded by a host of residents. It appeared as some form of recruitment. Curly, Mo, and Larry were lounging around taking it all in. Curly was the telegraph. He left the men's room as soon as she exited to warn the players in the cafeteria. He leaned on his mop with his right foot trying to appear innocent. His mop was in the yellow plastic bucket with wheels. Larry stood outside the group seeking to appear disinterested. It was a ruse. Ms. Bichette has seen before their juvenile efforts at pretense. Larry was one of Marty's biggest fans. Mo was seated at a nearby table eating bacon and eggs. He offered no subterfuge. She appreciated that about the man. On her order, the residents were once more denied the delicacies of bacon and eggs. But Mo was staff. His pay wasn't good and bacon tended to make up for the shortfall. Besides, he was formidable and she didn't want to upset him. Heaven forbid that he get angry.

When she was around, each of these three adopted the role that management imposed. They were employees, and she issued their daily orders. At best, they must stay neutral. But when Marty was lucid, he was such a damn nice guy. How could anyone stay neutral, let alone oppose him?

On most days, she was content with the standoff. This morning, Marty appeared in good form – neither quiet nor comatose. Rather, he was talkative and gesticulating. He appeared to have spruced up. He was clean shaven. From a distance, Ms. Bichette could smell a slight whiff of cologne, Elsha for Men. His hair was wet and plastered back. He wore his usual red speedo, with red swimming goggles on his head and flippers on his feet. Added to this uniform, he wore a large bath towel tied at his skinny neck. It was taken from Physical Therapy and striped vertically with magic marker: red, white, and blue. It flowed down his back and waved with his movements like a victory flag.

As she approached, the crowd of residents hushed and separated to allow her entry. Marty quieted and stepped down from the table. He stood straight to face her. She refused to acknowledge that he could intimidate her – but he did. Curly, Mo, and Larry each stiffened to attention. Some kind of confrontation appeared imminent.

"Mr. Markham, may I ask just what is going on here?" she commanded.

"Uh...we're waiting for breakfast. Peach yogurt and bacon", he smiled. The crowd muffled a few giggles.

Ms. Bichette's face reddened. She was in no mood. Her chest began to heave. She struggled to calm herself, to abate her breathing.

For a moment, her breathing slowed but only for a moment. Then, Larry chimed in.

"Ms. Bich...umm Bichette..." He almost sunk himself at the outset. "Ms. Bichette, I mean...well, the Director authorized an extra pallet of peach yogurt. Would you like some?" He stifled a giggle.

Larry was never any good at humor and, for him, the effort went completely flat. Mo yawned. Curly kept watching as if still expecting a punchline. Marty and the ladies were caught up in their own conversation and paid no attention. The humor may have never left the gate, but the attempt at humor was not lost on Ms. Bichette. Her face reddened. Her breathing hyped up. The top button on her uniform popped and went bouncing across the floor. Curly watched as it hit a small chip in the floor tile and bounced high. Like a major league 3rd basemen, he backhanded with his left, caught it on the bounce, and with one smooth and single motion, he deposited it into his left front pocket without breaking his stance on the bucket. Ms. Bichette felt her bosom release and heard the button bounce. She quickly turned toward Curly. But he was stationed just as before – holding the mop with his foot on the bucket and appearing oblivious.

She became more exasperated. Her breathing came even more rapidly. She sweated heavily. The serpent tattoo that appeared to enfold her seemed to move as if to coil for a strike. Rather forcibly, she strove to calm herself. She inhaled and exhaled quickly over and over in an effort to control her breathing. She straightened her blouse to better confine her escaping breasts. Larry and Curly lived in expectation of this long awaited reward. Marty's own expectation was heightened. As for Mo, he remained at the table and continued to eat. His love stayed firm for his bacon and eggs. The serpent continued to fight the hackles that confined it and seemed to undulate, up and down Ms. Bichette's entire frame, from her neck and shoulders all the way down to her toes and back. She struggled valiantly.

"Larry", she exclaimed loudly now. "Take these residents to the counter. Tell the cooks to give them some of your precious peach yogurt. Tell them the bacon is again on the menu for today only. Tell them anything, but get these people away from here". She exhaled sharply, purposefully until her breathing began to abate and control returned.

Larry wasn't sure whether he might endure Le Biche better in her wrath. When she was in full control, she could be exceptionally dangerous. He rounded up the spectators and herded them to the counter. Marty could be a hoot and his challenge exciting, but Ms. Bichette held sway. To him, and to most of the residents, she was unbeatable. As much as they might enjoy a good fight, the outcome was fixed. The promise of peach yogurt and bacon tipped whatever balance. Larry directed the crowd out the fire exit behind the kitchen at the rear of the cafeteria - including Trudy and Maggie, who had been sitting with Marty at his table in the rear. They were not prone to leave with an altercation brewing. Trudy, in particular, pressed to stay, but Larry insisted that she help with Maggie, herself comatose in her wheelchair.

Receiving no instruction from Ms. Bichette, Curly and Mo remained stationed. They looked at each other, nervously. Neither knew what to do now. Curly shrugged. Ms. Bichette took one final breath- deep and controlled. She cricked her neck, straightened her hair, pulled at her uniform, straightened her top, and brushed out her skirt. Her breathing returned; her color normal, she once again was master of this universe. She motioned Mo to leave his breakfast and to join them at Marty's table. She stationed him to the right of Marty just outside his immediate reach. Marty remained at attention. She directed Curly to take up watch at Marty's left – again, just out of reach. He rolled his bucket with his mop and took up his station. He looked again at Mo. Trepidation was heavy on both.

"Now, following that brief, but inconsequential interruption, I must again inquire: Just what is going on here?" Ms. Bichette demanded.

Marty responded, "As I said previously, we are...or were...waiting for breakfast. But it seems that we await yogurt and bacon no longer. Thank you so much for the hospitality", he said with some perceived sarcasm. He grinned. Both Curly and Mo stiffened. Surely Marty could set her off and the explosion would rain hell. Surprisingly, Ms. Bichette retained her composure. Marty always seemed composed, but the events of this day would echo a new norm. Neither had ever been in direct confrontation. Oh, sure. Marty was somehow cognizant of her exasperation with him. He often joked about it in his more lucid moments. But today, he obeyed and stayed at attention. Still, he was not inactive. His mind was turning, thinking, planning. He felt nervous; this feeling was new.

He really should take this contest "drug free" as it were, he thought. After all, he had made a commitment but as the button bounced and all eyes turned to Curly's athletics, Marty's resolve weakened. He swiftly retrieved a few pills, a purple from his goggles, an orange and blue from his speedo. These, he swallowed surreptitiously. Then, he waited. He had no clue as to what to expect. He'd never gone with this particular combination. Except for his own daily dosages, he had stopped taking pills altogether. Well...okay, he still took the pink pill made from jellyfish to help his memory. He still took that. And, of course, there were various vitamins and other pills that different women here at the home would offer to him. They liked his stories when he remembered. They wanted to help him to remember. Except for these more innocent pills, he hadn't touched the medications he kept stashed in his speedo and goggles. The pills that he took today were the first pills that he had taken for a week now outside of his normal routines.

Momentarily he began to feel it, the low buzz of "white noise" and the slight glow of blue light. Minutes, if not seconds later, a narrow laser beam of light jetted from within the blue glow like a quasar on display, then a second, and a third. LASIX surgery to his right eye when he was 50 produced the electronic display. Marty's optometrist, a friend from junior high school, had asked if he had worked in steel fabrication around an industrial oven, something to do with the type of cataract that was forming over his lens. Huh, what? The nature of the cataract serves to better identify its cause. Who the hell cared? Just replace the lens which he did. His otherwise "bionic" eye now fired laser like rays in all directions. The laser shots continued with mind numbing speed. With each piercing ray, the plaster on the walls splattered, the overhead lights exploded, the acoustic ceiling tiles shattered into small pieces and fell.

Marty's display was sudden. Mo, Curly, and Ms. Bichette each reacted reflexively. Curly barreled under a nearby table with a few of the residents who remained. Ms. Bichette stood atop the salad bar at center cafeteria. Trudy and Maggie had ditched Larry's efforts to absent them and shrunk beneath the counter to avoid detection.

Ms. Bichette refused to acknowledge that she had lost all control. Still she remained speechless, unable to plan or to even think. The best she could do was exit. On her way out, she left the details to Mo.

"Mo, I will hear your report later. Please take care of this matter- the sooner, the better. She chose not to watch the unfolding drama and left the cafeteria. Mo was surprised at her retreat but not unprepared.

CHAPTER XXVII

As Mo staked out his position to intercept, he waited for Marty to calm down and began to daydream. For some strange reason, he remembered second grade. Mrs. Burns was his teacher. She liked to sing opera style. She was very pretty, and he was smitten. Mrs. Burns could warble, her ruby lips intrigued. Her wide open mouth, especially with the higher notes, revealed her uvula. The uvula wasn't new to him. He'd already found one in his own throat, and he'd seen it in some of the other kids when they screamed at times whether in pain or for delight. But the name was new to Mo. For Ms. Burns, he had looked it up to include in his vocabulary notebook:

"Uvula - a conic projection from the posterior edge of the middle of the soft palate, composed of connective tissue containing a number of 'racemose' (huh?) glands, and some muscular fibers (musculus uvulae). It also contains a large number of 'serous' (again, wha..?) glands that produce a lot of thin saliva".

Of course, none of this made any real sense to Mo. He simply chose to call it "that thing that dangles at the back of the throat". At times to impress, he would throw the term around during playground conversation. He was fascinated by that small dangling thing there at the back of Mrs. Burn's throat. It was somehow sexy, somehow seductive. It wobbled reflexively, more quickly with the higher notes than with those lower on the chromatic scale. Mo loved Mrs. Burns and her uvula. He hung onto every word she said and taught, and he was always mesmerized when she sang.

Mrs. Burns had taught them the rules of one, two, and three. When she stood at the front of the class and signaled with her index finger, the class was to be silent and wait for instruction. When she signaled two, the class was to line up at the side of the room, stand silent, and await instructions to exit. When she signaled three, the class was to duck under their desks. In the west, near the Rocky Mountains, signal three most likely meant earthquake, and earthquake meant the class needed to shelter now. Mo speculated that in the eastern states, where earthquakes rarely ventured and instead tornadoes dominated the news, that a three was not a good idea. He speculated that for a tornado, an elementary school desk offered little to no shelter. At the arrival of a tornado, he could envision himself stuck under his desk and sailing through the skies, much like Dorothy sailing in her bed toward Oz. But in the west, a three was the best idea. The earthquake drill was definitely Mo's favorite. Throughout his second grade year, he cherished the earthquake drill and would watch with anticipation each time Mrs. Burns stood at the head of the class to signal three. Unfortunately, such a well-made set of plans was doomed to fizzle and by choice Mo had purposefully chosen to forget all about second grade. So why now should he remember?

As happened one day in the late spring while Mo was mesmerized by Mrs. Burns in the exercise of her uvula, the large windows at the side of the room began to wobble, the desks -filled with second graders- began to bounce across the floor, and the entire room shook, noticeably. Mrs. Burns stopped her warble and stood dumbfounded at the head of the class watching windows move, desks bounce, and the hanging lights slide back and forth. The entire class could only gawk, mouths open, but no one spoke. All, -including Mrs. Burns – just gazed about the room to watch it sway. Following what seemed like eternity, but in reality was no more 10 to 15 seconds, the wobbling stopped. The class stayed silent for a moment longer. Finally, Ms. Burns came to and told the class to pull out their notebooks. It was now time to take down this week's words for the spelling bee on schedule for next week. With Ms. Burn's return to business, this remarkable scene was forgotten until Mo returned home to find his mom cleaning up broken dishes in the kitchen cupboards.

"Mom, what happened?" he asked curiously.

"Didn't you feel it? We had an earthquake today", his mom explained.

At this revelation, Mo was dumbfounded. He was angry. All season long, he had practiced for this very event. Each time Ms. Burns had signaled three, he dove with alacrity underneath his desk. Each time she had signaled three, he sought the only protection available to him in the event of an inevitable earthquake. Her failure to signal three told Mo that the threat was not real but fabricated. His experience with this earthquake jaded him to the associated dangers and from that day forward, Mo stubbornly refused to participate in any supposed "earthquake" drill. This included all those as called by the "number three".

"Mo, darling," she would say. "Three means take shelter. You need to seek protection under your desk".

Mo would sit stubbornly at his desk, teeth clenched, arms folded tightly across his chest. To this day, in an exercise of free will, Mo expected to be killed in an earthquake. He would tempt his fate. He would dare those in charge. No more would he stoop to dive under a desk but would face the music regardless. Should an earthquake take him home, only then might he forgive Mrs. Burns for all of those wasted drills she had made them take while there in the second grade. For now, Ms. Burns could wait. But Marty could not and Mo's second grade training took hold. For whatever reasons, Mrs. Burns was now being vindicated. Marty was the earthquake!

Mo moved throughout the cafeteria signaling the residents there at breakfast to seek shelter beneath the tables, under the chairs, or behind the front counter and cash registers. Those nearest the entrance leading from Hallway B, he instructed to line-up at the far wall. He wasn't sure what was happening. He knew only that light bulbs were popping; fixtures were shattering. The ancient residential electrical wiring there in the cafeteria was kaput. But, replacement would wait. The wallboard was exploding as if fired upon by a shotgun. Safety to the residents was the priority. He signaled the line of residents to exit. He closed and secured the doors behind them. Those who had taken shelter, he instructed to hunker down and await an all clear. He then fixed his attention on Marty.

Marty wandered slowly throughout the open cafeteria, fins down, and skidding across the floor, goggles on his head, his cape folded across his chest. He moved slowly in the direction of Hallway B apparently unaware that Mo had secured the doors. His movements were slow, mechanical -like those of Gort, the mighty robot commanded by Klatu in The Day the Earth Stood Still. Those still present watched in amazement from behind whatever shelter they had taken, some behind overturned tables, some behind the cash register and front counter. Some had found refuge in the recreation room adjacent to the cafeteria where they sheltered under the ping pong table, others behind the pool table.

Marty continued to rumble and fire. Laser- like shots emanated from his right eye in every direction. Then suddenly, he stopped. His eyes searching, seeking for something, seeking for a way out- for an escape. But the doors were barricaded and Mo was not set to open them anytime soon. The laser shots were entertaining but by no means destructive. Marty directed a few at the doors in an apparent effort to burst them open. No luck. The old wooden doors absorbed the energy; the door handles vibrated; the hinges creaked, but the doors held. Marty's eyes moved right, his head followed slowly mechanically, then stopped at 90 degrees. His eyes came back again followed by his head which passed front, moved to 180 degrees, and then stopped. His eyes continued to scan – first right, then left and back. Once more, in the same manner, his head followed his eyes left to stop at front. Then, his head flowed left to 90 degrees and his eyes followed. His eyes then flowed past 90, to 100, then to 110 degrees where his head caught up, and his eyes lingered, perusing the wall to the left.

The lens in his bionic eye opened and closed seeking focus until he found what he was searching. His head stayed fix. His body turned to follow. His feet moved stiffly. His feet with flippers stayed glued to the floor as he pressed his skinny legs forward, one after the other. His movement took him to the fire hose kept housed in an old fashioned glass covered cabinet approximately three feet square. The writing on the glass said, "In case of fire, break glass".

Mo froze, his jaw dropped. He wasn't sure what he was witnessing. Was any of this real? Could he swear to any of this? Would it come to that? He looked around in an attempt to find Ms. Bichette. Maybe she could help. But he remembered her hasty exit and wished, for once, that she was present. Curly remained under the table. He offered a silly smile with a quick "thumbs up" to Mo. For once, Mo wished again that he could pass the buck to Ms. Bichette. That would be the right thing to do wouldn't it?

Marty stopped. His eyes, or his eye rather, was focused on the fire hose. He shot a laser beam at the glass. The glass shattered. With robot-like movement, he reached in with both of his skinny hands and secured the hose. He lifted it out. He pointed the nozzle toward the doors and turned the lever. Water exploded from the brass nozzle. Skinny Marty, though powerful in appearance, was still skinny Marty. The nozzle erupted and began to spit water like venom from a giant snake. Marty clung to the hose for dear life. The hose coiled and struck, coiled and struck. Marty rode bareback for all he was worth. The nozzle continued to spray as it banged off of the ceiling, the walls, and erupt from the rising flood. Marty continued to ride, his mood and expression unchanged. One burst felled Curly who had just left the safety of the cafeteria table under which he had taken refuge. He easily surrendered and returned to the shelter of the table. Another nearly nailed Mo - a rather selective shot considering that he stood just behind Marty, out of the normal working zone of fire.

After a Time, Marty regained a semblance of control and rode the snakelike hose, like a bull rider at the Fourth of July Rodeo. With the doors closed, the water rose - first two feet, then four feet and continued. In this, Marty found his element. He directed the force of the hose at the closed cafeteria doors. Wave after wave struck at the doors' center until with six feet of water pressing at the threshold, the doors burst open and a Tsunami-like wave flooded into Hallway B.

Like the centerpiece in a wild but wet fireworks display, Marty rode the resulting wave like a surfer on fins. Marty let go of the hose. Like a snake confronted, it rose and spit, rose and spit as it sprayed across the cafeteria's expanse shooting burst after burst. The wave took him out through the broken doors. Both hung askew at either side on busted hinges. The wave scattered a host of curious residents who had been stationed at the door jambs outside of the doors at both sides seeking to spy on the curious events inside. Some were holding drinking glasses pressed to listen. One had found a stethoscope to find some type of heartbeat. A few were stationed, bent to the floor, their skinny backsides exposed, and trying to peek under the doors. The wave sent them all drenched and tumbling down and through Hallway B, and into the main reception.

Marty rode the crest and when the energy waned, he stood drenched and dripping, hands on hips, goggles on his head, fins askew – there in main reception. Ms. Bichette had returned to her desk. She spectated from her desk there at the front entry. Marty stood erect like a statue in front of her desk. He stared longingly out the glass front doors. The bewildered residents, whom the wave had scattered with him down the hall, stumbled to their feet; coughing; and choking. Each was soaked to the skin, their pajamas; robes; and other hospital attire disheveled and dripping. Mo and Curly took up the rear. Larry, recently returned from helping residents back to their rooms, soon joined them. Trudy and Maggie found their way to the front. Larry sneered over at them and stuck out his tongue.

Ms. Bichette stood at her desk in reception. She completed her bookkeeping entry and looked up. She left the reception desk to confront the crowd. She was again in charge. Her white dress was neatly pressed, buttoned up, and spotless, her bosom at front and center, her hair pinned back, herself, orderly. She signaled to Mo, Larry, and Curly. Each came forward to stand at attention there in reception. Curly tried, as usual, to appear to be prepared. He came with mop and bucket.

"Well, Gentlemen, what must we do now?" she asked with practiced condescension.

"Mo", she said, "it would seem that you were less than successful in curtailing the antics carried on by the residents there in the cafeteria. What a shame. I had seen so much promise in you", she emphasized with a "tsk, tsk, tsk".

The three looked back and forth at each other but stayed mute.

"Gentlemen, I will ask again....What must we do NOWWWWAH!!!?" she emphasized dramatically. "Why are these people wet and dripping?"

She waved her hand in the direction of the drenched residents who stood together with Marty in the center of the reception area. Her stare remained firmly on Mo, Larry, and Curly. Each looked, again, at the other. None were certain exactly what had happened. None was sure just how to respond. Marty had always been an enigma, but this was ridiculous. Had they lost control? If so, how? How had he gotten himself here? Indeed, how had they come to be here? How best to explain? Where could they even start?

"Please..." she said impatiently as she looked up at each over the top of her reading glasses. She peeled them off with heightened impatience and said, "Mo and Larry, please get these people back to their rooms and into some dry clothes. It is medication time. Naptime follows shortly. Get them cozy. Now, do your jobs gentlemen".

"...and oh, you can leave Mr. Markham with me", she stated insistently. Her tone was disconcerting. The three of them hesitated. She looked at them again over the top of her glasses and impatiently waved them off.

"Curly," she directed, "Mop up this floor. Be sure to put out the yellow cones and otherwise mark off the water hazards. Visitors' hours come early tomorrow morning. I'm counting on you to keep this place safe. Now let's get to it", she said.

Mo shrugged and turned to leave. He saw Trudy pushing Maggie in her wheelchair. Surreptitiously, the two had been taking it all in. Trudy remained utterly confused by the days' events. For all purposes, Maggie was disconnected. Mo took Maggie's chair and together with Trudy returned to the cafeteria to commiserate.

Curly left and went to the closet to retrieve the safety cones. He stepped inside and closed the door. He needed a toke to clear his head.

Larry looked to Marty who stood alone like a statue there in the front entry. Once again, he was catatonic. Larry rounded up the dripping and bewildered residents. He patted Marty sympathetically on his back and led the others back to their respective rooms. Soon each was warm, dry, and tucked into bed waiting for Ms. Bichette to distribute their medications. Tomorrow they would remember little.

As Larry was shuffling the residents off to bed, Ms. Bichtte looked down Hallway B to see Trudy pushing Maggie – both of them leaving with Mo. She had seen neither Trudy nor Maggie during the exasperating ruckus. Always, these two were involved in every significant event at Golden Hills. Nothing of consequence occurred here without some involvement or dealings by one or both of these two women. This was curious. She made a mental note to check in with Trudy before the day was through. In the meantime, something had to be done with Mr. Markham. She liked the man and appreciated his humor, but he was beginning to get out of hand causing the residents to riot, water everywhere. The escalation in his behavior was disconcerting.

But then again...what was "escalation" anyway? What behavior? She, herself, could not explain exactly what had happened. She did not witness and would never fully know what had occurred in the cafeteria that day. She could only assume that Marty was at the center of the day's events. Wasn't that usually the case? She reached for the phone and punched in the number for his wife. She should meet with Mrs. Markham and her family. Visitor's day was coming and that would be a good time to discuss alternative plans.

Meanwhile, Trudy and Maggie sat at Marty's table in the back of the cafeteria. It was mealtime. Curly had repaired the doors and had just finished mopping. Mo was angling again for some more Smokehouse bacon – standard fair for Mo whenever he was near the cafeteria. Larry was ispo facto the cafeteria manager. He was present and on the job. The five of them were discussing the day's events. Mo was munching. Like Ms. Bichette, Trudy and Maggie had missed most of the excitement.

"Man, I tell ya, he was out of his element", Curly related. "Our Swimmer buddy was dressed...well, like a swimmer, you know: speedo, fins, and those goggles. But he sure didn't move like one. He didn't move at all like...you know...well...like Marty. He...He moved like some kinda robot thing; you know, stiff and...and, slow. I never saw Marty move 'slow' like that, no, not so much 'slow', but 'clunky'. You know what I mean?" He looked around for confirmation – almost begging- first to Trudy, then to Maggie and back to Trudy.

Maggie muttered her confirmation: "No, I never saw Marty move 'slow' like that". She was beginning to wake up. Both Trudy and Curly looked over at her, a bit stunned at her seeming illumination.

"Yeah, see? I told you guys!. Yesss!", he pointed to Maggie and balled his fist. He pumped it celebrating Maggie's less than audible vote of confidence. "Okayyy!", he said to no one in particular.

Mo added his confirmation. "Yeah, he was 'clunky', like a 'robot thing', like Curly said", he mumbled with a mouthful of bacon.

Trudy looked at Curly expectantly. He stared back at her and shrugged as if to say, "What?

"Curly," she said with exasperation. "Tell us the rest. What else happened? Don't spare the details. It's important". She needed to understand just what had occurred. She was worried. She knew that Marty was a target. Any behavior outside the normal – if there was such a thing here in Golden Hills – would give Ms. Bichette reason to act. She suspected, and correctly, that Marty's family would be advised and that alternative plans for Mr. Markham would be cemented. She looked again at Curly intently,

"Tell me everything that you remember", she said, "How he acted, what he said, what he did that was normal, you know, 'Marty normal', and what he did that was not. Tell me about anything out of the ordinary or unusual in what happened and the way it happened. And, give me a list of damages. I'm looking for the nature and extent together with any potential 'other' causes – you know, those maybe not related to Marty. It's important. Can you do that?"

"Well, I've told you pretty much what happened", Curly said. "I'll need to investigate the damages. It will take some time".

Trudy nodded. Curly reiterated the day's happenings with a bit more detail. At times, Trudy was forced to jump in to keep him on track. But for the most part, he stayed on point. She cogitated. The "blue light" was hard to explain. And the erratic laser-like shots from his eyes, for obvious reasons, were hard to believe, especially the shot that broke the glass and somehow set off the fire sprinkler to flood the room. Trudy suspected that the events of the day could be explained logically. Marty was almost magical and people loved him. But Trudy knew him best. She knew he was normal –whatever that meant. She would need to keep him normal. She would need to make sure that Ms. Bichette knew that he was normal, and that his family knew it. She would need to ensure that Marty stayed here with her at Golden Hills. She did not believe that he could survive outside the home.

Curly wrapped up his version of events, and Trudy nodded her thanks.

"Please, see what you can find out. Get back to me as soon as you can, Trudy directed. "And, again...thank you".

Curly set off determined. He was tasked to help Marty and he intended to do it right.

Trudy cogitated some more. The heavens only knew the number of different interpretations of the day's events floating among the residents by the time dinner was served. Maybe that was the answer. Let it play out. The residents of the home would spread only so much nonsense. They would remember nothing, really, about what happened, or would otherwise blast hyperbolic, so the truth would be irrelevant; no explanation required. Then again, few, if any, of the residents actually witnessed the happenings. There were Mo and Curly on the inside of the cafeteria and the few residents who had snuck back from the Larry-led evacuation to sneak a peek. On the outside in Hallway B, there were those who were swept away by the flood when the doors broke. One thing was sure: Ms. Bichette would use whatever story best suited her purposes, and her purposes surrounding Marty were not good. Trudy needed to find the truth just to be sure.

As for Curly, like a worthy investigator, he set about reliving the historical phenomenon of that day. Although he couldn't account for Marty and his strange behavior, he could review the respective conditions there in the cafeteria. He recalled that the glass that covered the fire case had shattered with an apparent shot from Marty's bionic eye. Some acoustic ceiling files had been broken. Chinks were taken from the wall plaster as if by pistol shot. This damage might be explained as part of the aging process. The building was old and needed repair. Vibrations from the dance music might have caused old repairs to fail. Closer inspection of the walls and ceiling tiles confirmed this likely conclusion. A quick review of the electric bill confirmed a power surge during the dance. This would explain the broken fluorescent lights.

The "blue light" and "white noise" that emanated from Marty were harder to explain. Curly speculated that Marty's Monoi could explain the "blue light". He had recently received a package from Tahiti that contained several bottles of Monoi – Tiare Tahiti. It was scented coconut oil, manufactured in Tahiti, and very popular. He slathered some onto his balding head which caused his head to shine, to even glow. The reflection of the light blue tiles and paint in the cafeteria would give his head a blue like glow. Wouldn't it? At times, this glow could appear to envelope Marty. Couldn't it? The best he could figure was that the light that emanated was a reflection off of Marty himself. And, as for the "white noise", Curly was curious. This noise had been with Marty for a while now. He speculated that Marty wore a hearing aid which lacked good volume control. Likely the "buzz" was tied to the hearing aid. Curly would check it out and later confirm. He concluded that the hearing aid explained the "white noise". Yeah, well, there could be better explanations, but these came close and should work for now.

The glass front to the firehose was shattered. A few broken remnants were left around in place at the edges of the frame. The fire hose had been replaced on the squeaky metal wheel. Broken shards lay beneath. He carefully shuffled through the remains to inspect. There, he found a button. Hmmmm... he thought. He reached into his shirt pocket and pulled out the button he'd recovered from Ms. Bich's uniform when she shot it across the cafeteria during her recent tantrum. Curly had been quick to make the grab. A comparison showed them to be duplicates. Ms. Bich had lost her fair share of buttons from which the boys each had a collection going. With the last one Curly recovered from beneath Le Biche's desk about a week ago when he was cleaning out front office, he was plus three. This one made four. Mo and Larry each had one. This one gave Curly a commanding lead, unless of course you counted Marty. No one really knew how many buttons he had captured. But given the number of times he had pissed off Le Biche over the years, he should have at least a yogurt container full.

Curly concluded that Ms. Bich must have lost a second button during the day's excitement. She was expansive enough so that when the uniform burst, a button could take off as if shot from a gun. He had never seen her lose two in one day. But rumor had it that ,although rare, it did occur.The last recorded happenstance was a few months back. Nothing was impossible given Ms. Bich's impressive set. Curly took a pleasurable moment to ponder then quickly went back to work.

He wondered about the laser shots – one, to break the glass, the other to turn on the hose? He remembered that the fire hose had come alive when another apparent laser shot from Marty's eye had hit it. But a brief inspection of the handle revealed nothing. No burn marks, no scarring, or other signs of an impact – whether by laser or by button shot. Closer inspection showed not so much what was visible, but what was aromatic. He smelled a familiar scent only to realize that it was Marty's cologne – Elsha. He took an intentional sniff. A light and remnant scent of Elsha cologne again wafted past his olfactory, and he recalled the tender moment between Marty and his wife when they danced beneath the romantic light display put up by the slowly turning globe covered in small chips of mirrored-glass that reflected small dots –even laser beams- of light throughout the darkened cafeteria. And he knew!

An errant button had shattered the glass that covered the fire hose. When Marty started his rampage, Le Biche ducked and ran. At the moment, she must have lost a second button before she ran to the buffet table at the back of the cafeteria and stepped up on top to watch from a safe distance. It was not a laser shot from Marty's bionic eye that broke the glass despite the visible shot of light from the mirrored globe. And Curly was certain that Marty, himself, had turned on the fire hose, not some dart from a bionic eye. No magic. No mystery.

Marty's robot-like movements together with his surf ride out on the wave from the cafeteria and down the hall to the entry were otherwise explained by Marty's curious athletic acumen. The size of the wave was explained by the folks outside the doors who had jammed towels, toilet paper, candy wrappers, and napkins – just about anything – under the doors at the threshold and at the door jambs to seal up the openings. They were as much interested in having fun as anybody. The rumor mill that accounted for his reputation only enhanced his exploits to make him not just a celebrity but a super hero there at Golden Hills. Curly needed to report back to Trudy. They might be able to capitalize on Marty's new found fame.

Problem was that Trudy had left the cafeteria. She was not in her bedroom, Bedroom 11 in Hallway B. She was not with Maggie in Bedroom 12, next door. He couldn't find her with Marty in Bedroom 13 down Hallway A. He took the stairs from Hallway A to the downstairs to the temporary morgue. He opened the basement door ever so slightly and peeked into the temporary morgue. He saw the Death Squad dealing with a stiff lying there on a slab,and for a moment, his heart stopped. No, it wasn't Trudy, and no it wasn't Marty either.

A closer look told Curly that it was Barney Brewster. Barney was – or had been – a very long time resident. He never came out to play. Most of the folks figured he had passed on years ago. Oh, sure, the fact that Barney finally died was no big deal. No one really knew how old he was. Bets had him easy at 100. The house put 2 to 1 on him at 106. The best odds put him at 111 and anyone who knew him would make that bet. Curly figured that his age registered higher than the temperature gauge on the hot tub in PT. The fact that he died was a given.

What Curly hadn't expected was that he would lose his dealer so abruptly. After all, he had only recently learned that Barney grew some pretty powerful pot beneath his bed. He had stumbled upon the plants with his dust mop while sweeping for bunnies under the residents' beds.

Barney had told him that by using a blue light and a few plants, he could harvest a worthy stash every 3 months or so. Water he supplied by poking a hole in the copper waterline that ran to the miniature swamp cooler that was placed in bedroom window from which he would sprinkle the plants during the midnight hours. When not in use, he would plug the line with a chaw of heavily gnarled chewing gum that, since he had no teeth, he was forced to purchase with a 12 percent share of the proceeds from his bunkmate. His bunkmate, at 98, was amazingly capable of chewing a stick of Wrigley's with a decent set of false teeth that he had borrowed from his 78 year old son who would sometimes come to visit.

"Scuttah", Curly whispered hard under his breath when he saw the Death Squad working up Barney. He'd need to go easy on his remaining stash until he could find another source. "Bon Voyage, my good friend" he whispered and blew a silent kiss to his friend. For now, he needed to find Trudy. He headed back upstairs.

"Scuttah", he muttered again to himself as he continued his search for Trudy in the bedrooms and hallways. "That is a good word", he thought. Marty had taught him that one.

He checked for Trudy in her bedroom, Bedroom 11, with Maggie next door in Bedroom 12, and stuck his head into every bedroom up and down Hallway B – nothing. He walked past Marty's room, Bedroom 13 in Hallway A. He poked his head inside. Marty was snoring. He'd been here, pretty much, since the dance. Curly recalled that in the days following, things had settled back into their more sedate routines. But Marty's exploits the day following the party still formed part of the daily conversations and contributed to an ongoing excitement unusual for the sedate setting of a senior residence.

As Trudy had predicted, the rumor mill ran rampant. The three most popular versions went something like this:

- Curly had mistakenly "hot boxed" Marty accounting for his aberrant behavior the night of the dance. The rumor was that Marty was high after Curly had mistakenly locked him into a stall while Curly was cleaning the men's room.

- Larry had misinterpreted the yogurt logs to somehow allow the yogurt to ferment, that Marty had taken an extra cup that morning for breakfast, and he was drunk.

- Ms. Bichette had juiced Marty with a witches' elixir in an attempt to calm him, permanently; the attempt somehow backfired, and either her pill selection was wrong or someone had unknowingly swapped out the peach punch from the punch bowl for homemade wine fermented by one of the residents - which dimmed Marty's senses and slowed his reflexes.

Of these three versions of events, this third one was, of course, the most widely disseminated only because it was the most outlandish. Everyone sought to ascribe superpowers to Marty.

The second was just not credible. Few, if any of those who knew Larry, believed that he could somehow "misinterpret" his own yogurt logs, and if he did, it was no mistake. Yet, no one would ascribe a malevolent motivation to Larry so an intentional mistake was unlikely.

The third was not really a rumor. Marty had been victimized, at least one time previously, when Curly took a toke in the men's room. In fact, whenever Marty's unusual behavior required an explanation, the most practical was the likely bet.

Curly was tired and needed a toke. He would celebrate Barney. What better reason to retreat to the men's room.

CHAPTER XXVIII

Trudy, herself, was the only female to have visited Curly's men's room to share some rather high grade weed. She had to admit that the experience was liberating to say the least. She trusted that Curly would offer this as the more "practical" explanation for Marty's behavior during clean-up the day following the dance. It might even explain Marty's rather unusual behavior overall. She had expected that following investigation, Curly would supply a logical explanation for the otherwise magical events of that evening. Some explanation would be needed to combat Ms. Bichette's efforts to send him home. Curly was cleaning the restroom. She figured it was Time for a second –more unadulterated- visit with the good Mr. Curly.

The most popular but least used men's room at Golden Hills was located in Hallway B, just down from the reception desk and head office at the front reception area. This restroom was used mostly by visitors and only then on the handful of annual holidays when Golden Hills was open to the families. On any other day, the nicely furnished front reception that looked out onto the beautifully landscaped front entry, with its ornate fountain, covered with tiles of all colors, bordered with flowers and surrounded by maple trees, stood locked. Entry was allowed at the rear delivery doors only through the morgue in the basement, or – to serve the legalities – at a side entrance used by the employees and otherwise restricted for use by the residents except for emergencies. The near location of this men's room to the front desk allowed Curly and his visitors to "hide in plain sight". Today, the orange cones were posted in the hallway at either side of the doorway to the men's room. A yellow sign reading "Slippery

When Wet" was posted in the open doorway to the restroom. Trudy heard male voices coming from within. She entered to find Curly, leaning on a mop with his foot on a bucket and conversing with Larry who was holding a cup of peach yogurt and licking a spoon. Curly was loudly exaggerating yet another of his youthful exploits.

"Curly, hold it down" she shushed with a finger to her nose.

Curly and Larry both jumped, startled. "WTF", Curly halted. "Where have you been? I've scrubbed this place high and low for you" he said with some indignation.

"Keep it down", Trudy urged quietly. "D'you want Ms. Bichette to find us all in here together?" Ms. Bichette was taking lunch in the cafeteria. "Look", Trudy began. "I was hoping that you two might help me explain Marty's strange behavior recently. I mean, stranger than normal....or – not normal, but strange...stranger...than usual... oh hell, you know what I mean", she babbled.

At that moment, Mo entered pushing Maggie in her wheelchair. "Hey", Mo said quietly. "I brought her like you asked. She was difficult to download from her bed into that chair". Trudy nodded. To no one in particular, Mo exhaled, "Whoa, Jake" as he wiped his brow for emphasis.

"Really,", Curly inquired, somewhat surprised, "You found her in bed; actually in bed and not in her wheelchair?

Mo nodded agreeably.

"Who'd a thunk it", Curly responded.

"Now look", Trudy began but was interrupted.

"Hey", Maggie said. All eyes turned to Maggie, surprised. Mo stood dumfounded. Curly burped up a puff of smoke. He quickly put his hand to his mouth to cover. Maggie had not spoken for some time. Her friends had begun to think that she had permanently faded.

"Hey" they each muttered in surprised response.

Even Trudy viewed Maggie's return with skepticism. She missed the girl. She wished and had long felt that the Maggie had taken her leave to greener pastures. She worried that Maggie had cheated Death for too long in exchange for what was a very small and otherwise worthless piece of the life that was left to her. She worried that Death grew impatient and would take it out on Maggie. But now she wondered.

"Maggie. Are you....okay?" she asked. "I..I've missed you. I've missed you very much".

"I've missed you too, my sister. I'm sorry I haven't been around much. I've been away visiting. I've learned a great deal. I can guess where Marty goes when he...closes down. I even suspect that he might 'swim', perhaps even the oceans of the world", she smiled. "Now, take me inside. We need to talk". Trudy looked at Curly, shrugged her shoulders and raised her eyebrows to inquire. Curly puzzled and shrugged back.

Larry interrupted and said, "I was going to send Curly to get you. Maggie called the meeting. Sorry." He looked apologetically to each.

The group moved inside. Although the two had not spoken, Maggie knew of Trudy's concern. She knew that Ms. Bichette was planning to dispense with Marty. She wasn't sure just what that meant, but she did know that Marty's exit from Golden Hills would occur one day in short order; and, if his permanence here was not properly choreographed, would serve a great loss to Golden Hills and to Marty's memory.

Curly reported the results of his investigation. Like kids who just learned that Santa had other plans on Christmas Eve, each was disappointed to learn that Marty was more normal than they had hoped. Still, each was convinced more than ever, that Marty was a superhero who would one day be legendary.

As for Marty, for a while, he had settled back into bed and had been comatose for some time. Currently, he was again away on what all knew to be "a long swim" as he called it. But they needed to probe his memory of things. If he was fading, they needed to know so they could bring in help. Each knew that Ms. Bichette was pushing and that time was short.

"Hey, wait a minute", Larry said. "What was it that Marty would mumble when sometimes in his coma...something about Time? How you could slow down and even stop Time, as it were, and if you could stop Time, you could reach into Eternity or what he preferred to call 'No Time'?"

"Sure, yeah, I remember him going down that road more than once" Curly added. "I thought that he was nuts, but no more than usual". He looked around for agreement. Mo and Larry nodded in response.

"But I thought he said that trying to reach eternity by monkeying with the clock would be like building the Tower of Babel to try to get to Heaven. No matter how high you stacked the bricks, you could never get to Heaven. The entire effort would be just a long...or rather... a high dead end", Curly chortled quietly to himself.

"Whoa, hold on", Mo chimed in. "That would explain a lot. Could it be that Marty is attempting to stop Time? I mean his behavior, of late, just might be some kind of effort on his part... you know...to stop Time? Think about it. He keeps toying with his meds. Why is he doing that? And, he keeps pushing to get out. Over the past few years, he's been more than content to kill it with us in the cafeteria, to try to sneak a peek at Le Biche's cleavage, or to just relax in the tub in PT. He's never been as impatient as he has been lately. What is it that he's trying to find"?

Trudy recalled that she had seen him a few nights prior, apparently returning from the downstairs morgue.

"I was dispensing medication with Ms. Bichette", she began. "I saw him enter Hallway B from the stairwell up from the basement morgue. He headed to his room just as Ms. Bichette had moved into the room next door - room 14. He saw me and put his finger to his nose. He quietly 'shushed' me, and whispered that he'd had a nice visit with Eldon", she reported. "Isn't Eldon the guy who drives the hearse that takes us home... I mean, the hearse that carries us... each of us...you know...home?" she asked nervously. Nobody really wanted to consider the long ride home.

Curly nodded. He knew Eldon. Nice guy. He didn't like so much what he did for work. But he was a good guy. Curly was aching for a smoke.

Trudy mused, "He seemed like good 'ole' Marty. But I couldn't say what he had been doing in the morgue. I don't know. Death occurs so regularly here at Golden Hills, but Time sometimes refuses to take us". She continued, "I'm not sure what, but I suspect that Marty knows something and is searching. I don't know why he was down there? I don't know what he wanted. But he sure looked like he was looking for something".

She turned to Maggie and smiled sweetly, "I also suspect that Maggie has been searching, even learning, and may have something to share". She nodded to Maggie as if to introduce her.

All eyes turned. Maggie rolled her wheelchair on up to Curly. She reached up and pulled a joint from his shirt pocket. He looked down and belatedly reached to cover his pocket. He thought she would trash his stash. Instead, she placed 5 tightly rolled sticks to her lips and asked -out of the corner of her mouth "Light?".

With some hesitation, Curly pulled a lighter from his pants pocket and struck a flame lighting each one in succession. She took a long toke and held it until she had passed 4 of the 5 to those in attendance. She blew out and coughed hard once. Somewhat unexpectedly for her, she coughed again. She picked a few seeds from her tongue and summarized.

"Well... I have learned that Time is relative; that it can be slowed and accelerated and, even stopped. It will even move backwards. I've been there when it slows. I've been there when it has moved backwards. I've moved through both the past and the future. I've seen bits and pieces of both. The vision was blurred and cloudy, somehow distorted. Nothing was ever clear, but somehow, at any given moment, I knew what Time and what place that I was in. I know what Marty wants. He is looking to find that point where Time stops, or at least, unites. Not sure what that means exactly. I haven't been there. I wouldn't go. But I suspect that Marty has come close. My own guess is that when Time stops, it's just over; life that is. Marty, on the other hand, thinks that when he finds that place – that place he calls No Time, that place where the light beam and the train travel together at the speed of light so that the light beam no longer bounces between the mirrors but runs parallel with the train– that he will find No Time. To him, he'll find Eternity". She looked at each for comprehension.

Curly looked around at those present in the men's room. No one spoke. Trudy took a drag and choked. Larry patted her on the back. Mo stood silent. Curly stared back at each.

"W-T-F?" Curly was incredulous. "A speeding train, mirrors and a bouncing light beam? No Time and Eternity. I don't understand a lick. You guys are as crazy as Marty."

Maggie went on. "To me the best option in dealing with Time travel is to stay with Time, to stay away from No Time. Once Time stops, it's over. Think about it. If you've found No Time, you're Out of Time, and absent Time....you're just dead". She paused. The others said nothing, but felt a foreboding.

"The problem is that Marty has been experimenting with his meds, the dosage, the order, and mixture of any or all together of his vast array of prescription meds. That is how he is trying to find No Time". She fell silent to let that sink in.

The men's restroom was quiet for a long moment except for the periodic sound of dripping water in the number three toilet. The stopper at the bottom of the tank was unsealed. Water dripped constantly. As sufficient water escaped, the valve would open to refill the tank. A few residents in the front bedrooms in Hallway B had complained to Ms. Bichette about the constant drip...drip...drip. Sleep was difficult enough to come by without the need to entertain plumbing noises in the wee hours of the morning.

Larry looked at Curly and tilted his head to toilet number 3 as if to say: Are you going to take care of that?

Curly frowned. He sensed the foreboding, but only because he had yet to seal the tank stopper as directed by Le Biche. Otherwise, he was wholly confused by the current topic of discussion. Somehow, when he took on tasks in the front bathroom, he would always get sidetracked. He pondered this apparent phenomenon as he took another toke and blew a few smoke rings to exhale. As for this Time/ No Time stuff, he really didn't know what to think about it.

"Gentlemen, are you finished?" Maggie gave a hard look to the two conversationalists and asked indignantly. "May I continue?"

Larry and Curly nodded sheepishly.

Maggie looked back to the group at large to continue, "At least that's my best guess. I've seen places and known people – glorious places, wonderful people. At times, I've wondered if I could get back. Sometimes I've wondered whether I even wanted to get back. Yet it would seem that something always pulls me back...back to here... back home". She paused. "What I don't know is how to manipulate Time to my advantage", Maggie said. "I suspect that Marty has gained some measure of control by playing with his meds".

Trudy nodded. That made sense. The puzzle was falling together. Marty was a "swimmer" -as it were- who was somehow "swimming" in and through Time. Perhaps this was his secret. At least it might explain why he always wore his swim gear.

Maggie went on, "Neither do I know just what happens when the speed of Time is changed or stopped nor can I say that if stopped, Time can be restarted. I have enjoyed those moments in which I was able to insert myself, if only for a second or two, but I can't say that I was truly lucid. The experiences were short, fuzzy, and often wholly incomprehensible. Yes, I believe that Marty has figured some way to fully immerse himself into the experience, to "swim" through Time?" Maggie looked at Trudy and nodded. She looked at the others quizzically awaiting some sort of response. Each looked to the other. No one spoke. Maggie's revelation was a bit much to ponder.

"Anyone for chips?" Curly asked. "I'm hungry".

Mo nodded. He had figured on bacon and eggs. He leaned on the handles of Maggie's chair and pushed her into the hallway. Larry was always up for some peach yogurt.

Trudy stopped Curly as he started to exit. "Use bleach", she said and pointed to the inside of the restroom. "Be sure to get the smell out so the visitors don't complain. Ms. Bichette could be trouble and you know it".

"Yeah", he muttered. "Don't I know it." He dropped what little was left of his joint into the bucket and pushed it into the men's room to go back to work. The redundant noise in the plumbing was again active, but soon muffled as the door closed behind him.

A member of the night crew was headed home following dinner in the cafeteria. She passed by Physical Therapy and thought that she'd heard a splash. She stuck her head in the door to investigate. She clicked on the light and saw water splashed on the floor surrounding the therapy tub. The water inside the tub rocked back a forth and was calming as if someone had just exited. She called out, "Hey, anybody here?" Strange, she thought. She'd better report this to Ms. Bichette. She would tell her on her way to her car in the front lot. She flipped off the light and headed to the front desk.

Of course, she was mistaken. No one had recently exited the tub. Rather, Marty had just entered. He needed to get out, to get back to the South Pacific, to get back to his island. He dove deep and swam steadily with intention, unlike when he had first left his island. He was not sure why he felt this need to get back. But it did seem that he hadn't been there for some Time. Quite frankly, he missed it. Last Time, he had no reason for "being". But today, he was here. This Time was different. Of late, things were looking up. Life at Golden Hills was almost pleasant. At the Spring Dance, he had rekindled romance with a beautiful young woman. The relationship was new and fresh, although it seemed to Marty that he had known this beautiful blonde girl for a long Time. On that night, at least, he had felt like a hormone-driven teenager newly acquainted with love.

Not so strangely, he had little, if any, recollection of what had happened after the dance. This bothered him. He first thought that he must be out of practice. He had failed to get her phone number. He had no way to contact her and unless she returned for a visit, he couldn't be sure that he would ever see her again. Still, even with the burden of a Swiss cheese memory, he could always rely on instinct and, his instincts never before let one get away without him getting a phone number. No matter. The memory that he made that night he would cherish for a good long while or at least as long as he could remember it. Regardless, Marty figured that this would stick because, as far as he was concerned- whether in or out of No Time - he would find this girl again, date her, and marry her!

Yes, indeed! Marty was in love and boy did it feel good, and he knew that if he could successfully plug himself in to No Time, he would have no further need to "remember" because he would get to know her, date her, and live with her – all in the present. This singular memory that stayed with him would drive him, keep him going, get him up in the morning, and – in essence - keep him alive until he could find his way into No Time.

Besides, with his new; refurbished; attitude, many of his old ways came back into focus. He had come to realize that futzing with his pills, the quantities, the timing, the order in which he ingested would not lead him into No Time. All it really did was to screw him up and get him into trouble with Ms. Bichette.

Yes, he was disappointed that his memory failed to bring back the lovely woman at the dance, but he was not disappointed that he barely recalled the events of the next day. He could vaguely recall and was not proud to remember feeling heavy and plodding unlike anything he had ever felt previously. He recalled flashing light like shattered glass cascading down around him as he lumbered slowly, boom, boom, across the cafeteria floor. His motions were stiff and stilted, wholly at odds with the smooth and supple athleticism that was his trademark. He recalled shooting buttons, broken glass, and a wave of water. Thankfully, he thought, the wave had reinvigorated his reflexes. The surf ride down was, well...memorable, beyond Swiss cheese.

He stopped swimming and began to tread water. He rolled onto his back and floated there beneath the azure sky, thinking. The day was well...glorious. Marty smiled. He was alive and knew that he was on a mission. He knew what he needed to do. He must find a way into No Time. He also knew that pills would not take him there. Truth was key, but how much truth? After all, he was just one of the seven blind men on the elephant. His perspective was limited. He wondered, must he acquire all truth before he could get to No Time? He didn't know but was determined to find out. He lowered his red goggles and fitted them into place. He took a few deep breaths. He inhaled slowly, deeply; then exhaled. And, again, slowly he inhaled. He paused, held it, and then exhaled. He stretched out and lay flat on the water's surface. The sun warmed him, and he relaxed. He paused for a moment longer, and then he kicked out.

For the first Time in what seemed like years, he set out on a serious swim. His arms began to stroke like the pistons of an engine, first slowly then harder and harder until he churned like a 427 engine in a '67 Corvette. His flippers synchronized to churn with his arms. He had a purpose. He had a goal that he could remember and, this Time, he would meet it.

He joined a school of dolphins; they, too, were swimming with direction and purpose. They chittered and chattered, and invited him in. He smiled and swam with them at the head of the pod, his flippers spinning. Two young males, appointed him to lead. They presented him with a long vine made of seaweed and with the vine, he harnessed both – not so much to lead, but to hold on. The two juniors virtually galloped over the waves. The thrill vanquished every concern.

He had no way to know that their speed was approaching the speed of light, except that to Marty, Time had slowed to a virtual stop. His vision cleared dramatically. It seemed to him that he could literally see things in his past, set together with things in his present. Other things: people, places, events, he saw as well-things he did not recognized but which were also familiar to him, as if they belonged to him. These must be his future, and he saw it together with both his past and present. The view was unfathomable, but somehow glorious! He found no more need for the support offered by medications. By contrast, the vision he had attained in reliance on such artificial support as medications was nothing compared to what he was now witnessing. He realized suddenly that the combinations of medication on which he had relied were nothing more than an artificial replacement for reality. They were a false reality. In his quest for Truth, they were the Tower of Babel. He chose to return to the real view where he found Truth to be fresh, clean, and utterly delightful.

Unfortunately, with the excitement that came from swimming with these magnificent creatures and the revelations about Truth that his swimming had engendered, Marty easily forgot his most recent vow. He forgot the exact purpose for and the goal to which he now swam. His current purpose, his only goal, was to swim, to play, and to enjoy the company of these dolphins. He had come to know that the glory of Time was in its individual moments, not so much in its expanse.

He listened so as to better acquaint himself with their language. The dolphins' voices were knit with a crackling laughter that was cheerful yet argumentative; scolding but reassuring; cynical and sympathetic. They were a family. They interacted with each other. Each had his or her own unique personality. The young were vibrant, assured but oft times overconfident and irresponsible: these, the pod kept close. The mature were burdened with responsibilities, yet they were secure in themselves and swam with confidence in solidarity with the others, and the aged: these were watchful, protective, and shrewd – these took up the rear of the pod. Not often, one would drop behind...to rest, as it were; never to be seen again. But something here was different. The pod began to swim. The dolphins swam faster and faster, first across the waves; then, above them, skimming the occasional crest of the biggest and bluest. They would dive suddenly to explore the depths, and just as suddenly would resurface to reach for the sky, climbing higher and ever higher. Then almost as if bored, they would splash back to the oceans to play. They travelled so fast, so high, and so far, in an instant. They swam so effortlessly through Time itself that Time, the measure of Time, seemed to stop. Marty could not say whether he had been with them for a few hours, a few days, or for even years. He cherished each moment that he spent with them, and each moment was enough.

Marty learned something more. He came to see that the thing that brought to him so much encouragement was that he had been here before- not so much here with the dolphins – but here in this moment, in this feeling. Was this No Time? He kept mental notes. So now that he was in this Time, he knew it instinctively. He felt it; He possessed it and it him.

Speed seemed to be of the essence but not so much in the temporal or physical sense. Moreover, he wasn't sure, but...had he been here before? Possibly, but he couldn't say for sure. He may have been, but... not exactly. Still, for reasons that were not yet clear, he doubted that he had found this exact place even as familiar as it was to him. He had been in a place similar, very similar but not the same. But it was not so much the place bounded by a past, a present, and a future as it was this singular feeling; not so much a specific Time as it was this experience.

Marty felt a pressing need to stay with these dolphins in this space he chose to call No Time. But something pulled at him and he dropped behind, to rest, to disappear, to step back. Maybe he was just tired. Who knew? He whistled a reluctant goodbye to the dolphin's pod. He stopped to tread water and watched the pod disappear into the horizon. He lay back and floated. He was disappointed. After a Time, the sun began to set,and Marty saw a stand of coconut palms spread across a low lying atoll silhouetted against the shimmering red and gold horizon. He stopped to gaze. In his younger years, he had spent some Time on Makemo, one of the largest of these atolls.

His reminiscence was interrupted by a loud cackle shouted out loudly by one of the dolphins. He had returned to check on Marty.

"My dear boy, are you alright?" he asked. "I trust that we haven't offended you in any fashion. Why is it that you have left us?"

"No, no..." Marty rushed to assure the old boy. "You guys are the best. It's just that...well...I thought that I was slowing the pod down. I had read somewhere that it was appropriate, somehow...for the slower ones, the slower dolphins to withdraw and stay behind... you know, as a last goodbye, if you will"

"Well, of course you were slowing us down. I must say Mr....uh, what is your name, sir?"

"Marty", he repeated.

"Well, yes...Marty. Uh, I mean really...uh, Marty did you say? That is your name? Interesting...in any event, as I was saying, don't be arrogant, my young fellow. Of course, you can't swim with the dolphins. Don't get me wrong, you are good with the flippers and, you swim like a...well, like a fish. But no fish can swim with the dolphins. Facts is facts, as they say in the vernacular". He offered an obnoxious sort of smile.

Marty could barely keep pace with his syntax. Still, Marty liked the boy.

"Well then, I will be on my way. But please....uh, Marty... feel free to join with us again. The old dolphin bowed. "We so much enjoyed your run with us though short lived as it seemed. Perhaps, in No Time, we will see you again. Now, is there anything I may do for you before I leave?" he asked.

Marty was uncertain whether he had heard the old boy make reference to No Time and couldn't think quick enough to ask what he knew. He felt somewhat obliged to acknowledge the dolphin's gentlemanly offer so he asked about the Tuamotus.

"Yeah, hey...uh, from what I know, the Tuamotu Archipelago or Islands is a French Polynesian chain of almost 80 atolls that form the largest chain in the world. The Archipelago lies north of Tahiti in the South Pacific and stretches from the northwest to the southeast over an area roughly the size of Western Europe. The total area of land within this chain is 328 square miles. Its' major islands are Anaa, Fakarava, Hao and Makemo. The Tuamotus are sparsely populated with approximately 16,000 inhabitants. The islands were initially settled by Polynesians, and from them, modern Tuamotuans share a common culture and language. The people of Tahiti originally referred to the islands as the Paumotus, which means the "Subservient Islands", until a delegation from these islands convinced the French authorities to change it to the Tuamotus, which means the 'Distant Islands'".

"Yes, well" the old dolphin smiled widely as he danced backward on the water and cackled. "I see that you have been studying. Let me offer a tidbit. As you swam, you passed numerous of these atolls, each one covered with coconut palms, silhouetted in the setting sun, and spread across the horizon. Am I right? I am right." he dove deep and immediately launched himself skyward, stood on his tail in the water and danced backward, smiled and bowed again deeply

"Yes well, let's say, I read about them", Marty said.

The old dolphin continued, "As you swam you sought to explore. You swam in and out of each of the deep blue lagoons that are held captive within that ring of sand covered 'low islands' in these varying island groups. You didn't swim far. You didn't need to. Despite the vast spread of the Archipelago, it covers a total land area of only about 345 square miles. Shall I continue?"

"Please" Marty smiled. He spread out his hand in offering, and bowed deeply.

The old boy finished, "The climate is warm and tropical without pronounced seasons. The annual average temperature is a relatively continuous 79 °F. Water sources such as lakes or rivers are absent. The only fresh water is supplied by rain that is captured by and held in catchments. The annual average rainfall is about 55 inches. Rainfall is not markedly different throughout the year, although it is lowest during the months of September and November.

The archipelago is geologically stable. No volcanic eruptions have been recorded historically.

The sparse soil of the coral islands does not permit diverse vegetation. The coconut palm forms the basis for copra production. On a few of the islands, vanilla is also cultivated. Agriculture is generally limited to a simple subsistence which can include: yams, taro, and breadfruit, as well as, a range of tropical fruits. Coconut palm fronds – or Pandanus leaves - are traditionally woven together to form roof thatch or other items such as mats and hats. Nowadays, corrugated sheet-metal roofs cover the majority of the otherwise limited housing.

These 'low islands' are home to a diverse range of underwater fauna. Surface creatures are primarily limited to seabirds, insects, and lizards. The Tuamotus have only 57 species of birds, but ten of these are endemic, including the Tuamotu kingfisher, the Tuamotu reed warbler, and the Tuamotu sandpiper. Thirteen species are globally threatened and one is extinct".

The old boy stopped to inhale through his blowhole at the top of his head.

Marty signaled his approval with a sharp salute and wished him well.

. The old boy smiled, "You are welcome to swim with us anytime, my good friend. For now, I shall bid you adieu ". He turned and glided away across the long and smooth ocean swells.

Marty was left alone on the water. He had enjoyed so much his swim with the dolphins but floating here now, the Time had seemed so short. His visit with the old boy came and went in a blink. His swim with the dolphin pod lasted but an undefined moment; his cruise through Tuamotus was over before it started. At this moment, Time seemed untrustworthy. Marty puzzled.

The dolphins' pod returned and circled around him. The old boy leapt from the waves.

"We shall leave you with a gift", he said, and suddenly, it felt as if Time had returned. Marty could feel it and for no good reason that he could think of, he was grateful.

For a Time, Marty tracked with them. How long, he couldn't say. But it was difficult to say goodbye. His mind was no longer clear and for the first Time in a good long while, he felt old. The azure sky had clouded. It was dark and foreboding, and he began to fear. Like an old dolphin, he felt that it was best to drop back and leave the pod. The dolphins seemed to sense that he had aged. They surged forward, plunged, and resurfaced as they circled around him a final farewell. Then, they skipped across the water at what seemed to be the speed of light and disappeared.

He felt again like he once did when he first left the island, no goal, no purpose, no reason to live. His prior cure was to swim, to dive deeply. He chose that cure now. He filled his lungs with the crisp and crystal clear night air and he dove. He dove for all he was worth. He dove fast and he dove deep. His temptation was to go back to the island. But that would reveal nothing. Rather, he dove now in what must be his best effort to confirm the Truth, not to hide from it. He dove to ponder the speeding "light clock" that moved quickly to light speed. He dove to ponder, if only to see "but through the glass darkly" and down he went.

He dove deeper than he had ever gone. He stayed longer - longer than he had ever done on previous dives, and he felt strange. He lost his senses. He began to fade. He abandoned himself to Time and passed out.

CHAPTER XXIX

Ms. Bichette had finished lunch. She walked up Hallway B. Most of the residents were napping. She poked her head into Marty's room. She saw him on the top bunk, again with the goggles on his head and those silly flippers. She supposed that if he could sleep like he did, they must not encumber him too much. Oh well, she thought. She was headed back to the front office when she encountered "the troublemakers". Aside from Marty, these five - no, it was only 4 that were here now in the hallway - gave her a world of grief. Mo was pushing Maggie in her wheelchair. Hmmmm? Wasn't she up and at 'em? She had been down for some Time. It was surprising to see her now. Ms. Bichette had thought that she may be calling on the recovery team aka the Death Squad anytime soon to pick up Maggie. In fact, she had even advertised her space to be available next month. She would need to give more thought to Ms. Maggie. With Marty again in deep mediation, she should have sufficient time available to rethink the bedding arrangements here at Golden Hills.

These four appeared to have some agenda, and Ms. Bichette steeled herself for the encounter. Mo steered Maggie and the two peeled off to escape down the hallway.

Trudy peeled to the left side of Hallway B and appeared to be searching for her own bedroom. She purposefully avoided eye contact as she passed Ms. Bichette. This behavior was not typical for Trudy. She mentally catalogued this to investigate further.

She failed to catalog Mo. Ironically, as big as he was, she rarely took note of the man.

As for Maggie, she appeared deadpan and lifeless. Perhaps, whatever outing the 4 had pursued had taken its toll.

Larry saluted as he passed down the right side of the hallway – directly past Ms. Bichette. "Ma'am", he nodded. She looked at him, but did not acknowledge his salute.

This entire encounter was just plain odd. More and more, she was troubled by the unknown machinations that seemed to center around Marty, but likely involved these other four...no five.

She should not forget Curly. Where was he anyway? Likely he was taking a blow again in the front men's lavatory. She set out to make sure that he used enough bleach to take out the smell.

As had been discussed back at the men's room, the four quickly reconnoitered to meet up with Curly in Marty's room. Curly had suggested that they meet under the bed. It had proven to be a successful conference room on prior occasions. Somehow – even when comatose-Marty had proven to be an effective watchdog. For reasons, yet to be explained, Curly felt safe and free from intrusion with Marty around. Even without Marty, his room proved second best.

Larry was hesitant only because the last time, he had found himself in that room to be entangled with the drop down safety rail. Curly smiled. He crossed his heart and hoped to die in promise to Larry that it wouldn't happen again.

Mo could barely fit under the bed. He didn't like the idea. He would rather meet anywhere else and stay standing. But Curly insisted,and if Larry had to meet under the bed, so did Mo. Before Mo crawled under, he stationed Maggie in her chair at the front of Marty's bed as if she was keeping vigil. Mo pretty much knew what Maggie was going through of late. She had asked him to take notes. The two of them had become close since their night Time battle over the TV remote. She had pretty much relayed her rather vague experiences with this Time thing when back with the crowd at the men's room. Mo could elaborate a bit if it became necessary. But if he was asked to lend some kind of understanding... well, good luck.

As for Trudy, she didn't see the need. But Curly was insistent. She crawled in under the bed next to Mo. His girth and the warmth he exuded were comforting. Surprisingly, she felt a sense of peace, a sense of security there next to him.

"So...", Trudy asked as the four of them snuggled in, "What do we do now?"

"I don't know" Mo said. "What do we do now?" he asked Curly.

"I don't know", Curly said with some exasperation. "My job was to find a place to meet. So, we're meeting", Curly said.

"Oh for hell sakes", Trudy said, exasperated. "Who - on earth -called this meeting?"

"I did", a voice woke up from the corner of the room. The four of them froze.

"Who, what, whoa...", Curly muttered. "God. Is that you? "Damn!" he exclaimed to the others, "God has descended. Hallelujah! He has come down here...or, wait", he stuttered. "Did we go up?" he asked the others.

"Oh hush...pipe down Curly. It's me, Maggie. I'm over here". She shushed them from the corner of the room where Mo had parked her. "All of you pay attention." She directed them from her seat in her wheelchair. "Larry, you skinny mutt, reach somewhere there above you beneath the springs of Marty's mattress. You should find stashed there some rough notes scribbled on a few torn pieces of a large brown grocery sack".

Larry turned his head to look up. There, just above Curly, he found the pages described. "Safeway", he read slowly. "It says 'Safeway'.

"What is so magical about 'Safeway', Curly asked, puzzled.

"Turn it over", Maggie responded patiently. "There on the back you'll see some notes; most are illegible. Marty wrote them. Some of it is too incomprehensible to be of much good for now. But you should find something there about a rocket ship, a bouncing beam of light...something about Time travel".

"Yeah, yeah, I see it", Trudy said. "So, how is this supposed to help us?"

"All I can say for sure is that Marty is right and I am wrong. No Time is a reality. Read! You should see something there about a storm sewer beneath the freeway that runs past the mouth of Parley's Canyon. That part, I could make out". Her voice was hopeful.

"Wait...", Trudy said. "Yeah, okay. So, what is going on?"

"I'm not sure, but if I'm right...or more accurately, if Marty is right, we may be able to zoom our way out of here and back to a Time where life was good and sweet; where we were healthy and strong; and, maybe – just maybe – if we can live our lives over...or somehow differently, we can make it...well, better". Sadness invaded her voice as it trailed off. Maggie fell silent.

"Whoa Jake" Curly crowed! "How cool is that? But why not go forward in Time? That is where I want to go – things to see, places to go, people to meet!"

"Yes, that would be nice", Maggie agreed. "But as you might surmise, none of us has much Time left to enjoy in our futures. Marty's proposed experiment is untested, and it's likely that we'll get one shot at Time travel. Yes, if we go forward into the future, we should see some interesting things. But the way I figure is that the future takes faith; faith that death will have been conquered. Otherwise we'll be there for but a short Time, as it were. We'll likely die there in short order, or theoretically, we'll be dead on arrival. As for me, I just want more of that Time about which I know more of the familiar things, people, and places; more Time to get it right, to make up for my mistakes, Time to repent as it were".

No one spoke. The only sound in the room was Marty snoring loudly and long. A snort startled those under the bed. Each of them jumped. Each bumped their head on the underside of the bedsprings. One at a time, they crawled from beneath the bed.

"Okay, I'm in!" Curly volunteered enthusiastically. Marty was here and as far as Curly was concerned, he had voted.

They all stood there as if at attention listening for a time, for the right "Time" to which they might travel. Curly started a military salute that Larry quickly squelched with a slap. Curly was 4F for the Vietnam draft. Marty continued to snore.

"Sorry", Curly whimpered. "I felt it was appropriate".

"You're forgiven already, idiot. Don't do it again", Larry responded.

"Alright", Maggie directed. "One week. Be back here and ready to roll at 3 a.m. Curly, what's the best way out of the facility?"

Larry grew concerned. "How do you expect to get out of here", he asked. "There is only one key and Ms. Bichette keeps it on her person". Mo and Curly nodded their understanding.

Trudy responded quietly, "I suppose I can try to get it from Ms. Bichette during rounds. Perhaps she'll be distracted and I can lift it off of her".

"Naw, too risky", Maggie said still thinking.

Suddenly, Curly snapped his fingers and exclaimed, "Wait...", and immediately, the others sshhusshed him.

"Keep it soft", Trudy held an index finger to the side of her nose as she patted downwardly with her other hand and whispered.

Curly lowered his voice, "Look, we can go out through the basement morgue. It will have to be on a day after one of us passes away– or I should say - one of our residents". He felt sheepish. "Ms. Biche places a call and The Death Squad appears for pick-up. They will take the body to the basement, prepare it, and dress it for burial".

He continued softly, "Eldon Jones drives the hearse part-time. He gets a call for pick-up and comes alone. He is supposed to bring an assistant, but he doesn't want to share the retrieval fee. We can convince Eldon to take us out in his hearse. We'll need him to deliver us to Parley's Canyon. It will take a bribe. But he'll do it. And remember: this plan requires the passing of one of our residents – one of our own. We cannot kick it off absent that, and when that happens, I will know and can spread the word. It can work. But we should each be prepared at a moment's notice to leave this place, head downstairs, climb into a drawer to hide where we will then wait for Eldon to take us out. We'll convince him to drive us to Parley's. You should all be prepared to ride with a real 'stiff' together with Eldon in his hearse".

Curly searched the faces, looking for weakness, searching for a chink in the assembled armor. He found none. "Huddle up", he said.

They circled around Maggie's chair. Maggie put her hand in, and each placed theirs on top of hers. Each bowed their head. No one spoke. Marty gave a snort as he rolled over in bed. Silence prevailed for a long Time until each knew intuitively that the pact was confirmed. They would await Curly's call. His call came sooner than expected, and the message was devastating.

Maggie died in her sleep. Curly was running a quick broom down Hallway B when Ms. Bichette exited Maggie's room. He was startled to see her stop a moment just outside the door. She appeared to wipe a tear from her eye. She paused; her head down. She whispered something and crossed herself before hurrying to the front office. Curly knew what she would do next - The Death Squad! The Death Squad was nothing if not efficient. They would be here in short order. He must hurry. He had promised Maggie.

Curly enlisted Mo. The two met at Maggie's room. She was there in bed, wearing a warm cotton robe and a sweet smile. She was out like a light, apparently at peace. Mo stood dumbfounded. Curly poked him in the ribs and pointed to the closet. The two worked quietly. Mo found Maggie's "double wide" wheelchair, folded, and standing just inside the closet door. He drew it out, opened it, and parked it next to and facing the bed to receive its' occupant. They negotiated how best to maneuver such a large load. Mo managed the heaviest load which was the top half. Maggie was buxom to say the least. Curly could offer no real help. He would nudge a little here or there until Mo had her loaded. Mo lifted one large and varicose leg, and then the other onto the metal footpads. He pulled a worn pair of slippers from beneath the bed and put them on her feet. He waited for Mo to catch his breath. Mo nodded when he was ready. Curly checked the darkened hallway. The coast was clear. He held the door as Mo pushed. They rolled the wheelchair into Hallway B and headed for the stairs.

"Wait", Curly whispered. "What are we thinking? No way can we use the stairs."

They would need to take Maggie to the man lift. Mo turned the chair around and headed for the cafeteria. The manlift was located behind the refrigerators. They had to hurry. Breakfast was in just over an hour. The staff typically arrived one hour early or six a.m. to prepare the morning repast. Curly ran ahead to open the doors. Maggie had gained momentum. She had reaffirmed Newton's second law of physics. It had taken effort on Mo's part to get her up to speed but now that she was there, it was going to take a significant effort to stop her. Mo couldn't think about that now. For now, all that he could do was enjoy the ride. He put his feet up on the back crossbar installed there between the back wheels to reinforce the frame. He cruised on into the cafeteria just as the doors opened. Curly's timing was impeccable. Inside, Mo found an open pathway clear through to the chrome railings that separated the counter area from the dining facilities. So far, so good, but Mo knew that he would need to make an almost 90 degree turn to gain access around the railings to the passage way next to the exterior wall that to the stock room behind the refrigerators. In the stockroom, he would find the manlift that would take him to the basement. The kitchen staff used the manlift to retrieve canned and dry goods delivered weekly to the loading dock downstairs.

Maggie's momentum was fast, but the speed exchange allowed Mo to move spectacularly. As the wheelchair approached the chrome railings, Mo transferred his entire weight to the cross bar immediately behind the large left wheel as he pulled upward on the right side handle. The momentum and weight transfer lifted the right side of the chair. The move caused almost an immediate 90 degree turn of the chair to the left. With neither wasted motion nor wasted speed, the wheel chair pivoted to move left and straight at the exterior brick wall of the cafeteria. Mo readied himself and again with impeccable precision and timing, he executed a similar maneuver to cause the wheel chair to turn to its right and down the hallway to the stockroom behind the refrigerators. The two maneuvers lessened the chair's momentum to give Mo the opportunity to brake. He jumped from the back support bar and landed both feet onto the linoleum floor. The black rubber soles on the bottoms of his shoes laid skid marks to bring Maggie and her wheelchair to a smooth stop. He had executed this ride with aplomb. He was rather proud of himself. Curly arrived to find Mo breathing heavily and smiling. Curly had been impressed by the maneuvering. He had to hand it to Mo. He offered in applause, gave Mo a quick two finger salute, and pointed to the manlift. Curly moved to the lift and opened the gate. He held it open for Mo to push Maggie's chair forward onto the lift.

Whatever was the weight limitation for the manlift, Maggie's weight alone exceeded it. Mo and Curly looked at each other and shrugged. They didn't dare ride. Mo closed the gate. Curly pushed the button. The elevator squeaked, clicked, and squealed to suggest that it was under loading pressure. But there was no turning back now. As Maggie descended slowly, the two boys ran back through the cafeteria. They ran past and waved at Trudy who was just sitting down to eat.

"Hi, what are you two do...;" she started to say as they rushed past her headed to the stairs at the other end of Hallway B. They hoped that they still had enough time before sunlight, before new breakfast deliveries, before meals were prepared and eaten by people who might put their plan in jeopardy.

As they arrived at the door to the basement stairs, Curly fumbled with his keys. He was a bit nervous and trying too hard. He fumbled with one, then another and another. His hands began to shake.

He wasn't used to being this close to Le Biche's office without the benefit of a toke. He dropped the keys to the floor. They made a collective clink that echoed through the abandoned hallway. Both Mo and Curly stopped. Each was silent. Curly's breathing was tight. Mo pulled a brown paper lunch sack from his back pocket. He never really thought that this would ever come in handy. Thank gawd for paper bag lunches. He opened the bag, held it to his face to demonstrate for Curly, and signaled him to inhale and exhale slowly both into and out of the bag. Curly place the bag over his face and breathed as instructed. His breathing began to moderate when they heard Ms. Bichette's voice. He choked and stopped breathing altogether.

"Who goes there? Breakfast won't be for another hour. Music appreciation and exercise are set for one pm and three pm respectively. Visiting hours began at five pm. You'll enjoy. Until then, back to your rooms or go to the cafeteria to awai...". She stepped quickly into Hallway B in hopes of startling someone. She was surprised to find no one there. She shrugged and headed for the cafeteria.

Curly found the correct key. Mo and Curly ducked to make it safely into the stairway to the basement morgue. Mo had grabbed Curly by his shirt collar and literally bounced him down the stairs. Curly caught his breath as the two of them moved immediately through the darkened hallway that led from the temporary morgue to the downstairs delivery area in the back. There, they found Maggie, her broad backside facing them from her wheel chair parked on the manlift. When they loaded Maggie, Mo had asked Curly to affix the chair's brake. The single lever to set the parking brake on the large back wheel was affixed on the left side of the chair beneath the left armrest. The lever was buried now beneath a mountain of flesh. Unlike the first floor on which the lift stood gated but otherwise open on all sides, access to the lift here was restricted on three sides by the walls of the elevator shaft in which the lift travelled. There was no way to maneuver from any location except from the open front. Access to the brake release was buried beneath Maggie's girth and otherwise protected by the cinderblock walls of the elevator shaft. The clock was ticking. Mo was not happy, but he knew what he had to do.

Mo took deep breaths, in and out, to prepare himself to dive beneath Maggie to find and release the parking brake. He knew the routine. By now, Curly had recovered. He had refocused, but grew confused as it became apparent just what Mo intended to do. Curly moved to the wheelchair. He grasped both handles and tugged. The chair rolled easily off of the lift, bounced, rumbled, and creaked a bit under Maggie's weight as it slowly rolled to a stop right there in front of Mo. Mo heaved a heavy sigh and look to Curly with some exasperation.

"Didn't set the brake, did you?" Mo said to Curly.

"Ahhh...I forgot", Curly responded sheepishly.

Mo should have been exasperated. But all he felt was relief. He nodded to Curly, grabbed the handles at the back of the chair, and turned it to head down the darkened hallway toward the basement morgue. He grunted as he set the wheels in motion. He reminded himself about the necessary distance required to stop this heavy load. The wheelchair squeaked and moaned under the weight. Mo worried that the chair would give out before they could unload her. They could hear activity upstairs: the staff awakening those residents who had signed up for breakfast; and some - for their own benefit – who had not; visitors arriving before work to bring toothpaste, peanut butter or something other to mom and dad; miscellaneous deliveries; etc. They needed to hurry. Sound echoed loudly down here. Mo worried that they might be discovered soon.

He rolled with Maggie into the morgue. He jumped to set both feet to brake. The chair came to a skidding stop. Again, Mo proved proficient. He immediately opposite the front of Drawer A – Double Wide; specifically meant for people like Maggie who – let's just say – who needed the extra room. He signaled Curly to open the Drawer while he spun the chair around to put Maggie's back against the front of the Drawer. He set the brakes and signaled to Curly to grab a few dusty medical books on the office desk. He directed him to stack them beneath the pull out table extend out from Drawer A. These drawers were more than sturdy, but for one with Maggie's tremendous girth, additional support couldn't hurt. He set additional books at the wheelchair to secure the large wheels, in place, so he could then release the brakes to allow the axis to spin. He waved Curly over to help him hoist. The two grabbed the front foot pads and lifted. Maggie tilted backward as intended until she sat face up, with feet skyward and the wheelchair balanced at the handles on the pull out table extended from Drawer A. Maggie's full weight now rested on the leather back portion of the chair.

Mo instructed Curly to hold the chair up while he moved to the Drawer side. He grabbed Maggie's robe at both shoulders and pulled. He pulled and pulled again. No luck. He worried now that they would never get her into the drawer. He inhaled to set himself as he prepared to pull again.

Without warning, the leather back split. They heard a loud rip. They saw the rear handles separate: one fell off to the right side; the other to the left. They heard a thump as Maggie's head and back fell another 4 inches to the table top. The additional inches allowed gravity to help so that Maggie slid out partially onto to the table. Mo took the advantage. He grabbed Maggie by the back of her cotton gown at the shoulders, and pulled. Maggie slipped easily across the polished metal table until she lay peacefully in place.

Curly heard the key turn in the lock on the door upstairs.

"Shhhh", he quieted Mo. Someone was coming down the stairs. Mo slid the easy glide table with Maggie on it quietly back into Drawer A- Double Wide. The two silently tiptoed out of the morgue and back down the hallway to the delivery area in back. They rode the man lift back up to the cafeteria.

Ms. Bichette stepped into the morgue to make her morning inspection. She found it to be clean and tidy, except for what appeared to be some kind of skid marks near Drawer A. She made a note. She would talk to Eldon. He should be more orderly.

CHAPTER XXX

Later that day, Curly called an emergency meeting. The crew had reconvened under Marty's bed. Marty was in bed, but incommunicado. Ms. Bichette and Trudy had distributed the nightly vitamins and Ms. Bichette was again back in her office filing the bed check report. Trudy had just left her there to join the meeting. She slid in under the bed next to Larry. Curly had summoned Mo and Larry who had been waiting for some Time now. Curly gave Trudy a quick update on the most recent events; how they had stolen Maggie from her bedroom and secreted her into Drawer A in the temporary morgue downstairs. Trudy was shocked at what she heard.

"You did what with Maggie? She is where? What do you propose that we do with her?" She asked, flabbergasted. "We can't leave her there! What about her family?"

"Cool your jets" Mo tried to calm her. "She is safe....for now", he soothed. "Look..." he began, "She's got no family. Maggie told me, a long time ago, that she wanted...well...a Viking funeral pyre; more than anything, and well...I just thought that...it might be nice" his voice trailed off. He looked sheepishly at those assembled with him under the bed. Those convened stayed silent awaiting further explanation.

When none came, Trudy exploded, "A what!?"

Mo quickly shushed her with a finger to his nose and a gentle hand across her mouth.

She pushed his hand away and in a harsh whisper, she asked, "Are you guys nuts? What on earth are you thinking? A Viking funeral pyre...of all things! And, how do your propose that we get her a pyre?" she asked, incredulously.

"Well...I'm not sure, but..." Larry thought out loud. "A pyre does sound kinda nice. I vote we do it". He smiled a broad smile at the assembled crowd beneath the bed.

Curly and Mo nodded with hopeful concurrence.

Trudy glanced harshly at Larry and asked again to those convened, "So! Let me ask again: how do you propose that we do that?" she asked. She searched the faces there beneath the bed. Her neck was getting stiff as she tried frequently to peer into the eyes of each person there assembled. She couldn't believe that they were serious.

Larry continued, pondering mostly to himself, "The grounds crew replaced an old fence along the back lot. They pulled down the old fence and tore out a bunch of railroad ties that had been used as a retaining wall to support it. They poured a concrete wall in its place and built a new fence on top. The ties, together with all of the scrapped fencing, are stacked out back waiting to be hauled off".

"Okay?" Trudy shrugged, "What do you suppose that we can do with a bunch of scrapped railroad ties?" As she found their eyes, she could read their thinking.

"Oh no, not a pyre?" she shook her index finger at them like a young mother telling her to stop eating from the dog dish. "And...where might we build this pyre? How do you propose that we build it? Doesn't a Viking funeral require the pyre to be put on a boat and sent out to sea? We don't have a boat. We don't have a sea. And...even if we did, how would you propose that we set the whole thing on fire? My, gawd...a fire! I can't believe we're even talking about this".

Curly piped in, "An Archer! An Archer can set the fire! That would be cool! A fire lit pyre at sundown!" He clapped his hands together like a small boy with a new toy at Christmas.

Trudy's will was weakening. "Well, Robin Hood is not registered at Golden Hills. I don't suppose that you know anyone who can shoot a flaming arrow into the pyre to set it on fire?" Can any of you shoot an arrow?" She figured that this logic should completely dissuade them.

Larry raised his hand, "I earned an Archery Merit Badge in the Boy Scouts. I can shoot the arrow. My daughter is coming to visit today. She can bring a bow and some arrows. I'll text her right now". He pulled an old phone from his jacket pocket that his daughter had given to him. He never called anyone except her. They kept in touch. She visited often. The phone was old. He had to pick one of 3 letters from every numbered key. The going was slow, but Larry was proud to be "conversant" with all of the new technologies.

S-w-e-e-t-i-e. N-e-e-d B-o-w & A-r-r-o-w. B-r-i-n-g w-h-e-n y-o-u c-o-m-e.

"There" he said as he punched in the last letter. He looked up and smiled.

"An Archery Merit Badge!...You're kidding right?", Trudy said. She was getting desperate. "C'mon, you guys. You can't be serious." She made one last attempt at logic. "What about the boat", she urged, "...and, the sea? There's no sea around here. Where do you propose that we find a boat? And, even if we could find a boat, where would we float it?" She paused. "Huh?" Her resilience was depleted, almost gone. For a moment the collective crowd was silent. Each was thinking. She tightly closed her eyes and crossed her fingers to hope. Suddenly from above a familiar voice responded. The assembled group lurched in unison, startled by the voice from atop the bed. Marty poked his head over the side. He looked upside down to the folks there beneath the bed.

"Hi guys", he waved with a grin. "I vote we do it. Sounds like fun."

" "Heeeyyy, Marty!!" they cheered. "It's...it's you", they breathed a collective sigh of relief as each welcomed him back. "Sure is good to have you with us" Curly was the spokesman. "We need your help. Have you been listening? You got any ideas?" he asked.

At first, the idea had been wishful, tinged with a smidgen of hope. As the discussion progressed, Trudy scored some points; and, Larry began to see the absurdity in his thinking. Besides, this had begun to sound like an awful lot of work. Curly was on board, but he too needed a vote of confidence. Mo hadn't yet spoken. Larry needed desperately to pass this baton. Then, his mobile phone rang.

He flipped it open. "Hello? Who is calling? Oh hi, Sweetie. Mmmm huh. Rubber tipped?" He looked searchingly at Marty. Marty nodded. Larry put his thumb up to the assembled group and smiled. "Yeah...of course", his hope was rekindled. "Great!" His daughter would supply rubber tipped arrows; not as dramatic as the real thing, but they would work. She'd bring them by later today.

"Hey doll?" he inquired. "Will I see you here for lunch, maybe? Uhhhhmm. Well, I don't know. I'll need to check. But we do have peach yogurt!?" he volunteered enthusiastically. "Great. See you soon...and, thanks, doll", he closed the cover and pocketed the flip phone.

"Sorry, no way she can bring real arrows", he shrugged to the group there under the bed. "Rubber tipped should still work, huh?" He glanced inquisitively at Marty who nodded. Larry grinned. He smiled a self-congratulatory smile as he looked to the assembled group.

"I got it from here, Larry", Marty took the helm. "The lake at 'M' street, it's just down the street from here. There is an old wooden rowboat lying in the weeds at the back of the lake. Used to be owned by someone from here, from Golden Hills; someone who is now... shall we say...indisposed. The boat hasn't been used in ages. May float long enough to say our farewells to dear old Maggie? Let's discuss the details over breakfast", he jumped out of bed, his flippers spinning, goggles on his head. The crowd scrambled from beneath the bed. Trudy was consigned. She exited stage left from under the bed, followed by Larry, Mo, and then Curly. They all stood and brushed the dust from their clothing. Each looked to Marty. He fluttered out from his bedroom and into Hallway A where he headed toward the cafeteria. The crowd followed, again amazed at his seeming ability to hover.

At breakfast, Larry got his Peach Yogurt. That "treat" was getting to be a bit boring to the rest of the crowd. To Larry, it was his crowning achievement. Marty spelled out the details of his "plan". Someone would need to secure Eldon's cooperation. Curly was elected. For obvious reasons, this was critical to the plan. Each of them agreed to meet at the back stairs behind the cafeteria at 7:30 pm. They would help get Maggie from Drawer A there in the morgue and into Eldon's hearse. Curly was nervous. He took leave to take a few tokes. Mo and Larry agreed to haul the railroad ties from the back lot to the park at M Street. They would make the wooden rowboat "seaworthy" and set it to float on the pond there at the park. They would stack ties in the boat and get it ready to "set sail". They should be able to get it all handled after work tonight. They left to finish work for the day. Larry would meet with his daughter in short order to secure the bow with arrows – albeit rubber tipped. He left to wait for her up front. Trudy reluctantly agreed to keep Ms. Bichette occupied this evening to distract her. She wasn't quite sure yet what she could do. But she agreed to try. She headed to the front office to report in. All had agreed to meet back at 8:00 pm – bedtime.

Marty was satisfied that all necessary arrangements would be made. He headed for PT. Right now, he needed another swim. Sky Blue!

CHAPTER XXXI

Ms. Bichette made a mental note. She should deal with Mr. Markham. She had pretty much decided to check him out of Golden Hills. She liked him, but he was getting to be too much. Besides, more and more, he challenged her authority in front of residents and staff. She stepped into her office, pulled up a chair at the front desk, and picked up the old rotary phone. She reached for an equally old "roll-a-dex" that sat on the desktop beneath the public window. She fingered alphabetically through to the "M"-tab to find "Markham". She dialed the number listed. Mrs. Markham answered. Following a brief conversation with Mrs. Markham, they set up a time to deal Mr. Mark, Mark, Markham. She hung up and paused for moment, hand on the phone. Sad, she thought. But it was time.

Mrs. Markham arrived smartly at her scheduled appointment with Ms. Bichette. Her daughter and son accompanied her. Trudy was measuring out the night's medications in the front office. She knew right away that something serious was soon to take place. Ms. Bichette showed them into the front conference room next to her office. Preliminarily, she asked if they would take some coffee or tea. Mrs. Markham asked if she had any hot chocolate with whipped cream on top. Ms. Bichette smiled weakly, a bit unnerved by the odd request, and excused herself to accommodate the request. She called back to the kitchen with no success. No one answered the phone on the back wall near in the kitchen. She wondered with some aggravation, where the hell was Larry? She quickly rejected the notion that he could be of any help and instead high tailed it back to the cafeteria. She would prepare the hot chocolate herself. Where do I find whipped cream, she wondered?

Trudy took advantage. She caught Curly in the front men's room in the front hall, again stationed on the toilet seat, a cloud of smoke circling near the ceiling.

"Curly, we've got trouble" she shouted. She heard a thud as Curly fell from his neatly balanced position on the seat. She bent down to peer at him beneath the stall door. "Get up and come out of there. Marty's family is here. That can only mean one thing: Ms. Bichette is angling to check him out, to remove him from Golden Hills. Dammit!" she said to no one in particular.

"Oh, hey" Curly said sheepishly as he scrambled to stand up. He opened the stall door, shyly stepped out, and extended a bullet that he held between his finger and thumb to Trudy. He asked, "D'ya wanna take a toke?"

"Oh, put that away!" she scolded. "We've got some work to do!"

"Okay. What do you want me to do", he asked less than enthusiastically. He looked at her with an inquiring an eye, the best that he could muster. She could only look back at him. The pause between them perpetuated and the silence deafened.

"Oh, c'mon Curly, think of something" she finally said almost desperately. He shivered but could think of nothing. Then he said, "Maybe Marty would know what to do. We could ask him?" It was more of a question than a statement.

"Right," she pointed at Curly and her eyes lit up. She smiled as she bolted out the door and down Hallway B to PT. "C'mon Curly", she shouted back to him as she ran. "We need to catch him before he swims out of here". He followed her on the run. The two hoped to catch Marty in the hot tub, and before he dove deep, too deep to reach him.

Their luck held. They found Marty in PT. He was in the hot tub. He looked asleep and they worried. Were they too late? They called out and tried to wake him. Nothing. Trudy patted him lightly on the face with no effect. She continued to pat, pat, pat, until Curly became exasperated and slapped him hard, still nothing. Trudy wrung her hands and began to fret. Curly pulled from the wall the hose that he used to wash down the floor tiles and turned the cold water tap to full pressure. He held his thumb over the spout and sprayed Marty with full force. Surprisingly, he began to arouse. He never awoke fully, but he did speak while still in his sleep.

"What's that he's saying? Trudy wanted to know. "Time?...uh, pages? Pages of Time. He's talking about Time again Curly...do you know what he's talking about?"

"Not a word," Curly answered as he shook his head slowly.

Trudy continued to chatter worriedly as they pulled him from the tub. For all purposes, he was incoherent.

Curly looked at her, "We need help! Hold him up. I'll be right back". Trudy steadied him while Curly ran to find Mo.

Mo was in the storage room downstairs from the kitchen where Curly found him bent over and unpacking boxes of kitchen supplies for Larry. As he unpacked, Larry took inventory. The inventory included: flour, cooking oil, cold cereal, bacon, eggs, frozen veggies, potatoes, cream of wheat, boxes of spaghetti, and – of course – peach yogurt. Curly whistled down the elevator shaft from the kitchen above. The inventory stopped in mid-count.

"Mo. C'mon. We gotta help Marty...I mean, you gotta help Marty!" Curly shouted down through the elevator shaft from the kitchen above. Mo stood and looked over at Larry. Larry nodded in the direction of the shaft, "Go. I'll get this".

Curly filled in Mo with current events as they scrambled through the cafeteria on up to Physical Therapy where the two of them joined Trudy. She continued to steady Marty who remained incoherent and was babbling something about Pages of Time. She was at her wits end. Mo hoisted Marty onto his broad shoulders and they all headed off on a run up Hallway A to the conference room. Mo figured that

Curly had a plan. Trudy breathed a bit easier. She also figured that Curly had a plan and that he was in charge. Curly was in charge, but he had no real plan to speak of. The best he figured was that he would play it by ear. He had no real confidence in this non-plan. But, at least, he had brought along reinforcements.

They moved quickly up Hallway A. As they approached the front office, they saw Ms. Bichette leave the office and step around the corner and into the conference room. They peered around the corner to catch a glimpse through the glass. Marty's wife, his son, and his daughter were seated at the conference table. Ms. Bichette seated herself at the head of the table. She opened what appeared to be a brochure. Marty's wife began to tear up. Ms. Bichete handed her a tissue, and she wiped her eyes. Of a sudden, Marty seemed to come alive - kind of. He seemed to sense the import of what was happening inside. He eased himself down slowly from Mo's shoulders. He creaked as he walked to the conference room doorway. He did not enter.

Some might argue that he acted to protect his own interests. Others would say that he acted to protect the woman that he loved, even if he couldn't fully remember that he loved her. As he stood in front of the conference room, a "white noise" began to buzz and crackle as a blue light filled with jagged bolts of electricity surrounded him. The energy appeared to lift him off of the floor. The field of vision inside the conference room and those surrounding the conference table began to blur and moved in and out of focus. Those seated at the table appeared to freeze in place, to stop dead still, and move again, haltingly.

Ms. Bichette had been speaking. She was standing at the table, a sheet of paper and pen on the table in front of her. She held her finger out as if gesturing to make a point. She was frozen in the position and appeared to be in mid-sentence. Marty's wife was seated to her right. It seemed that she had been placing a tissue into her purse. She, too, was frozen in place. Her purse was open, her hand clutching the tissue was partially inside. His son sat with his arms folded across his chest, his face in a grimace, eyebrows knit with mouth tight, lips firm and in a straight line. He was not interested in what Ms. Bichette was trying to say. His daughter was partially standing and in the act of getting up from the seat next to her mother. She, too, was frozen in place. A second glance corrected the perception to show that she was actually taking her seat after having handed the handkerchief to her mother who was just then tucking it into her purse.

Several minutes passed. Nothing changed inside the conference room. The vision continued to move in and out of focus, but the conference participants remained frozen in place. Blue light surrounded Marty as it cracked and fizzled. The "white noise" buzzed. Then Marty held his hand out and he pointed to the large clock on the wall of the conference room immediately behind Mrs. Markham. He rotated his index finger and the large hand on the clock rotated with it. He licked his fingers and flipped them backwards or counterclockwise and the conference room participants appeared to move backwards, a scene or two at a Time…or through Time as it were. First quickly, then more slowly, each movement in sync with Marty's efforts to turn the clock. As he rotated his index finger, the occupants around the table fidgeted and stirred from the positions in which they were first captured, each moving backward through Time.

Ms. Bichette first seated herself from her standing position at the table, then stood and moved backwards, apparently pushing her chair away from the table, then tucking it back in beneath the table, and then walking backwards again from the head of the table and backward to the conference room door. Here, Marty reversed the rotation of his index finger and the conference room clock moved in sync, forward in Time, and Ms. Bichette also moved forward with the clock. When he spun his index quickly, those people in the conference room moved in sync. When he spun his index more slowly to allow him to examine the positioning and people in the conference room, the conference room participants, again, moved in sync. The action in the conference room continued, backward and forward, moving back and forth through Time; sometimes in fast motion as Marty spun his finger quickly; and sometimes more slowly and slower still when he sought to focus the movement so as to place the participants in just the right place in Time.

As he continued to rotate his finger, the conference participants appeared to fidget at the table, change positions, and gesticulate as they engaged in discussion until Marty found the moment in Time that he wanted, and he made a fist to reset Time at that moment that he had selected. Ms. Bichette had picked the pen up off of the table and was holding it out to Mrs. Markham who was seated and appeared hesitant, her son and daughter were there to support her but were seemingly not knowing how to help. All were now frozen in Time there at the conference room table. Marty continued to glow blue, to snap, crackle, and buzz. But he too, seemed frozen.

As they watched these events unfold, Mo could only scratch his chin. Curly was dumbfounded and could only stare. Trudy saw what Marty was trying to do and acted. From the hallway, she stepped into the front office and rummaged through the desk drawers. She thumbed through stacks of paper on the shelves overhead. She looked into the file cabinets on the back wall and found what she knew Marty wanted. She smiled. This felt very much like Marty hiding his pills from Ms. Bichette.

In a hurry, she ran to the conference room. She stepped around Marty's blue glow as she entered being careful to avoid the blur that surrounded him. She leaned over the table and swapped the paperwork on the table for which Ms. Bichette was seeking a signature, for the paperwork in her hand. She lifted the first document and replaced it with the second in the exact same position. She then ran quickly back out of the room and stooped behind Mo to watch what came next.

Marty lifted his index finger again to point it at the clock. He rotated his finger forward slowly. The conference room patrons moved forward slowly, frame by frame. Curly, Mo, and Trudy watched as Marty's wife affixed her signature to the pages presented to her, then a couple more turns of his finger, and they saw Ms. Bichette leave the conference room to return to her office where she retrieved a manila file folder from her desk. She placed the folder into her in-basket for later review; and finally moved back past the three conspirators hiding behind a potted plant there at the door, and back into the conference room – all the Time smiling and shaking hands with those who had come to visit. She moved slowly in sync as Marty rotated his finger. She jumped forward quickly and slowed; jumped again as Marty searched for the exact spot. The process took uh...shall we say, it took Time.

At one point, Ms. Bichette spoke kindly and smiled to those in attendance; at another, she spoke very slowly in a voice deep and low; and at another her voice reached a fever pitch, high and squeaky as Marty spun his finger forward and backward through Time to make his adjustments. As Marty finished his work, Ms. Bichette smiled sweetly as she escorted his family to the front door in halts and fits. Marty's wife and kids appeared puzzled throughout as though they had no idea as to why Ms. Bichette seemed suddenly so lighthearted and serene. They shook hands ever more slowly with her at the front door. They began to depart, but the front door had not yet fully closed when all action froze once again. Marty stayed fixed, his finger out as if to count some invisible second. The blue light continued to crack and fizzle around him. The air stayed blurred.

"Mo" Trudy directed, "Grab him. We need to hike him back to PT. He'll need to be in the tub".

Both Mo and Curly were wholly confused and remained stymied. She snapped her finger in front of each. "Mo, grab him now and bring him with me back to PT. C'mon".

Mo did as directed. Curly followed en suite. The three of them successfully delivered Marty to the tub in PT. By the time they reached the hot tub, the blue light and fizzle had resolved. They put Marty back into the tub. Almost automatically, he ducked his head into the water and dove. Within moments, he was back up and alive.

"Gentlemen and ladies, how may I assist you?" he asked as if he had met them here for the first Time. They looked at each other, then at Marty.

"C'mon Marty, let me help you out of there", Trudy said and he obliged.

At the front entry, Marty's wife and adult children seemed to jolt awake. They looked at each other quizzically. They shrugged to each other and then nonchalantly moved on their way.

Ms. Bichette snapped out of what seemed to be some kind of "phase". She too shrugged. She checked her buttons, brushed her skirt and adjusted her cap. Feeling "ship-shape", she walked back to the front office where she pulled from her desk drawer what she thought to be a fully executed "Waiver and Permission to Transfer". But upon opening, she was stunned to read what had been signed: a "Contract to Provide Continuing Care" for Mr. Mark Mark Markham, fully executed by Mrs. Markham, and witnessed by her two children.

She was confused. She thought that she had called them in to get Marty moved. But now...she was perplexed. Her head had been spinning from the first part of the meeting. Looking back, things had seemed unfocused. That annoying buzz with the blue light likely accounted for her apparent confusion. At present, she could not recall just why or even if she needed him moved. After all, he was a source of entertainment around this otherwise morose environment. She determined that she could put up with his idiosyncrasies and would let the matter drop. For now, she had work to do.

As Ms. Bichette filed her morning tallies and balanced her medication records, she heard commotion in the hallway. She poked her head out her office doorway to see, there assembled en groupe, the good ole boys and Trudy. They had just exited PT and were headed for the cafeteria. What are they up to, she wondered? This was the second Time in one week; except now, Marty was with them.

Soooo, he was again up and at 'em, she thought. The contest begins anew. She smiled. He appeared energized, flippers spinning. No telling what he had in mind. Something was cooking. She was determined to find it out. She could not endure another day like the one following the ballroom dance. She had to admit that Marty's behavior on that day was an aberration. Under normal circumstances – and aside from his quick wit and fast flying speed - she was glad to have him back to…"normal", as it were. Nevertheless, his most recent behavior was a tough wrestle.

But something else was amiss, she thought as she watched them move from PT into the cafeteria. *Hmmmm...* She thought for a moment, and it came to her: Maggie. She jotted herself a note to contact them tomorrow morning. Maggie had moved on.

CHAPTER XXXII

Curly was sweeping Hallway B late at night. It was almost his bedtime. He was tired and in no mood to mop down and clean PT. He poked his head in to take a quick peek around with the hope that it could wait until tomorrow. Satisfied, he reached to turn off the light switch.

Then, across the way, he saw the top of head in the therapy tub. "Sheesh!" he thought. Now, he'd need to ring for the Bichette to come and rustle the boy back into bed. He sighed deeply. This had happened before. The old folks sometimes sleepwalked. The peach yogurt was popular and some would get mislaid on their way back to the cafeteria for a late night sneak attack on the refrigerator. Most recently, Curly had found a few night owls in the kitchen. He herded them back to bed. Likely they never knew they had been out or that they had partied. A while back, an old dude had managed to lock himself inside the bathroom nearest the front desk. Why Le Biche had not discovered him was a good question. Curly supposed that this was one of the reasons that he still had his job. She knew that he knew about this specific glitch in the functioning of her otherwise finely oiled machine. He knew of a few more glitches. That bathroom dude was a strange one since the door locked on the inside where only he had access to the lock set. He could have clicked over the lock and walked out on his own at any Time. Yeah well, as they say: what the mind can conceive, it can achieve. Poor dude just didn't have the mind to conceive how to unlock the door from the inside. Curly had to use his key to open it just to get the old boy out. Go figure.

Besides Marty, this one here in PT was a first. No one had ever either intentionally or in his sleep approached Physical Therapy. It wasn't so much that it was haunted. It was just that...well, Physical Therapy meant work: dressing down, filling the tub, setting gauges, climbing in, climbing out, toweling off. And the old folks here avoided work like the plague. Marty was the only patron that he'd ever seen in PT.

Curly looked over at the tub with increasing trepidation. He did want to be sure that he had seen someone there. If he did, it could only be Marty. He didn't want to find him there. But before he could ring for Le Biche, she arrived on scene. Curly puzzled. He ducked behind the weight machines to hide and watch. What was she doing here, he wondered?

"Mr. Markham? Is that you?" she said. "Are you alright?" She grunted loudly as she pulled his face out of the water there in the tub. She pulled off his goggles and began slapping his face. She rang the red emergency button on the wall next to the therapy tub and continued to slap. The button was intended to summon the medical staff – which meant Trudy with a first aid kit. But here, The Death Squad materialized well regimented and neatly dressed– dark suits, dark hats, and dark glasses. They had been making themselves indispensable to Ms. Bichette of late. They pulled Marty from the tub and laid him on the floor. He was dripping wet and limp. Curly, too, went limp. It was Marty. The Death Squad was hovering. He wondered again why they were here. Why not the EMT unit from the nearby fire department? Marty wasn't dead yet, was he? And, if he was, how did she even know to summon them. Curly couldn't help but recall his own dance of death with Ms. Bichette in the PT therapy tub. Marty had saved his life.

Ms. Bichette slapped him again and asked, "Mr. Markham, are you okay? What on earth are you doing here? You should be in bed. Why are you up so late?" The smallest of the three Death Squad members sat down on Marty's chest and began to pump. The second of the three started mouth to mouth. *If this was an act*, Curly thought, *it was a good one.*

Curly wondered again. Why were these guys here? Where were the EMT's? Marty hadn't died yet, had he? Oh, my gawd! What if it was true? What if Marty was gone? Curly began to tear up. He couldn't bear the thought. How would he tell the others? They still had to deal with Maggie. Now they had both to send off. This could not be happening! He wiped his eyes and left to go find the others. They'd need to meet yet again under Marty's bed in emergency session. One thing he knew for sure. They must get to both of them in the morgue before Eldon arrived to take them home.

As Ms. Bichette worried, Marty surfaced with a huge breath intake, followed by a blow out and hard cough, "Buh...hhhaaahhh!, coff, coff, coff...Huuuuhhhhhh, coff, coff, aaahhhhggg.......". He was back in the lap pool at the Country Club. He gulped, lifted his goggles, wiped his nose, and took another moment to gather himself. He stood up in water to his chest and looked around. This place was familiar. There across the way at the family pool sat the pretty blonde with whom he had danced...what was it...a few nights back, maybe? She was accompanied by that familiar blond young man who stood next to her as she sat there at a patio table next to the family pool. They were accompanied by a third person who sat across from the pretty blonde. Marty could tell by her profile that it was a woman... nicely built, he must admit. A large umbrella shaded the table. The shade overshadowed the mystery woman so he couldn't see her face, only her profile. She was talking rather intensively with the pretty blonde. The blonde did not look happy. She hid her face in her hands. She seemed to be crying. The young man placed his hand on her shoulder to comfort her. He looked concerned.

Marty exited the pool and moved closer to eavesdrop. He took up an empty chaise lounge near the table. He covered his face with a small towel left on the lounge. He lay on his back to sunbathe.

"Mrs. Markham. I am sorry to deliver this news to you. I had intended to meet with you concerning better, uh, more sophisticated arrangements for Mr. Markham". The pretty blonde and the young man looked at each other. To them, this somehow felt rehearsed. The young man scrunched his face as if to inquire further. The mystery woman continued, "Uh, I was saying...well, that you would need to make..., ummmm...more specialized arrangements for Mr. Markham; that we can no longer keep track of him at Golden Hills; that he...ummm, well this is hard to admit because we are all professionals at the home, but...uhhh..."

She went on, "He sometimes goes missing despite our best efforts". She finished abruptly. Her attempt to explain had failed miserably.

The young man interrupted, "What do you mean, he goes missing? He is old and crusty; and wears those swim fins everywhere. He doesn't ever go very far, maybe from his room to the kitchen, sometimes to the family center up front. How can he simply 'go missing'?"

The sexy shadow hesitated. Marty could tell from her demeanor that she had more to say, but really didn't wish to share this next part. "The other night....we pulled him from the therapy tub in Physical Therapy. He was in bad shape. This was following bed check and medications. He was sleeping soundly no more than an hour earlier", she said.

"Medications, What medications!?" the young man asked, surprised. He was having a difficult time processing.

"It's alright honey", the pretty blonde patted his leg to calm him. I know about his medication chart. You do too. He's been taking meds for years: blood pressure, thyroid...he's getting...well, old...you know sweety", she explained. "They keep me updated".

The sexy shadow sighed and stood up to adjust her chair. Marty heard the chair scrape on the stone patio. He peeked over from under the towel. The sun glinted off of her back. There - undulating from the top of her right shoulder, across her bare back to hide briefly beneath her tight white skirt, only to continue down and around her long left leg to end at the outside of her ankle –was a serpent tattoo.

Marty puzzled. This was Ms. Bichette! Or at least, she was the Ms. Bichette that he sometimes dreamed about: poolside in a bikini and wearing a serpent. But what was she doing here? In his waking moments, she came fully dressed albeit still sexy. She wore a tight white nurse's outfit: miniskirt to expose the legs and tight top to expose some cleavage, but nothing like this. Her cleavage was on full display. She wore a miniskirt with white stockings attached to a white garter belt. This had to be another dream, the kind of dream that Marty had not had in a long, long time. He smiled to himself as he watched the serpent undulate each time she breathed. He had only ever seen the serpent in his dreams. When he was awake, the serpent was always a mystery except on a few occasions when she'd lost a button. Boy, those times were memorable. He smiled to himself. Here, she was scantily clad with the serpent out in the open. Marty cherished these small moments, the type of moment that could bring interest to an otherwise drab life at Golden Hills and, yes, he was certain of one thing. This was a dream and a damn good one. He'd stick around to watch it unfold.

"Please", Ms. Bichette said softly. "There is more".

"More? More what?" the young man asked. The pretty blonde inquired, as well, "More what?"

Marty played along. Now that he knew he was dreaming, he sought to be entertained. Yeah, he thought, more what?

Ms. Bichette looked sincerely at them both across the lounge table. She sighed, took a deep breath and said, "As I was saying: The other night we pulled him from the therapy tub. He was not breathing. We did our best for him, but..."

The young man interrupted urgently. "What do you mean 'We did our best'". I thought we were talking about more specialized arrangements? I thought we were talking about moving him to a different home, you know, one with a better...I mean...a more experienced staff. You sound as if you're trying to tell me that, well.... that he died". He began to choke up. He stared intently at her, urgently seeking some kind of reassurance. Ms. Bichette was not good at reassurance.

"I apologize. I am bad at this. Mr. Markham did not survive." The Death Squad appeared at her shoulder as she spoke. They smiled eerily. She continued, "You will need to make arrangements through our temporary morgue facility downstairs at Golden Hills - Mr. Eldon Jones. I have his number right here". She handed a card to the pretty blonde who reached out her hand without looking up. The young man intercepted the card and placed it into his shirt pocket. He scowled at her, still not fully comprehending.

Ms. Bichette continued uncomfortably, "He will need to be picked up. Eldon can help you make...", she paused. "You know... whatever final arrangements you may wish for Marty...uh, I mean, Mr. Markham". Her slip into informality betrayed her respect for the man who had been a worthy foil. "Please, call Eldon". She pushed her chair back and stood to leave. She paused for a moment with her back to them as a son held his mother. "I'm sorry", she said and hurriedly left poolside.

Marty was confused. This was becoming a nightmare. Had he just heard Ms. Bichette tell this pretty blonde woman that he had somehow "passed on", "kicked the bucket", "gone belly up", "assumed room temperature"? Had he heard her correctly? He thought back to recount the interchange. Yes, he had just heard Ms Bichette tell this pretty blonde woman that he had died.

My gawd! This was not a problem with his Swiss cheese memory, a more familiar problem with which he sometimes struggled. With that, he had learned to cope. But this...this was unsettling. The Death Squad, holy hell, are they kidding?! His confusion stemmed from the simple fact that he was still living, moving, thinking, and breathing. He felt up and down his chest as he inhaled quickly and blew out several times. He looked around to reassure himself that he was indeed alive. For the moment, he was reassured. So okay, he was alive.

Then, almost instantly, the sunlight began to fade. The large family pool disappeared. The pretty blonde and young son vanished. The table, the chairs, the entire surroundings slowly darkened and faded to black. The chaise lounge, on which he had hidden to spy, disappeared. Silence enveloped. Once more he wondered, was this a nightmare? He couldn't say. It felt so much like one of his deeper dives. He half expected to see a manta ray or a tiger shark. No such luck. He heard nothing and saw only darkness,and the secure sense that he craved with the surrounding water in which he typically swam was wholly absent. Where was he?

Was this "hell" or "purgatory"? Nah, he rejected the notion. This was more like...well, "limbo", he guessed. He thought for a moment. He didn't follow the doctrines but if he was asked to describe "limbo", he would use one word: "boredom". Ouch. Could that be an eternal consequence? Oh c'mon, he thought. If "limbo" was just "boredom" and if "limbo" could be eternal, then "limbo" was "hell". Besides that, he wasn't bored. He was way more than that. He was nervous, even scared. Rarely, had he been scared. He remembered a Time when he was a child, his mom and put him down for nap. As he slept, she walked to the grocery store a couple of blocks away. While she was gone, he awoke to hear water begin to fill in the washing machine. He thought the world would flood,and it scared the Beejeesus out of him! He wasn't used to that feeling. The Catholics had it wrong! This was more than "boredom''. It wasn't "limbo". This was more like fright, but not quite; nerves maybe or anxiety? Still, it was more than boredom. Score one for the Protestants.

With that thought, Marty earned some enlightenment. He could deal with "hell" on Protestant terms, at least as that term was used as an invective to best describe how one felt or as an utterance in surprise. You know like, "I feel like hell today" or "What in the hell was that?" On those terms, Marty concluded that he was more nervous than scared. It was bigger than "boredom" more like, "he felt like hell, and therefore he must be somewhere back at Golden Hills". This logic was irrefutable. If he waited long enough, he'd figure out where he was: whether in PT, in the cafeteria, or even in bed. But for now, he'd do what he always did when befuddled. He'd dive deep and take a nap.

Momentarily, an intuition troubled him: The Death Squad. What were they doing in this nightmare? Granted, a nightmare is where they belonged. Still, he refused to allow such a peaceful rest to be interrupted by any Death Squad shenanigans. He took another deep breath and blew it out slowly. He quickly fell asleep and began to snore. His sleep was deep, but troubled.

CHAPTER XXXIII

Miss Lauren Bichette, head nurse at the Golden Hills Senior Residence, was flummoxed. This was not a condition with which she was even vaguely familiar. The Mortician's Assistants aka The Death Squad accompanied her. (Yes, she knew the nickname that the residents had assigned). She had summoned them. They had come to care for Maggie. She had passed away unexpectedly – if there were such an adverb for dying in a place like this. Ms. Bichette felt that once they dealt with Maggie and got her tucked in, as it were, that things here at Golden Hills would soon be back to normal. But she was mistaken. Mr. Markham had now gone missing,and she was loath to admit that he had gone missing – again.

He had been acting close to his "normal" self, and she had hoped to restore some semblance of control here at the old folks' home. She was proud that she had not lost her temper through these recent days, and that she had passed on the temptation to strike back at what seemed to be purposeful attempts by Mr. Markham and his crowd of rowdies. When it came to Mr. Markham, she was never really sure whether his conduct was purposeful. She was glad that she had acted patiently with him. But this time, her patience had worn thin.

In this new round of folly, her search had taken her to PT where she had found him in the therapy tub. She had checked his pulse and breathing. She had pulled him from the tank, laid him on his back, and pounded his chest. She had administered mouth-to-mouth, repeated several times over. She was unable to revive him and had directed the Death Squad to deposit him to the mortuary downstairs where she thought that he had been tucked in, soon to be delivered to his maker. That was the same night Maggie had passed. She had been caught by Marty's coincidence and was unable to focus on Maggie.

Now here she was, forced to leave Maggie in bed and cold, just so she could meet yet another of Marty's "emergencies". She was not sure that this "emergency" even existed. She was miffed at Marty for putting her in this circumstance. After all, he was dead wasn't he? What the hell was he thinking? She did like him, but she must be more cautious when dealing with that man. Now, here he was taking precedence, again. She reminded herself from his earlier history that he was hard to kill and she worried. Damn it, should she ever get through this, she should write a book. She summoned The Death Squad who had cared for Maggie. She left instructions with the front desk that when they arrived to have them report to Physical Therapy to help her with Marty.

She went to the office for Eldon's phone number. With so much confusion, she'd forgotten his contact information. This wasn't like her. Perhaps now with Mr. Markham really gone and, once she could deal with Maggie, things here at Golden Hills could get back to normal. She crossed herself, looked up, and pointed skyward like a pass receiver following a one-handed catch in the end zone.

She figured that The Death Squad had performed admirably,and that they had properly cleaned and tagged Mr. Markham. She had instructed them to leave him with his goggles, his speedo, and his fins. She thought that to be a nice touch and had been pleased with herself to have thought of it. The Death Squad had wheeled him to the basement and placed him into Drawer 13, this Time for good. They smiled at this instruction. It seemed this old boy had a standing reservation. By their own report, they had delivered him to Drawer 13, pushed in the drawer, and bowed to him in unison as a final payment of respect. Little did they know that this was not the last they would see him, and that their respect for him soon hereafter would expand exponentially.

As they bowed, Number One noticed that the extra wide drawer at the bottom row and one column left of Drawer 13 was not fully closed. The steel cupboard doors that covered the extra wide slab inside the drawer were slightly ajar. Number One stood left of Drawer 13 and was closest. Casually, as he worked to place Marty, he reached over with his left foot to close the steel cupboard covers to the extra wide opening. "Drawer A Extra Wide" would soon come to be known as "Maggie's Drawer". He pushed with his toe, but the drawer didn't budge and the covers would not close tightly. Funny, he thought. He whispered to the other two and pointed. They secured Marty, closed him up tight, and moved in unison to the front of the extra-wide.

"One, Two, Three", the First commanded. This was as much a countdown as it was a specification of each of them present: Numbers One, Two, and Three. It was a call to arms, to each when extra effort was required. Each grunted as they maximized there singular effort to close the drawer. They pushed in unison at the steel cupboard covers. But the drawer would not fully close.

"Hmmm, something must be caught or the drawer is off of its rollers", Number One observed. Two and Three nodded back. Number One thought for a moment and shrugged. Two and Three shrugged back. Maintenance was neither their bag nor their assignment. They decided to post a note with the front office for Eldon. He should handle such trivial details. As for them, they had bigger fish to fry.

They giggled quietly with each other as they thought of Ms. Margaret Lassiter. "Bigger fish", they chuckled in unison. Maggie was awaiting their service. She would be a challenge. They headed upstairs to oblige. They bumped into Ms. Bichette at the entry to the stairway in Hallway B. She was on the hunt. She could not find Maggie. She was not in her bed. She was not in her room. She asked the respective numbers whether they had seen her. Of course, they had not. They were headed to her room now to deal with her.

"Forget the room, she's gone", she told them. Where could a four hundred pound dead woman hide? She wondered. The fact that she had wondered such a thing was distressing. But then...

"Wait a minute", she exclaimed out loud to no one in particular. "A dead woman does not hide. She doesn't walk away. She can't!" She cogitated. She must have been taken, removed. Someone must have taken her. Plus, she weighed four hundred pounds...FOUR HUNDRED POUNDS!! They could not have taken her far. She paced as she cogitated there in Hallway B. The Death Squad had come to attention and quietly waited.

"My gawd, there I go again!" Ms. Bichette thought. "What in the hell am I thinking. 'She' – the dead woman, Maggie - couldn't have gone anywhere. SHE WAS DEAD!"

Ms. Bichette pounded her brain. "Think! Think! Think!" She crossed her arms and squeezed to calm herself. She took a few deep breaths, in and out, in and out. She exhaled and held. She inhaled and held. She squinted hard and pinched at her temples. She blew out loudly, relaxed, then concentrated. Slowly she calmed. That was better.

No one person took her, she confirmed to herself, as her thinking began to clear. Logic began to govern. Her mind opened and expanded.

The Death Squad hadn't taken her from her room. Check.

Eldon was only recently summoned ,and anyway, he never came upstairs. Check.

No one else had checked in at the front desk at any time today. It must have been someone from within. Check.

It had to have been...what? A resident? Only Marty had the stones to do such a thing. But, he was dead. Wasn't he? Her suspicions grew. Nah! C'mon, he couldn't have; not without help. More than one had to be involved. It would take... numerous.

Then, BAM! The answer hit like thunder. It would take MO! He was the only one here who could manage. With a little help from

Curly, it would be cake. She liked this logic because it kept Marty confined to the eternal realms. Where were Mo and Curly? Where were they now? She hadn't seen them since lunch! She started toward the lunchroom to find Mo, but stopped suddenly and turned back.

Wait... she thought. There's a better way. The only way out of here for a four hundred pound dead woman was via the basement morgue. Eldon would need to haul her out of here in his hearse and he was already here! She had already issued an order for him to pick up Marty.

As for Maggie, she must be in the extra-wide drawer at the bottom row! That is the only drawer big enough to house her. The question for Eldon is whether he brought help. Almost always, the tightwad picked-up and delivered on his own. It didn't matter. She had the Death Squad. There would be plenty of help to get Maggie into the hearse. Once she could ensure the delivery of Ms. Margaret Lassiter to the Elysian Fields, she would relax. All would be well! She would deal with Mo and Curly later. She remained troubled by why they had felt it necessary to move Maggie in the first place. She was more trouble by why they felt that they could work outside of the chain of her command. This challenge to her authority was a serious breach. But,... no matter. Maybe if they confessed, she would go easy. She felt good. She still had time to rectify this mess. She smiled. Order had returned to her Universe! She closed her eyes, crossed herself and pointed to Heaven.

"Let's go!" she signaled to the Death Squad. They followed directly down the stairs to the basement mortuary.

Eldon Jones arrived for the night shift at the Golden Hills basement morgue. Good news, bad news. Tonight was easy. No scheduled deliveries, but no delivery bonus. No $300. He could get out of here early. He'd check with the staff upstairs to better assess next week's pick-up and delivery schedule. The schedule was difficult to predict. There were always several residents hovering on the brink. But one could never predict their passing. Like the one 78 year old dude- he was still active with the ladies, favored bourbon over scotch, and was a favorite with the staff. They figured he'd be around for a while. He'd lost his wife several years back. The two had raised their own kids, raised an adopted set of kids, lost their daughter, and chose to raise her kids. Let's face it. The boy was tired. He sat down one day to watch the World Series. An autopsy revealed that he had felt a heart attack coming on in the top of the 7th. The score and his pitch count suggested that he could easily have taken the bench to await the win coming his way. Instead, he chose to remain to the end of the 9th. He took the win, but his season ended. He was stiff by the end of the game.

Then there was the 86 year old woman and her husband. They'd been married for a good half century or more. They were friends with his wife's aunt. He met them when he and his wife stopped by to visit. She was a pretty lady, red hair. She kept herself up real nice. She was pleasingly plump and healthy. Folks had figured that she'd be around for a good long while. He – on the other hand - was pushing 90. He was in bad shape: shingles, weak heart. He was transported around in a wheel chair. Folks said that he was "on death's door", set to go at any time.

Eldon smiled at the memory. During the visit, the women sat around and chatted. He and the old boy sat at the kitchen table listening to the chirping going on. Eldon was bored. He kept looking to his wife, pointing to his wrist watch as if there was some place important for them to be. The old boy just sat, stoic – no movement, no sound. He was easy to overlook and had been for several years now. The women's conversation turned to birthdays and the significant number about which they knew that came in December. Wasn't that odd? How curious was that? Stuff like that. Seemingly out of nowhere, the old boy raised his head and spoke.

"March must have been a cold month", he said and then like a turtle, he retreated back into his protective shell.

The women were stunned. The silence was deafening. They were surprised that he could speak, more surprised that he had been following the gist of their conversation. Eldon grinned today at the recollection. For whatever it was worth to him, the old boy had outlasted both. Eldon sighed. Yeah, well. Eventually, even the old boy finally checked out.

Eldon parked the hearse in the garage bay and exited. He pulled a ring of keys from his pocket, fiddled with the ring to find the proper key and opened the door to the temporary morgue. He flipped on the lights as he entered. The overhead fluorescents flickered slowly on. As expected, the various slabs were empty. No transports; no preparations necessary. He laid his keys on the front table, scooted over a small, three-legged stool, and took out his lunch to eat. He wondered. The old boy, - Marty - would he ever see him again? Would he ever see any of these stiffs...ughh...these people again? Eldon caught himself. He didn't want to be disrespectful. If one day, down the road, he just happened to bump into any of these folks that he'd been hauling out of here, he would hope that their meeting would go favorably. Spirits or Zombies or whatever, he'd certainly hope that they could be friendly. He crossed himself, clasped his hands, and whispered a short silent prayer with a brief look to Heaven.

This kind of thinking could get philosophical. Aside from the question of how and in what form, would he – or maybe even should he – return, he wondered: If he could come "back", where did he come back from? Was it back from the "dead"? And, if he came back from the dead, was it a resurrection? What was that anyway? Or was it just a simple, well... he paused again -he couldn't think of a good word for it....a "refreshment", maybe? Yeah he concluded. It was a: "refreshment". From the stories in the Bible, no one except the Main Man was ever "resurrected" as it were. He was the first. He kept the big one for himself. Before that happened, He made a bunch of smaller miracles. Water to wine, that was cool, but not as big a Lazerus. Lazerus was probably second to resurrection. He brought that boy back from the dead. Eldon remembered the story from Sunday school. The rule was that ole Lazerus would have to kick again sometime later. He got only a temporary reprieve, at best, from the in-laws.

Eldon concluded that Lazerus had been "refreshed", not "resurrected". He surmised that ole' Lazerus still needed to learn how best to put up with his wife's family, you know, as part of the test. When he passed – and everybody did – he'd then get the bigger prize: resurrection that part seemed sure, at least according to Sunday school. Eldon smiled at his own solid reasoning. He didn't mean to diminish Lazerus' miracle. By all accounts, it was big, just not as big as well...as resurrection. From what Eldon understood, resurrection was the end-game. It would last for a helluva long Time. Whereas, "refreshment" could last maybe 30, 40, or more years; or until a person plumb wore out. Not long when compared to forever, he thought. He guessed that Lazerus got a second chance of maybe another 40 years to get to better know his in-laws. Hopefully by then, he'd be well versed as to how best to please his wife's mother and how not to piss off his wife's dad. Eldon shuddered to think that he may spend forever with his in-laws. Brrrrrr.

He stopped himself. Realistically, he only saw any of these dead folks here at Golden Hills, but one Time – at pick up- and one Time was plenty. "Refreshment" –if there was such a thing – was as rare as "resurrection". It'd be most unlikely that he might bump into some Lazerus whom he had transported on the first go round, only to be shocked to see him for a second Time. That thought was reassuring, at least.

Cl-clickk; Creaaakkkk. Eldon's thoughts were interrupted as the upstairs door leading to the main lobby clicked open. He heard some hushed whispers at the top of the stairs. The door creaked and clicked shut followed by several pairs of footfalls down the stairs. This was not the night for visitors. He'd been thinking about spirits and zombies, death, refreshment, and resurrection. He was a bit worried about just who had come to visit. One at a time, a skinny woman with a cane came through the downstairs entry. She smiled nervously and waved. Then, a huge black man filled the doorway opening and virtually poured into the basement morgue. He nodded and a third, Curly - he knew this guy - the custodian. He saluted and Eldon took some reassurance. Curly was buddies with the old dude who had cursed him not to speak. He had been mute from the day he'd pulled the guy from the drawer. Eldon was getting impatient. The head nurse was not a frequent visitor. He hadn't seen her yet to deliver the message. The old boy told him to "testify" to the head nurse; something to the effect that Marty should stay at Golden Hills in perpetuity. But he was in no real hurry. Nobody said much in the morgue anyway, not much need for conversation.

He shrugged at his visitors and held out his hands to say, "What are you doing down here?"

The fact that they had come down the stairs and under their own power told him that it was a little early for them to be here anyway. He laughed quietly to himself. "They were here, in the morgue, a little too early...because they weren't dead yet", he chuckled again at the thought. That was funny. It was too bad that he couldn't speak. He'd make a good comedian. Besides, he had several questions to ask of these jokers.

He nodded toward the lockers that lined the nearby walls and waved his arm in an expansive gesture over the tables to offer welcome.

"Sorry Eldon. We didn't mean to interrupt", Curly said. "But... well, we've got a bit of a dilemma, and...ummm". He paused. Mo leaned over and whispered into his ear. Curly nodded and looked again to Eldon. "Maybe you could help us?" he asked.

Eldon offered a theatrical bow. Whatever delivery he was supposed to make had not arrived, and he found no ticket to verify it, anyway. He smiled to the assembled crowd, clapped his hands together and rubbed them as if to say, "Go on. I'm waiting".

Curly nodded to Mo directing him to the large bottom drawer. Mo nodded back and moved to the wall of drawers. He reached down to Drawer 1A- Extra Wide and pulled. Maggie was there as if asleep and smiling sweetly. She'd only been there a few hours. Thankfully, she had not yet, well..."aged" as it were. The laundry may not be fresh, but – to the guys, at least – it could still be worn for another day.

Eldon's face registered surprise as if to say, "What the F...?"

Trudy couldn't hold back and began to tear up. She already missed Maggie. It was different when she was around, even though she couldn't really visit back. Her recent resurgence to what had seemed like full vigor had been a pleasant surprise. It was almost like old times. Then, Bam! She was gone, this time for good. Trudy put her face into her hands. She could barely cope.

Curly put his arm around her shoulders to bolster her. He whispered into her ear to offer support and a consoling word. She looked up, wiped the tears from her eyes, and smiled weakly. Curly handed her a clean rag from his back pocket. She blew her nose loudly and handed it back. He took it back and put it into the opposite back pocket that he used for the dirty rags. He was nothing if not circumspect.

Larry too was overcome with emotion. He and Maggie had been good friends. She had helped him figure out that Ms. Bichette was color blind and had supported his push for Peach Yogurt. It was difficult to see her this way. He knew what they were there to do. He knew that it was for Maggie, and that it was her final wish. He'd rather attend a normal funeral. He'd seen plenty of those and knew what to expect. But this was different. This was what she wanted. He would help to grant her request.

Eldon lifted his eyebrows and shrugged. He pointed to Drawer A. They looked at him quizzically. He held up a palm toward his face and acted as if he was writing on a pad. He looked at each of them inquiringly.

Curly pulled a pen and scrap of paper from his pocket and handed them over. Eldon wrote, "How did she get here? I've seen no order. For one as big as this, I'd have brought an assistant." He handed the note to Mo and looked around at the faces of Maggie's friends as if to say, "What do you want me to do?"

"We need you to help us transport her out of here" Mo said.

Eldon took back the pen and paper. He wrote, "What do I do with her? How do I do it by myself?". He looked at Maggie, blew out his cheeks and spread his arms wide as if to say, "She's huge". His inquiry was legitimate.

All responded at once: "We're going with you! We'll do the big job, but we need your wheels".

Eldon grimaced and began to shake his head – No! No! No! Rules were rules.

For purely practical reasons, he could have no recourse with the patrons here at Golden Hills unless, of course, they were dead. And, even if he could, he did not want to absorb the legal responsibility that could accompany. Mo and Curly were employees and could hold their own. But if he was caught riding around with them in his hearse, it would still mean his job. Trudy was obviously a resident. Larry was a maybe. If anything happened to them while on board, he could be sued and even go to jail. No. No. No. He continued to shake his head emphatically from side to side.

Larry piped up. "Look", he said, "How about this?" He looked over to the table where Eldon had been seated. He saw his lunch spread there. "You go take lunch. You never heard us. You never saw us. Mo is almost big enough by himself to handle Maggie. Curly and I can take up the slack. We'll handle her from here. We'll roll her on out and load her up into your hearse..."

"Is it open?" Mo asked. He was following Larry's thinking.

Eldon nodded. Who would steal a big ugly hearse?

"Good", Curly interjected. "As I was saying...we'll get her into the hearse, make our delivery nearby, and have her back here in 30 minutes".

Eldon wrote on the pad, "Where is 'nearby'?" He searched the blank faces in front of him. Suddenly, his realization dawned. He shook a finger at them from side to side and shook his head as if to say, "Never mind". He really didn't want to know. Still... he thought. He didn't really know any of these old folks. He didn't want to be a drag on some worthwhile adventure, and this was business after all. He wrote, "What is in it for me?"

Curly looked to the assembled group and smiled. They had hit Eldon's sweet spot and were on their way. "How much?" he asked Eldon.

Eldon hesitated. He was thinking.

"C'mon. How much? Your trouble is worth something, right? We can pay", Curly affirmed. "How much"? Curly kept eye contact with Eldon as he reached his hand behind him to the others. The others -except Trudy - put in bills. Trudy added a bottle of coins: pennies, dimes and nickels. Curly looked at her quizzically.

"How much will you take? Curly asked.

Eldon looked back. He liked these folks. He showed three fingers on his right hand to signify: $300 per delivery. He then brought his left hand to his chin and scratched. He was thinking. He pointed to Maggie, opened wide his eyes, blew out his cheeks spread his arms wide in an awkward attempt to show what a load Maggie would be,and he put up two more fingers on his left hand, held them together with the three on his right, as if to say: this "wide load" should run another two hundred for a total of $500. He smiled at the crowd as if to say, "I like you guys" and held up a total of four fingers on one hand to signify $400 total. He then nodded confirmation and waited.

"Done", Curly announced confidently as he confirmed with the group. He counted out the bills: "Two hundred eighty-seven, eighty□eight, and eighty-nine dollars even", he announced proudly until it dawned on him and the others that he was short.

"Trudy..." he looked at her hopefully. 'What do you have?"

"Twenty three dollars and seventeen cents," she reported confidently, her chin out.

Larry added quickly, "Three hundred twelve and seventeen cents". He looked around hopefully. The group looked at Eldon and begged. He shrugged and shook his head. He felt bad, but he had some risk here.

The assembled group was crestfallen. Curly was quickly considering other options if any. Larry figured that he could put his hands on some more money, but it would take Time. He wondered: Would Eldon take credit? He raised a finger to catch Eldon's attention when suddenly from Drawer 13, they heard: "BAM, BAM, BAM". The group jumped in unison. "BAM, BAM, BAM", Drawer 13 rattled. Then, within seconds, they heard the hallway door open at the top of the stairs.

Curly put a finger to his lips and shushed the group. He waved them to the back receiving area where they crouched in darkness behind yogurt boxes, recently delivered.

Ms. Bichette bounced into the basement morgue from the stairway. She was in a hurry and more impatient than was usual. She looked to see Eldon, his feet up on the table, his face behind a newspaper. He was playing it cool.

"Excuse me", Ms. Bichette demanded. Eldon peeked from behind the paper. "Are you here to take delivery?" she asked. He shook his head truthfully.

"Are you holding anybody?" she asked. Eldon sat mute, first because he couldn't speak, and second because he didn't know what to say if he could. Her stare drilled down. She was getting impatient and he had heard rumors. Don't mess with Ms. Bichette. But he needed her help. He took a deep breath and loudly sighed. He put down his paper, set his chair forward, and stood. He signaled for her to follow him to the dry erase board affixed to the wall directly across from the metal drawers. He wrote: "Are you Ms. Bichette?"

She inhaled deeply in exasperation blew it out. "Yes, what might I do for you?" she pressed emphatically.

"Ms. Bichette-head nurse at Golden Hills?" he wrote again. He had to ask to assure himself.

"Yes! What is it!" she said in frustration and trying hard to stay patient.

Eldon wrote: "Marty was here. He is a god – of sorts, and he should be spared a space here at Golden Hills in perpetuity". He watched her a brief moment then added, "Although you may think differently", he grinned uneasily.

She looked at him quizzically. He shrugged. She took the meaning, waved him off, and hurried back up the front staircase in a huff.

Eldon didn't really know why she had come. She was scary, but he did get his voice back. He had nothing to lose, so he "testified" – as it were – as he had been instructed. No one told him just when he would get his voice back once he had testified. He expected he would need to be patient, to bide his Time. As he thought what he might do until his voice came back, he suddenly gagged, choked up a large spit wad, and coughed violently for a long while. Eventually, the fit calmed. He stayed silent for a moment longer. He coughed purposefully, a few Times, to clear his throat; and miraculously, he sang: "♪Do, Re, Mi, Fa, So, La, Te, Dooooooo♪". He grinned again, and looked around sheepishly as the group crawled out of the shadows.

"Sweet", he said hoarsely, "Now where were we?"

"Drawer 13", the group responded in unison.

To Eldon, this was déjà vu all over again. With some trepidation, he approached Drawer 13. He took off his shoes and kneeled again reverently before the drawer. He wasn't going to take any chances. He turned to the crowd assembled, signaled them to shush and to remove their shoes. He then signaled for them to kneel. They did as they were directed.

The last time he'd confronted this dude left him speechless... literally. Now, here he was again. He knew to be careful in front of Drawer 13. Who was this guy? He took the normal precautions associated with deity. He kneeled again in front of Drawer 13, crossed himself, and said:

"Speak, Lord. Thy servant heareth". He said it as reverently as he could muster.

"Damn is that you, noble knight?" a familiar voice came from inside Drawer 13. Curly and crew were nicely surprised. They "high☐fived" each other all around, and watched expectantly.

"This is the second time I've awakened from a peaceful and relaxing sleep to find myself here in a refrigerated crypt with you inquiring at the outside. What goes - Sir Smith and Jones is it? I ask you"?

"Uh, well", Eldon was flummoxed, not sure what to say.

Trudy spoke up, "Marty, we need your help. By the way...why are you in there?"

"Silly question... I've been napping. Please...just get me out". Marty responded rather magnanimously. Trudy nodded to Eldon. He shrugged and pulled open Drawer 13.

"Thank you, my fine knight", he said. "Oh, I see that we have company". He smiled and waved to the group at large. His friends smiled and waved back. Like before, Eldon heard something best described as "white noise". The others didn't seem to notice. But Eldon was forced to put a finger into each ear to get some relief from the subtle tickle. He saw also that Mr. Markham was again enveloped in a blue light. And, like last time, his flippers fluttered allowing him to hover just off of the checkered tiles. This Markham dude was a cool customer. But business was business.

"Ummm, now that the gang is all here", he said. "May we get back to business?" He tested his voice, again, "Meee, meee, meee....

do, re, mi, fa, so, la, ti, do...do, ti, la, so, fa, mi, re, do". Good, he thought. It was working.

He looked to the crowd. "So, what do we do now? For $400 we're a go. If not, I'm outta here. There is way too much excitement for me in this place – a mortuary at an old folks home no less?"

"So, how may I help?" Marty smiled to the group.

Curly nodded to the extra-large drawer that had been pulled out. It was located just one column over and two rows down from Drawer 13. Marty looked to see Maggie.

"Oh my", he said matter-of-factly. He understood life and death at Golden Hills better than most. Curly explained that they needed $400 to borrow Eldon's hearse to take her to the park at M Street where they would honor her with a Viking funeral. The best they could come up with was $312.17. He wasn't sure just how Marty could help. His speedo didn't look like it could hold much more than few cents. But Marty lit up. He was ever ready for an adventure. He reached into the pocket of his speedo. He dug deep. That pocket seemed a bit like Mary Poppins bag. He dug ever deeper and almost lost himself inside his own pocket. Soon, he emerged with a handful of bills. He reached in again and fumbled around. His hand came out clutching some change. He laid his money on the metal table-slab for Curly to count.

Curly counted once and appeared confused. He counted again, still stymied. Mo pushed him gently aside and counted out an even $88.83 in small bills and change. Marty was indeed a walking bag of miracles, he thought. Mo put Marty's contribution with the others and slid them across the table to Eldon. Eldon had seen the count. He pulled the keys to the hearse from his pocket, handed them to Curly, and sat down at the slab to take his lunch. He put his headphones back in place, leaned his stool back, kicked his feet up, and looked to snooze. To him, these folks never existed.

He would expect to see his keys here on the table within the next 30 minutes. He flashed ten fingers, three times at Mo to remind him. He pointed to his wrist watch as if to remind himself of the Time. The others got the message. Mo, Larry, and Curly managed to get Maggie out of the drawer and onto a cart to wheel her to the hearse. Trudy took the lead. She unlocked the door to the garage where they found the parked hearse. She confiscated the keys to the hearse from Curly and jumped into the driver's seat. Curly didn't complain. The crowd jumped into the back and surrounded the coffin. Space was tight. But they rode together royally with Maggie. Marty fluttered outside, near the front of the hearse to guide Trudy to the park at M street just a few blocks over. She drove with the windows down. Curly rode shotgun. He was enjoying a smoke from what looked to be a rolled joint.

Trudy smiled as she recalled Maggie. In her early days, she smoked her fair share. The two of them would go to her private room when they needed a good girl talk. She would park her wheelchair sideways and up close to the narrow horizontal window. Each time she needed to exhale, she would hoist herself up on the side handle of her chair to get close to the window screen. There, she would blow out a cloud of blue smoke that would circle around her for a moment until it escaped on a cool breeze. Tonight, the air was also brisk. It felt good to be out...and free. The moon was full and bright.

Mo and Larry posted themselves on the back of the hearse with the doors open and their feet on the bumper. Mo was simply too large to ride inside. Larry took his own advantage of the sweet night air and squeezed in next to Mo. They chittered about nothing in particular. Trudy was looking forward to paying her respects to her good friend, Maggie. She was also very pleased that Marty seemed to be back to his more normal self – if there was such a thing. The headlights shimmered on his skinny backside there in front of the hearse as she drove. He seemed to paddle himself through the air. She still marveled at his apparent athleticism. She smiled. Even now, he reminded her of high school.

CHAPTER XXXIV

Eldon finished his sandwich. He kicked back on the stool. His feet were up on the steel slab. He had no work today. For the first time in a long time, He was just chillin'. He wore headphones and was listening to Huey Lewis and the News:

♪♪ ...Don't bet your future, on one roll of the dice
Better remember, lightning never strikes twice Please
don't drive at eighty eight, don't want to be late again
So take me away, I don't mind

But you better promise me, I'll be back in time... ♪♪
-Huey Lewis

The door slammed at the top of the stairs. He pulled off his phones and heard several pair of footsteps clamoring down. He looked up to see Ms. Bichette and The Death Squad. She was intimidating. The boys with her were spooky.

"Ms. Bich...I mean Bichette", he stammered nervously. He'd picked up the slang used by Curly to describe the head nurse. She stared back at him. Now was not the Time. He'd already dealt with her once today and once was one Time too many. Her second visit of the day was the equivalent of a 500 year storm. Even in her niceness, she scared the beejeesus out of him. And, he didn't like those Death Squad boys, either. Normally, he never had to deal with them.

"What do you guys want?" he asked again, his voice quavering. "I mean, how may I help you today?" He used his most professional voice. He glanced at The Death Squad. A slight shiver moved down his spine.

"Where is Margaret Lassiter?" Ms Bichette demanded flatly.

Eldon was prepared for this. His confidence returned, "Who?" he asked.

"Maggie, the dead woman - all four hundred pounds of her. She is not in her room. Now where is she?" she pressed.

"Look, before I came today, I received no orders, none, nada, zippo. Now, you come lookin' not for one, but for two stiffs. Not my iaob mang. Let me know when you figure it out.

Ms.Bichette was not happy. "Now look here..."

Eldon played his hand. "No, you look. If you have an order for me and can produce a stiff so I can do my job, then I will. For now, I don't know any Margaret Lassiter. I don't know any Maggie. I've never been to her room. I've never even been upstairs. I would only know her if she was dead and your boys there had put her in my basement. Did your boys put her in my basement?" he asked as calmly as he could muster. His knees began to shake, but so far he was holding up well.

Ms.Bichette struggled to offer a defense to this logic.

"Okay. So, Mr. Smith and Jones is it? I'm sorry. Let me start over. My 'boys' did not put her in your basement", she said. "I wrote out the transfer order and faxed it over to them just this morning. They arrived here expecting to find her in her bed. They did not find her in her bed", she recited.

The Death Squad all shook their heads in unison. Number One was staring forward to the rows of drawers with stainless steel faces. He suddenly remembered. He walked over to the extra wide drawer on the bottom shelf. He stood at the front with the cupboard slightly ajar. He opened the steel covers, set his feet, and pulled on the drawer slab. The slab didn't budge. He looked to Numbers Two and Three. They nodded and joined. Ms. Bichette hustled over to see.

Number One counted them down: 3-2-1 and they pulled together. The door screeched and waffled. It appeared that the drawer had come off of its rollers. The Death Squad was undaunted. They pulled again and the slab released. The Death Squad fell backwards to the floor. Ms. Bichette watched them tumble. She turned to see an empty slab.

"Where is she?" she shouted incredulously to no one in particular. The Death Squad together shrugged their respective shoulders. Eldon replaced his headphones. Huey Lewis continued to sing. Eldon tried hard to stay cool. He was almost free and clear. But Ms. Bichette wasn't finished. She ran to the garage. The garage was empty. The hearse was gone.

"Damn", Eldon muttered under his breath.

From the garage, Ms. Bichette shouted to The Death Squad, "Saddle Up"! Numbers One, Two, and Three quickly left the morgue and followed her in. Her loud voice echoed again from the garage. "Mr. Eldon Smith and Jones, I will deal with you in Time".

"Ouch," he thought. Whenever she used his full last name, it meant trouble. Oh well, can't do anything about it now. Huey Lewis sang again: "♪♪Back in Tiiieeiimme!♪♪" Eldon figured that he'd be happy to go "back in Time"...maybe by a few days, even by a few years. "Damn", he repeated to himself. He put his headphones on, tipped back his chair, propped up his feet onto the table slab, and quickly went back to sleep. He would deal with it all later or, if lucky, not at all.

CHAPTER XXXV

Trudy pulled the hearse into what was the upper parking lot for the city park at M Street. She parked at the edge of the lot, next to the curb, and got out. It was early morning. The full moon still lit the parking lot and the expansive lawns. The park sat at the top of a long grassy hill that dropped from the lot to a large pond maybe 100 to 150 yards below. The slope was, well... steep. The pond was large, more like a lake. It sat in the center of residential neighborhood. People would ice skate there in the winter time. When it was frozen, the nearby elementary school kids would shortcut across the ice to make it home in time to watch cartoons on TV with Fireman Frank. Each season the Fish and Game would stock the pond with Rainbow Trout. It was a popular place for school kids and nearby neighbors to fish and play. A large tree stump sat near the shoreline – a good place for parents to park three or four small ones to better watch them as they fished. A large axe was stuck in the center of the stump. Chips, splinters, and several split logs lay on the ground surrounding the stump. A single odd railroad tie lay on the small, wooden dock, a few yards away from a stump that carried the large axe. Someone had been busy. The dock was long enough for one boat. An old wooden row boat floated next to it secured by a rope at both stern and bow. Firewood filled the entire inside. Railroad ties rode over the firewood, atop the boat in a criss-cross fashion, 3-rows high. Thoughtful as always, Mo had placed a small mattress for Maggie to lie on at the top of the pile. Mo's executive judgment was on display with his selection of railroad ties. He had brought sufficient, plus one extra. The ties were heavy and the boat sat low in the water. But it was ready for the torch. Mo worried that Maggie's weight would sink the whole endeavor. For what it was worth, they had done their part.

Trudy watched from the parking lot above. She knew of Maggie's dying wish. This seemed to fit the bill. She and Maggie had shared their dreams together on numerous occasions. Maggie's passing had been a surprise. Trudy never really expected that she would go so soon. Even so, Maggie had seemed to sense it. She spoke often of her Viking heritage. She wished to be sent home on a Viking raft and set ablaze. Fat chance, Trudy thought. Yet, here they were thanks to Mo and Curly. She looked over at Mo and smiled. He was a good man, she thought. Trudy stood at the back curb and looked out over the park below. They had made it this far. She still found it hard to believe that they could pull this off.

Usually, Marty directed such things. But more and more, he was off somewhere and "out of Time" as he would say. She looked down to the lake. He was far out on the pond doing the backstroke, seemingly oblivious. She watched as he flipped over to the butterfly. Today, he was awake and alive. She smiled again. She had to give it to him. He had been instrumental throughout in bringing this crowd together. Truly, he led this fast group of friends.

There, standing next to Trudy in the upper parking lot, Mo made his own cursory review of the landscape. All was going according to plan. "Hop in", he said to Trudy. "Flip it around and back up to the curb", he directed. She gave a quick salute, jumped in, and backed the hearse to the concrete curb closest to The Hill at M Street. She was perplexed. The current circumstance posed a problem, not the least of which was a 400-pound dead woman who needed to be moved down a steep grassy hill. But Mo seemed confident.

"Wait here", he said as his eyes searched across the parking lot to the concession stand. The stand was closed, but soon to open for the weekend. Mo had had scouted a large steel chest next to the stand. The chest was painted white with large red letters on the side: "ICE". He didn't know but had trusted that by this time of year, the chest would be stocked with blocks of ice. The park rangers put ice blocks on sale for those patrons who caught fish. The rule was: "You catch, you keep it". It proved to increase the revenue stream for Park Services since they charged $5 per pound for each fish caught. Parents took the brunt when they brought their small ones to fish for the first time. The smallest fish in the pond ran three to four pounds. $20 bucks plus $10 bucks for the block to keep it cool on the drive home. It was a racket. This was the one part of the plan that he assumed could be met.

Mo ran across the lot to the ice chest. He stopped and grimaced when he saw the door handle. The horizontal handle had a key lock. Mo hadn't planned for this either. He had no keys and he couldn't pick the lock. He didn't have any real tools. He was beginning to stress when Curly approached.

"What's the matter", he asked. "I thought you said we'd get some ice for the transport".

Mo pointed to the lock on the ice box. It was not a padlock, but was set inside the horizontal handle. It was key-locked.

Just then, Marty buzzed up to settle in front of the ice chest. "My fine friends, how may I assist your noble efforts?" he inquired.

"Uh, Marty..." Mo began. "I'm not sure that you can help, and it's a long story". He was growing impatient. "The 'short' is that we need to open this ice chest and..."

"Why of course the ice chest is locked." Marty interrupted. "I can see that. Donnez-moi un moment mes beaux amis", he grinned. Mo and Curly said nothing.

Marty closed his eyes, moved his head from side to side, interlocked his fingers and placed his hands backwards to crack his knuckles. He pressed quickly and the knuckles popped. He took a deep breath and exhaled slowly. Suddenly, to Mo and to Curly, he appeared to fade in and out. His image became more and more distorted like the image on an old television that had lost its antennae. Each scratched his respective ears at the emanating sound of "white noise" that grew louder as Marty continued his ritual assault. At the height of the distortion, Marty appeared to flip through what seemed like pages in a book. He would look over an unseen page, as if searching for specific instructions. All at once, he seemed to find the right page and his eyes focused. He nodded slightly as if he'd found what he needed. He reached out with his right hand; his left still held the imaginary book,and he pulled the handle to the icebox. The image was not clear, and they couldn't be sure, but the handle clicked and the door popped open. Within seconds, the distortion ceased. Marty faded back into full view,crystal clear. The white noise stopped,and, the night came to a soft and peaceful rest. Crickets were chirping. Frogs were croaking. The sky was clear and beautiful; the moon still full and bright.

Marty saluted. "See that", he said. "No meds". He smiled, turned and fluttered back to the pond.

"Hey", Curly noted. 'Wasn't that moon higher in the sky just now? I could swear we picked up some Time". Mo Check his watch. "Damn", he tought." Daylight savings. Looks like w picked up an hour or more". Neither could know that the ice delivery service only recently paid a visit just over one hour earlier.

Mo and Curly were stunned. "What just happened?" Curly asked. Mo shrugged his response. They remembered nothing of the past few minutes. They watched Marty flitter over the pond. He was staring down into the water as if searching intently for something. He apparently found it and submerged. For a Time, he did not resurface. Curly started to worry but caught himself. "What are we worried for" he scoffed. "It's Marty. WTF anyway", he said.

Mo nodded his agreement. He turned his attention to the icebox. The heavy insulated door was closed. Mo wasn't sure what Marty did. He wasn't sure whether he'd even been up there with them in the parking lot. He thought that he had seen the icebox open, but now he wasn't sure. He reached to test it worried that it may not open, but his worry was short-lived. He reached for the handle and pulled. It clicked and came open easily. A treasure trove of large ice blocks lie within.

"C'mon" he said to Curly. He waved to Trudy across the lot and directed her to bring the hearse over. She waved back and arrived quickly. Curly pulled a hand truck that Mo had told him to bring along from the back of the hearse. As he hoisted it, he nodded his silent approval to Mo for his foresight. Mo nodded back.

The three of them loaded ice blocks into the back along each side and on top of Maggie. They didn't think that she would mind. They filled the hearse with what they thought to be enough. They left the hand truck and sat on the open back of the hearse. Trudy hopped into the driver's seat. They headed back across the lot to the grassy slope where they off loaded the blocks. This final assault would be the tricky part.

"Where's Larry?" Mo asked glancing over at the hearse.

"There", Curly pointed.

Larry was at the boat launch. He appeared to be watching Marty swim. But his gaze was fixed to a certain spot on the lake. In fact, it seemed that he was peering intently into the water, somewhere beneath the surface as if he had seen something of interest.

Mo whistled to Larry, "Hey, we need you up here. Bring Marty", he shouted down.

Larry looked up. For a moment he stood quietly as if lost in thought.

"Hey, Larry. C'mon" Mo called again. "All hands on deck. Bring Marty. We need your help".

Larry looked up and saluted. He turned to the water and called out to Marty. Marty had resurfaced. He stopped swimming and sat up on the lake. He quickly puttered over to the dock, exited the pond, and flittered on up the hill. Larry followed on his heels. They arrived in short order and Mo issued his instructions. The four of them laid out ice blocks: five-rows wide; five-columns deep, a nice ice bed for Maggie. They put another in front on the downhill side. This was for Mo. He would sit in front and hold Maggie by her feet. The plan was for him to guide, assuming that was even possible. He would use his feet and overall weight to slow the drift. He would serve to anchor. The hope was to deliver Maggie lakeside at the row boat. If they could do that without fuss, Mo would then need to come up with a way to hoist her up onto the railroad-tie pyre atop the boat. Right now... he had no idea.

They placed another block at her right hand side for Trudy to sit on; and, a third at her left hand side for Larry. The two of them would help to steer. The plan was for Marty to ride a block at the back, above Maggie's head. He would captain. Should Maggie begin to drift one direction or the other, he would signal either Trudy or Larry to set their feet. The thought was that if Trudy set her feet, Maggie would turn her direction to the right; if Larry set his, she would go left. Rudimentary, but hopefully steerage would not be needed. The slope was long; the shot to the boat was straight. The real concern was speed. The slope was very steep. The plan was crude, and...not really a plan. The attempt was untested. Mo was certain that no one had ever tried to slide a 400 lb. dead woman down this steep, grassy slope on a bed of ice blocks – all in an effort to place her onto a Viking funeral pyre built with railroad ties and laid on the back of an old wooden row boat that was barely floating next to a small dock, lakeside, in the park at M-Street. Yes. He was absolutely certain.

The crew was now stationed. Mo gave the signal and Marty nudged the ice-block platform. The platform barely budged. "Everybody, lift your feet", he shouted.

Each of them raised their legs to bring their feet off of the ground. Marty nudged again and the platform, made of loosely fit together ice-blocks, began to slide. Quickly, Maggie picked up steam. Almost immediately, Mo set his heels into the turf. He was barely able to control the speed on descent. He was dug in for the entire ride. His burden was to keep control of the 400-pound load that rode behind him. His size worked to counter balance Maggie to offer just enough control on the way down to keep the raft in one piece and to otherwise allow for steerage. But Mo's brakes were smoking and he was looking for an exit ramp. Marty deftly guided the ice raft down the slope. "Trudy", he would shout and she would set her heels into the grass. The ice raft would drift easily, almost imperceptibly to the right. As the ice raft adjusted, Marty would shout "up". Trudy would lift up her heels, and the ice raft would straighten. Similarly, if they needed to adjust left, he would shout "Larry", and he would set his heels until told to lift them up.

The ride took less than a minute to pass 100 yards. To the drivers, it seemed a lifetime. Mo pressed his legs hard into the slope. His heels bit into the grass. But before the ride could end, his legs gave out. He was spent. "Damn", he thought. "We were so very close".

Trudy lost her grip. Her ice block floundered from beneath her and deposited her on the grass short of the pond. Her block tumbled into the pond with a loud splash. Larry's block hit a bare spot in the grass. The dirt stopped him abruptly and he sailed head first. He somersaulted safely away to land downslope, feet first and standing. He was quite proud of his landing. He had never before done much athletically. This was a first. He had to smile.

The ice blocks had served the purpose well. As planned, the ice-raft would deliver Maggie to the funeral pyre. Oh, it was a good plan. Too bad, no one thought about how to slow her down. With her weight and at her current speed, she would crash with the ice blocks into the boat, shatter the pyre, and sink with a boatload of firewood to the bottom of the pond. Damn", he thought again. "Damn, damn, damn". He clambered away to his right, as quickly as his 300 pounds would let him, to keep from being crushed between the boat and Maggie's ice raft.

Mo was not prepared for a disaster of this proportion. All he could do was close his eyes. He could not watch. But Mo had forgotten about Marty. He'd forgotten that Marty was in charge. It was easy to do. Marty was eccentric for sure, often, "away" as it were, always, on the edge of things. Mo should have learned by now that Marty was capable of just about anything. From his vantage point at the back of the ice-raft, Marty had correctly assessed Maggie's speed. He accurately gauged both her take- off and her landing. More importantly, he had accurately identified the moment when their clumsy ice-raft would first arrive at the water's edge and the element of Time that would be required to deliver Maggie to her place of rest. In the seconds before the ice-raft reached the pond, Marty focused and "white noise" echoed. The light surrounding Maggie and the ice□raft distorted. He reached out his right hand and appeared again to flip through the pages of a large book that he nestled against him with his left hand. As he did, Time slowed, stopped briefly, and then moved fitfully backwards as if being slowly adjusted.

The boat, the dock, the pond, and the surrounding park – all blurred and electronic snow clouded the scene. Static electricity crackled and popped. Marty looked to find the odd railroad tie that a very short Time ago, lay on the dock, a few feet from the chopping stump.

He seemed to want to recheck a reference, a few pages back, in the invisible book that he held. The crew watched closely as blurred visions of both Mo and Curly seemed to unload ties from off of the boat; ties that they had laboriously loaded onto the boat seemingly moments prior, until in swiftly moving, fuzzy and broken views, the ties were offloaded and strewn across the grass in front of the launch.

Marty grimaced. His neck tightened. He stretched out, cricked his neck, and rolled his head back and forth across his shoulders. He set himself and tried again. He riffled pages, back and forth, as if seeking to find focus. No one could figure, but what he was doing was trying to fiddle with Time. Now slowly, page by page, he flipped the pages forward. In broken images that stopped and cleared only to reset to a new view a few seconds more current, Mo and Curly moved forward with Time. In these broken images, they slowly loaded the ties, frame-by-frame, back onto the boat until the pyre was fit together and recognizable; until only one odd tie lay on top of the deck a few feet away from the stump and axe. Here, Marty paused. He breathed out a sigh and flipped one more page. He looked back to see now that the railroad time, once on the deck and close to the stump, was now lying on the grass immediately in front of the boat launch and in the direct path of the Mo's ice raft, soon to plummet down the remainder of the hill and directly into the left-over railroad tie. Here, Marty closed the book and opened his eyes.

From their respective locations, now slightly readjusted, they watched as Maggie's ice-raft, moving rapidly with Maggie on it and crashed into the odd tie left abandoned there on the grass immediately in front of the boat. The ice-raft exploded into separate blocks and pieces of ice that flew in all directions, and Maggie launched. Upward and outward, she sailed. A slight breeze rippled, caught her bathrobe, and caused her to turn over in mid-air. She rotated easily on the wind. Those watching would swear that she smiled. The wind gusted and her silk pajamas billowed. She parachuted down onto the small mattress left conveniently atop the pyre. She landed lightly, softly with hardly a ripple on the water. The billows in her pajamas deflated, and her pajamas and robe settled nicely to surround her in luxury. She was–at last, at rest.

Mo stood up and brushed himself off. His knees ached. He kicked his feet on the ground to bring back some feeling. He looked to see Maggie atop the pyre, smiling sweetly. He scratched his head. He could not recall anything since the ice-raft had crashed to send them all sprawling. He must have been knocked out for a short time. Larry and Trudy joined him. They too were baffled. They all looked at each other and wondered what had just happened. All they could see was Maggie lying peacefully atop the pyre.

"C'mon, my friends", Marty called to them from dockside, "Maggie awaits us". He waved them over. The group joined him at the dock. He bowed his head. The others followed suit, and Marty whispered a sweet prayer. Trudy began to tear up. Mo held her close to console her. Marty finished and nodded to Curly. Curly put a match to the paper and kindling they had left beneath the firewood in the bottom of the boat. The firewood soon caught and fire spread swiftly to the pyre. The old, thick, and heavy ties began to burn.

The ascending fire was hot. Its orange glow lit up the night sky. The full moon had set leaving the star-filled night dark and peaceful, even reverent. Maggie ascended in sparks of glory with the burgeoning flames until she reached to the stars where she departed with the rising cinders that floated and twisted upward until they disappeared. They all stood in silence and watched her go. Soon thereafter, morning sun broke the horizon to the east. The crickets began again to fiddle, the frogs to croak. Newly stocked trout jumped, here and there, at gnats just above the surface of the pond or for no better reason than to exercise. The pyre soon burnt low. It was very hot. Ashes and cinders filled the boat. The old wooden rowboat burnt to water level until all that remained was the charred keel filled with ashes that floated forlornly on the water. Later in the day, once the coals had cooled, Trudy would return to scatter ashes across the pond in Maggie's honor and to bid farewell to her friend. She would sink the burnt keel to hide the remnants of their worthy collaboration. But now they needed to hurry. Eldon was waiting.

Trudy put the pedal to the metal on the near ancient Pontiac hearse, so much so that the chrome railings around the top deck rattled and shook, and the large chrome capital "R" in "Heavenly Rest" fell off and hit the pavement as Trudy bounced the hearse over a speed bump on the way out of the parking lot. Mo and his crew rode in the back and held on for dear life - all except for Marty. True to form, Marty was in no real hurry. He bid them adieu and excused himself to return to swim. They had watched him take a deep breath and dive. They did not see him resurface. They worried, but Trudy couldn't wait. Besides, Marty could take care of himself. She was more concerned about Eldon, or rather, what Eldon might do. They all needed to get back to the home before Eldon's shift was over, and they were found out. She didn't know if he would wait for his hearse before calling Ms. Bichette. If he called her, there could be some 'splainin' to do. But as it stood, she needn't have worried.

The gold painted hearse with its gaudy chrome ornamentation was easily recognizable and could be seen for miles. Not long after Ms. Bichette and the Death Squad left Eldon Jones in the basement morgue, she had spotted the hearse with its large and shiny chrome medallions, parked in the lot at the top of the grass hill in the park at M Street. She arrived with the Death Squad in time to see Curly light the torch. Upon witnessing the funeral pyre climb into the moonlit night, she chose to dismiss The Death Squad. They wouldn't be needed. The scene was somber and dramatic. Ms. Bichette was touched by the love and dedication of Maggie's friends. She felt the need to be alone. She watched as the flames grew to eventually engulf dear Maggie and had stayed on to see the fire ebb and eventually die. She sat there on the hood of the hearse and watched ,in reverence, Maggie's send off. It was sweet, these folks –impressive, and, for a long moment, she had let the peace and the freedom associated with Maggie's release wash over her. For the first time in a very long time, she had snuffled, pinched at her nose, and wiped her eyes. When Maggie's admirers came back up the hill, she hid in a small copse of trees next to the lot near the hearse. Oh, yes, she thought as she waited for them to leave, there were many number of violations, even a host of illegalities associated with Maggie's Viking Funeral, but Ms. Bichette was nothing if not a pragmatist. Maggie had no one to care for her. No family ever came to visit. She had been committed to Golden Hills with sufficient retainer to eventually take her home to her grave, as it were. But the retainer was now depleted. Golden Hills was required, by law, to keep her until she passed, but they had no obligation to pay for her burial. Until her friends had intervened with the Viking Funeral, Maggie had been destined for a pauper's grave. As it was now, the earth; the wind, and the fire had taken her. It was as if Maggie knew that she had overstayed her welcome.

Her final days at Golden Hills had been lonely. She had no family. No one had ever called upon her or had come to visit. Old age had taken its toll on her relationships with Trudy and the others. Over almost this entire past year, she slept through the day, sitting in her chair, and rarely taking meals. In the early spring and fall, Mo would place her near the window in the front lobby so the sun could warm her. In the colder months, he lit the gas log on the stone fireplace and parked her close. Sometimes, he would turn on the TV to watch some football. Periodically, throughout the day, he would check on her. He would help to ensure that she stayed... well, tidy. At night, the staff would trundle her back to her room. Sometimes they could get her into bed; sometimes not. She was well cared for, considering. Four hundred pounds was a challenge to the best of caregivers. As it stood now, Ms. Bichette could simply close the book on this resident. No fuss; no muss. She would mark her as "deceased" in her book; dictate direction to the staff to clean out her room; and, publish a vacancy notice. Several young families needed help with an aging parent. Golden Hills and Ms. Lauren Bichette would serve to meet that need.

But at present, Ms. Bichette had another issue that required her attention: Marty – priority number 1. She had seen him at the Viking funeral which surprised her considerably. She thought that he had "drowned" in Physical Therapy. Sheesh, she thought. She had helped to pull him from the hot tub. She had witnessed The Death Squad pound his chest and administer mouth-to-mouth. She had personally assured herself that he was indeed...well, dead. As difficult as that was to believe, she had filled out the paperwork and called upon The Death Squad to deliver him to Drawer 13 in the basement morgue. Still, he had been at Golden Hills long enough now that nothing he did ever really surprised her.

She wondered, if perhaps it was resurrection, maybe? She'd read about it, but certainly had never seen it before. It was hard to believe. But here he was, sitting at lakeside: red speedo, goggles, fins and all. She had no doubt. He had been here and paying his respects with the others at Maggie's funeral.

So, where was he now? She thought on this a bit and realized that she did not see him exit in the hearse with Trudy. She puzzled as she walked down the grassy hill to stand lakeside. A slight breeze stirred to gently push the ash-filled keel into the dock with a soft bump, bump. She peered out over the still waters. There, far across lake, just where the lake jogged back to the east to disappear around the hillside and nearest to the southern shore, she saw what appeared to be a large trout break the surface and leap for a small fly. She rubbed her eyes to look again. But the fish was gone as the ripples widened. She could have sworn that the fish was wearing red, as in goggles and a speedo, maybe. She watched a moment longer as the waters stilled. She rubbed her eyes once more, but saw nothing. Marty could wait, she thought. One thing she knew for sure, he'd be back. The walk back to Golden Hills proved restful and invigorating.

Heaven knew that she needed it.

*****No Time by the Guess Who*****

♪♪ (No time left for you) On my way to better things; (No time left for you) I found myself some wings; (No time left for you) Distant roads are callin' me; (No time left for you)

No time for a summer friend; No time for the love you send; Seasons change and so did I;

You need not wonder why; You need not wonder why; There's no time left for you; No time left for you;

(No time) No time, no time, no time, no time
No no no time, no no time, no time, no time

I got, got, got, got no time
I got, got, got, got no time for you, woman
I got no time for you, woman
I got no time for your stupid games anymore
No, no I got no time for you, woman, no
I got no time for hangin' around
For gettin' stepped on;
For gettin' pushed around, woman
I got no time for hangin' around them kind of things

(No time left for you) I found myself some wings; (No time left for you) Distant roads are callin' me. (No time left for you) Time, time, time, time, time

No time for a gentle rain; No time for my watch and chain; No time for revolving doors; No time for the killin' floor; No time for the killin' floor; There's no time left for you; No time left for you. (No time left for you) On my way to better things; (No time left for you)

I found myself some wings ♪♪

****

CHAPTER XXXVI

Marty knew that it was Time; Time to learn the secret of 1967; Time to learn a secret that he had feared all of his life; Time to discover the secret that had kept him bound, stultified his mind and limited his exploration of the world in which he lived. Anxiety overwhelmed, but he had to go. He must. It was Time.

Maggie's send-off had been perfect. How better than to go out in the manner and style that you had chosen, the fashion that suited you? Marty couldn't say where she had gone. That was contemplation that he should make some other Time. For now, he needed to visit The Library.

From his earlier visit, he knew that the dive was a deep one. He fixed his goggles over his eyes, adjusted his speedo, and tightened his flippers. He inhaled slowly and blew it out once to clear. He inhaled again deeply and dove. He kicked and paddled for all he was worth. After a Time, his mind caught sight of a light way down and away. He kicked harder and paddled furiously. There, still far away and deeper down, he thought that he saw an exquisite light tinged with the color red which he knew must come from the beautiful Cherrywood shelves taken from the sparkling reflection in the elegant wall sized mirrors that graced all four sides of that peaceful and most reverent "sanctum santorum" that Marty had once discovered.

This dive seemed longer than he had previously taken. His lungs were set to burst. He swam up to what he had supposed to be the front entry. As before, he stepped through from water into light and cool dry air.

Again, with that first step, the sign lit up; "Please, remove your footwear. Our Library is a clean Library. Thank you". Marty pulled the flippers from his feet, removed his goggles, and placed them together in the small box provided. Once again, the box and sign disappeared. As before, he took another step to the second sign: "Take the robe made available for your comfort. Place the socks on your feet to protect The Library floor". He found the white, silken robe on the elaborately cushioned bench together with the fluffy white cotton socks, marked at the bottom for safety to help prevent slipping on the highly polished marble flooring tiles. He put on the robe. He sat on the bench and put on his socks. These instilled in Marty a tremendous sense of peace and contentment. As with the earlier sign and shoe box, the bench also disappeared.

Marty did not waste a moment. He did not explore, but went directly to the set of two Cherrywood bookshelves on the shiny crème colored, marble tile floor inside The Library. The beautiful bookshelves carried a complete set of tightly bound books, large like encyclopedias together with periodicals, magazines, newspapers – an entire history of Time in various and differing segments as may be requested. He noted again the signs posted at the top, outside of each shelf at the entrance to the aisle way the granted access. The sign on the shelf to the left read: Truth/Light – Access Restricted. The sign on the shelf to the right read: Observation Only.

His last visit had intrigued, but was somewhat misguided. Performances by both Heston and Bales were interesting and noteworthy. But his visit to Egypt was a bit of a waste. Granted, the Red Sea was beautiful; the turquoise waters, delightful but so much sand. If you have seen red sand once, you've seen it all. He'd have much preferred to visit the Great Pyramids and encounter the Pharoahs. He knew better this Time. He closed his eyes to focus so as to remember explicitly why he was here. He remembered that as he now strode these aisles between the bookshelves and among the vast array of knowledge, instruction, legislation, maps, movies, photographs, periodicals, letters, and personal notes and diaries, that he was walking in No Time. He also remembered that the endless array of knowledge and instruction that lined these beautiful and deeply rich Cherrywood shelves constituted the makings of Time itself, not just a historical review but the exact moments of Time in terms of years, months, days, hours, minutes, seconds and even milliseconds. Think of it. Should he be a better student while here in The Library, should he become better versed in the research and study of Time, should he stay worthy to remain here in this No Time, better known as The Library, then all light and truth might be his to possess and to share so that he might rally the seven blind men on the elephant to learn, at last, the creature's true nature: to become light and to learn, at last, the fullness of all truth.

Marty looked back at the shelves and wiped the Cherrywood gently, lovingly with the tips of his fingers. Surprisingly, he remembered how to bring up a reference. He had yet to experiment with the shelf on the left. But he was sure that he was after "Truth/ Light". He wondered what "Access Restricted" was about, but he figured that he would find out soon enough. He knew from his earlier experience that he needed to be a bit more specific with his entry and so, he thought: 1967 together with a date and Time: October 2. He paused. He had no idea which hour, minute, or second that he should request. He decided to let it ride and with that last thought, a complete schedule of books and other source material appeared on the shelf in front of him – all from the specific date and Time he had thought about. A single large encyclopedia sat immediately in front of him; one book with the reference marked on the spine: 1967.1002.00:25:19, 20, 21, 22...the countdown had started and continued. From what he could see, he figured that he had been under the Time clock for 25 minutes and moving to 26. He pulled the encyclopedia from the shelf and started to turn the pages slowly, one by one. A few pages in and he flipped the book to see the spine. The spine now read: 1967.1002.03:13:09, 10, 11, 12... Marty was getting the hang of this, but he still had yet to jump. He figured he might need a bit of Time to himself, to study some of his surroundings, to figure things out while there. In fact, he figured he might need maybe a full day.

He replaced the encyclopedia for 1002 and watched as it vanished back into the bookshelf. His mind went to 1967.1001.13:00:00 to earmark that page. Immediately, the bookshelf delivered all resource materials. This Time, however, the materials were marked for October 1, 1967. And, as expected, the materials included a large, tightly bound, hard cover encyclopedia with a spine that read: 1967.1001.13:00:00, 01, 02, 03, 04...and counting.

He decided to waste no more Time. He pulled the encyclopedia from the shelf and opened it. He closed his eyes to focus on the Time he had set for himself and...nothing. He tried again to focus. He tightly closed his eyes and concentrated. The sign appeared. The wording flashed red: "For Self-Help, Access Restricted to the Speed of Light". Somehow, it seemed that the bookshelf knew that his mission today was personal, that he was intent on changing his own Time in the past for his own purposes. True. He had been allowed to "Observe Only" as the sign read on the companion bookshelf when he had travelled to the Red Sea to visit with Moses. But as he recalled now, he had made no attempt then to change or alter Time when he was there. He had been tempted to bring back Moses' staff that he had found at the bottom of the Red Sea, but instead had replaced it. Who knew what might have happened had he attempted to bring it back with him.

He puzzled somewhat over his minor flirtations with changing Time when he unlocked the ice-box in the parking lot at the park on M-street, and he had pushed it a tad further when he rearranged the rail road ties and toyed with putting Maggie to bed peacefully. But the more he thought about it, the more he concluded that neither of these efforts should be construed as "Self-Help". In essence, he figured that he didn't need the speed of light to access Time through No Time, that is when he had come to help others. But as the sign said for "Self-Help" well...it appeared that the speed of light was a prerequisite.

From what Marty could see, he'd needed to register the speed of light. All this Time, he had assumed that the speed of light somehow constituted a "fullness" of Truth, and as he only now recognized, he wasn't there yet. He'd need to chance it. He would need to change venue. He surfaced to breath then he dove again to swim eastward to Parley's Canyon. It was Time to change the past. It was Time for Marty to repent.

CHAPTER XXXVII

Marty was missing! The news had gone out. The entire old folks' home was abuzz. The prevailing thought was: how did he do it? By now, Maggie's funeral was front page. No one had seen him since then. Thanks to Curly, rumor of his rather magical help in opening the ice box had spread. But as of yet, he hadn't figured how best to interpret just how it was that Maggie came to rest on top of the funeral pyre. Curly didn't like ballet, but ballet best described her graceful movements from the ice blocks to the top of the pyre where she was so gently deposited – all 400 pounds of her. In the mind of most, these rumors had transformed Marty from mere mortal and had cemented his reputation as a god on earth.

Even Ms. Bichette, an avowed pragmatist who usually confirmed that he was in bed, could not account for him. She, too, had witnessed Maggie's rather unusual delivery from the ice blocks to the pyre, although no one knew that she had been there. She, too, was mystified by Marty's most recent antics. She was hesitant to call the authorities. His disappearance would not make her look good. She determined to first search the grounds and cover every inch of Golden Hills. She would call out The Death Squad to search the place top to bottom. She hated to think that they might find him dead in the Physical Therapy tub -yet, a second Time - especially if this Time was for real. She had to admit, Marty was...well, he was precious. She hated to admit it, but she liked him.

She was scheduled, once more, to meet with his wife and daughter tomorrow afternoon. If he didn't turn up by lunchtime, she would call the local authorities and report him missing. She would report her own efforts to find him prior to the call. She could justify 24 hours in the name of efficiency. But this might put a blotch on her otherwise spotless record. Damn that man! She muttered to herself.

Trudy was seated in the cafeteria. Curly had sought to convene another emergency meeting in the front restroom. He was anxious and Trudy knew that it was an excuse to light one up. Larry suggested reconvening in Marty's room, under his bed. Mo was reticent. He had a tough time crawling underneath. Trudy had vetoed both suggestions.

"How 'bout the cafeteria and breakfast?" she asked as she hastily scooted back her chair and stood to leave. "Larry...peach yogurt; Mo....bacon; Curly...?" she hesitated. "You do whatever", she waved him off. Larry and Mo nodded their agreement. Curly went with the consensus.

They convened and she began, "Look, he had often spoken of Parley's Canyon and a small stream that runs through a long storm sewer beneath the conjunction of the various freeways that converge there in the mouth of that canyon". She spoke to herself mostly, wondering if Marty was truly gone, trying to convince herself that she could find him.

The scraping of tables across floor tiles and the sudden movement of metal chairs interrupted, and she was momentarily distracted. She heard voices and looked to see Ms. Bichette and The Death Squad effectively "sweeping" the cafeteria, opening the cupboards, unlocking the freezer box, looking under tables and chairs. They were searching - or better still - they were hunting. Trudy knew for what or rather, for whom. The three stooges, too, were distracted momentarily by the racket and had looked to the front of the cafeteria. Trudy snapped her fingers in the faces of her audience and brought them all to attention.

"Gentlemen, listen!" she snapped her fingers loudly, several times, in their faces (a. following faces). "We don't have much time. You three wait here for ten minutes then meet me in the basement morgue. Make sure that you are not followed, and no matter what...don't let them (she pointed to The Death Squad) leave here (she waved her hand across the cafeteria). Got it?" She looked at each of them for a nod. They each complied.

Curly moved to the entrance with his mop and bucket. He placed a few cones directly in front: "Caution. Slippery When Wet". He would stand guard. Mo got up from the table and headed back for more bacon. Larry began to inquire, but Mo cut him off, "yeah, yeah, I'll grab some yogurt – peach, since it is all that we have here anymore", he muttered to himself.

"Ten minutes!" she hollered over her shoulder as she hit the exit and headed up Hallway B. She knew where to find Parley's Canyon. She was sure that Marty would be there. But first, she needed to hitch a ride: Eldon. She needed his hearse. But would he give it up? She hustled on up Hallway B to the front desk. She had to make a call. Eldon wouldn't show without an order.

A new attendant was on duty. He was standing in the lobby at the glass front doors peering out and daydreaming. She stopped near the door to the stairway to the temporary morgue in the Hallway B. From there, she tiptoed ever so quietly up to the front office. She reached the front office and crouched to stay low behind the counter just inside the doorway. Slowly, she reached inside the office for the desk drawer and quietly pulled it open. An old-fashioned dial telephone was inside. She pulled it from the drawer along with a phone book. She found the number for the Heavenly Rest Mortuary and quickly dialed. Eldon answered. She announced that she was with the Golden Hills Rest Home, that they had a deceased, and needed a pick-up. She gave him a fictitious name with otherwise irrelevant information.

"Ten minutes", he said. "I'm leaving now".

She quietly hung up the phone, placed it back into the drawer, and slowly slid it closed. She stayed crouched in the doorway. She looked back to see the three stooges coming up Hallway B. Mo, Larry and Curly were creeping up, doorway by doorway in the surrounding rooms and trying not to be noticed. Larry spotted her there in the office. She signaled for them to hit the stairway and was just about to leave her roost when the stooges froze. Instinctively, she froze too. Larry pointed to the front entry. The attendant was through daydreaming. He was moving directly toward her position. Trudy stepped back inside and closed the door. This was a bad choice. What would she say if he caught her here? She supposed she could act demented. Sounded good for a patron here at the old folks' home.

As the attendant moved to the office, he was momentarily preoccupied. He bent to fiddle with his trousers and held himself at the zipper. Trudy bolted for the men's room. Mistake! The attendant headed there directly. His zipper was stuck and he had to pee. Trudy hit the men's room only steps ahead of the attendant. He didn't notice that the door had not yet fully closed when he reached to press it open. He was pressed for Time.

Once inside, Trudy darted to her right to hide in the first stall. The stall reeked of marijuana smoke. From here she could push open the door ever so slight to catch a peek.

The attendant whistled as he relieved himself at the urinal: ♪♪ Smoke on the water...a fire in the sky ♪♪.

Trudy knew it. Catchy, she remembered. She almost joined in. Just outside, she heard Ms. Bichette and The Death Squad pass together, en force, toward the front office. The attendant finished zipping. He'd be at the sink soon. He began to futz with something in his pants pocket. He pulled out a small bag and loosened the draw string that sealed it. From his shirt pocket, he pulled some tobacco papers. Hmmm, she thought. He and Curly could partner in a plantation. She waited for him to seal his doobie. She knew that the jig was up. He'd open the stall door and catch her...in the men's room no less. As it turned out, she was saved by his nonchalance. Unlike Curly, the attendant's favorite stall was the middle stall whereas Curly preferred the end stall. Trudy was safe. When she heard the bolt click over to ensure the attendant some privacy, she bolted out of the men's room and across the Hallway B to the stairway. Mo had already stepped in and was headed down. Larry was right behind him. Curly was also inside and holding the door for her. Trudy stepped inside and the door closed behind her, only seconds before Ms. Bichette, with her accompanying Death Squad, exited the front office and headed down Hallway B calling out for the attendant. The men's room doorway opened just as the stairway doorway closed.

The attendant stood there, choking back smoke, and holding a joint in one hand behind his back, "I'm here ma'am... I mean Ms. Bichette. Wassup?" He burped a small cloud of smoke and fought to hold back the remainder in his lungs.

She asked if he'd seen anybody. He told her that he hadn't seen anybody here at the front in over an hour,and certainly nobody in the last ten minutes. She frowned. She turned and signaled her minions to work the right side of the hallway back toward the cafeteria. She instructed them to check every room, under every bed, in every closet, and to be thorough.

"Swallow that damn thing!" she growled at the attendant. She fixed him with a snarl as he quickly gulped down the newly lit joint with a hard grimace.

"Go, go!" she commanded The Death Squad as she waved them off. They swept down the right side of Hallway B. She swept down the left side. As they headed back toward the cafeteria, Trudy and her crew landed in the basement morgue where they waited for Eldon to arrive. They heard him pull the hearse into the garage. A few minutes later, he opened the door and came inside only to see four smiling faces, looking rather uncomfortable as if they had to pee.

"Hey", he said. "I hope you didn't come to tell me that the little skinny god himself is back down here in Drawer 13. That would be way too cruel."

Trudy stepped up. She told him that she had placed the call to bring him here. No, Marty wasn't here for pick up, but she did need his help. Marty was gone. She thought that she knew where he was headed. She....they, needed the hearse. She thought they would find him at the painted rock in the mouth of Parley's Canyon.

"The painted rock!" Eldon exclaimed. "What in hell would he be doing there? How would he get there? Fly?"

"Weellll..." Curly started to respond. Mo put a large hand over his mouth.

"Look", Mo said. "Can you help us or not?" Mo was getting impatient with the delay.

Eldon thought for a moment. He'd come here to transport one body out of here for which, he now learned, he would not get paid. "What's in it for me", he asked.

Mo had had enough. Time was a-wastin'. He stepped forward – all 6'3" and 300 pounds of him. "The pleasure of our company", he said as he fixed Eldon with a gaze that could freeze fire.

Eldon thought again. "Uh yeah, sure", he said with some trepidation. "No problem. I can use a worthless tour around town" he added sarcastically. He looked at Trudy and urged, "But I am driving".

She frowned. "Just open the garage door and take the front passenger seat." Her stare could melt ice.

He shrugged as he opened the door from the morgue to the garage. "All yours", he said in surrender. She bowed and exited. The others followed. They all piled into the hearse. Trudy took the driver's seat; Eldon, the front passenger seat; Curly and Larry found room at either side of Maggie; and Mo was again forced to ride with the back open, his foot on the bumper. Trudy found I-80 east. She liked the feel of this ride. She was getting used to it.

CHAPTER XXXVIII

In the mouth of Parley's Canyon, accessible from I-80 eastbound and a good 200 feet below the surface of the various freeways that converged there, sits a large painted rock. The rock has been decorated over and over through the years by local high school and college kids, who have some rock climbing skills, with painted messages and designs- some intended to celebrate, some to mourn, and some to honor. The only consistent thing about these messages is how frequently they are painted over and changed.

Few if anyone travelled to the base of the painted rock. Few knew of this location nor of the small stream that meandered down from the Canyon to the mouth of the large storm sewer line that ran beneath this freeway junction. The large storm sewer pipe that ran beneath the freeways was made of concrete and corrugated iron, approximately six feet in circumference, and placed to accommodate the occasional flash flooding caused by summer thundershowers.

Following the summer of 1971, the local authorities had closed access to this playground made here by the local high school kids. The authorities built a fence and padlocked the gate, and for the first several months following that summer, the local sheriff patrolled to ensure that the kids learned to stay away. But the summer of 1971 was one hellacious summer for Marty and a few of his friends.

Mostly, the storm sewer line carried only a small stream that ran year-round at maybe three inches deep and two to four feet wide. The line ran a good 1000 feet from east to west at about a 30-degree angle down through the storm sewer from one side of the freeway junction to the other. The playground included, at the mouth on the upper end, two half sheets of ¾" plywood affixed by wire at one corner on either side of the mouth opening.

Someone had placed these to serve as flood gates at the upper end of the storm drain to stop the flow of stream water before it entered the line. Typically, it would take about 20 minutes to block a pool of water maybe four feet high behind the plywood dam. Two local boys controlled these flood gates and would release the dammed-up waters on cue. During that summer, on any given day, there would be upwards of a dozen kids or more at that playground. At the inside of the storm drain, on the other side of the plywood, kids would line up their large rubber inner tubes to wait for the dam to open to form a train of sorts. The tubes carried one, sometimes two per tube. The kids would wait on their tubes for the waters to gather on the backside of the plywood dam. Here they laughed, cajoled, and otherwise visited. One of the gate guardians kept a transistor radio with him, but the signal was weak this far below the freeways. No matter. The kids didn't need this distraction.

At the lower end, the waters exited the end of the line approximately ten feet above the surface of a small pond. Local kids created the pond to capture the fast-flying train of inner tubes and riders pressed by the rush of the newly freed mountain waters that spewed from the bottom end of the large concrete and corrugated iron pipe ten feet up. They built the pond by stacking large boulders, three rows high into a semi-circle at maybe 30 feet out from and surrounding the storm sewer's exit. The boulder dam brought the depth of the pond to about five feet nearest the storm sewer's exit where the topography was lower. Further out, the depth lessened to only two or three feet. Overall, there was plenty of water in the pond to slow and capture the fast-flying inner tube train of passengers. At the end of the ride, kids and tubes would spew from the end of the storm drain. They would fly out over the pond. The first to splash down quickly scrambled to get out of the way of those that followed. The pond's waters sloshed back and forth testing the strength of the boulder dam which sometimes required repairs following each 20-minute surge.

Marty surfaced in this pond. The dam was constructed with stone and cement. A beautiful lawn surrounded the wall. A picnic table decorated the greens. A large aluminum building with a sign that read 'Road Maintenance' sat next to the lawn. Sidewalks and an asphalt parking lot with nicely painted stalls and a handicap parking space decorated the front. Large dump trucks, snow plows, and various tractors and road equipment sat in the back, locked behind a large chain link fence.

"This was new.", Marty observed. But he was in a hurry. He saw the lower mouth of the storm drain that under rode the freeways high above. He climbed into the pipe and hiked to the top where he squatted at the upper end of the line.

Two sections of plywood were hung at either side of the circular opening by bailing wire attached at one corner. A large rubber inner tube lay nearby begging to be ridden. The stream was alive and running maybe two to three feet wide and through the corrugated line at two to three inches. Yes, Marty knew this place. He remembered it well. He sensed somehow that he had "remembered" himself here; that his ability to recall this place and Time had brought him here; and here was the summer of 1971 – or, at least, it would be soon enough. And, from there – assuming he could reach the speed of light – onto 1967.

He pondered a moment more. What to do now? He was here wasn't he? Yes. He had been here in the summer of 1971. He remembered that summer with profound affection. He was close. Why not chance it? Kids were here with him enjoying the last summer for this awesome homespun event. The guardians were at the gates. Water was rising behind the plywood. He grabbed the lone inner tube. The water was deep enough to keep the gates from jostling when he stepped over. No one seemed to mind. He could hear the static from a transistor radio. He put his tube in line. No one objected; no one called him out. It seemed that this ride was made for him. The other kids in the train were laughing and visiting there on the inside and at the top of the storm line. No one seemed to notice him.

He wondered about speed. He had contemplated swimming through the wave to the other end, but he might catch a fin on the corrugate piping. He could swim fast, but the "speed of light"? He was not so sure. Besides, it could make for a bumpy ride. But Marty somehow felt that in this "here and now", he should ride this train. Marty had learned that "truth" was the same as "light",and that as he acquired "truth" – as he accepted it - he would absorb its "light" until ultimately – if he could absorb a fullness of light and truth- he would become light. He would become a source of all light; or more likely, he would join with others to become the source of all light, of all truth. In this way, should he obtain a fullness of all truth to become the source of all light – indeed, should he become light itself, he could then attain unto the speed of light. There would be no need to jump on a train capable of reaching the speed of light; no need to fool with a light clock; no need to experiment outwardly in theory; no need to ride the wave down the storm drain. He could simply accelerate naturally to enter No Time.

Still, like Einstein, he felt it necessary to hop onto the less than theoretical train that could, itself, reach the speed of light; a train that carried a light clock to measure Time; and a light clock that would slow as the train itself moved faster to toward the speed of light when, at that point, the light beam that marked off Time inside the train ran at the same speed as, and parallel to, the train itself. No more ticks. No more tocks. So, as the theory goes, when Time is no longer measured, Time would be no more.

Of course, it would take Time to absorb truth. After all, he could only learn "bit by bit; line upon line" as they say. His search for a fullness of light might never end. But the more truth that he discovered, the more truth that he accepted, the closer he could approach the speed of light.

This could work, assuming of course, that the Time clock would indeed slowdown when the speed increased as Einstein had theorized. Still, Marty was impatient; and anyway, he worried. He felt that any attempt to build a train so as to reach the speed of light was tantamount to building a Tower of Babel to reach heaven. It would be an affront to the powers that be, a puny human effort to confront a godly enterprise. After all, a fullness of truth was immortal wasn't it? It was eternal, n'est pas? A fullness of truth was...well, it was beyond human understanding. It was more of a...a heavenly pursuit. But why worry about it now?

The music on the radio blared but was otherwise inaudible, sounded a bit like...The Guess Who, maybe?

The scraping of plywood on concrete awakened him to the moment. The gate guardians had decided to release the backstopped waters. The tube train was about to roll. Marty's ride against Time was launched. He held onto the inner tube with all of his strength. He locked his feet onto the tube in front of him. The folks behind him locked their feet onto his tube. A loose tube could derail the tube train. Each weld or bolt, loose joint or corrugation in the line could strip the clothes off of any passenger who came loose from the tube train. As the gates blew open, a huge wave of water immediately scrolled beneath each tube and passenger, one by one, and lifted them almost to the top of the corrugated line. The rising tide from the cold mountain stream roared down the line fast and foreboding as if the tube train was reaching into Time, itself.

But Marty's Swiss cheese memory made it difficult for him to discern it, let alone to reconstruct it ,and he was stymied by this apparent ability to actually manipulate it. To think that he could move Time back and forth, up and down was...well absurd to say the least. Still, credible experience was that he had done it. According to his No Time theory, absent a fullness of truth, he should not have been able to attain the speed of light and could not, therefore, enter into No Time. But if he could not enter, how had he played with Time? Was a partial fullness of truth sufficient to bend or to even slow it down? This had to be a working theory, otherwise how had he unlocked the icebox? How had he laid Maggie gently to rest? How had he manipulated Ms. Bichette into keeping him here?

Somehow, he had within himself enough understanding of the truth as light itself, that he had been able to slow Time enough to perform those....well those "miracles". How else should he characterize them? He pondered for a moment. One thing he knew: the thought that had driven him now for so long was that the certainty he craved would be found in 1967. That much was clear... or, at least, he thought that it was. How or why he would get there was still unknown, but he knew that he was now closer than ever; and to have a chance, he must get there. He must get back to 1967.

*****

Trudy drove the newly paved maintenance road below the freeway interchange there in the mouth of Parley's Canyon. She stopped at a newly installed maintenance gate with a sign posted that read: Private Property - Keep Out. Mo stepped out of the hearse and walked to the gate. He reached with his bare hands and broke the chain that secured the gate. Larry and Curly exited the hearse to help. They grinned at the effort. Mo shrugged, "I didn't think I had it in me". Larry lifted his eyebrows as if to say, "Oh, brother".

Eldon reached over from the passenger seat and honked for them to get in. They headed on up the newly paved road towards a parking area that had been carved out years ago by the kids. This too was newly paved. White lines were painted to designate parking spaces. A spot for the handicapped was reserved closest to the metal work building with double glass front doors and an office. Eldon pulled some headphones from the glove box together with and old portable cassette player. He plugged the phones into the player, pulled one of various cassette tapes from the glove box, placed it into the player, and popped it closed. He adjusted the volume, sat back, and enjoyed the ride.

A few minutes later, they arrived to find a permanent pond stocked with fish. Trudy wasn't quite sure what she had expected to find. Her own memories of this place were fondly colored by reminiscence of one summer afternoon with Marty. The boulders that had been placed to dam the small stream were gone. Instead, the water that trickled from the storm drain ten feet up, fell into a permanent pond. The trickle was minimal, at best. The pond pooled behind a permanent concrete wall, approximately four feet high and nicely tiled along the outside. The semi-circular wall ran approximately 50 yards from the parking area to the edge of the large, aluminum maintenance building. Parked out back were maintenance vehicles, a backhoe, an asphalt paver, a variety of dump trucks with snow plows and other salting equipment for the winter months. Two wooden picnic tables with benches had been placed upon a strip of lawn that surrounded the low concrete wall. This place was a roadway maintenance yard with a couple of tables reserved for the crew at lunch. But the crew appeared to be "out to lunch". A sign on the door of the aluminum shack read: "Closed for County Seminar".

Mo figured that they were darn lucky to be here, and even luckier not to have been arrested for trespassing onto county property. Curly was not so sure. He knew that Marty had brought them here. He felt it in his bones.

He must have known that the place would be vacant, and that the crew would be away. He was certain that Marty came here for some specific reason. Still, whatever was the reason, it had him stumped. This place was far below the freeway interchange that ran above into the mouth of the canyon. He had driven the freeways many times. But he never knew this place existed. He smiled at the puzzle presented. He was up for the challenge. He would solve it. He looked over at Larry with a smile, a wink, and a thumb's up. Still, why this place he wondered?

Trudy didn't wonder. She knew. She had been here before with Marty - one day in the summer...1971. She knew where to find him. He was thirty degrees up and a good thousand feet further east at the other end of the storm drain. He was preparing to ride the tube train. She had done it with him back in 1971. But as to why, she didn't have a clue.

"C'mon", she said. She pointed to Mo and directed him into the pond. "Stand there beneath the trickling water", she directed. He could see that she was in no mood for an argument. He waded into the pond, placed his hands on the concrete wall from which the storm drain exited ten feet up, and leaned in. Cold mountain spring water dripped onto his head and back. Trudy waded in. She directed Larry and Curly to boost her up onto Mo's back. Eldon sat at one of the picnic tables to enjoy the show. From Mo's back she was able to reach up to the corrugated line. Mo put a big hand on her skinny butt and hoisted her in. Without her cane, the going was slow. As she limped on up the line, she feared that the gate guardians would pull the plywood. For now, she chose to be fatalistic. If it was her "Time", she would go easily. That is...if it was her "Time", she thought. She continued upward toward the light. She limped onward and upward. She paused to catch her breath.

In between breaths, she thought she heard the faint sound of a CD player or a radio. The sound came and went, sometimes loud and somewhat clear, at other times, faint and fading in and out. She listened intently. She recognized the song: A Madman Across the Water by Elton John.

> ♪♪ I can see very well,
> There's a boat on the reef with a broken back
> And I can see it very well,
> There's a joke and I know it very well,
> It's one of those that I told you long ago
> Take my word I'm a madman don't you know

Once a fool had a good part in the play
If it's so would I still be here today?
It's quite peculiar in a funny sort of way
They think it's very funny everything I say
Get a load of him, he's so insane
You better get your coat dear
It looks like rain

We'll come again next Thursday afternoon
The In-laws hope they'll see you very soon
But is it in your conscience that you're after
Another glimpse of the madman across the water

I can see very well
There's a boat on the reef with a broken back
And I can see it very well
There's a joke and I know it very well
It's one of those that I told you long ago
Take my word I'm a madman don't you know
The ground's a long way down but I need more

Is the nightmare black
Or are the windows painted?
Will they come again next week?
Can my mind really take it? ♪♪

The radio had sounded far off, not so much distant, but far away...in Time, as if it was coming from somewhere back from the 1970's. Trudy puzzled. A breeze began to blow inside the storm sewer. It quickly gusted and increased in velocity. The distant music that she previously had heard only faintly was now loud, almost deafening. A piano thrummed inside her head. The music was loud and hurt her ears.

♪♪Nothing can stop a MADMAN ACROSS THE WAAAUHTERRRR...♪♪♪.

She put an index finger into each ear to block the volume. She wedged her cane between the corrugations and held on. The harsh wind became a driving mist. The mist blinded her. She closed her eyes, held an arm across her face, and held onto her cane for dear life. A wave, it seemed, passed through her, lifted, and jostled her.

She felt out of focus like the picture on an old black and white TV when little brother strikes out with a plastic bat but misses and instead, knocks the antennae off of the top of the set. Then, as quickly as it had come on, it all blew past her, almost pulling her down. The music that had sounded out so clear and so loud was gone. In its place: silence. The corrugated walls dripped, wet with mist. She was soaked from head to toe. For a moment longer, she held tight to her cane. She wobbled, but she didn't fall. She looked up toward the top end of the tunnel. Sunlight beckoned her. She could hear birds and the sounds of summer. The freeway noises were audible, but far distant. She looked down toward the bottom end. She could see Curly silhouetted there in the backlight. He must be standing on Mo. Mo must be cold and shriveled. She felt badly for Mo. He was a good friend. They were all good friends. She thought a moment longer. Somehow she knew that if Marty had been here at all, he was gone now. Yeah, well...never mind.

"I'm coming", she shouted down.

*****

Marty rode the inner tube train with the rest of the crowd. Elton John rode with them. Madman Across The Water echoed off of the corrugated steel. The surge was a big one – maybe a bit more water than usual. A wave had formed inside the storm line and crested. Marty rode the break, faster and faster. The passengers that rode with him on the tube train – one by one – faded and disappeared. Then, for a moment ever so briefly, he felt "blurred" or "fuzzy". First he wondered whether he had posted to No Time. But no, the "moment" was too sudden. Then, again, ever so briefly, he thought he saw Trudy there in the pipeline, clinging to the side. He watched her as the wave washed over her and she was gone. The Tsunami like wave broke at the end of the storm line, blew out of the mouth, spewed out, and crashed into the pond below. But Marty....well, Marty didn't follow. He blew out of the storm line and...

"Pop"...

He disappeared.

Curly felt the surge before Mo. But it hit them both like a ton of bricks. To Curly, it felt like an invisible ocean wave had launched him out from the mouth of the storm sewer and backward into the pond with a loud splash. A six-foot high wave formed-up, washed forward over Curly, and left him lying on dry ground. The wave continued forward like a Tsunami over the top of the concrete wall, ricocheted off of the concrete barrier, backwashed over the top of Curly to again knock him down, and hit Mo squarely in the chest.

Mo had seen Curly sail from the mouth of the storm line. *Why did he jump?* Mo wondered. He turned to watch him splat. He watched as the wave moved out and ricocheted back. It happened so fast, he had no time to react. The six-foot monster hit him smack in the chest and drove him back into the concrete wall beneath the storm drain. As the water rocked forward again, he sat flat and out cold. The water sloshed back and forth to eventually calm. Curly sat in water up to his chest. He wiped his face and eyes.

Mo was still out like a light, seated with his back against the wall. He was in it up to his face and eyes. Quickly, Curly waded over to him. He slapped his face a few times. Mo slowly came around.

"Trudy", he exclaimed. He stood back up and pressed himself to the concrete wall. Curly climbed upon his shoulders and stretched himself up to peer into the storm drain. "I can see her", he said. "She's almost here", he told Mo.

It took about another 20 minutes for Trudy to work her way back down the storm sewer line to the mouth opening. Curly was there and helped her climb down onto Mo's broad shoulders. From there, Larry and Eldon helped her down and took her out of the pond to the hearse. Eldon pulled a blanket from under the seat and wrapped it around her. She was wet and shivering. Curly climbed down over the top of Mo. The two of them left the pond and came to the hearse.

"Let's get out of here", Mo said. "Eldon, you drive".

Eldon had his earphones in. He sat in the front seat, listening to a tape, oblivious to Mo and the events of the day.

"ELDON!" Mo shouted.

Eldon jumped. He pulled the earphones from his ears. Scratchy music trickled out from the headphones and passed through the hearse:

♪♪ We'll come again next Thursday afternoon

The In-laws hope they'll see you very soon

But is it in your conscience that you're after

Another glimpse of the madman across the water ♪♪

"Wassup!" he responded rather naively. He turned his head and leaned back. He intended to stay uninvolved.

"Drive, please." Mo directed. His impatience was showing. He was weary.

Eldon popped open the cassette player, took out the tape and put it back into its box. He stashed the tape, the player and the headphones into the glove box. "Yeah, sure", Eldon muttered. He slid across the seat, adjusted it to fit, started the engine, and the crew headed back to Golden Hills.

CHAPTER XXXIX

Eldon dropped Trudy and the crew at the senior residence. He unlocked the door to let them into the basement morgue and, bid them adieu, for now. Who knew when he might see any one of these folks again? After all, he'd already seen this Marty dude twice over there in Drawer 13. Who was he to say that he wouldn't see him again sometime soon?

Trudy thanked him for his help and quickly stepped through the door before it closed. Mo was in a hurry. The night shift was coming on and he needed to get to the front lobby to clock them in. Curly too had responsibilities. The men's front men's room needed attention and he needed to "choke a fat one"; to "chief out"; to "fire one up"; to "poke smot" – as they say. Trudy needed to run "bed check" with Ms. Bichette. She would be waiting for her up front. Larry needed to place an order for kitchen supplies – including yogurt - with Ms. Bichette. He wasn't looking forward to meeting with her. None of them were. They were due for a stern rebuke, and they knew it. None of them had a good answer.

What could they say? They had gone looking for Marty whom they believed had gone back to an old favorite playground from his youth. Never mind that they had taken Trudy – a resident of Golden Hills – with them. It was the truth, but it wouldn't sell. As it turned out, it wouldn't be necessary.

Ms. Bichette was finishing up with some bookwork in the front office. She intercepted them in the front hallway as they approached.

"Gentlemen...and lady, I presume that you took a day off. In fact, I presume that you took an entire year's worth of your available days off because, I'm sure you will agree, that you will have no more for the remainder of this year", she dictated calmly in her most officious voice. They all looked at each other.

"And, Ms. Trudy....you are doing well, I presume?" she nodded to Trudy. Trudy nodded back weakly. "You have been promoted. You will now assist me with all of my duties. That is to say that during the daylight hours when you are neither taking meals nor sleeping, you shall remain with me, right by my side. I have much instruction to share", she smiled sardonically.

"My friends" she announced, "Marty has gone missing. We all know what a dear treasure Mr. Markham is, and has been, to this facility; and, just how much it would mean to us all should he return in short order. All of us would rejoice to have him home". She looked at each intently with a serious touch of sincerity. "Do you agree?" she inquired.

Each nodded. They sensed a ray of hope.

She continued. "Now, should he fail to return by tomorrow morning, I shall be forced to report his absence to the local authorities. I am sure that none of you want that to happen. I am scheduled to meet with his wife and family tomorrow at 10 a.m. to report either that he has gone missing – which I am sure you would agree, would be a sad, even frightening report for the family - or that he has been such an inspiration to each of the members of the entire home, that we would beg their permission to celebrate with them at a party – to be sponsored by Golden Hills Residential Community – to name the cafeteria in Marty's honor. The 'Mark, Mark, Markam Mealtime Menagerie'. Catchy, wouldn't you say?"

Curly started to respond, "Nah. Not so mu...." This time Trudy popped him in the face with the back of her hand. "Shh", she swiftly stifled him.

Ms. Bichette stood firm and still, her hands behind her back. She was all business. "Now, I trust", she said, "that we will be able to celebrate with the family tomorrow morning". She emphasized 'tomorrow morning'. "*N'est ce pas?*" she barked. They all knew that when she said this – the only French that she knew – the conversation was over. She quickly turned and retired to her office. "Trudy?" she commanded without looking back.

Trudy waved weakly to her friends and surrendered. She followed Ms. Bichette to the office. The others returned to their tasks as if nothing had happened over the past 24 hours. Curly reported to the men's room. His nose was bleeding and he had Trudy to thankbut mostly he needed to take a "bullet". *Right now, he thought, it may as well be literal.*

CHAPTER XL

"Pop"...Marty's exit from the present was an immediate entrance into 1967, or so he thought. He found himself in mid-air over Bell's Canyon Reservoir that sat in the canyon above Dimple Dell. He slowly began to fall. He adjusted his goggles and dove. The water was ice cold and bracing. The reservoir fed the small stream that flowed past his childhood home. He didn't know it yet, but he had missed October 1967 by a few months shy of a year. When he failed to enter the hour, the minute, and the second into the book for October 2, 1967 that was presented to him on the Cherrywood shelf in The Library, he failed to secure the page and inadvertently allowed the page or pages to slip as if a stray breeze wafted through The Library to lift and turn one or several pages from October 2, 1967 to somewhere maybe days, weeks, or even months later in Time.

To Marty, the day felt like June...maybe July. The sky was blue and cloudless. The desert air was thin and light. He could smell the sagebrush. The bright sunlight painted the shimmering leaves on the scrub oak and quaking aspen in different shades of green. The day was mild, comfortable – a perfect day on the Wasatch front, a perfect part of the world. Marty's mind was open and clarifying. As if in a vision, he watched himself progress. He knew where he was going and he knew why he was going there. From the reservoir, he found his way to the stream that ran along Dimple Dell Road in the days of his childhood. Soon, he was paddling the open creek that ran across the lower pasture in front of what was his home.

Dad had focused his attention on this stream and the lower pasture there at the front of the property below the barn. The stream that Marty swam in ran the entire width of the front property. In an ongoing battle with the local irrigation department, dad would use a portable pump to steal water from the stream. He frequently sparred with water master who routinely drove up and down Dimple Dell on a small Honda 50 to monitor the stream flow and to catch water sneaks. He routinely caught dad. During the day, he would ride to the property and pull the foot valve from the stream. When dad got home, he would put the foot valve back and watered at night.

Marty reached up for the lodge pole fence that bordered the newly paved asphalt drive. The drive ran over the creek that flowed through a large corrugated storm sewer pipe. He pulled himself up and out of the water and stepped onto the unshaded paved drive. His feet were bare and the pavement burned. Ouch, the pain surprised him. His flippers were gone. He no longer wore a red speedo, but a pair of cutoff jeans. His goggles were gone. He wore no shirt. His skinny frame was tan all over. His hair was thick and lush.

He no longer felt old and sluggish, but...well...he felt pretty damn young. In fact, he felt alive! He smiled as he inspected his arms and hands. They were the arms and hands of a boy. He looked at his legs. These too were boyish, no hair to speak of; except for some dark, manly hair from the ankles to the shins. This troubled him, but he didn't know why. He pulled the waistband of his cutoffs away from his waist. He smiled to know that the important parts were covered. He shook water from his thick head of hair. He ran both hands through it. Without a mirror, he knew that it was dark brown. Except for a brief space under his cutoffs, he was tan all over.

He grinned. He was pretty sure not so much of "where" he was, but of "when" he was, and it pleased him. Okay, so he missed his target. But this was terrific anyway. His intention had been to come back to October 2, 1967. He was twelve years old back then, and pubic hair and zits had yet to manifest. Upon re-examination inside his cutoffs and again there at his shins and ankles, he was sprouting. He felt his back. Ouch. Three large zits: one on the shoulder, two closer together at mid-back - told him that he had reached thirteen. He put the date at around late July 1968. He wondered not so much "how?", but "why?"

Yeah, well...I'm here, he thought, and he began trapesing up the long twisting driveway. He passed the barn – more of a carport with a total of eight stalls, four for autos on one side and opposite, four more for the horses. Each horse stall held a large hay bin for feeding. The first auto stall housed a large haystack with bales of alfalfa. In the fourth auto stall was a stack of firewood lined against the western wall. The horses - Toro and Princess - neighed and whinnied at him as he walked up the drive. The area in front of the barn sloped downward from the driveway and was unpaved. Marty looked to see the basketball backboard, rim, and net affixed to the barn. A cinder block wall bordered the upper edge of the unpaved entrance and angled back and upwards toward the house. Marty pretended to shoot and swish a shot. He made a fist a pulled back hard. "Yessss!" He raised his arm to signal two points. Three point shots had yet to be awarded in 1968; except in the ABA. And anyway, Marty thought, the ABA was using red-white-and blue colored basketballs. That game felt more like the Harlem Globetrotters, not so much like real basketball ,or at least that's how it felt to Marty.

He continued to walk up the drive. He passed the white fence that bordered the small patch of lawn that sat between the concrete parking area in front of the home and the white fence that sat atop an escarpment that sloped steeply to the cinderblock wall that bordered the unpaved basketball court below. In the hillside escarpment, Dad had planted 3 quaking aspens. Years later, the septic tank beneath the lawn had failed and began to drain across the grass. Dad had directed the flow with a hand shovel into a small ditch that fed down the slope and into the middle aspen. He dug a huge circle around the base of the tree and bordered it with a high mound of dirt and boulders. Marty remembered how, in future years, the quake had grown twice, maybe three times, as high as the other two quakes, one on either side.

Marty passed the basement door that served as the main entrance to the home from the upper parking area. The home had no garage. Covered parking was available only at the barn down below. He passed beneath the large picture window that dominated the front of the home and walked up the concrete walkway to the front door. The window provided an expansive view of the eastern slopes of the Oquirrah Mountains that ranged across the western side of the Salt Lake Valley. From this window in his living room, Marty could see across the entire "dell" that continued its brief run, north to south, past Marty's house before it turned west on Dimple Dell to parallel the large gully that led down to White City.

Dad had hammered together a wooden ladder made of 2x4 lumber: two 12 foot pieces for rails and ten-one foot sections to serve as rungs. The damn thing was heavy, and once or twice each summer, Marty was required to set up the ladder at the window to clean the glass. Sometimes, his mom would help him. He remembered how much he had loved her for it.

His mom was pretty and young, but somehow careworn. She was always tan in the summer. She would lay on a chaise lounge that she set on the lawn in the back yard. For a Time, she bleached her hair and wore it in a large beehive-like hairdo. Marty remembered a picture of her wearing the hive, a formal dress, and chewing on a tooth pick. She and dad were seated at a club table in Las Vegas. She really didn't like it – any of it. She did it for dad. She did like to ski, but what she liked best was to golf. At one point, she joined a club and golfed every week. She won several tournaments.

Dad had taught both mom and him to golf. At least, there was that. When she and dad divorced, she got a Camero and took a job. She worked to support a small family of...of three. Three? Marty caught himself and for a moment he faltered. His mind fogged over.

He felt fuzzy, insecure. Quickly, he reminded himself why he had come. His mind cleared and he felt young again.

His mom, he remembered was a classy lady. He knew somehow that she had brought him here today. He was amazed at just how much he could recall. He was still stumped as to both why and how he seemed to be thirteen years old. But, never mind. He felt a freedom that he hadn't felt in years. He would ride this bull as far as it would take him, he told himself and shivered.

As he walked up the concrete ramp, he came to a small concrete porch. At 90 degrees, several steps led up from the porch to a second higher porch that served as entry to the front door. Marty remembered a day filled with fluffy, white cumulus stacked high over the valley floor and swiftly moving. He was seated right here on the front porch just outside the door. The air was fresh and electric, in anticipation of a coming cloudburst. He watched as the large clouds darkened as they marched in from west to east where the wind squeezed them against Lone Peak. He usually enjoyed spectating at these large summer storms.

Typically, he would sit here on the porch to let the brief torrent wash him clean. But on this day onward marching and ever darkening clouds blocked the sun to overshadow the porch on as they marched across the valley. Jagged bolts of lightning began throwing brilliant flashes against the house. For a time, he felt that the bolts were aimed at him. The air was heavy and reverberated. Suddenly, a brilliant flash blinded him and KABOOOOMMMMMM! The thunder was immediate. No counting seconds to determine how many miles away. The heavy air knocked him backwards; a deluge broke from the skies and nearly washed him from the porch. As Marty recalled this, he began to understand that this had been heaven sent; sent for some reason to warn him or better still, to direct him, to set it right. He believed that he would soon come to remember whatever it was that he was now being called upon to remember; that for his salvation, he needed to remember.

He reached the corner of the house and turned east toward the back yard. Lone Peak in the Wasatch Range dominated the view, silhouetted against the deep blue sky. Even in late July, the 11,000 foot peak was snowcapped. The peak shaded the backyard in the early morning hours. In the summertime, at night, Marty would throw a stuffed cotton sleeping bag onto the back lawn where he would sleep like a baby. In the morning, he would lay on his back until the sun moved away the shadows so as to reach down and touch him. He would yawn, pull himself out of the bag, roll it up and stash it on there on the patio to be used again later that night when the moon and stars again dominated the skies. The open skies above and soft grass beneath, offered some of the best sleep he had ever experienced.

Hmmm...he wondered? What was it about age that made it so difficult to find rest? He thought about Golden Hills. His mattress was lumpy and felt like rocks. He hadn't had a good night's sleep in...well, he couldn't say how long. Suddenly his vision blurred, his head buzzed, and he felt as if the portable antennae on top of his old black and white TV set had been knocked out of proper angle to skew his horizontal hold. He was discombobulated; out of focus. Marty squinted, pressed his temples, and focused again on his home there in the mouth of Bell's Canyon. After a moment, his mind cleared as he returned. He told himself to avoid any thoughts about or comparisons with his present circumstance at Golden Hills.

In the years before Marty and his family took up residence at Dimple Dell, rattlesnakes had taken over Bell's canyon behind the home. Word was that the local ranchers had let a number of mink loose in the canyon to solve the snake problem. In all of his exploration up and down Bell's Canyon, Marty had never seen a rattlesnake. He did recall one small baby rattlesnake that his little brother had captured and placed inside the milk box that he pulled from the front porch. Inside it he put sand, planted a piece of cactus, and placed a few stones to serve as a home. He tried to show off his find to mom who just about wet her pants to see her little boy with a baby rattlesnake. She took him and the milk box with his snake up into the back pasture where they let it go. Frequently Marty did see and had to deal with mink and other critters that the cats at the home would corner in the deep window well next to the back door. Such critters included: a large skunk, a muskrat, and two or more mink. He recalled how, the cats – Tiger and Pepper – had cornered a great big skunk in the window well next to the back door. Dad was yet versed in how to deal with the local wildlife. He elected to shoot the thing with a .22 caliber rifle – single shot.

The thought of this rifle suddenly caught Marty up short. He coughed, lost his breath and dizziness overwhelmed. A small piece of memory, vivid and stark caught a hold of him; paralyzed him. He recalled the little bed wetter. It was funny that this little bed wetter whom Marty had struggled for so long to remember turned out to be his own little brother, the little brother about whom he had all but forgotten. His name... was Brandon.

Strange, Marty thought, that he should recall him here. But then again, maybe it was not so strange at all. Suddenly, he gasped. A faint blue light began to glow around him. He again began to pop and fizzle. He lost a piece and couldn't capture fully the memory of his little brother. A piece of him was glad for that. Then, as suddenly as it had come, the memory was gone. He didn't try too hard to recapture it. The blue light faded and he steadied himself. Peace returned. Marty knew that – at some point – he would need to come to grips with this. He coughed again to clear his throat as his breathing slowly came back. Marty had come here for a specific reason and he had some work to do.

He walked timidly into the back yard. By way of detour, if only to buy himself – what?...Time? He weaved his way through the colored bed sheets that mom had hung out to dry on the line that was there in the side yard. Four "lines" made of wire, stretched between two, T-shaped iron poles, cemented into the ground approximately fifteen feet apart from each other. The lines were not set to spin on a single pole like the one at grandma's house. These were not as fun to play on. But he enjoyed the cool, clean, freshness of the sheets, and the sweet memories that they carried with the breeze that helped them to dry.

He felt a tinge of confidence return, but as he stepped from beneath the sheets, trepidation bounced back. To his right, a pathway stepped up to an upper pasture. The pasture was enclosed by a lodge pole fence. Just outside the fence and nearest the home was a 50 gallon, metal trash bin rusted and shot full of holes. It served as an incinerator. It also served for target practice. Frequently, Marty would empty the "burnable" trash, old newspapers and magazines, and stuff from the bathroom. The bathroom stuff was fun. Purposefully, he would overlook any of the aerosol cans that were deposited. When dumped into the incinerator, as the fire grew higher, a can would explode and rocket upward. Marty would stomp out any residual fire when it fell to earth. He didn't worry much about starting a ground fire on the sandy ground of the upper pasture. He was more concerned about the large paper ashes that glowed red with the wind that pushed them up and far away; just not concerned enough to care.

Once more, he started top fizzle and pop. The blue light grew brighter and began to strengthen. When he turned away from the rusted trash barrel, the noise stopped and the light faded. When he turned to look again at the barrel. He looked away and the noise and light quickly stopped. He worried. He had experienced this blue light and buzzing in earlier attempts to reach No Time. These attempts had been aided by some experimentation with his medications. He had tweaked the order, the combination and amounts. But he no longer played with his meds. He hadn't played with them for some Time and he believed that this was the reason for how he found himself here. Still, he knew that his memory was diminishing, fading, returning to Swiss-cheese. Damn, he was worried. Until now, the memories of this Space and Time had flowed easily through his consciousness. They were maybe not new, but different ,or better still – just unfamiliar. He squeezed his eyes shut and rubbed his temples. He rolled his head from shoulder to shoulder. He breathed in deeply and quickly pushed the breath out to better relax.

With continued trepidation, while standing at the rusted trash bin at the top of the steps, he looked down into the backyard. Like the barn at the front of the home, the backyard was protected by an escarpment. This one was also approximately fifteen feet high. It dropped into the lower backyard from the upper pasture. Large tams and other shrubbery that dad had planted to hold back the sandy soils from sliding help to keep the slope from eroding. The upper pasture was also fenced with lodge pole to better characterize the old west view of Bell's Canyon and Lone Peak. Dad had struggled for years to raise alfalfa there, but the sandy soil was poor and water was not immediately available and difficult to supply to the thirsty grasses of the upper pasture. Planting had proven too difficult so this pasture was rarely used.

A retaining wall, constructed with granite boulders curved around the backyard between the sandy escarpment and the back lawn. The largest boulders, at the base, averaged two to three feet around. The smaller boulders closet to and at the top of the wall ranged roughly from one to two feet in diameter.

The former owner had aligned these boulders vertically at the escarpment. Over the course of several years, during the wet winter months, different sections of the wall would slide and fall. Seasonally, Marty would repair, refit, and reset these various sections. He reconfigured the heavy stones at a slight angle against the escarpment. The angle added enough stability to prevent further collapse so that over the years since then, the entire semicircle of granite boulders, both large and small, had been arranged into a more or less permanent retaining wall. He hadn't seen it at the Time, but being here now and looking back, he could see that this work, done by him and on his own at a fairly young age, was quite an accomplishment to be admired by even the best of wall builders. Marty smiled at the thought. But with that thought: a recollection back, the blue light flickered and dizziness returned. For a moment, he was back in the underwater library. Marty focused hard to return again to his backyard, the way it was when he was thirteen. He looked around to admire the dandelion -free back lawn. It was lush and green. Nicely placed quaking aspens were planted beside three large granite boulders placed strategically throughout the back yard into two separate flower beds to decorate. Mom usually planted different colored petunias in the rich topsoil that Marty had placed around the boulders; and which he tilled and fertilized each spring. To Marty, the backyard was truly a work of art.

Marty looked to the back patio. He puzzled as to why the far end opposite the incinerator was blurred and grey. Here, his memory was unclear; out of focus. This part of the back yard was altogether missing, vacant and undiscernible. He took a step forward to inspect further.

"Mark", he heard his mother say. He turned in surprise. She was seated cross legged on the lawn opposite, picking peas from a small garden planted next to the patio.

"Mom!" he exclaimed, surprised and happy to see her. "Where have you been, I have missed you".

"What do you mean – where have I been?" she asked him curiously. "I've been here at the house all day. If I remember correctly, I helped you clean your room this morning. If I further remember correctly, you asked me if I needed milk and told me that you'd be happy to take my car to get some at the store. I trust that you remember that I gave you my keys, told you to be careful and to be back soon, and – of course you remember that I kissed you 'good bye' ". She smiled sweetly at him. "You do remember that don't you?" She reached out and grabbed his long, dark brown hair and gave it a tug.

"Oh, yeah", he answered. He remembered her handing him her keys. He remembered saying, "thanks mom" and kissing her on the cheek. He remembered the exhilaration he felt while driving. He was 13 years old. He remembered driving carefully, both hands on the wheel. He drove the approximate 12 miles down the hill to Safeway to buy a gallon of 2 percent milk. In his mind's eye, he could see the blue and white carton. It read: Highland Dairy. He returned and parked the Camero in the driveway. He walked the ramp in front of the home, entered the kitchen just inside the front door, and put the milk in the fridge.

"C'mon. Help me pick some peas", Mom smiled up at him and patted the lawn next to her for him to sit.

He walked over and gave her a kiss on the cheek, "Hi, mom. Thanks for letting me take the car". He sat down with her on the lawn next to the garden. It wasn't a garden really; more like a patch of peas. They were the only thing planted there. Several months back, Marty had helped her plant them. Now, here they were ready to harvest.

"You're welcome. Did you get the milk?" she asked with a smile.

"Yep...he saluted. "And I got a dollar's worth of gas for the car. Where are the girls?"

The girls were his younger sisters: Deedee was 8, the oldest girl and the middle child. She was solemn and smiled little. But she was wide open to brotherly kindness. It was hard to give only because her well was deep, even endless. Marty loved her, but she really didn't fit the family dynamic, and it was hard to craft a space for her. Marty recalled the night that he had shouted at her to turn down the television. She was seated on the floor directly in front. The volume was booming. Marty had come from downstairs. He needed to use the phone next to the couch.

"Deedee, turn down the TV. I need to make a call", he'd said absentmindedly as he plopped himself down. She remained still. The TV continued to blare. "Deedee, please turn down the TV', he had asked. No response. Marty was getting aggravated which seemed to occur more and more with her as she got older. "DEEDEE" he shouted. She jumped at the sound, startled. She turned innocently. "What is the matter with you?" he asked with more than a hint of irritation. "Can't you hear?" She looked at him, dumbfounded. He let his agitation show if only to reinforce his righteous indignation before he took the phone into the front room and closed the door to make his call.

Several months later, at the school's recommendation, Mom had Deedee's hearing tested. The results showed a 70% hearing loss in one ear, a 20% in the other. Marty recalled shouting at her, if not this Time, then at various others. He felt bad to get the news. He had tried to be a big brother. He had tried to show her some understanding, to somehow apologize for his aggravation. He was sweet with her after that, but he never did get close to her. Come to think of it, he never got very close with either of his sisters. The family dynamic – particularly during the growing years - was much too complicated. It was survival of the fittest. Marty was fit and they were silly little girls. Shanna proved her fitness, but Deedee never did. Mom was fit and Marty figured that she could take better care of the girls than he could.

Shanna was Marty's baby sister. She was five, a pixie with short blond hair and shining blue eyes, energetic, and mischievous – the last of four kids in the family. Many times, over the years, Mom would tell the story of how – when Shanna was about three years old, Mom had discovered a handful of plastic army men and a few small plastic airplanes at the bottom of the toilet bowl in the one bathroom in the house. Shanna was playing in the tub. Mom had asked Shan just who had put those toys into the toilet. Shanna responded nonchalantly, but with a sincere effort to help, "Pwobbably Mawwkiie did it". Thereafter, whenever anybody wanted to discover just who was responsible for just about anything that had happened, the response came back: "Pwobbably Mawwkiie did it".

Mom began to harvest the large green pods. Each had three or four large green peas. "Shan went to the Bonham's. I hope that her little friend doesn't lock her into the barn like last time. Dad was mad that she didn't come running when he called. You know how he gets", she said. Yeah, Marty thought, he knew how he could get.

She continued, "He ranted and raved at her around here for an hour or so until Ann called to say they had found her. She had heard her wailing and pounding the locked barn door from the inside. Ann reassured Mom that her little girl would be appropriately disciplined, which likely meant, not at all. "Your dad was a bit sheepish after that" Mom smiled to herself as she popped open a fresh pod from the bowl of newly harvested pods there on her lap. She broke it open, threw back her head, tossed in a few peas, and chewed contentedly.

The summer day was calm, the sky – serenely blue and cloudless, the temperature warm, but comfortable. He and Mom spent a length of time sharing fresh peas and enjoying the moment. No one spoke. Her bowl was now empty and the two of them had gone directly to the vines.

Once again, Marty's head began to spin. He felt quesy and began to spin. Blue light surrounded him. It popped and fizzled. Then suddenly, the realization dawned. Marty was given this moment. It was not a mistake that he had missed October 1967. It was not a mistake that he had found his mom on the back lawn in the pea garden, here in what was the summer following. Marty knew what he must do. He must do it now, what had been back then, the most difficult thing for him to do. He must do now what he did not do back then. Yet, he also knew that he could not rectify what had happened. This was not about changing the past. He could not bring him back. "No Time" did not allow for that. But it did allow him to remove the darkness, to make room for the light, to give place for the truth. He knew that he must seek forgiveness from the one person whom he had hurt the most. He cringed and began to tear up.

"What is it Marty?" she asked. "Are you okay? Is everything alright?" She reached for him and pulled him to her. She hugged his head to her chest. She hummed a familiar song from his childhood, and held him close. The song was sweet; her voice soothing. "It's alright sweetheart. I'm here" she whispered as he sobbed. The dam that held back years of emotion burst wide open. As he stood there at the Cherrywood counters in the underwater Library, quesy, dizzy, and sick, with blue light buzzing and popping all around him, wave broke upon him and he floundered. He gasped and tried to speak. He could not. He struggled to bring back a semblance of calm. He could not. He could only struggle to choke back the pain that he felt, the hurt that he had caused. But it was not to be. He was here to let it all go. Tears flowed down his cheeks, and he let them... wash him away.

No Time had brought him to be with his mom. She needed to know, and he must tell her. He must tell her that which for so long now he had withheld. He looked across the patio to the spot where he had fallen. Brandon, the bed wetter – he was ten years old. Marty was his older brother. He was twelve. The blue light rose as the recollection dawned. Brandon, the bed wetter, was his younger brother. Marty had named his only son, Brandon – after his little brother. From that day, Marty had somehow known that his own fist child would be a son, and that Marty would name him Brandon. So certain was Marty that when the obstetrician placed the blue little guy onto his mom's belly upon delivery, Marty never thought to look. It was his wife who contentedly commented, "It's a boy". Oh yeah, Marty thought. It's Brandon.

On that day, the 2nd of October 1967, the two had wanted to target practice. Mom had finally succumbed to their pestering. She had rather that dad deal with the "boys" and this "man" business. She unlocked the gun cabinet and removed both of the two .22 caliber, single shot rifles that Dad had bought for them. She gave five shells to each of them. Marty put his in his shirt pocket.

Mom had delivered one rifle to each of her boys from the cabinet and led them upstairs to the backyard. She sat them on the lawn at the north end just off from the patio. They had shot target practice several times previously from here with dad. The target was the rusted 50 gallon drum that served as an incinerator at the far south end of the property on the upper portion near the pasture. A few extra holes in the barrel never hurt to help the fire breath. Sometimes they would set up bottles on a 2x4 placed across the open barrel. Today, they just wanted to shoot at the barrel. Mom lectured them about safety. Of course, they had heard it all before and besides, she would be there with them to watch.

She pulled up a chaise lounge from the far end of the patio. She had just finished with her safety reminder and prepared herself to sit when the front doorbell rang. Marty had thought this strange. He was irritated and became impatient. People rarely came to visit midday and besides this Time belonged to him.

The neighbor, Afton had already paid her earlier visit. Daily she came up for coffee. She negotiated the long driveway on stubby legs from her home about a quarter mile further south on Dimple Dell. She had intrigued Marty. She was short at less than 5 feet and stout, not fat, but...stout. She wore blue jean coveralls. Her legs were stumpy and her leathery skin was wrinkled and sunburned. Her intrigue was not so much her skill with horses or her diminutive stature, but her report that Marty had overheard one day as she visited with mom. She and her husband Tom were nudists. Marty had only recently learned about nudists from a magazine that he had discovered a few Sundays back in his grandma's hall closet when he had gone looking for the family photo album. The magazine had intrigued him. But he found it much less interesting than the Playboy magazine he had already found under the mat in dad's truck when he vacuumed the carpets. The thought now that Afton was a nudist made the entire idea wholly unappealing. Marty shivered to even think about it.

Mom excused herself to answer the door. "You boys wait here. No shooting til I get back" she had told them. She opened the back door and stepped inside. The screen door closed with a clap. He sat there with Brandon on the back lawn. The two were quiet for a moment. The fall afternoon was pleasant. The leaves on the scrub oak that surrounded the property were turning orange. The birch leaves contrasted with yellow and gold. It was an "Indian Summer".

As Marty thought now, he wondered how through all of the years that followed, he had viewed Brandon as his "little brother". Of course, this was true. Marty had him by just over two years. But in large measure, the two were joined. They were equals and Marty didn't always like it. Numerous times in the years previous, before Dimple Dell, when he and Brandon were playing together with friends from the neighborhood, skating on Edward's driveway, or sometimes rolling down the small hill in Robert's backyard inside an empty barrel of oats, at the suggestion of his friends, he would try to ditch his little brother. The effort only succeeded in making Brandon cry. Marty would feel so badly that he would go back to Brandon who stood where Marty had left him and sobbed forlornly. He would hug Brandon and tell him that he was sorry. He'd tell him it was okay and would reach for him to bring him along. If his friends rebelled, Marty and Brandon would leave for home. It was better than having him cry. Marty didn't like to make him cry.

Marty recalled another Time, a few years later, one summer day there on Dimple Dell. Brandon Randy, -the kid next door- and he met to hang out. Randy had brought home two boxes of cigarettes that he had shoplifted: one Marlboro, one Salem. He told them to climb the tall Cottonwood tree at the base of the asphalt driveway where they all lit up. He said that the tree leaves would absorb the smoke so that it could not be seen and nobody could find them. Marty tried it. The Marlboro's gave no taste and held no appeal. With the Salems, he could taste the menthol, but he never inhaled properly to even choke. Anyway, the idea of smoking held no interest. His grandmother smoked four packs a day; his grandfather, another four packs. All he ever got out of that was burning eyes in the swirling haze of smoke at their dinner table. There was no intrigue to hold him. He had instructed his little brother that they were through with smoking. So he was wholly surprised about two weeks later when he saw Randy and Brandon sitting on the large granite boulder next to their mailbox across the street from Marty's driveway there on Dimple Dell. They were smoking. Marty was stunned. Brandon looked as if he had learned quite well just how to inhale comfortably. His little brother was gaining his own independence.

But here on the back lawn, Marty's impatience had grown. Where was Mom? Why was she taking so long? He reached into his shirt pocket for a bullet and loaded it into his .22 caliber, single shot, rifle. He closed the trigger slowly and laid the gun across his lap for safe keeping to wait for her. Of course, Brandon never did like the idea of Marty doing anything on his own and loading a shell was not just a breach of etiquette but smacked of outright defiance. He began to pester Marty. It was the usual: He would tell Mom. Marty would be in big trouble when Dad came home. Dad would take the guns away. The drivel went on but thankfully Brandon became bored with the harangue and fell silent. Birds chirped. A robin landed on the lawn and pulled a night crawler. Lone Peak rose majestically behind the house to display its fall colors against the deep blue background of a cloudless fall afternoon. The sun was setting to the west, and the backyard was shaded, cool, and peaceful. Brandon couldn't resist. After all, he was the little brother. "I'm telling mom", he said. "You're pointing your gun at me". Of course, he was right, the little irritant. Marty's rifle lay across his lap and was pointed directly at Brandon. Marty had become distracted and had readjusted a few times.

The barrel now pointed at Brandon, and it bugged Marty to be bested by his little brother. This seemed to be happening more and more these days. In frustration, he lifted the rifle, cocked the trigger, and pulled. He'd show him who knew best. He'd show him what an empty chamber sounded like. He would show him that the gun was harmless. But instead of the expected "click", the gun popped. Marty saw Brandon's shirt jump. He saw a tiny hole in the shirt just there in his chest next to his left shoulder. For a moment, Marty froze. What had just happened? It was not bad, was it? At least, he hoped that it was not bad. But his hope faded quickly.

"You shot me" Brandon said calmly. It was the last thing Marty would hear him say ever again. He had better get Mom. He reached for the door just as Mom stepped outside. She must have heard the report. She must have known. The door closed on the Avon lady who stayed inside. Stupid lady, Marty thought. If only she hadn't come that day....

Mom didn't ask what had happened. She seemed to know. Marty couldn't speak. He couldn't tell her. She picked up Marty's little brother in her arms and carried him into the house. She laid him on the carpet there in the TV room just inside the backdoor. The blood spot never fully came out, so Dad replaced the carpet. Marty didn't go inside. This wasn't his business. This was work for... well, for grownups. Mostly, Marty could not confront what he had done. He wasn't quite sure yet exactly what he had done. He went down to the barn and sat on the baled haystack to think, to hide. An ambulance arrived. He watched from the barn as Mom rode away with Brandon, his little brother.

A neighbor came to the house. She stayed behind to watch his little sisters, to watch him. After all, he was still just a little boy, wasn't he?

Later that night, Dad and Mom came home together. That was different. Marty rarely saw them together anymore. They rarely did anything as a family anymore. The local church authority was there with a few of the brethren. Dad sat with Marty on the couch. He told him that Brandon would not be coming home. That he had gone to Heaven.

Whoa, wait. What did you say? For years this didn't register. For years, Marty expected Brandon to meet him down at the barn to pester him to take him on a hike, to the pond, or to the reservoir in Bell's Canyon.

Neither Dad nor Mom, ever asked him just what had happened. Neither ever spoke of the accident again. Truly, no one wanted to know. That night, one of the church brethren told Marty that he was forgiven. Marty wasn't so sure. It was the only word that was ever spoken to Marty about the accident in any of the Time that followed. That was nice but still...Marty didn't know. In reality, he didn't think so. Why else would he have fought so hard to come back here, to come back to well...to 1968, to better deal with the personal disaster. Never mind that it happened in 1967 - October 2nd, to be exact. He thought he knew why he landed here in 1968 a few months following.

He needed to find his Mom at a Time when he found her to be most approachable, most forgiving. He needed to speak with her. He needed her to know what had happened. He realized now that his target date was wrong. It was selfish. He had targeted October 2nd with the hope that he could intercede, that he could change things. But he was wrong. He couldn't change things even if that was possible. Changing what had happened may change nothing or it could change everything. The No Time theory did not work to change events, things in the past, or to even give a benefit from knowing the future. It only served to change the person who found it. No Time worked for the individual to remove any darkness, to clarify events, to bring light, to tell the truth, to change the individual, not to change things. It served only as an outward guide to the inner person. It served to guide the soul.

"Hey, Mom?" he started tentatively. He was nervous. "I need to tell you something". She looked up and smiled. "It's something I've needed to say to you for a long Time now".

"Marty" she interrupted. "You don't need to say anything". She paused to collect her own thoughts. Then she asked, "Why do you think you've come to 1968? Why do you think that I brought you here"?

"Whoa... what?" Marty stammered. "What are you saying?"

I brought you here to tell you that I know what happened. Mothers know their boys. I know you. I know Brandon. I don't blame either of you. I don't blame you. I have blamed myself all of these years. I should never have left you alone with the guns. I should never had stayed away so long with the...the Avon Lady." She began to tear up. She grew quiet for a long while. In an instant, Marty was transported back to the Library. He sat there with his mother on a nicely upholstered bench, beneath a beautiful crystal chandelier. She held him close like she used to when he was small. She stroke his head and softly sang to him. At long last, he found peace. "I am so sorry that I never talked with you about that day, that I never held you, that I never comforted you", she continued. "And, I am so sorry that you needed to carry this burden for all these years. But..." she stopped once more and cried. "But I didn't know how...". She choked up and couldn't speak. Marty's eyes watered. Tears rolled down his cheeks. He couldn't find his voice. He wasn't sure what was happening, but he could feel the mists clear, the long held burden ease, the muddled thoughts realign.

She faced him and held him by his shoulders. She pulled him close and put her soft hands onto his cheeks. She looked into his tear filled eyes. "Marty, I am sorry, so very sorry that I wasn't there for you when you needed me the most, that I failed you as your mother. Can you ever forgive me? She broke down and sobbed. She sobbed for a long time and could no longer speak.

Marty was stunned. Never had he expected this. Never had he ever felt that she was to blame. Never! He cradled his mother to his chest. He bathed her head with his own tears and held her cheeks in his hands.

"Mom", he said to her. "Please, don't cry. I love you! You have been so good to me, the best mom a kid could have...ever. I am so very grateful for you. I am proud to call you my Mom. A kid could not ask for a better mom. Thank you for your kindness and optimism. Thank you for carrying me over the rough spots in my life".

He told her again that he loved her, more than anything. He told her again that he was forever grateful for the strength that she had brought to him.

She had defended him even during some of her own very darkest days with his Dad. Marty told her that he was thankful that she never tried to make his Dad an enemy to him, thankful that she never tried to glorify Dad's weaknesses to any of his kids. She let them love him in spite of his weaknesses. She let them come to know him, to understand him. She let each of them judge him accordingly. He told her again just how much he cared for her; and how sorry he was that he had taken Brandon from her.

She reached for his cheeks and wiped his tears. She wiped her own and smiled. They sat together in silence for a long Time. His Mom held him sweetly,and he hugged her close. He had never felt so much peace; so at peace with himself. He didn't want to leave her. He didn't want to leave this place. After a while, Mom let him go. She reached into the vine and pulled another pod. She popped it open and tossed the peas into her mouth. She smiled again at Marty as she lifted an empty pod in tribute to both of them.

And now, they were together back in the pee patch, back in 1968. The two sat and visited as they finished the pea harvest. He was glad that he had come home.

But then Marty knew that he was not to stay and after a peace -filled moment, the air around him began to vibrate and buzz. "White noise" began to build, increasing and decreasing in volume, building back and falling away, only to come back louder, over and over to where Marty was forced to hold his ears tightly against the pain. The view surrounding the mountains blurred and faded in and out of focus. His mom's pretty face dissolved into electronic "snow", and the scene that surrounded her and his childhood home slowly melted away. He reached for her one last Time, but she was gone. The "white noise" fizzled, and an eerie quiet returned. The scenes that had surrounded Marty faded to black, and he began to move faster and faster. A light clock appeared to him, the light beam bouncing more and more slowly as the track between mirrors grew longer and longer.

Marty knew that in the next several decades, the entire scene that surrounded his home would develop and change. Many of the friends that Marty had known would move, fade away, or die. Much of what he had loved in this place would become unrecognizable to him. Ultimately, this place as he knew it would disappear and die. This place that had held so very many of his childhood memories would fade away and vanish. Still, for Marty, many of his memories remained, caught now and held tightly within him, precious and unchanged. He had found them. He had rediscovered them. Upon his return, he had embraced them all. Now it was Time for him to turn the page.

As Marty reminisced, Time advanced and carried him forward. The train was rolling and moving faster and faster. Immediately it seemed, the train stopped and without warning, spit him out.

"Pop"...

Marty found himself skyward 10 feet over open water, most recently exited from a train made of inner tubes and now over the pond at the road maintenance yard. With Time, this place had changed. Most places do. Marty saw no tubes, no other riders. He heard no voices nor radio music.

Instead, what he saw below were road crews back on duty following a daylong seminar. They were taking lunch at the table next to the pond.

"Look", one of them shouted with a mouth full of bologna sandwich. He pointed skyward. His co-workers turned to see Marty execute a pinpoint dive into the open water. He struck the water with nary a ripple.

"Did you see that?" one said to the others. A supervisor stuck his head out of the office window in the office trailer and shouted, "Gentlemen, lunch is over, back to work! Andy just buried his rig under a load of hot asphalt at the self-loader".

The crew chuckled as each of them threw half-eaten sandwiches, sardines, and a homemade pie, back into their lunch pails. It was Time to rescue Andy again.

"C'mon you dolts, clean that up later" the super chastised. "Grab some shovels and hurry! Get his truck out of there before the tires melt."

EPILOGUE

Rumor was that Marty was back. Ms. Bichette would be the last to trounce the rumor. For some reason, she had become a bit of a celebrity associated with Marty's popularity. Who knew?

True to her promise, she moved the management committee for the Golden Hills Senior Residential Community to rename Physical Therapy in honor of Mark, Mark, "Marty" Markham or "Marty's PT" as the old folks here at the home called to it.

In addition, the committee purchased a new whirlpool tub made of fiberglass. This one could hold even Mo. Or, it would hold any three of the old folks there at the home.

In the days following Marty's return, rumors were that Ms. Bichette oft times used the whirlpool, late at night when the lights were down and the old folks in Hallways A and B muttered and puttered and otherwise tried to sleep. To date, her use of the tub remained a rumor, but that rumor was to be enjoyed thoroughly throughout the residence.

On a plaque affixed to the front side of the whirlpool tub was inscribed:

A purpose for life?

Search the soul, came the reply

A baby's toes gave me the hint
Clean as the future they held no lint
It is the past that makes lint new

To make for me, my present.
So, through countless times I've counted past
From my childhood and mounting fast

The answer can be found there in my tarsals.

So, go I again Counting backward from ten
And finding there a bit of hair
And lint from which to make new argyles

*****

Curly was on duty and had just finished mopping in Physical Therapy where he paused for a brief moment to reminisce. He leaned on his mop and thought about Marty. He wondered if he would ever see his friend again. The atmosphere around the home was heavy. People died here every day, but that was more or less a matter-of fact. No one really mourned for these poor souls; none of them were ever missed. Family – if there were any still around – most likely celebrated with a sweet "good riddance". But Marty.... He sighed a heavy sigh.

He put is bucket and mop away in the back closet. What he needed was a reefer. On his way out to the front men's room where he could find some needed rest, as he stepped back through the Physical Therapy and passed the whirlpool, he spotted a familiar wet trail from the tub out the door and headed toward Hallway A, Room 13. He broke out into a wide grin. He grabbed his mop from the back closet, cleaned the water trail from the floor; and redeposited it. Then, he ran as fast as his skinny legs would take him to the cafeteria to spread the news.

Marty was home!